5}

DARK NIGHT IN BIG ROCK

Center Point
Large Print

Also by William W. and J. A. Johnstone
and available from Center Point Large Print:

Rising Fire
Gold Mine Massacre
The Morgans
To the River's End
A Stranger in Town
Twelve Dead Men
Powder Burn
The Jensen Brand
Hang Him Twice
Evil Never Sleeps
Dig Your Own Grave
Pray for Death

**This Large Print Book carries the
Seal of Approval of N.A.V.H.**

DARK NIGHT IN BIG ROCK

The Jensen Brand

WILLIAM W. JOHNSTONE

and J. A. JOHNSTONE

CENTER POINT LARGE PRINT
THORNDIKE, MAINE

THE JENSEN FAMILY

FIRST FAMILY
OF THE AMERICAN FRONTIER

Smoke Jensen, *The Mountain Man.*
The youngest of three children and orphaned as a young boy, Smoke Jensen is considered one of the fastest draws in the West. His quest to tame the lawless West has become the stuff of legend. Smoke owns the Sugarloaf Ranch in Colorado. Married to Sally Jensen, father to Denise *"Denny"* and Louis.

Preacher, *The First Mountain Man.*
Though not a blood relative, grizzled frontiersman Preacher became a father figure to the young Smoke Jensen, teaching him how to survive in the brutal, often deadly Rocky Mountains. He fought the battles that forged his destiny. Armed with a long gun, Preacher is as fierce as the land itself.

Matt Jensen, *The Last Mountain Man.*
Orphaned but taken in by Smoke Jensen, Matt Jensen has become like a younger brother to Smoke, and even took the Jensen name. And like Smoke, Matt has carved out his destiny on

the American frontier. He lives by the gun and surrenders to no man.

Luke Jensen, *Bounty Hunter.*
Mountain Man Smoke Jensen's long-lost brother Luke Jensen is scarred by war and he's a dead shot—the right skills to be a bounty hunter. And he's cunning and fierce enough to bring down the deadliest outlaws of his day.

Ace Jensen and Chance Jensen,
Those Jensen Boys.
The untold story of Smoke Jensen's long-lost nephews, Ace and Chance, a pair of young-gun twins as reckless and wild as the frontier itself . . . Their father is Luke Jensen, thought killed in the Civil War. Their uncle Smoke Jensen is one of the fiercest gunfighters the West has ever known. It's no surprise that the inseparable Ace and Chance Jensen have a knack for taking risks—even if they have to blast their way out of them.

Denise "Denny" Jensen and Louis Jensen,
The Jensen Brand.
Denny and Louis are the adult children of Smoke and Sally Jensen. Denny is the wildcard tomboy, kept in line by the more level-headed Louis. The twins grew up mostly abroad, but never lost their love of the Sugarloaf Ranch or lost sight of what it means to be a Jensen.

CHAPTER 1

Misery Springs, New Mexico Territory

The new century might be a couple of years old, but in this wide spot in the trail, nothing had changed because of that milestone. Just as they had for years, saddle horses stood tied at the hitch rail in front of Frenchy Lafors' Gay Paree Saloon, which was constructed of warped, unpainted planks and, despite the name, wasn't fancy enough for even the most squalid of Paris's slums.

Of course, that description fit all of Misery Springs, which *did* live up to its name. The pioneers who had founded the settlement hoped that the springs gushing out of a rocky bluff would be a never-ending source of good water, but they quickly discovered that the stuff smelled bad and tasted worse.

Still, the water wouldn't kill you to drink it, and in this mostly arid stretch of southern New Mexico Territory, that counted for something.

Six horsebackers and a man in a buggy arrived in Misery Springs on a blistering hot afternoon and came to a stop in front of the Gay Paree. The riders wore range clothes, but a close look at their hands revealed none of the calluses working cowboys usually displayed. Those supple hands, their hard-eyed faces, and the well-cared-for revolvers that rested in well-oiled holsters on their hips testified as to their true profession.

One of them, a sinewy man with a lantern jaw and a permanent squint in one eye, leaned over in his saddle and spoke to the buggy's occupant.

"You want to come in with us?"

The voice that replied was quiet and mild. "No, I believe I'll stay here in the shade. It's terribly hot, and the man we're looking for may not be here, after all."

"That fella back in Lordsburg said he was. Got kinfolks here, he said. Planned to stay for a while." The rider ran his eyes over the dismal surroundings and shook his head. "Kinfolks or not, if I ever got out of this place, I'd never come back, that's for sure."

"Perhaps the man in Lordsburg lied."

The rider snorted. "You know better than that. Once you start asking a fella questions, he don't lie for very long. The truth comes out in a hurry."

"Well, there *is* that. But I'll still remain here, out of the sun, until we're certain."

"Sure, that's fine." The rider swung down from his saddle and looped his reins around the hitch rail. "Come on, boys."

The other men dismounted, and all six of them trooped into the Gay Paree.

• • •

Frenchy Lafors had never been closer to Paris than New Orleans, and he didn't speak a word of French. His mother, who worked in one of the houses on Bourbon Street, named him Antoine and insisted that his father was a down-on-his-luck French nobleman who had somehow wound up in New Orleans and fallen in love with her before getting himself shot over a poker table. Growing up, the boy had called himself Tony, but that name never stuck. Frenchy did.

He'd decided that if he was going to have the name anyway, he might as well put it to good use. So he dressed well, slicked down his hair, grew one of those little mustaches that curled up on the ends, and learned how to gamble and woo the ladies.

The latter skill had prompted him to skedaddle from the Crescent City when a particularly jealous husband sent men to kill him and dump him in the Mississippi. The former had supported him until a good hand—and surprisingly an honest hand, at that—had won him this saloon. He had been here a couple of years. Misery Springs was a terrible place, but nobody bothered him. There was something to be said for that.

Frenchy was standing behind the bar when six men walked in. He caught his breath and pressed his palms against the hardwood. They reminded him of the men who'd come after him in New

Orleans. This couldn't be his past catching up to him. Surely not after all this time.

He glanced down at the sawed-off shotgun resting on a shelf under the bar. If they came at him, he hoped that he'd have time to grab the scattergun and take a few of them with him.

But the man who seemed to be their leader just looked around the room and then headed for a table where four hombres were playing poker. Frenchy breathed a little easier, but only for a moment.

Then he started worrying that his place was about to be shot up, and while it might not be much, it was his, by Godfrey. He might have need of that scattergun after all.

But for now, he could afford to wait and see how things played out.

"Jake Farrell?"

Jake glanced up from the cards in his hand, annoyed at the interruption. "Yeah?"

"Need a few words with you."

"If you ain't blind, you can see I'm a mite busy right now."

The man who had spoken to him rested a hand on a gun butt. "Oh, I can see just fine. Well enough to shoot, anyway."

One of the other players, a fat little man who called himself the mayor of Misery Springs, cleared his throat. "I, ah, I'm sure we can

10

postpone the rest of this hand if you need to speak to these gentlemen, Jake."

Nobody minded him declaring himself mayor because nobody else wanted the job of running an awful settlement like this, although running Misery Springs didn't really take much effort. Nothing happened here.

Until today, looked like. Six gun-hung strangers riding in didn't bode well for Misery Springs or anybody in it.

Jake knew that and decided he'd better tread pretty carefully. He had strayed over onto the wrong side of the law a few times. He knew what sort of men these were, just by the look of them.

Slowly, so as not to spook them with any sudden moves, he placed his cards facedown on the table and sat up straighter, an affable-looking man with curly fair hair under his thumbed-back Stetson.

"I'm Farrell." No point in denying it now. "I don't think we've met before. What can I do for you?"

"You know a man named Martin Delroy?"

So that was it. Farrell frowned slightly to make it look like he was thinking about the question before shaking his head.

"No, can't say as I do."

"Fella in Lordsburg told me you were acquainted with Delroy and that you'd headed in this direction."

"That hombre in Lordsburg made a mistake. I never heard of anybody named Delroy." Farrell smiled and shook his head again. "Sorry."

"Not as sorry as you're gonna be."

That open threat changed things. Jake had let this go as far as he could. His hand darted for the gun under his coat as he started up out of the chair.

The boss gun-wolf was faster. His left hand grabbed Jake's right wrist and stopped him from pulling iron. His right fist slammed into Jake's jaw and knocked him sideways out of the chair.

Two of the other men grabbed the poker table and upended it, sending money and cards flying. The rest stepped back a little and drew their guns to cover the people in the room. One of them leveled his Colt at the man behind the bar, who had started to reach for something under the hardwood.

"I wouldn't do that, mister."

The barkeep nodded, stepped back, and raised his hands. His jaw trembled, and that made the curled ends of his little mustache jump up and down.

Jake was groggy from the punch, but it hadn't knocked him out. He felt a hand reach inside his coat and take his gun. Then more hands took hold of him, hauled him to his feet, and shoved him toward the door. He stumbled and might have fallen, but the hands were there to steady him and force him to keep moving.

One of his captors pushed the batwings aside. Jake stepped out and squinted against the sunlight. The man who had hit him moved up beside him, looked around, and pointed to the livery stable owned by the mayor of Misery Springs.

"That place looks like it ought to do. Take him over there."

A couple of the men grabbed his arms and marched him toward the stable. As Jake's wits started to come back to him, he looked around and saw the leader talking to somebody in a buggy. The man climbed down from the vehicle, and he and the leader followed Jake and the others.

Even though the man from the buggy was small and dapperly dressed, something about him made a ball of fear explode in Jake's stomach. He didn't give a damn about Martin Delroy. Not selling out somebody you knew was one thing, commendable but not absolutely necessary, and certainly not at too great a cost. Whatever they wanted to know, Jake would tell them, right up front and as honestly as possible.

Thing of it was, he didn't know if that would be enough to satisfy the appetites of the man from the buggy.

The men inside the Gay Paree could hear the screams coming from the livery stable as they picked up the scattered cards and money and set the overturned table on its legs again.

Frenchy expected the screaming to stop after a few minutes. He didn't know Jake Farrell very well, but he didn't figure the man would hold out for long before he answered the strangers' questions.

When the shrieks continued for a quarter of an hour, though, Frenchy started to get sick to his stomach, and a little mad, too.

"We got to do something, by Godfrey. We can't just allow this to go on."

With a glum expression on his round face, the mayor shook his head. "You saw those men, Frenchy. No matter what they're doing, do you really want to tell them they have to stop?"

"But . . . but . . ." Frenchy drew in a deep breath. "If we all go—"

"We'll likely all get killed."

Frenchy couldn't argue with that. But neither could he forget all the taunts and bullying he had endured when he was growing up, the child of a prostitute. He looked at the scattergun under the bar, reached for it, then drew his hand back. If he walked up to the stable holding that weapon, more than likely the strangers would just shoot him on sight.

He had a pistol in his trousers pocket, a hammerless Smith & Wesson .32 caliber Safety First model, also sometimes known as a Lemon

Squeezer because of its small size. He was pretty good with it and had shot two men in gunfights, maybe even killed them. He didn't know because he had rattled his hocks out of those places as fast as he could once the shooting was over. He didn't advertise that fact, because bragging about how good you were with a gun never failed to bring trouble.

The Lemon Squeezer's five-round cylinder was fully loaded. That wouldn't be enough to save his life if any gunplay ensued with the strangers, of course, but it was better than nothing. He stepped around the end of the bar and started toward the door.

"Frenchy, don't . . ."

"I can't just stand by and listen to it, Mr. Mayor. Anybody who wants to can come with me."

He pushed the batwings back and stepped outside. He didn't look behind him as he started toward the livery stable.

He didn't have to. He knew he was alone.

They saw him coming. A man stepped out and raised a hand to stop him.

"Best hold it right there, friend. This is none of your business."

A bubbling moan came from inside.

"You have no right to—"

The gunman raised a hand again to forestall Frenchy's protest. "Wait right here."

Frenchy didn't know what the man would do

next, but he swallowed and nodded. The man disappeared into the shadowy livery barn. A moment later, the lean, squinty-eyed man who seemed to be the boss sauntered out.

"My friend says you're a mite upset about what's happening."

"It's not right. Whatever you want from him, Farrell's given it up by now."

"Somebody else has to be the judge of that, and as long as *he's* not satisfied . . ." The man's narrow shoulders rose and fell. The phony smile he had given Frenchy went away. "Now, here's the way it's gonna be. We're going to do what we came here to do, and then we're going to ride away. We can ride away without any other trouble, or we can ride away with bodies scattered around and every building in this Godforsaken hole burning." Again the shrug. "It's really up to you. But if you decide you have to start something . . . we'll finish it. I give you my word on that."

Frenchy stood there staring at the man as several tense seconds went by. Then everything went out of him in a long sigh.

"Nobody here knows Farrell all that well. And this is our home, miserable though it may be."

The phony smile came back. "Now, that's the smart way to be, *amigo*. You go on back to the saloon now, you hear?"

Frenchy nodded. As he started to turn away, another scream ripped from inside the stable.

16

For half a second, Frenchy thought about jerking out that Smith & Wesson, spinning around, and squeezing some damn lemons.

Then he kept moving, his feet raising little puffs of dust as he plodded toward the Gay Paree. He hoped the squinty-eyed man kept his promise about not burning Misery Springs to the ground.

CHAPTER 2

Big Rock, Colorado

Without taking her eyes off the traffic in the street, Sally Jensen said to her daughter, beside her on the buggy seat, "My goodness, Denise, you're squirming around like a six-year-old."

Denise Nicole Jensen—Denny to her father Smoke and certain friends—tugged at the lacy, high-necked collar of the stylish sky-blue dress she wore.

"I don't see why I couldn't have just worn my regular clothes and ridden horseback into town."

"On that wild Rocket horse?" Sally shook her head. "I don't think that would have been a good idea."

"Rocket's not wild. He's just . . . high-spirited. Sometimes he just needs a little room to run."

"Which he wouldn't have here in town."

Denny supposed her mother had a point. Big Rock's main street was fairly crowded as the buggy approached the big, redbrick train station at the end of it. Wagons and buggies were parked in front of the businesses along both sides of the street. Other vehicles moved here and there, as did men on horseback. And there were plenty of pedestrians, including men, women, children, and dogs. If she'd been mounted on Rocket and the black stallion took it in his head to run, that could mean trouble. Denny could control him most of the time, but not always.

"Maybe you're right about Rocket, but I didn't have to get all dressed up. It's just *Louis*."

Denny's voice held the disdain that most sisters felt for their brothers. She loved him, but he could be a stuffed shirt sometimes. She figured that tendency might be even worse now that he was coming home as a lawyer with a degree from Harvard.

"It's not *just* Louis," Sally responded as she brought the buggy to a halt at one of the hitch rails in front of the depot. "Melanie and Brad will be with him, too."

"Sure, but Melanie's not one to put on airs. And Brad's just a kid. He won't care whether I'm dressed up or not. In fact, he likes it when I'm wearing my usual duds and we can go riding."

"When we get back to the Sugarloaf, you can put on your usual *duds*. I know by now there's no point in arguing with you."

Denny smiled. "You just don't want me mentioning all the times you put on trousers and rode the range with Pa and Pearlie and the rest of the crew."

"You weren't around for that."

"No, but I've heard stories. Lots and lots of stories—"

19

"There's Mr. Morgan," Sally interrupted her. She nodded toward the young man approaching them.

"Mrs. Jensen," Conrad Morgan said as he swept off his flat-crowned black hat. "And Miss Jensen. Good day to both of you."

Denny didn't respond, but Sally said, "Hello, Conrad. How are you?"

"I'm fine. And I'll bet I know what brings you both to town. I heard that your brother's coming home, Denny."

"That's right," she allowed.

"I'm looking forward to meeting him. He was already back East at school before I came to Big Rock."

Conrad wasn't telling Denny anything she didn't already know. She remembered quite well when Conrad Morgan arrived in Big Rock with a business partner, both of them bent on opening up and restoring to operation with new-fangled methods a number of long-closed gold mines they had bought. That venture had caused all kinds of trouble, and the partner was long gone, but Conrad was still in town, and the mines were still producing ore. It looked like he would be staying in these parts as long as that was the case.

Having Conrad around wasn't too big a chore, she supposed. He was tall and broad-shouldered, with dark blond hair, blue eyes, and regular features that most women considered handsome.

His clothes were expensive but not fancy: dark blue trousers tucked into high-topped black boots and a lighter blue work shirt. He had a black gun belt and holster buckled around his hips.

He was also incredibly rich, although that didn't mean much to Denny, who came from a family that owned one of the biggest, most successful ranches in Colorado and wasn't hurting for money at all.

Despite his advantages, Conrad wasn't the spoiled, pompous Eastern windbag he could have been. From what Denny had heard about him, in his younger days that description had fit him all too well, but tragedy and hardship had forced him to grow up. He came from good stock, too. His father was Frank Morgan.

Frank Morgan . . . Denny had heard her father speak of him. The Drifter, men sometimes called him. One of the fastest guns the West had ever seen. Some said *the* fastest. Denny didn't believe that for a second. Smoke Jensen was faster. But she would have hated to see the two men go up against each other in a fight. Smoke himself had said that he wouldn't want that, so it was a good thing the two of them were friends.

Conrad Morgan had inherited a lot of his father's gun-skill. Denny had seen proof of that with her own eyes. But she was another apple that hadn't fallen far from the tree. She could draw a gun faster and was a deadlier shot than all but a few people. Smoke and Frank Morgan were in that number who outclassed her when it came to gun-handling, for sure.

Conrad . . . ? Maybe. But she felt about him the same way Smoke felt about Frank. She wasn't certain she ever wanted to know who was faster.

And, for that matter, she mused now, she was pretty sure Conrad prompted a few feelings in her that her father never felt toward Frank Morgan!

Those thoughts went through her head in less than the blink of an eye. She pushed them away as Conrad went on, "That's a beautiful dress you're wearing today, Denny."

"You think so? I figured I ought to dress up a little, you know, to welcome Louis and his family home."

She saw her mother smiling, and willed Sally not to say anything about her earlier complaints.

Conrad put his hat back on and asked, "Where's Smoke?"

"He and Pearlie and Cal are riding in separately," Sally answered. "They'll be along soon."

"I was inside the station a few minutes ago, checking on some equipment that's supposed to arrive, and I was told that the train's running about an hour late. You two ladies might as well come over to Longmont's with me and have some tea while you wait, instead of sitting out here in the heat."

"Why, thank you for the invitation, Mr. Morgan. If we can have coffee instead of tea, I believe we'll take you up on it."

Denny resisted the impulse to kick her mother on the ankle for speaking for her like that. But, to tell the truth, some of Louis Longmont's superb Cajun coffee sounded pretty good right now.

Conrad stepped up to the buggy to help Sally down. Dress or no dress, Denny wasn't going to wait. She hopped down agilely on her side of the vehicle and then went around the back to join her mother and Conrad Morgan, who had taken the buggy horse's reins and was tying them to the hitch rail.

When he finished with that task, Conrad linked his left arm with Sally's right and then offered his right arm to Denny, who hesitated—but only for a second—before taking it. Arm in arm, the three of them strolled toward Longmont's, which was both a saloon, albeit a refined one, and one of Big Rock's finest restaurants.

The owner, Louis Longmont, had a long and storied career as a gambler and gunman before settling down in Big Rock, and more important, he was one of Smoke Jensen's oldest and staunchest friends. In fact, Smoke's own son had been named for him.

As the trio reached the boardwalk and started toward Longmont's, two men rounded the corner at the far end of the block and started toward them. One man walked slightly in front of the other. He was hatless, with lank, dark hair and dark stubble on his hard-planed cheeks. He wore a nondescript shirt and jeans, and his hands were held out in front of him, linked together by a short chain that ran between the cuffs snapped tight around his wrists.

The second man was a little smaller, compact but muscular, with slightly wavy brown hair under his light brown Stetson. His right hand rested on the walnut grip of a Colt revolver holstered on his hip. The badge of a Deputy United States Marshal was pinned to his butternut shirt. His young, handsome face was set in determined lines.

"Looks like Deputy Rogers has himself a prisoner," Conrad commented. "He must be taking that man to the station to put him on a train."

"Yes, I think I heard Smoke say something about that," Sally said. "I believe he's wanted in Utah. Brice arrested him last week, and he's been locked up in Monte's jail since then."

Neither small group had slowed, so the gap between them on the boardwalk was closing rapidly. Then Brice Rogers said, "Hold it, Fenner. Stop here and we'll move aside to give these folks some room."

The prisoner stopped and sneered back over his shoulder at Brice. "Figured you were in a hurry to get rid of me, Marshal."

"As soon as the train gets here, I'll be more than happy to turn you over to those guards Chief Marshal Long's sending from Denver to escort you to Salt Lake City. But until then you're in my charge, and I don't see any reason why we can't be courteous."

"Yeah, I wouldn't want to be impolite on my way to the gallows."

"That's enough."

The two men moved to the outer edge of the boardwalk. Brice lifted his left hand—the right had a habit of not straying far from the gun on his hip—and pinched the brim of his hat as he nodded to Denny and Sally.

"Ladies." Brice paused a second, then added, "Morgan."

"Hello, Deputy," Conrad said.

Denny was waiting for him to say something else. Since Conrad's arrival in Big Rock, some tension had grown up between him and Brice Rogers, and Denny knew that she was the cause of it.

In the past, she and Brice had carried on a sporadic, somewhat awkward romance that had developed as much from the two of them facing danger together and fighting side by side against deadly enemies, as from any real attraction. Then Conrad had come along and flirted shamelessly with her on numerous occasions . . . and she had responded in kind.

Brice knew that, and he was jealous. Conrad knew what had happened between Denny and Brice in the past, and *he* was jealous. Most of the girls Denny had grown up with in England and on the Continent would have been giddy with glee to have two such handsome suitors vying for them. Denny just felt vaguely annoyed by the situation most of the time. Annoyed with herself, too, for not knowing what she wanted to happen.

So she wouldn't have been surprised if the two young men had traded barbed comments. However, that didn't happen because the outlaw named Jess Fenner didn't give it a chance to.

Instead, Fenner lowered his shoulder and, with no more warning than that, lunged across the boardwalk and bulled into Conrad Morgan, driving him backward and knocking him loose from Denny and Sally. Fenner's cuffed hands shot forward, and one of them plucked the gun from the holster Conrad wore. He caught his balance and spun toward Brice as he shouted, "Now, boys, now!"

CHAPTER 3

From the corner of his eye, Conrad saw three men on horseback who had been passing by in the street suddenly lunge their mounts toward the boardwalk as they yanked guns from holsters. One of them was leading a saddled, riderless horse. Conrad knew instantly that this was a planned attempt by Fenner's men to rescue the outlaw from custody.

It might work, too, because Brice Rogers would hesitate before starting any gunplay on the crowded boardwalk, especially with Denny and Sally Jensen right in the line of fire.

Fenner wouldn't be that cautious. He raised the gun he had taken from Conrad and pointed it toward Brice.

But then he fumbled with the weapon and yelled, "What the hell is this thing?"

Conrad had caught his balance by now after the collision with Fenner almost knocked him down. A split-second's glance was enough to tell him that Denny and Sally were all right for the moment.

He dived at Fenner from behind, tackling the outlaw around the waist and driving him off his feet.

At the same moment, the mounted outlaws

opened fire, spraying bullets around wildly so that the people on the street and the boardwalk yelled and scrambled for cover.

Fenner hit the boardwalk hard with Conrad on top of him. That jolted the pistol out of his hand. It slid along the boardwalk. Conrad planted a knee in the small of Fenner's back, clubbed his hands together, and brought them down on the back of Fenner's head. That smashed the outlaw's face against the planks. His nose broke with an audible *pop!* and a spray of blood from both nostrils.

A bullet fired by one of the outlaws whined past Conrad's ear. He crawled over the half-conscious Fenner and sprang toward the pistol, reaching out to grasp its round wooden handle.

Meanwhile, Brice Rogers had drawn his Colt. As Conrad tackled Fenner, Brice called, "Stay back!" to Denny and Sally Jensen and turned toward the riders attacking from the street. They were shooting wild, but some of the bullets were coming too blasted close. Brice felt the wind-rip of one of them as it passed by his cheek.

An even bigger worry for him was that one of the slugs would strike Denny, Sally, or some other innocent bystander.

Brice dropped to one knee to make himself a smaller target. It was good that he did, because just then one of the shots found the crown of his hat and sent it flying off his head. He lined his sights on the outlaw who had almost ventilated him and squeezed the trigger. The Colt roared and bucked against his palm as flame spurted from the barrel.

The shot nicked the man's shoulder and caused him to twist in the saddle as he grimaced in pain. But it didn't put him down; in fact, it barely seemed to bother him as he swung his revolver toward Brice again. The gun boomed. Splinters flew from one of the posts supporting the awning over the boardwalk and stung Brice's cheek.

Brice fired again, and at the same time, a series of sharp cracks came from his right. He didn't have time to look in that direction to see if he was under attack from a new threat or if someone else was getting in on the fight. He squeezed off a third round just as the outlaw fired again.

The owlhoot's slug ripped along Brice's left forearm and threw him off balance so that he fell back on his butt. From there he saw that his third shot had found its target. The outlaw who had wounded him pressed his free hand to his chest. Crimson blood welled between the spread fingers. His gun slipped from his other hand and fell into the street. The dying outlaw toppled after it and landed in a limp heap.

Ignoring the pain from his wounded arm, Brice surged back to his feet to continue the fight.

They had happened to be passing Hukill's Barber Shop when the trouble started. The door into the shop was open, since it was a very warm day. Denny noticed the smell of bay rum drifting out and thought that it was odd, the things that stuck in a person's mind at moments of great stress and danger.

Less than a heartbeat later, she had hold of her mother's arm. Denny pulled Sally toward her, pivoted, and let go. That swift thinking and instinctive burst of action propelled Sally through the open door and sent her stumbling toward a startled barber, who dropped his scissors and reached out to catch her.

Satisfied that her mother was at least safer than she would have been outside on the boardwalk, Denny swung around and yanked up her blue dress's long skirt.

Strapped to her right thigh was a holster holding a .38 caliber Smith & Wesson revolver, the short-barreled model known as a Baby Russian.

When she was packing iron on her hip, she normally toted a .41 Colt Lightning. Smoke sometimes commented skeptically that if you were shooting anything smaller than a .44, you might as well just *throw* the weapon at whoever you were up against, but Denny figured it was a matter of placement. If you were accurate enough with a .41 or a .38, you could still do considerable damage.

She was accurate enough.

Which she proved by yanking the Baby Russian from its holster, straightening, and drilling her first round through the upper right arm of the outlaw closest to her.

That happened to be the man leading the riderless horse intended for Jess Fenner to use in his getaway. The man yelped in pain but didn't drop the gun he held. He must have known that he couldn't maintain his grip with that hand, however, because he let go of the extra horse's reins and reached across his body to take the gun in his left hand. He snapped a hurried shot in Denny's direction.

The bullet missed her and struck the red-and-white-striped barber pole mounted on the wall beside the door. Colorful splinters showered around Denny as she crouched. She thumbed back the Baby Russian's hammer and fired again. Her target howled as the bullet ripped away a good chunk of his left ear.

More shots roared nearby. Gun-thunder filled the street and made it hard to concentrate. Denny willed herself to ignore everything else that was going on and focus on what she needed to do. Her adversary got off another left-handed shot. This one shattered the barber shop's front window.

Denny didn't allow herself to think about the fact that her mother was in there. She could only hope that Sally and everybody else in the shop had dropped to the floor to get out of the line of fire.

She squeezed the Baby Russian's trigger again. The .38 cracked. The outlaw's head jerked back as a red-rimmed third eye appeared in the center of his forehead. It was a fatal shot, and odds were, he was dead already before he fell from the saddle and crashed to the street. His spooked horse kicked him a couple of times before capering away.

Denny straightened from her crouch and turned to see how Brice and Conrad were doing.

Conrad closed his hand around the fallen gun's handle and rolled onto his right shoulder as bullets chewed into the boardwalk beside him. He kept rolling and came up with the gun extended in his right hand. He thrust it toward the outlaw who was trying to kill him and started squeezing the trigger.

Five sharp reports sounded, crowding even closer together than they would have from a double-action revolver. The leaden messengers stitched a path across the mounted outlaw's chest, each wound blooming like a crimson flower on the man's shirt. Those bloodstains rapidly ran together as he rocked back in the saddle and dropped his gun. He managed to open his mouth in shock, but no sound came out before he swayed and then toppled off to the left.

Conrad got to his feet. Close beside him, Fenner started to stir. The outlaw got his hands under him and tried to push himself up as blood still dripped steadily onto the planks from his broken nose.

Conrad kicked him in the head. Fenner slumped back down, senseless.

Kicking a man while he was down wasn't very sporting of him, Conrad thought . . . but he didn't feel very sporting right now. What he felt was angry that this outlaw had set in motion a chain of events that threatened the life of Denny Jensen.

But Denny was all right, Conrad saw. Relief surged through him at the sight of her standing straight and defiant on the boardwalk in front of the barber shop's bullet-shattered window. She had a gun in her hand. A wisp of smoke still curled from the muzzle. Since all three of the outlaws who had been on horseback were now lying motionless in the street, Conrad figured Denny was responsible for one of them.

Brice Rogers had taken care of the other one. Brice still held his Colt, too, and seemed steady enough on his feet, but Conrad spotted a trickle of red worming its way down the back of his left hand to drip onto the boardwalk.

Denny saw the blood at the same time and exclaimed, "Brice, you're hurt!"

"It doesn't amount to much," Brice replied. "Bullet just grazed me, that's all."

Despite that, when he started to slide his Colt back into the holster, he missed on the first attempt and had to try again. Conrad noted that and knew it wasn't like Brice Rogers to be that unsteady. The shock of being shot and possibly the loss of blood must be affecting him.

Brice stepped closer to Denny and asked, "What about you? Were you hit?"

She shook her head. "No, I'm fine. I need to check on my mother, though."

She turned and hurried into the barber shop.

Conrad said, "You'd better have a doctor take a look at that arm, Deputy."

"I will, when I get around to it. I need to check on my prisoner first, though, and those men who attacked us."

Conrad hooked a boot toe under Fenner's shoulder and rolled the outlaw onto his back. The way Fenner's arms flopped loosely told him what he needed to know.

"He's out cold," Conrad said. "Why don't you keep an eye on him and I'll have a look at the others?"

For a second, Brice looked like he wanted to argue, but then he nodded and said, "All right." He leaned against one of the posts along the edge of the boardwalk.

With his gun still in his hand, Conrad stepped down into the street and moved quickly from body to body. All three outlaws who had tried to liberate Jess Fenner were dead, just as Conrad expected. He, Brice, and Denny had each accounted for one of them.

Now that the shooting was over, the townspeople were starting to emerge from cover and look curiously toward the scene of carnage in front of the barber shop. A few even approached, eyes wide at the sight of the corpses.

Rapid footsteps made Conrad look behind him. An older, gray-haired man was hurrying toward him, carrying a shotgun. The man sported a tin star pinned to his vest.

"It's all right, Sheriff," Conrad said to Monte Carson. "Everything's under control."

Monte, who had served as Big Rock's sheriff for more than two decades, slowed to a stop and nodded. His gaze moved back and forth between Conrad and Brice.

"Did these fellas try to spring Fenner from your custody, Brice?" he asked the federal lawman.

"That's right, Sheriff," Brice replied.

"But you and Mr. Morgan took care of that little problem, I reckon?"

"We had some help," Conrad said dryly as he nodded toward the boardwalk where Denny and Sally had just stepped out of the barber shop. Denny still held the short-barreled pistol she had used to gun down one of the outlaws.

Monte Carson chuckled. "Yeah, I'm not really surprised. I knew Louis was supposed to be back today and the rest of the family would be coming in to meet him. Jensens seem to attract trouble most of the time."

"I heard that, Monte Carson," Sally called to him. "You've been known to attract some trouble yourself."

Monte had been a hired gun before meeting Smoke and coming over to the right side of the law, so there was no disputing Sally's claim. The wan smile she gave the sheriff took any sting out of the words, though.

"What in blazes is that?" Brice asked as he nodded toward the gun in Conrad's hand. "It sounded almost like a Gatling gun when you started shooting."

"Well, it's not quite that fast." Conrad lifted the long-barreled pistol. It had a round wooden grip and a box-like magazine just in front of the trigger. "It's a Mauser C96. A German pistol I picked up a few years ago."

"Double action?" asked Monte.

Conrad shook his head. "Semi-automatic, they call it. The recoil moves the bolt back, ejects the empty cartridge, and chambers a fresh round after each shot, so it'll fire just as fast as you can pull the trigger. It's a new design, less than ten years old. It'll throw a lot of lead in a hurry, and the magazine holds ten rounds." He shrugged. "I still have a fondness for a good Colt revolver, but I like to carry this broomhandle part of the time.

It came in handy today. Fenner grabbed it away from me, but he wasn't familiar with it and was too clumsy to get it going before I tackled him."

As if aware that he was being talked about, Fenner groaned and stirred again.

"I need to get him up and take him on to the train station," Brice said. "He's going to Utah to answer for his crimes there. There are supposed to be a couple of deputy marshals on the train to take charge of him."

Monte said, "No offense, Brice, but you're looking a mite green around the gills. You'd better get that arm tended to. I'll take over for you and make sure Fenner gets on the train with those marshals."

"It's my responsibility—" Brice began.

Denny took his uninjured arm and said, "Sheriff Carson can handle it just fine, and you know it. You won't be doing anybody any good if you pass out and fall down."

"I'm not going to pass out and fall down," Brice replied, clearly irritated. But he didn't pull away from Denny. He sighed and nodded, instead. "Thanks, Sheriff."

"I'll go along and help keep an eye on Fenner, too," Conrad offered.

That brought another grudging nod from Brice. "Obliged to you, Morgan."

Conrad clapped a hand on his shoulder. "Go get yourself patched up."

Denny and Sally led Brice away toward the doctor's office. The crowd that had gathered parted to let them through. Monte Carson tucked his shotgun under his arm, watched them depart, and said quietly, "I'm a little surprised at you, Mr. Morgan."

"Oh? Why's that?"

"Sending Brice off with Denny like that. I'd gotten the idea that you were interested in her."

"Even if I was—and I'm not admitting that I am, Sheriff—sometimes a fellow has to be practical. Deputy Marshal Rogers needs medical attention, and he's more likely to get it with Denny helping him to the doctor's office. The way he's sort of leaning on her . . . Well, that might be worth getting shot."

Monte laughed. "If I was forty years younger, I'd agree with you, son. And if her pa wasn't my oldest friend. Speaking of which . . . here comes Smoke now."

CHAPTER 4

"It'll be good to see Louis again," Calvin Woods had commented as he approached Big Rock a few minutes earlier, riding alongside Smoke Jensen and Pearlie Fontaine.

They were a formidable trio. Smoke was now a successful rancher and family man, but once he'd been the most famous gunfighter on the wild frontier. If he had lost even a fraction of his speed with a gun, nobody wanted to find out for sure. That would be just too risky.

Pearlie was a fast gun himself who had met Smoke first as an enemy. It hadn't taken him long to realize the error of his ways. As one of the first cowboys on the Sugarloaf, Smoke's vast ranch, it was a foregone conclusion that Pearlie would boss the crew of salty top hands who rode for the Jensen brand.

One of those top hands was Calvin Woods, who had come to the Sugarloaf as a young man and become part of the family. When Pearlie decided to retire as the day-to-day foreman, it was only natural that Cal, now in the prime of adulthood, would take over for him while Pearlie still functioned as an advisor and troubleshooter for Smoke.

Together, they kept the Sugarloaf operating

at a high level, and as Smoke glanced between his two old friends, he was mighty grateful for everything they had contributed to the ranch.

Still, something was missing . . .

Smoke hoped to fill in that piece today.

"I'll be glad to see Brad again," Pearlie said. "That young'un's always full of questions and wants to know everything there is to know about cowboyin'." His leathery face creased in a grin. "Gives me a good excuse to ramble on for a spell."

"He's a good boy," Smoke agreed. "Louis is a lucky man, getting a wife like Melanie and a son like Brad in the same deal. I expect Louis and Melanie will have kids of their own someday, too."

"That ranch house will be plumb full before you know it," Pearlie said.

Smoke didn't respond, but he thought Pearlie was jumping to conclusions. Louis had never said that he intended for him and his family to live at the ranch, and certainly not in the main house. If Melanie was like most women Smoke had known, she would want her own house. The question would be whether or not it was on the Sugarloaf.

A lot of legal matters were involved in the operation of a spread like the Sugarloaf. Ever since he'd started the ranch, Smoke had handled those things himself, with the occasional assistance of lawyers in Big Rock. But the place really needed a full-time manager for the business end of things, and with a law degree and a head for numbers, Louis seemed perfectly cut out for that job.

Smoke had known for years that Louis, with the medical problems that had plagued him since he was born, wasn't suited to run the ranch on a daily basis. Such a life didn't fit his personality, either. But in recent years, since Louis and his twin sister Denise had returned from England to live full-time in Colorado, Smoke had realized that Denny *was* equipped, in both skills and temperament, to take charge of the Sugarloaf someday.

Smoke wasn't ready to let go of the reins just yet—he was only in his fifties and looked and felt considerably younger—but that day would come, and he would feel better about things if he knew that he could count on *both* his children to preserve and expand the legacy he and Sally would leave them.

So, at some point he would have to have a talk with Louis and find out exactly what the young man's plans were. But that didn't have to be today. Business could wait. Today was for welcoming Louis, Melanie, and Brad back home. Sally and Denny had taken the buggy into Big Rock earlier. Smoke was looking forward to having everybody together again.

The church steeples and the roofs of some of the buildings were in sight when gunshots began to roar up ahead in the town. The three riders stiffened in their saddles, and Pearlie exclaimed, "What in tarnation!"

"Come on!" Smoke called as he dug his heels into his horse's flanks. The animal leaped ahead in a gallop. Pearlie and Cal followed close behind him. To all three of these men, the sound of trouble was a clarion call that couldn't be ignored.

They were still far enough away that it took them several minutes of hard riding to reach Big Rock. During that time, the gun-thunder welled up and then began to subside. As Smoke and his companions slowed at the edge of town, they realized that the shooting had stopped.

"Sounds like the war's over," Pearlie said. "Don't know if that's a good thing . . . or a bad one."

"It may be over, but I want to know what it was all about," Smoke said. "Sally and Denny should have been in town by now, and they could have been in danger."

"No offense, Smoke," said Cal, "but if Denny had anything to say about it, she was probably smack-dab in the middle of that ruckus."

Smoke nodded. He knew that as well as Cal did, and the knowledge just increased the worry growing inside him.

He spotted a crowd gathered near the far end of Big Rock's downtown section, where the railroad station was located. Smoke knew it wasn't quite time for the westbound train to have arrived, but if it was on schedule, it would be rolling in soon. At least, whatever the trouble was, it had erupted before Louis, Melanie, and Brad arrived.

Unless the train had been early. That was rare, but it had been known to happen.

The three men rode toward the depot. While they were still a couple of blocks from the spot where the townspeople had gathered, the crowd parted and three people emerged: two women helping a man between them who seemed to be injured. Smoke recognized the lustrous dark hair of the older woman and the blond curls of the younger one.

"There's Miss Sally and Miss Denny," Pearlie said. "Appears they're all right, thank goodness. But who's that fella with 'em?"

"Brice Rogers," Smoke said, his keen eyes having picked out the features of the young deputy marshal. "Looks like maybe he's wounded, but not too bad. He's moving under his own power. I reckon they're helping him to the doctor's office."

"Like I said," Cal put in, "Denny must've been in the thick of whatever it was."

"Let's find out," Smoke said.

The bystanders had started to disperse, and as

the crowd thinned out more, Smoke saw three motionless forms lying in the street in front of Hukill's Barber Shop. Pools of blood had formed around them, although the thirsty dirt was soaking up the dark liquid fairly rapidly.

"There's Monte," Pearlie said. "Who's that with him?"

"Conrad Morgan," Smoke said, wondering what part the young businessman had played in whatever happened here. Not that long ago, Conrad had been at the center of a lot of trouble in the valley, although to be fair most of it wasn't his fault.

Conrad and Monte Carson were standing on the boardwalk in the shade of the awning. Monte had a shotgun tucked under his arm, aimed in the general direction of a man who sat with his back propped against the building wall. That man's nose was swollen, and blood smeared the lower half of his face.

Smoke hadn't heard the distinctive boom of a scattergun as they were riding in. The racket had sounded like several different handguns going off. Monte must have arrived after the trouble was over, Smoke figured.

Conrad had a gun holstered on his hip, which wasn't unusual, but it had an odd-looking, round wooden handle instead of the usual curved grips of a Colt, Remington, or Smith & Wesson.

The three newcomers reined in and swung

down from their saddles. Smoke nodded to the sheriff and said, "Sounded like you had yourself quite a fandango here, Monte. We heard the gun-music all the way outside town."

"It wasn't my fandango, Smoke," Monte replied. "But Mr. Morgan here can tell you all about it."

"Conrad," Smoke said with a brisk nod to the young man.

"It's good to see you again, Mr. Jensen."

Smoke wasn't one to mince words when he was worried about his loved ones. "Are my wife and daughter all right?"

"They're fine. Neither lady was injured."

Pearlie pointed at the red-and-white striped pole with a chunk knocked out of it by a bullet. "Somebody shot up the barber pole!" The front window was busted, too.

"What happened?" Smoke asked.

Monte nodded toward the sullen, bloody-faced man sitting on the boardwalk. "This fella is an outlaw named Jess Fenner. Brice ran him to ground and arrested him last week. Utah wants him on a heap of charges, including convictions for murder, so Brice planned to put him on the train when it gets here. But three of Fenner's pards figured different."

"Those three?" Smoke leaned his head toward the dead men in the street.

"Yeah. As it happened, Sally, Denny, and Mr.

Morgan were on hand when all hell broke loose."

Smoke grunted and glanced at Cal, who nodded as if to remind him of what he'd said earlier.

Conrad said, "Denny made sure her mother was safe inside the barber shop, then exchanged shots with one of those outlaws. He came out second-best."

"She's good with a gun." Smoke frowned slightly. "But I thought she was wearing a dress today. Didn't see a gun belt on her when she left the ranch earlier."

"She had a pistol, ah . . . under the dress. As well as a pair of jeans."

Smoke felt the urge to chuckle, although he didn't do it with three dead men lying a few feet away. Instead, he said dryly, "I'm not surprised."

"Deputy Rogers took care of another outlaw, and I dealt with the third one, as well as corralling Fenner," Conrad went on.

"He got his nose broken in the fracas," Monte added, "but at least he survived. That's more than his friends can say."

Cal pointed at the gun on Conrad's hip and asked, "That's what you used in the fight?"

"Yes. It's a Mauser C96." Conrad drew the pistol and displayed its features.

"Impressive," said Pearlie with a nod, "but I reckon I'll stick with a good old-fashioned Peacemaker."

"They're hard to beat," Conrad allowed, "but

the Mauser holds four more rounds and has a higher rate of fire."

Smoke said, "Most problems don't need ten shots to take care of them . . . but now and then, that *could* come in handy." He held out his hand. "You mind if I get the feel of it?"

"Of course not." Conrad reversed the Mauser and extended the handle to Smoke, who took the gun and weighed it in his hand. He tilted it up and down, gauging the balance of it, and sighted down the barrel.

"Fine weapon," he told Conrad as he handed it back, "but I'll stick with a Colt, too, like Pearlie."

"Then you should try the Colt 1902." Conrad holstered the Mauser. "It's a semi-automatic, self-loading pistol like this, only designed by John Browning. The magazine is in the butt, not in front of the trigger like the Mauser. I tried one not long before I came out here and was impressed with it. I could have one sent to you, if you'd like."

Smoke nodded. "Wouldn't mind giving it a try. Revolvers have served me pretty well, though."

"That's an understatement," Monte said. He nodded along the street. "Here comes the undertaker's wagon." Raising his voice, he went on to the townspeople still standing around, "You folks move back now. Man's got work to do."

Dr. Enoch Steward plucked another splinter out of Brice Rogers' cheek, looked over at Denny, and said, "It seems that a physician will never run short of patients while you're around, Miss Jensen."

"Doctor, what a terrible thing to say!" Denny exclaimed.

"He's got a point, though," Brice said. He felt considerably better now. The doctor had given him a shot of whiskey—"Strictly for medicinal purposes, as a restorative, you know"—and then stitched up the bullet gash in Brice's arm. Steward had offered to use chloroform and knock him out before patching him up, but Brice had refused, preferring to keep as clear a head as possible.

Denny made a scoffing sound and said, "You're a fine one to talk, Brice Rogers. You seem to attract just as much trouble as I do. Maybe even more, since that's sort of your job, isn't it? Hunting trouble?"

Brice shrugged in agreement, or at least non-argument.

"It's safe to say you keep the undertaker busy, too," Steward said. "But there was really nothing else you could do, was there?"

"Not the way those fellas were throwing lead around," Brice replied as a grim note entered his voice. "We had to act fast, or innocent folks might have been killed." He looked at Denny. "With you and your mother there . . ."

He drew in a breath and didn't say anything

48

else. He wasn't sure how things stood between him and Denny, but the thought of anything bad happening to her was intolerable. Yet, every time gunplay broke out while she was around, she seemed to rush right into it.

Dr. Steward stepped back from the examining table where Brice was sitting and said, "That takes care of you, Deputy. I want you to stop by tomorrow so I can change the dressing on your arm and see how the wound looks. Your arm will be very stiff and sore, so don't try to use it any more than you have to. In fact, it would be best if you didn't use it at all. I'll give you a sling, and I want you to keep the arm in it while you're up and moving around."

"For how long, Doctor?"

"At least a week."

Brice frowned. "It's going to be hard to ride a horse with my arm in a sling."

"Good, because you don't need to be riding a horse. You should rest, instead."

"I don't know if my job will let me do that."

"Well, do the best you can," Steward said. He turned to Denny. "Now, Miss Jensen—"

"I'm fine," she interrupted him. "I don't need any medical attention."

"You have a cut on your cheek from a splinter, just like Deputy Rogers does."

"It's nothing," Denny insisted. "It won't leave a scar, will it?"

"Well, no, it's not that big, and it doesn't need even a single stitch. But it should be cleaned and bandaged."

Denny sighed. "All right, go ahead. But you—" She looked at Brice and jerked a thumb toward the door. "You can go out and wait with my mother."

Brice wondered if she wanted him to leave because she needed to talk to Dr. Steward about something else. Her being a woman, that led down trails Brice didn't particularly want to follow, so he nodded and slid off the table.

"We'll wait for you," he said.

He pulled down his bloody, bullet-ripped sleeve over the bandage Dr. Steward had wrapped around the wound and went out into the front room. Sally Jensen stood up from the chair where she had been sitting.

"Are you going to be all right, Brice?" she asked.

He nodded and said, "The doctor seems to think I'll be fine. He sewed me up and told me to take it easy for a week while I keep my arm in a sling."

"Where's Denny?"

"He's cleaning that little cut on her cheek she got from a flying splinter." Brice smiled. "She tried to argue with him."

"Of course, she did. If you need someone to look after you, you're welcome to come out to the Sugarloaf and stay with us. Inez Sandoval is quite a competent nurse, and I've dealt with quite a few gunshot wounds myself."

"I appreciate that, ma'am, but I'm sure I'll be fine in my room at the boarding house."

"Well, if you change your mind—"

Denny came out of the other room and asked, "If he changes his mind about what?"

"I just told Brice that he could come recuperate at the Sugarloaf if he wanted to."

Brice watched Denny to see how she'd react to that, but instead, she lifted her head—which sported a small bandage on the left cheek—as a shrill whistle drifted through the office's open front door.

"That's the train coming in," she said. "Louis is back!"

CHAPTER 5

"I hope they brought a horse for me," Brad Buckner said as he gazed eagerly out the window at the Colorado landscape rolling past. "I want to ride out to the Sugarloaf on a horse, not in a buggy." He turned his head to look at Louis. "You think maybe Denny brought Rocket into town?"

"You mean Aunt Denise," Brad's mother Melanie corrected him.

Brad had a serious look on his ten-year-old face as he said, "I don't think she cottons much to being called Denise."

Louis managed to keep from grinning, but it wasn't easy. He said to his wife, "You can take the boy out of the West, but you can't take the West out of the boy. Brad *was* born out here, you know."

"Yes," Melanie said dryly, "I was there."

But Louis hadn't been. He hadn't known Brad until the boy was eight years old. He had met the two of them together, Brad and his beautiful widowed mother, during an eventful and dangerous trip over the Sierra Nevada Mountains in a stagecoach. Louis had fallen in love with Melanie almost at first sight, and he had come to love Brad like the boy was his own son.

Louis intended to make that the case, legally, by adopting Brad. He hadn't discussed the idea with Melanie yet, but he couldn't imagine that she would object. She knew how close Louis and Brad were. The three of them had been a family all the time that Louis had been at Harvard, getting his law degree.

Brad was sitting on the backward-facing seat across from Louis and Melanie. When his attention was back on the landscape again, Melanie leaned closer to Louis and asked quietly, "Do you think they brought a horse for him?"

"Oh, it's certainly possible," Louis replied. "That sounds like something Denny would do. Pearlie, too. He and Cal are both unofficial uncles."

Melanie lowered her voice even more to a whisper and asked, "Are your parents going to be terribly upset with us when they find out our plans?"

Louis sighed and shook his head. "I don't know," he told her. "I really don't."

She slipped her arm through his, squeezed it, and rested her head on his shoulder. "But it's for the best. I really believe that."

"So do I," he said. "I wouldn't be doing it if I didn't." He looked at the youngster watching intently out the window beside them. "He's liable to be disappointed, though."

"I don't think so. He'll still be able to spend a lot of time on the ranch."

Louis hoped that turned out to be true. His mother and father had gotten quite attached to Brad. Smoke and Sally didn't have any grandchildren of their own—yet—but Louis was sure they regarded Brad in that light.

The locomotive's whistle blew, the sound coming in through the window that was open a few inches along with the smell of smoke from the engine. Brad sat up even straighter and grinned.

"That whistle means we're getting close to town," he said. "We'll be in Big Rock in just a few minutes."

"That's right," Louis agreed. "You're looking forward to seeing everybody, aren't you?"

"I'm looking forward to being *home,*" Brad said.

Louis and Melanie glanced at each other, but neither spoke. Louis saw the worry lurking in his wife's eyes, and he supposed it was reflected in his own.

Denny stood with Smoke, Sally, Pearlie, and Cal on the station platform as the train rolled in with smoke belching from the diamond-shaped stack on the massive Baldwin locomotive. Other people waited on the platform, too, of course, either to board the train or greet other passengers disembarking, but the five of them were the only ones there to greet Louis, Melanie, and Brad.

With a squeal of brakes and a clash of metal, the train lurched and shuddered to a halt. Steam billowed from relief valves. The conductor swung down from the platform at the front of the first passenger car, where he'd been waiting for the train to come to a stop. Porters hurried to put steps in place for the travelers to descend to the station platform.

The blue-suited and black-capped conductor recognized Smoke and smiled. "Hello, Mr. Jensen," he said. "I reckon you're here to meet your boy. I know he's traveling with us today. Spoke to him a couple of times. That's a fine-looking wife and boy he has."

"That they are," Smoke agreed. "Had any trouble on the run so far?"

"A couple of mechanical issues that have put us a little behind schedule, but that's all."

"Glad to hear it."

Sally's hand tightened on Smoke's arm. "Smoke, there he is!"

Several passengers had already come down the steps. Louis appeared behind them, on the car's platform. He waved at those who were there to welcome him, then turned and held out his hand toward the door into the car. Melanie took it and came out onto the platform.

Brad was with her, holding her other hand. It appeared that he was doing that under protest, because as soon as he was clear of the door, he pulled loose from her and bounded down the steps.

"Denny!" he called.

Smiling, she bent down to hug him as he threw his arms around her. "Welcome home, Brad."

"It's mighty good to be here!" He turned and gave Sally an equally enthusiastic hug, then hesitated in front of Smoke for a second before he stuck his hand out. "Mr. Jensen."

Smoke gave the boy a solemn nod and clasped his hand. "Mr. Buckner. Welcome back."

Brad pumped Smoke's hand and asked, "How are things on the ranch?"

"Going along just fine, but I reckon they'll be even better now that you're back." Smoke's face was still serious, but a smile twinkled in his eyes as he added, "Pearlie and Cal will have plenty of chores for you to do."

"We sure will," Pearlie declared as he thumped Brad on the back. "Place has plumb been fallin' apart without you there, kid."

"I wouldn't go so far as to say that," Cal put in. He shook hands with Brad, too. "But I'm sure glad to see you anyway, Brad."

By this time, Louis had helped Melanie down the steps from the train. There were hugs and handshakes, smiles and laughter, all around.

"Inez and I have been getting ready for this celebration for days now," Sally said. "It's going to be quite a welcome home feast." She smiled at Brad. "Everything you like, in fact."

"Bear sign?" the boy asked excitedly.

"Plenty of bear sign," Sally confirmed with a nod. "And deep-dish apple pie, too."

"Oh, boy!"

Sally turned to Louis and Melanie and went on, "And of course, we have your rooms ready for you, so you'll be comfortable."

"About that . . ." Louis began.

He stopped when Melanie squeezed his arm. "We can talk about all that later," she said with a smile. "Thank you, Sally. It feels just wonderful to be back."

Denny knew her brother pretty well, though, and she had seen the look on Louis's face and heard something in his tone of voice when he started to respond to Sally's comment about their rooms at the Sugarloaf. Something was going on. Louis was worried about it, too. Denny had recognized that.

But Melanie didn't want to talk about it now. That was pretty clear, too. Denny supposed she ought to honor her sister-in-law's wishes . . . for now.

But before too much longer, Louis was going to spill whatever it was he had on his mind. Denny would see to that.

Farther along the platform, Monte Carson stood with the twin barrels of his shotgun pointed at Jess Fenner's back. Fenner's head drooped forward disconsolately. He continued to complain about not getting any medical attention for his broken nose.

"It needs to be set so it won't heal crooked," he whined.

"I don't figure you'll have to worry too much about that," Monte said. He knew that a gallows was waiting for Fenner in Salt Lake City. Fenner had been tried and found guilty in the robbery and murder of several Mormon families and had chosen hanging over a firing squad as his method of execution. But he had escaped before his sentence could be carried out.

"Can you at least see that my pards are buried proper-like?"

"They'll be buried," Monte assured him. "In Potter's Field, maybe, but they'll be laid to rest."

"Better than being left for the buzzards, I reckon," Fenner muttered. "This nose of mine hurts like blazes."

"Should have thought of that before you tried to escape."

Monte spotted two men in tweed suits and flat-crowned hats approaching them. Each of the strangers carried a Winchester and wore a holstered revolver. They had the same sort of deputy marshal's badge pinned to their vests that Brice Rogers wore. One sported a mustache and the other was clean-shaven, but they both had tanned, rugged features.

The one with the mustache nodded to Monte as they came up and stopped. "We were expecting a colleague of ours, Sheriff," he said, "but this looks like the prisoner we're supposed to take charge of."

"This is Jess Fenner, all right. We had a little trouble earlier."

"Hence the busted nose and dried blood," the clean-shaven deputy marshal said.

"Three of his friends tried to rescue him while Brice was bringing him down here to the depot from the jail."

Both federal lawmen instantly got grim expressions on their faces. "Is Rogers all right?" asked the one with the mustache.

"He is," Monte said, wanting to put their minds at ease. "He got a pretty good bullet crease on his arm while things were popping. But our local sawbones patched him up and says he's going to be fine. He's under doctor's orders to rest, though, which is why I volunteered to bring Fenner down here and wait for you fellas."

"What happened to the men who tried to rescue him?"

"They're at the undertaking parlor. They risked their lives for a worthless piece of trash like Fenner . . . and lost."

The look that Fenner gave Monte was pure hatred.

"All right, we'll take him off your hands," the

clean-shaven deputy said. "I'm Hal Goodwin, by the way."

"Ed Foster," the one with the mustache introduced himself. He reached inside his coat and pulled out a leather folder, which he flipped open to reveal an identification card. "Here's my bona fides."

Goodwin followed suit. Monte looked at both cards and nodded, satisfied that the men were who they said they were. It was a far-fetched notion that more of Fenner's friends might be masquerading as deputy U.S. marshals, but the possibility couldn't be ruled out.

However, Brice Rogers knew both of these men and had described his fellow officers to Monte when the sheriff talked to him briefly before Brice headed for his boarding house to rest, as Dr. Enoch Steward had ordered.

Confident that he was doing the right thing, Monte said, "He's all yours, boys," and stepped back as Goodwin and Foster fell in on either side of Jess Fenner to grip the outlaw's arms and steer him toward the train.

Fenner twisted his head to curse Monte. The deputy marshals tugged harder on him.

"Sorry, Sheriff," Foster said.

"Don't worry about it," Monte assured him. "I've heard plenty worse from the likes of him."

He stood there watching as the two lawmen and their prisoner ascended the steps at the caboose and disappeared into the car that brought up the rear of the train. Fenner and the deputies would ride there, rather than subjecting the regular passengers to the outlaw's presence. That was a good idea, especially considering Fenner's battered, bloody appearance. Looking the way he did, he might well frighten the women and children.

Monte turned away from the train and saw Smoke, Sally, and the rest of the Jensens leaving the platform, along with Cal Woods and Pearlie Fontaine. It was good that Louis was home, the sheriff mused. Now the Jensen family was complete again.

Brice Rogers was surprised to hear a knock on the door of his room in the boarding house. He wasn't expecting any visitors. He sat on the bed, with pillows propped up behind him against the headboard, trying to read a yellow-backed novel he held in his right hand. He'd been having a little trouble focusing on it, though, since Doc Steward had given him some pills for the pain of his wounded arm and the one he'd taken had left his brain a little fuzzy.

Not so fuzzy that he was going to be foolish, though. He set the dime novel aside and dropped his right hand to the butt of the Colt lying on the bed beside him. He had enemies—what star packer didn't?—and if any of them figured he'd be an easy target because he had a minor wound, they would find out different. Mighty different.

"Who is it?" he called.

"Me," a throaty female voice replied.

Brice recognized the voice and relaxed some, but not completely. He wasn't sure why Blaise Warfield was here. Somebody might have brought her to the boarding house at gunpoint, in an attempt to get into his room and take him unawares. Maybe he was being too suspicious, but that was better than being careless—and dead.

He was also surprised that his landlady would allow Blaise to come up here. She didn't exactly have the best reputation in Big Rock . . .

Those thoughts took only a second. Then he lifted the gun and called, "The door's unlocked. Come on in."

The knob turned and the door swung in. Blaise Warfield stepped into the room but stopped short when she saw the Colt pointed at her. It was hard to throw Blaise for a loop, though. She smiled and said, "Is that the way you always greet a lady when she comes calling, Brice?" Her voice had a mocking tone to it. "Or maybe you don't consider me a lady. I don't think that old woman downstairs does, but at least she didn't point a gun at me . . . just a look that could kill!"

Brice didn't see anybody else in the hall. He lowered the gun and said, "I'm sorry. About the gun and about the landlady. I reckon she doesn't want to see any more harm come to me."

"Well, I won't bite," Blaise said as she reached back to push the door up. She didn't close it completely, but almost. As she sauntered toward the bed, she went on, "Unless you want me to. Bite, that is."

"Sit down," Brice told her with a curt nod toward the room's lone chair, a ladderback that sat over by the window.

She pulled it closer to the bed and lowered herself onto it. "Seriously, how badly are you hurt? I heard that you'd been shot, and I got away from the saloon as soon as I could to come check on you."

"I appreciate that," Brice told her. "And I'll be fine. I just got winged a little when all the lead was flying around."

"I heard the shooting. I didn't know you were involved, of course."

"You heard that ruckus all the way over in your saloon?"

She smiled. "Blaise's Place may be on a side street, but it isn't *that* far removed from the rest of downtown Big Rock. I heard the shots, and so did my customers. Some of them went to find out what had happened, and when they came back, they told me all about it. Including the fact that you'd been hurt."

"So you had to come see about me?"

"I did." Blaise's voice softened. "Is that all right?"

Brice looked at her. With her thick, light brown hair, green eyes, and intriguing beauty mark near her mouth, she was one of the most attractive women he had ever seen. She wore a simple, dark blue dress, which meant she must have changed out of one of the more provocative gowns she usually wore in the saloon she owned. The garment didn't do much to conceal the appealing curves of her body. As always, Blaise Warfield took his breath away, just as she had ever since she'd shown up in Big Rock months earlier and taken over the old Double or Nothing Saloon, renaming it and fixing it up.

"I'm very glad you came to see me," Brice said. "In fact, you can, ah, come and sit on the bed and make yourself comfortable if you'd like to talk for a while."

"That sounds nice," Blaise said, then suggested, "but you should probably move that gun first."

CHAPTER 6

Smoke had arranged at the livery stable for a second buggy to carry Louis, Melanie, and Brad out to the Sugarloaf, along with some of their bags. The other bags would be delivered to the ranch later.

Brad asked his mother, "Can I ride with Miss Sally and Denny instead?"

"Well . . . I suppose that would be all right," Melanie told him. "As long as they don't mind."

"Of course, we don't," Sally said. "You're always welcome to ride with us, Brad."

"I was hopin' I could ride a horse, but I guess this is all right."

He climbed into the buggy and sat between Sally and Denny, who leaned over to him and said, "I'd rather be on horseback, too."

Brad grinned. "I thought you might ride Rocket into town."

"That would have been fun."

"I'd like to see him run again. He sure is fast."

"I'm sure you'll get the chance to," Denny told him.

The group left Big Rock with Smoke, Cal, and Pearlie leading the way on horseback, followed by the buggy with Louis and Melanie and then the buggy holding Denny, Sally, and Brad. The

Sugarloaf's headquarters lay seven miles west of the settlement, and the road was a good one the whole way, hard packed and easy to follow.

Remembering the look she had seen in her brother's eyes earlier, Denny said to Brad, "Have Louis and your mother been talking much about their plans? What are they going to do now that they're back?"

"I don't know," Brad replied with a shake of his head. "They don't talk much to me about things like that." He paused. "But they said some things on the train, when they thought I wasn't listening. I think they're worried about something."

"Goodness, what would they have to be worried about?" Sally asked. "It seems to me that everything is going just fine for them. Louis has his law degree now, and you're all healthy and happy."

Brad shrugged. "I dunno. Like I said, they don't talk to me about important stuff."

"Maybe Melanie's expecting," Denny suggested.

Sally looked over at her with excited hope leaping into her eyes. But then she glanced at Brad and gave a little shake of her head, indicating that such a possibility wasn't a suitable thing to talk about in front of the boy.

Denny thought maybe her mother was a little too cautious about that. Brad had spent time on the ranch before, and he would again. If he didn't already know how such things worked, he would before too much longer.

When they reached the Sugarloaf, most of the crew—except for a few men out on the range—were waiting along the lane leading to the main house. They whooped and hollered and waved their hats in the air as Smoke, Pearlie, and Cal led the little procession between them.

At the house itself, Inez Sandoval stood on the porch, along with several young women hired to help out for the day. Tables had been set up in the shade of the trees near the house, and soon those young ladies would begin trooping from the house to the tables, carrying platters of food for the big dinner Sally and Inez had put together. There had been quite a celebration the day Louis left to go back East, which also happened to be the day he and Melanie had gotten married, and although today's fandango wasn't the equal of that, it was still very impressive.

The cowboys who had been waiting for the group hurried up to the house. Inez got her helpers busy bringing out the food while the men lined up to shake hands with Louis and bid him welcome home. He wasn't really one of them, but they knew his health had never allowed him to ride the range like they did. They didn't hold that against him. He was Smoke's son, and that was all that was necessary for them to like him.

Not only that, but several times in the past,

Louis had buckled on a gun and ridden out with his pa and the others to battle the plans of evil men. Louis Jensen's heart might not be as strong physically, but it wasn't lacking for courage.

While that was going on, Denny slipped into the house to get rid of the dress and slippers she wore. When she came back down, she was in boots, jeans, and a white shirt with the sleeves rolled up a couple of turns on her tanned forearms.

She found Brad, who had shed his coat and tie and unbuttoned his collar. With a motion of her head, Denny said to him, "Let's go out to the barn. You can say hello to Rocket."

"Yeah! As long as we're back for that feast Miss Sally and *Señora* Sandoval are putting on."

As they walked toward the barn, Denny said, "Since Louis and your mother are married now, you could call *my* mother Grandma, I suppose."

"Yeah, I thought about it," Brad said, frowning now. "Somehow it just doesn't seem right, though. I mean, Louis isn't my pa. Not really."

"He could be. Maybe he's thinking about it."

"That would be something," Brad said. "Something grand."

Denny heard the awe and hope in the youngster's voice and thought that if Louis wasn't considering adopting Brad, he blasted well ought to be. But her brother could be awfully thick-headed sometimes, she reminded herself.

She would have a talk with him, she decided, and make sure he knew what he ought to do.

The shade inside the barn felt good, and Denny liked the smell of fresh straw even though it was mixed with other, earthier smells.

They spent several minutes standing at the gate of Rocket's stall. The spirited black stallion came over and allowed Brad to reach through the bars and rub his nose.

"I've missed you, Rocket," Brad told the stallion. "One of these days, I'm going to ride you."

"You have a considerable amount of growing to do before you're big enough for that," Denny cautioned.

"I'm not that much younger than you."

"I'm more than twice your age!"

"Yeah, but just barely," Brad insisted. "And I plan on growing fast."

"You do that," Denny told him.

"Hey, Denny . . ."

"Yeah, what is it?"

"My ma says I should call you Aunt Denise. Is that what you want?"

Denny snorted. "I don't care what you call me, kid. But I won't be offended if you call me Aunt Denise while your mother's around. There's something to be said for keeping peace in the family." She laughed. "I know, that doesn't sound much like me, does it?"

"All right, I'll try to remember. But when we're out here in the barn, or riding the range, I'll just call you Denny."

"That sounds like a good idea to me," she assured him. "Now, they're probably getting ready to eat, so I suppose we should mosey on back."

"Yeah! Bear sign!"

"You'll have to save that for dessert," she cautioned.

The afternoon passed very pleasantly with good food and conversation. Some of the cowboys broke out their guitars and provided an impromptu concert. The young women Inez had hired to help with the meal wound up dancing with the ranch hands, as well.

Denny sat at one of the long tables with Smoke, Sally, Louis, Melanie, Brad, Cal, and Pearlie. The former foreman said to Smoke and Louis, "You fellas ought to get up and dance with your wives."

"I think my dancing days are over," Smoke said. "I'm too old."

"Yes, you're positively ancient," Sally said with a smile. "Of course, since I'm not that much younger than you, I wonder what that makes me."

"Just as young as you ever were, like you always will be," Smoke replied without hesitation.

Melanie waved her hand in front of her face

and said, "It's a little warm out here for me to be dancing, I think. It's going to take me a while to get used to the weather here again."

Denny suspected she said that just to give Louis a good excuse for not dancing, since he had to be careful about how much he exerted himself. The doctors had told him that he could live a reasonably normal life and not expect to have it shortened too much by his condition, but in order to achieve that, he had to be cautious about what he did. When Denny saw him reach over and briefly squeeze Melanie's hand, she knew that her hunch was right.

Smoke was sitting on the bench beside the table with his back to it and his legs stretched out in front of him, appearing completely relaxed. Denny knew he was alert, though. The prospect of trouble cropping up this afternoon was pretty slim, but Smoke didn't ever let his guard down all the way. He couldn't. He had spent too many years on the razor's edge of danger.

But he sounded as if he were just making idle conversation as he said, "We're going to have to have a long talk, Louis. I have plans for this ranch, and you're a big part of them. But that can wait until you and Melanie and Brad have moved back in and gotten settled down a mite."

Denny saw her brother look at Melanie, and once again she spotted something in Louis's eyes that made her sit up straighter and tense her muscles in anticipation, especially when Melanie shrugged slightly and gave Louis a tiny nod.

He drew in a deep breath and said, "Actually, Pa, the three of us aren't going to live here on the Sugarloaf."

Smoke's eyes narrowed as he turned his head to gaze at Louis. Sally exclaimed, "No!" Everyone else at the table looked at Louis and Melanie, including Brad.

"I think I should explain—" Louis began.

"Yeah, you should," Smoke broke in. "Your mother and I assumed you were back to stay."

"We are. I mean . . . we're back in the valley to stay. But we're going to live in Big Rock, not here on the Sugarloaf."

"Why are you going to do that?" Sally asked.

"Because that's where my law practice will be located," Louis said with a solemn expression on his face. His voice was firmer as he went on, "We need a home of our own, Mother. We can't stay here on the ranch from now on."

"You could if you wanted to," Smoke said.

Louis said, "And be dependent on you?" He shook his head. "I don't think so."

Smoke pulled his legs up, sat straighter, and clasped his hands together in front of him. "That's what I wanted to talk to you about," he said. "I have plenty of work for you to do. Legal work. You wouldn't be dependent on anybody. You'd earn your keep, I promise you that."

72

Louis shook his head. "I'll be glad to handle any legal affairs for the Sugarloaf, of course, but even with a ranch of this size, there wouldn't be enough of those to keep a law practice busy all the time. That's why I want to open an office in town where potential clients can come to see me."

"Shoot, I'll build you an office here," Smoke offered with a wave of his hand.

"It's not the same thing, and you know it, Pa."

Denny knew her father well enough to recognize the frustration on his face. When she looked at her mother, though, she was surprised to see acceptance in Sally's expression.

Sally reached over to rest a hand on one of Louis's hands. "I understand why you feel that way, dear."

Smoke frowned at her. "You do?"

"Of course. Louis is your son, Smoke. He's got an independent streak in him."

"And a stubborn streak a mile wide," Denny added. This was family business, and she had a say in it, too.

Louis glared at her for a second, then laughed. "I won't deny it," he said. "I'd say we're both pretty stubborn, wouldn't you?"

Denny shrugged.

"Well . . ." Smoke was struggling to accept this decision, Denny saw, but he was trying. "Where are you going to live?"

"I've already made arrangements to buy the old Livingston house."

Denny knew the house he was talking about. It was a sturdy, two-story structure a few blocks from downtown. It wasn't new; in fact, it was one of the first houses built in Big Rock more than twenty years earlier, when the honest citizens of the outlaw town Fontana had established the new settlement. But it had been well cared for, and Denny recalled that the elderly widower who lived there had passed away a few months earlier.

"None of Bob Livingston's children are interested in living in the house," Louis went on. "They've all moved away and have lives of their own elsewhere. So they were very happy to sell the place to me for a decent price. I've also agreed to rent office space downtown."

Smoke nodded slowly. "Sounds like you've given this a lot of thought. Reckon you could have told us about it and talked it over with us, though."

Melanie said, "I suggested that he might want to do that, but you know how he is."

"I was afraid you'd talk me out of it," Louis said bluntly to his parents.

Sally squeezed his hand again. "Not if it's something you really want to do."

"I feel like I have to," he said, nodding. "I thought about settling somewhere else, striking out completely on our own, but . . ." He smiled.

"I'd miss all of you too much. I'd miss this place too much. And I know Brad loves it here, too." He looked at his stepson. "What do you think?"

"I thought we'd live on the ranch," Brad said. "I was looking forward to it."

"You can still spend a lot of time here," Smoke told him, clearly trying to make the best of the situation. "Big Rock's less than ten miles away, and it's an easy ride. That is . . ." He glanced at Melanie. "If your ma agrees."

"Of course, I do," she said. "You and Sally gave Bradley and me a home when we didn't have one. I'll never forget that, Smoke. The Sugarloaf will always be a part of us, and we'll be part of it whether we're living here or in town."

Smoke drew in a deep breath and nodded. "All right, then, I reckon it's settled." He pointed a finger at Louis. "But no matter where your office is, I'm still counting on you to give me a hand with all the legal folderol that comes up. Why, at least half the papers that cross my desk just look like gibberish to me. I need you to translate them to plain old English."

"I can do that," Louis replied with a smile.

Denny was proud of her father for not arguing more and for supporting Louis's decision. She knew it wasn't easy for Smoke to step back and allow other folks to make up their own minds, especially when it came to family.

She felt a little twinge of guilt for realizing

that Louis's decision was a welcome one to her. She loved her brother, but he had been gone long enough that she had gotten used to not having him around on an everyday basis. And even though her father had made no secret of the fact that he intended to turn the running of the Sugarloaf over to her someday, that would be easier on all of them if Louis was busy elsewhere with a successful career of his own.

She supposed she could understand why Melanie wanted her own home, too, instead of sharing one with Sally.

Brad was the one losing out here, since he wouldn't get to spend as much time on the ranch he loved, riding and roping and growing up to be a top hand like his late father had been. But as Smoke had said, Brad could still be around the Sugarloaf quite a bit. It would all work out.

"Think you'll be able to get enough clients in town?" Smoke asked.

"They won't just come from town," Louis said. "I expect the other ranchers in the valley will need legal help and advice from time to time, too." He smiled. "After all, it's not like the old days, when most disputes out here were settled by the firm of Colt and Winchester!"

CHAPTER 7

Chet Holloway had been riding for the Box RG, Roy Gardner's spread, for six months now. It was the best job he'd had in several years of cowboying across Montana, Wyoming, and Colorado. Mr. Gardner was a good boss, and the rest of the hands were friendly . . . for the most part.

One of them, Andy Simons, liked to hooraw the other fellas and play tricks on them, especially the younger ones who hadn't been part of the crew as long. Chet had woken up one morning to find a rattlesnake in bed with him. It was dead, thank goodness, but Andy had tied a string to its rattles and was shaking them from across the room to make Chet think the snake was alive and about to strike him.

Chet jumped about four feet off the bunk, straight up, yelling all the way. When he came down, rolled off onto the floor, and wound up lying there on his belly with his heart pounding wildly in his chest, he heard the roars of laughter filling the bunkhouse and realized what had happened.

He knew who was to blame for it, too. For a second, he wanted to leap up, charge across the room, and whale the tar out of Andy Simons.

But, in the long run, it was easier just to grin sheepishly, pick up the dead rattler, and toss it back at Andy as he said, "Here, I reckon you lost somethin'."

That just made the other fellas laugh even more. But Chet figured it was better for them to see that he could take a joke, instead of getting mad or sulling up.

Now, as he approached the waterhole near the northern edge of Mr. Gardner's range, he wondered if somebody else was playing a joke on him. He couldn't see any other reason why anybody would stick posts in the ground and string wire between them so Box RG cows couldn't get to the water. There was a drift fence between Mr. Gardner's spread and his neighbor to the north, the Ace of Diamonds belonging to Tony Mullen, but that was a good quarter-mile from here.

Two other Box RG hands were a ways behind Chet, pushing a small group of stock this direction so the cows could drink at the waterhole. Chet had ridden ahead to make sure everything was all right. It had been a hot summer so far with very little rain, but none of the waterholes had gone dry. However, some of them were low, and the cattle were starting to get thirsty at times.

That was the case today, Chet knew. Those cows had been bawling when he rode ahead. They were eager to get to the water. Once they scented it, they would hurry even more and might even start running.

If that happened, there was a possibility they would plow right into that fence and hurt themselves. Chet saw the wicked barbs sticking out from the wire strands. Barb wire was a common thing now.

But it wasn't welcome around a waterhole where stock could get hurt on it.

Surprised, Chet had reined in at the sight of the fence. He looked back over his shoulder in the direction the cattle would be coming from. He couldn't hear them yet, but he knew they would be here soon. Without wasting any time, he swung down from the saddle and let his cow pony's reins dangle. The horse was well-trained and wouldn't wander off. Chet reached to his hip pocket and pulled out a pair of wire cutters. The hands carried them because occasionally a cow would get tangled up in a fence and have to be cut loose. It was considered bad form to cut another man's fence . . .

But this one was on Box RG range, blocking Box RG water. Chet didn't hesitate. He lifted the cutters and fitted them around the top strand of wire.

The sharp crack of a rifle shot sounded at the same instant as a bullet smacked into a fence post a couple of feet from Chet. He yelped and jumped back, so shocked that he dropped the wire cutters as he stumbled and fell down.

Three men on horseback spurred their mounts out of some trees not far from the waterhole and galloped toward Chet. One of them held a rifle. Chet felt certain that was the varmint who had just taken the shot at him.

He came up on one knee and reached for the six-shooter holstered on his hip. He had only ever used it for shooting snakes, but right now he felt like those hombres headed toward him sort of fit the description.

The Colt's barrel shook a little because he had never pointed a gun at another human being before. He gripped his right wrist with his left hand to steady it. His sights settled on the chest of the man holding the rifle, but he didn't squeeze the trigger. Instead, he raised the gun slightly and fired over the riders' heads.

The warning shot didn't make them slow their charge. In fact, the two flanking the rifleman whipped out their handguns and opened fire. Bullets kicked up dirt to both sides of Chet. He cursed as he scrambled to his feet and turned to run toward his horse.

Three-to-one odds were no good, especially when he wasn't any sort of a gunman to start with. He expected to feel a slug smash into him at any second, because the onrushing riders were still shooting at him. Thankfully, they didn't seem to be all that accurate. He wasn't hit by the time he reached his horse.

Unfortunately, the racket had spooked the animal, and it jumped away when Chet reached for the dangling reins.

"Blast it, come back here, you dang jughead!" he yelled. That was the wrong thing to do, because the shout made the horse even more skittish. Chet still had his Colt in his right hand. He jammed the gun back in its holster so he could use both hands to try to grab the horse.

His hat suddenly flew off his head, and a second later he heard the wicked whine of another bullet passing close by his ear. Those bushwhacking skunks were getting the range now. He made another awkward lunge after the horse. This time he snagged the reins. He dragged down on them, bringing the cow pony under control, and grabbed the saddle horn. A frantic leap brought him into the saddle. He found the stirrups, banged his heels against the horse's flanks, and leaned forward to make himself a smaller target as the horse bounded into a gallop.

"Hold your fire!" Orrie Striker called to his companions as he reined his horse to a halt. "Hold your fire, blast it!"

Quince Jessup hauled back on his reins and glared at Striker. "But we can still get him," Jessup protested.

"He's out of handgun range."

"Well, let me get my rifle out, and I'll plug the

son of a buck! I can shoot the eyes out of a gnat at a hundred yards!"

Jessup was young, a firebrand who figured he was a dangerous man. Striker, a lean man of middle years with silvery hair and mustache, said, "Just let him go, Quince. We scared him outta five years' growth, I reckon."

The third member of the Ace of Diamonds trio, a stolid puncher named Baxter, said, "He'll go back and tell Gardner what he found here."

"Hell, Gardner had to find out sooner or later, didn't he?" Striker shook his head. "You boys got a mite ahead of yourselves. The boss never said to kill any Box RG hands we came across, just to run 'em off if they came close to this waterhole."

"He shot at us first!" Jessup protested, which wasn't actually true since Striker had fired a warning shot a little wide of the Box RG puncher.

Jessup continued with a note of pride in his voice, "We ran him off all right. He won't stop runnin' until he gets back to Gardner's bunkhouse. And then he'll probably crawl in his bunk and pull the blankets over his head and cry for a while."

Striker stared at him and said, "You don't know a whole heap about cowboys, do you? Sure, he lit a shuck because he had sense enough to know he wasn't facin' good odds. But I'll bet a hat he ain't exactly shakin' in his boots right now." Striker rubbed fingertips over the bristly stubble on his chin. "In fact, he's probably already thinkin' about how he's gonna settle the score with us. So we'd better head back to those trees, because I reckon we ain't done yet."

Chet's horse was still running flat-out when he spotted the jag of cattle in front of him, being pushed along by Johnny Dolan and Ben Hendricks. The cows were moving along at a pretty good clip, still anxious to reach that waterhole. Chet waved at Johnny and Ben and yelled, "Stop 'em where they are!"

The other two cowboys didn't seem to grasp what he was saying, so he rode straight at the cattle, shouting and waving to try to get them to turn. If they did, they would start milling around and then stop in confusion.

Dolan and Hendricks got the idea then and spurred ahead to push the cows to the side. All three men were good hands, so it didn't take long to get the small herd stopped.

Then Ben Hendricks, thin to the point of gauntness even though he had one of the biggest appetites in the bunkhouse, with a drooping dark mustache that looked like it ought to weigh more than the rest of him, confronted Chet and demanded, "What in the Sam Hill is wrong with you? Them cows are thirsty!"

"The waterhole's fenced off." Chet was a little breathless. He dragged in some air before he went on, "I didn't want the cows hurtin' themselves on the barb wire."

Johnny Dolan came up in time to hear that. He said, "Fenced off! Who would do such a loco thing?"

"And where's your hat?" Hendricks asked with a frown. "I just noticed it's gone."

"That's because it got shot off my head when I went to cut that fence so Mr. Gardner's cows could get through."

Both his friends stared at him for several seconds before Hendricks said, "I thought I heard some shootin' a little spell ago. You mean to say that whoever fenced off the waterhole was guardin' it?"

"That's exactly what I mean to say," Chet confirmed with a curt nod. "And now that I've had time to think about it, one of 'em might've been old Orrie Striker, Mullen's foreman. I never had the time to take a real good look at the varmints, because I was too busy tryin' to get on my horse and get outta there before I got ventilated."

"They tried to kill you?" asked Dolan.

"If they weren't, they did a mighty good imitation of it."

"How many were there?" Hendricks wanted to know.

"Three that I saw." Chet shrugged. "Could've been more in the trees, I don't know about that."

"Three of them, three of us," Dolan said. "I say

we go back there and learn those boys that they can't shoot at Box RG hands and get away with it."

Dolan was the youngest and most hotheaded of the three hands, Hendricks the oldest although he hadn't seen thirty yet. He said, "Hold on. There's never been trouble between the Box RG and the Ace of Diamonds before. Fencin' off waterholes and orderin' his men to shoot at us don't sound like something Tony Mullen would do."

"Sound like it or not, the waterhole's fenced off and my hat's got a bullet hole in it, wherever it is," Chet said. "We can't just go chargin' up to that fence, though. Those boys have already shown that they'll shoot. We shouldn't give 'em easy targets."

Hendricks nodded. "Yeah, that's makin' sense, Chet. We'll leave these cows here and ride on to the waterhole, but when we get there, hang back a mite. I want to see if they'll talk instead of shootin'."

Johnny Dolan glared in obvious disagreement with that plan, but he didn't say anything, instead falling in with the other two cowboys as they rode north.

It didn't take long to come in sight of the fence, with the waterhole beyond it. The three men reined in and studied the layout. The fence ran as far as they could see east and west, with no breaks and no easy way around it.

"How in blazes did Mullen get this thrown up so fast?" muttered Hendricks. "He must've had every man on his spread workin' long hours to do it. I'm surprised we never saw them at it."

"None of us have been up in these parts for a while," Chet said. "The graze around here isn't very good. That waterhole is really the only thing that makes this area of the Box RG worth anything."

"And now it looks like Mullen's gonna try to steal it," Dolan said.

Chet was right about this being pretty sorry range. Much of the terrain was rocky, and grass was sparse. The trees that grew were scrubby. Farther north, across the line on the Ace of Diamonds range, some hills lifted in rolling waves, and the grazing was better there. In the past, when water had been more abundant and before the drift fence was built, Mullen's stock had wandered down here from time to time and used the waterhole. Nobody got upset about that, just like Mullen didn't care if some of Roy Gardner's stock meandered into the hills and ate some Ace of Diamonds grass. It all evened out in the end, both ranchers figured.

But then, several years ago, the state had gotten more particular about property lines. They wanted the boundaries to be cut and dried. The days of the open range were over. Nobody was particularly happy about it, but the times were changing and spreads could no longer operate the way they always had.

After a moment, Hendricks nudged his horse ahead of the other two. "We're in rifle range," he said, "but it'd be a long shot. You fellas stay here. I want to see if I can talk to whoever's on the other side."

"They'll shoot you, Ben," Dolan warned.

"Maybe not."

"They came mighty close to ventilating me," Chet said. "You'd best be careful, Ben."

"I intend to be. I'm not getting much closer than I already am unless I think it's safe."

Hendricks moved ahead another twenty feet or so and then stopped again. He cupped his hands around his mouth and shouted toward the waterhole, "Striker! Orrie Striker! Are you there?"

Faintly, a reply came back from the trees. "Who's that, and what do you want?"

"Ben Hendricks from the Box RG! Just figure to palaver a mite! No need for any shootin'!"

"Don't come any closer to that fence!"

"I'll wait right here," Hendricks promised. "Why don't you come closer so we don't have to holler so much?"

"So you can shoot me, you mean?"

"If I shoot you, your boys'll shoot me, won't they?"

"Dang right they will!"

"Well, I don't want to be shot, so let's do this without burnin' any more powder than what's already been burned."

Striker didn't answer, so the Box RG hands assumed he was mulling it over. Then, a tall, straight-backed figure on horseback emerged from the trees and rode slowly toward them.

Chet recognized Orrie Striker and knew his earlier guess had been right. Striker had been Tony Mullen's foreman for several years, from what Chet had heard. He had also heard that Striker was considered something of a fast gun and was rumored to have been an outlaw at one time. But many men went back and forth over the line that separated outlaws from honest men, and most folks tried not to judge anybody on their past but only on what they were doing now. As far as Chet knew, Orrie Striker was an honest puncher.

But that didn't mean he wanted to get crosswise with an old-timer like Striker, who could be rough as a cob when he wanted to.

As Striker rode forward and approached the fence, so did Ben Hendricks. Hendricks was just a regular hand, not the Box RG foreman, so he didn't have any real authority other than his age. Still, Chet was more than happy to let Hendricks handle the talking part of this confrontation.

The two men stopped, facing each other from opposite sides of the fence. They were close enough for Chet to hear the conversation.

"Looks like this fence is in the wrong place," began Hendricks. "That waterhole over yonder belongs to the Box RG."

"Not anymore," Striker responded. "The boundary line between the spreads has changed. The waterhole's on Ace of Diamonds range now."

"Who says so?"

"My boss. Mr. Mullen."

"He knows better than that," Hendricks argued. "He and Mr. Gardner got together and settled on the boundary line between the spreads a long time ago."

"All I know is that the man I work for told me to shift the fence a mile south. I'm in the habit of doin' what he tells me."

Chet couldn't control his temper anymore. He moved his horse forward a little and called, "Are you in the habit of tryin' to kill honest punchers just tryin' to do their jobs?"

Striker's narrow-eyed gaze swung toward Chet. "You ain't dead, are you?"

"What? No, you can see I ain't dead."

"Well, if I'd wanted to kill you, you would be. That rifle shot I fired was just to make you move on." Striker's shoulders rose and fell. "The two boys with me got a mite excited when you shot back at us, that's all. They threw more lead than I intended." Striker looked at Hendricks again. "The boss wants to keep the peace."

"Fencin' off our water is a mighty funny way to

go about it," Hendricks said. "I don't know what makes him think he's got a right to do it, but if he honestly believes that, he should've talked to Mr. Gardner about it first."

"I don't tell the man how to run his business," Striker said flatly. "But I'm tellin' you and the rest of Gardner's crew to stay away from this fence."

"And if we don't?"

"There'll be trouble."

"Gun trouble?"

Striker's lips curved thinly in a shadow of a smile.

"When you get right down to it, there's not really any other kind, is there?"

CHAPTER 8

Badger Gulch, Utah

The little settlement had gotten its name from a nearby gulch where somebody had once seen a badger or at least claimed to have seen a badger. Nobody knew the actual truth of the matter—or cared.

What was important was that the settlement just west of the border between Colorado and Utah functioned as a supply point for the ranches in the area, as well as for prospectors and other pilgrims passing through. The surrounding area was rugged country, with deep canyons carved out by streams that flowed between tall sandstone bluffs. The wind had also shaped and altered those bluffs, creating a landscape that was stark but beautiful.

The railroad passed through Badger Gulch on its way to Salt Lake City, but the settlement wasn't a regular stop. Bert Larsen, who ran the local Union Pacific station, had to raise a flag in order to have a train stop. That didn't happen often. Equally rare were those occasions when a train stopped to deliver some freight or allow a passenger to disembark.

Evening shadows had started to gather over

Badger Gulch as Larsen sat in his office at the depot, which consisted only of this room and a small waiting room, with a door and a ticket window in between, plus a shed for freight and a covered platform next to the tracks. The waiting room was empty because nobody had bought a ticket on the westbound, which was due in another half-hour or so. The train would slow as it approached the settlement so it would be able to stop if the flag was out, but as soon as the engineer realized that wasn't the case, he would pour on the throttle and the big locomotive would leap ahead again.

Larsen was looking over the latest paperwork Union Pacific headquarters had sent him. He was convinced the railroad employed at least a dozen people writing documents all day, every day, just to send out to fellas like him who kept the stations running. Very little of it was of any actual importance, but Larsen had to read it all anyway, just to make sure nothing vital slipped past him.

He raised his head when he heard the door into the waiting room open. Footsteps approached the ticket window. Maybe somebody wanted to travel on the westbound after all. Larsen, a big, heavyset man with a thatch of flaxen hair, heaved himself to his feet and went over to the ticket window.

One man had come into the waiting room, but

when Larsen looked past him, he saw several more riders just outside the station, still mounted on their horses. Larsen didn't recognize the man who walked up to the ticket window, but he smiled anyway and asked, "You fellas want tickets for the westbound? I don't know if there'll be a stock car for your horses, but I ought to be able to send a telegram back up the line and find out for you. It'll still be, oh, twenty minutes or so before the train gets here. Plenty of time."

The stranger nodded and said, "Plenty of time is right. We were a mite worried that we'd gotten here too late."

Larsen shook his head. "You might have, most times, but the train's a little behind schedule today. Are you headed for Salt Lake City, or are you going farther west?"

"Actually, we're not goin' anywhere," the man said. He was a burly hombre with thick red hair that he revealed by thumbing back his hat with a casual gesture. "We're meeting somebody."

"Oh? Not many people get off here."

"Our friend is going to." The stranger nodded toward the tracks. "Do you get the train to stop by raising the flag on that post outside?"

"Yeah, that's the way it works." Larsen frowned slightly in confusion. "But that won't be necessary if your friend has let the conductor know that he's getting off here. The conductor will make sure the train stops."

"That's just it. He won't be able to do that. We'll have to put the flag up."

Larsen shook his head. "I sure don't understand what you're getting at, mister."

"Maybe you'll understand this."

The redheaded man moved back a step and reached down. His hand came up with a gun in it, a gun that he pointed through the ticket window at Bert Larsen, whose eyes widened in shock.

A second later, Larsen glanced down at the shelf below the counter where a pistol lay. The man on the other side of the window eared back the hammer of the gun he held and said, "I know what you're looking at, and I know what you're thinking. And you're nowhere *near* fast enough to pull that off, friend. You reach for it and I'll shoot you. Somebody in town will hear the shot and come to see what it's about. Then we'll have to kill him, and somebody else will come, and before you know it, we'll wind up wiping out half the damn town. You don't want to be the cause of all those people dying, do you?"

Larsen had a lot of relatives and friends in Badger Gulch, so he definitely didn't want any of them coming to harm because of him. Maybe these men wanted to rob the train. There had never been a holdup on this run during the eight years Larsen had worked for Union Pacific, but that didn't mean it was impossible. The whole business about meeting a friend could be just a ruse to get the train to stop.

Nothing they might steal was worth his life, Larsen told himself, or the lives of folks he cared about. Keeping his hands raised above the counter in plain sight, he said, "Whatever you want, mister, just tell me. I'll be glad to do it."

The stranger's rugged face creased in a grin. "That's more like it," he said. "Come out of there. And if your hands aren't empty and where I can see 'em when you open that door, I'll kill you . . . and then our deal's off."

"I understand," Larsen said. "No tricks." He moved over to the door between his office and the waiting room, opened it, and stepped through, showing the outlaw his hands. Larsen had no doubt now that this man and his companions were desperadoes, like Butch Cassidy and that Wild Bunch of his. The Wild Bunch hadn't been heard of lately, but they might have come back from wherever they'd gone. Maybe this man holding a gun on him actually *was* the infamous Butch Cassidy.

Wouldn't that be something, Larsen thought.

The stranger motioned with his gun, indicating that Larsen should go out on the platform. The stationmaster did so, with his captor following closely beside him. The other men, who had dismounted, came around the corner of the building on foot. Larsen supposed the leader had signaled to them somehow, although he hadn't witnessed that for himself.

"One of you pull the rope on that post and raise the flag," the redheaded man said. "A couple of you go inside and watch the door." He poked Larsen in the back with the gun barrel. "Are you expecting anybody?"

"N-no," Larsen replied. "I was fixing to close up and go home as soon as the westbound came through."

"Well, you can still do that. Just don't give us any trouble."

"Not a bit," Larsen promised.

"When you raise the flag and stop the train, are you usually out here to meet it when it rolls in?"

"Sometimes, but not always. Sometimes I'm busy in the station when it gets here."

"So the engineer will stop whether you're in sight or not?"

"Yeah, he should, as long as the flag's up." Larsen turned his head to look curiously over his shoulder. "Why do you want to know—"

He realized why the outlaw would want to know that at the same instant as eight inches of razor-sharp steel slid into his back and reached all the way to his heart. Pain exploded throughout his body, and that split-second burst of agony was the last thing he was aware of as his knees buckled.

That and the distant, mournful wail of a

locomotive's whistle as the engineer on the westbound announced that the train was approaching Badger Gulch.

Jess Fenner sat next to a window in the caboose with Deputy Marshal Hal Goodwin on the hard bench seat beside him. Deputy Marshal Ed Foster was in the chair in front of the conductor's desk, with his hands clasped together on his stomach and his legs stretched out in front of him as he leaned back. The conductor was somewhere else on the train at the moment, tending to his business.

Foster's black, flat-crowned hat was tilted down so that the brim shaded his eyes. Goodwin knew his partner was snoring, even though the sounds were too soft to be heard over the clatter of the rails.

Fenner hadn't given the deputy marshals any problems since leaving Big Rock. He had even stopped complaining about his broken nose, although his breathing through it was harsh enough for Goodwin to hear it, sitting as close as he was.

They would reach Salt Lake City late tonight. Foster was getting a nap now so that they could switch places later and he would guard Fenner during the last part of the trip.

The chief marshal back in Denver had warned them about Fenner, telling them not to underestimate the outlaw. As far as Goodwin and Foster could tell, though, Fenner had had all the troublemaking knocked out of him by the violence that had taken place in Big Rock. Other than a little whining at the beginning, he had been very cooperative. He just sat there, peering out the window at the rugged Utah landscape as the day's lingering sunlight faded.

The locomotive's whistle blew, and a moment later, the train began to slow down. That was enough to rouse Ed Foster from his light sleep. He raised his head, looked around and blinked a couple of times, then said, "What's going on?"

"Seems like we're stopping," Goodwin told him.

"Where are we?"

"As near as I can tell, not far over the Colorado/Utah line."

Foster frowned. "There aren't any good-sized towns between here and Salt Lake City."

"No, but there are a few flag stops. Don't worry, Ed. We probably won't be stopped more than a few minutes, and then we'll be on our way again."

"The train's already late," Foster grumbled.

"Not much. Not enough to matter."

Foster squinted at him and said, "That's just it. You never really know for sure what's going to matter, and what isn't."

"You'll have to take it up with the Union Pacific."

Foster just shook his head and stood up. "I'm gonna have a look."

"Go ahead."

Foster moved toward the front of the caboose, turning his head back and forth to look out the windows on both sides as the train continued slowing. The tracks curved a little, and that gave him a view of some lights up ahead, yellow glows in the gathering dusk that came from the windows of a small town. Foster had been through here before and vaguely remembered a settlement being located in these parts. He tried to recall the name of it but failed.

He stepped out onto the platform at the front of the caboose and leaned to the right to look along the train. He saw the town and the small wooden building that served as the station. A water tank with an attached spout rose on stilt-like legs just beyond it, so a locomotive could stop and take on water if it needed to. In mostly arid country like this, such things were important.

Foster suddenly leaned forward and squinted as he stared at the water tank, which, like the station, was drawing closer fairly quickly. It was difficult to be sure in this gloom, but he would have sworn that he saw something—or some*body*—move on top of the tank.

Foster's heart slugged hard in his chest as he wheeled around, burst through the door into the caboose, and ran toward Goodwin and Fenner.

"Ambush!" he called to his fellow deputy marshal. "They're waiting for us!"

Goodwin leaped to his feet and exclaimed, "What are you talking about?"

"Up ahead," Foster said, waving his free hand in that direction. "I saw somebody on top of the water tank. Got to be a gunman waiting for us. You know what happened back in Big Rock. Fenner rode with a good-sized gang, and they're not all accounted for—"

With a slight lurch, the train came to a stop. It had reached the station.

Outside, gunfire shattered the evening calm.

Goodwin grabbed Fenner's collar and threw the handcuffed outlaw to the floor. "Get down there and stay down!" he ordered. He started to turn toward the nearest window, crouching slightly and lifting his rifle.

Instead of following Goodwin's order, Fenner came up on his knees and threw himself at the lawman's legs. Goodwin yelled as the impact from Fenner's body knocked him down.

At the same time, windows shattered as rifle fire from outside raked the caboose. Glass shards flew through the air. A bullet ricocheted from the iron potbellied stove in the corner, which wasn't in use at this time of year. More slugs thudded into the walls and desk.

Foster heard shots from elsewhere, as well as right outside, and knew the caboose wasn't the

100

only car under attack. If the gunmen were bent on freeing Jess Fenner, as he believed to be the case, they would want to keep the train stopped. That meant the engineer and fireman probably were in danger, too, if they hadn't been gunned down already.

He saw Goodwin and Fenner wrestling on the floor and ran toward them, crouching to try to avoid flying glass and bullets. It was a little surprising that the outlaws would pour such a barrage into the caboose and risk hitting Fenner, but he supposed they figured he would rather die from a bullet here than kicking out his life at the end of a hang rope in a few weeks.

Foster looked for a chance to use his rifle butt and knock out Fenner, but before he got it, the door at the front of the caboose slammed open. He twisted toward it and swung his rifle around as three men burst into the car. The guns in their hands roared and spurted flame.

Foster took a couple of jittering steps backward as bullets pounded into his chest. He had been about to squeeze the trigger of his rifle, and his finger still clenched spasmodically as he was hit. The rifle cracked and the recoil jolted it out of his fingers, as his nerves and muscles no longer worked. Fate guided that shot to the belly of one of the outlaws, who dropped his gun and doubled over as the slug punched into his guts. He collapsed.

Foster fell to his knees, managed to press both

hands to his bloody chest, and then toppled sideways. His eyes began to glaze over as he twitched a final couple of times.

A few feet away, Fenner got an opening to swing his clubbed hands into Goodwin's face. The blow drove the lawman's head to the side and stunned him. He lay on his back, unable to move for a moment, and that brief bit of time proved to be his doom. Fenner snatched up the rifle Goodwin had dropped. He lifted it with both hands and brought its butt crashing down into Goodwin's face. Bones cracked and blood spurted under the blow. Grating hate-filled curses, Fenner struck again and again with the rifle butt until Goodwin's shattered face didn't even look human anymore.

One of the outlaws stepped up to him and leaned down to grasp his arm. "You can stop hitting that badge-toter, Jess," he said, sounding amused. "His brains are running out all over the floor, so I reckon he's probably dead."

Fenner spewed a few more curses, then tossed the rifle aside. By now, its stock was broken although still hanging on to the rest of the weapon. He looked up at the man leaning over him and said, "He had it comin', Nick. He truly did. Both of these lawdogs did. But they're not the only ones."

"What are you talking about?" the other man asked as he helped Fenner to his feet.

"This isn't the only score I've got to settle," Fenner said. "There's another lawman back in Big Rock I want to see."

"Big Rock! That's where the boys who made the first try to free you wound up getting killed."

"You're not telling me anything I don't already know." Fenner drew in a deep breath filled with gunsmoke fumes and the coppery smell of freshly spilled blood. "I spotted Randall as these two were putting me on the train and knew he'd get word to you that the first try failed, Nick. So I figured you'd show up somewhere before the train got to Salt Lake City. Did you shoot up the whole train?"

"And half the town," Nick replied with a grin. "Figured that was the way you'd want it."

Fenner nodded in agreement with that statement.

From the other end of the caboose, the other outlaw said, "Wilkerson's dead, Jess. The one shot that lawman got off was a lucky one. Well, unlucky for Wilkerson, I guess."

Fenner ignored that and thrust out his cuffed hands. "Find the key for these damn things," he told Nick. "I want to get out of here."

As he started feeling through the dead deputy's pockets, Nick asked, "Are we going back to Big Rock?"

"Not right now. But when the time's right . . ." Fenner nodded. "When the time's right, I'm gonna settle the score with Brice Rogers and the others who got in the way. Some fella named Morgan, I think . . . and a blond girl who won't be near as pretty when I get through with her."

CHAPTER 9

Denver

Hannah Winslow went by the name Flossie here at Madame Dumont's Academy for Young Ladies. She didn't care for the name, but that was what Madame Dumont had decided to call her because she had a big shock of curly hair so pale it was almost white. So she was stuck with it.

Madame Dumont herself went by a name other than the one she was born with, which Hannah happened to know was Bertha Applewhite because she had seen it on a letter she'd found while poking around in the office one day when the madame had gone somewhere. Bertha Applewhite from Fulcher's Holler, Missouri. That was a far cry from Madame Esmerelda Dumont.

Hannah kept that knowledge to herself because if Madame Dumont ever found out she'd been sticking her nose where it didn't belong, that'd mean a whipping for sure. Hannah didn't mind too much if a customer swatted her on the rump now and then to get in the proper frame of mind to conduct business, as long as he wasn't too rough about it. The madame's hickory switch, wielded with savage efficiency and a considerable amount of passion, was a whole different thing.

105

Hannah had been working at the academy, which actually did teach the younger "ladies" a number of lessons they'd probably never dreamed of, for six months, so she should have been used to her nickname by now. But sometimes Madame Dumont would call, "Flossie!" in that mule's bray of a voice of hers that came right out of Fulcher's Holler, Missouri, and Hannah failed to respond because she'd forgotten that was what she went by now.

That was what happened this afternoon. The madame had to summon Hannah twice before she realized she was wanted. She jumped up from the chair where she'd been sitting in the parlor, pulled down the shift she was wearing so it covered a little more at the bottom and revealed a little more at the top, and started across the room with the forthright stride of the farm girl she had been back in Kansas, an eternity ago by one measure, less than a year by another. Halfway across, she caught the madame frowning at her and tried to make her gait more sensuous and seductive. Whenever she did that, she always wondered if it looked as ridiculous as it felt.

Probably not, because the gents all seemed to like it, including the one who stood next to Madame Dumont in the foyer, near the bottom of the staircase.

She couldn't tell for sure what the man thought of her because he was embarrassed and kept looking at the floor, glancing up only now and then. Hannah actually preferred the customers who acted like they were eight years old and mortified by the sight of female flesh and the prospect of what they were about to do. Those were the ones more likely to be gentle and undemanding.

She put a bright smile on her face and said, "Yes, Madame Dumont?"

"This gentleman would like to spend a little time in your company," the madame said.

"Why, that's just dandy, because as soon as he stepped through the door, I said to myself, now there's a gentleman I'd like to get to know better. I surely did."

That brought a shy smile from the customer, who was on the short and slender side. He had thinning brown hair, and a pair of rimless spectacles perched on his nose. He was well-dressed in a nice suit and turned his hat around and around in his hands.

Hannah hadn't noticed him at all when he came in, but the lie she'd told was harmless enough.

Madame Dumont, who was four inches taller than the gent and outweighed him probably by fifty pounds, put her hand on his shoulder and practically shoved him at Hannah.

"You two fine young people go on upstairs and get acquainted," she said.

Deftly, Hannah stepped forward and linked her

left arm with his right and steered him toward the stairs. "You just come on with me, Mister . . . ?"

"Oh, dear," he said. "I assumed that names wouldn't be necessary."

"It's so much more friendly when we know each other's names. Mine's Flossie. How about I call you . . ." She cocked her head to the side, pressed the forefinger of her left hand to her dimpled chin, and frowned slightly as if she were devoting deep thought to the question. "Mr. Smith! That's what I'll call you. Mr. Smith."

The man swallowed hard. "Mr. Smith will be just fine."

"And if we get to be *really* good friends, maybe I'll call you Smitty," she said as they started up the stairs. "Would that be all right?"

"Of . . . of course."

She hugged his arm with both of hers and laughed. "I can already tell that we're gonna get along just fine."

Like so many of the shy, embarrassed ones, Mr. Smith wanted to talk for a while first before getting down to business. That was fine with Hannah. He was paying for the time, so he could spend it any way he wanted to. And even if he was as gentle as he appeared to be, talking for a spell was that much less wear and tear on her.

She expected him to ask her where she came from and how she wound up working in a place like this. Those were the most common questions.

But instead, he placed his hat carefully on the dresser, turned toward her, sat down in the room's single chair, and said, "You must meet all kinds of men in your, ah, line of work."

"I suppose that's true." She perched on the edge of the bed and extended her stocking-clad legs, pointing her toes to make them look sleeker. She thought they were a little too skinny, but they weren't bad, if she did say so herself. She reached for the top of the stocking where it hugged her right thigh and went on, "You want me to take these off, honey, or leave 'em on? Some fellas really like to watch me taking them off."

Mr. Smith shook his head. "That doesn't matter."

"Oh?" She shrugged. If she'd been more abundantly endowed, such a gesture would have been more effective, but a girl did the best she could with what she had. "Well, I'll leave them on, then."

"That's fine. Do you ever get any gamblers in here?"

"Gamblers?" she repeated. He *was* a strange one. "Why, sweetie, I don't really know. Sometimes a gentleman will tell me what he does for a livin', but we don't usually get around to talkin' about that, if you know what I mean."

Mr. Smith put his hands on his knees. The fingers were long and slender, Hannah noted, but they looked strong somehow. He said, "Don't most gamblers dress in a certain style? Frock coats, fancy vests, frilly shirts? Maybe a top hat."

Hannah stared at him for a second, then she couldn't stop herself from laughing. That made his hands tighten on his knees. She had grown accustomed to watching for little signs like that, so she said quickly, "I'm sorry, honey. I didn't mean to laugh. It's just that the fella you described . . . well, he sounds like the villain from one of those melodrama shows. You know, the kind with a mustache that curls up on the ends. Like the evil banker who kicks the poor family out of their home, so the sweet, innocent daughter has to go out and do things she normally wouldn't do just to survive."

She grew more serious and frowned as she realized she had just described a situation similar to the one that had befallen her own family. The banker back home in Kansas didn't wear a top hat, though, nor did he dress all that fancy. But he *was* evil.

"All right, let's back up," Mr. Smith said. "So none of your, ah, gentleman friends ever told you he was a gambler?"

She shook her head. "Not that I recall. I'm sorry."

In truth, she didn't always pay that much attention to what the men told her. Smiling and nodding and occasionally saying, "Uh-huh, that's right, sweetie," went a long way toward making them believe you were listening.

"Well, then, let's take another tack."

Hannah said, "Are you sure you wouldn't rather come over here and sit next to me on the bed, honey? I mean, you can do whatever you like, but most gentlemen who come up here with me like to get to know *me* better."

"In a moment, perhaps." For such a meek-looking little fellow, he was a stubborn cuss. "You said earlier that you like to know the names of the men who visit you. Do you remember one named Martin Delroy?"

"Martin Delroy? It's a pretty name, Mr. Smith . . . but I'm afraid it doesn't ring a single bell."

That was the truth. She figured most of the customers gave her fake names, anyway. Like Smith.

"I have it on good authority that he was headed this way. A bartender at one of the nearby saloons directed him to this establishment. And I know . . . forgive me for speaking bluntly, miss . . . I know the sort of woman he gravitates toward."

"You mean what kind of gal he likes?"

"Yes, indeed. He doesn't have a particular . . . type, I suppose you could say . . . when it comes to hair color or age or appearance, except for one thing." Mr. Smith lifted a hand and pointed to Hannah's face. "He always seeks out women who have one of those."

Hannah raised her hand and covered the beauty mark on her cheek. She felt her face warming with embarrassment.

"I never liked it," she said. "It looks funny. It makes *me* look funny."

"Nonsense," Mr. Smith said. "There's nothing unappealing about it. It makes you . . . distinctive looking."

She gazed down at the rug on the floor, which was getting a mite threadbare in places, and shook her head. "Some men don't like it. Don't want anything to do with me."

"Some men are fools," Mr. Smith said. "But now do you understand why I believe there's a good chance Delroy paid you a visit?"

"I guess. Can you describe him better? Not like some silly melodrama villain?"

"I certainly can. He's forty years old, has dark hair with a liberal sprinkling of silver, and wears a mustache that's not as silvery just yet. He has brown eyes, is medium height, and is stockily built. He wears a ring on each hand and often sports what appears to be a diamond stickpin in his cravat. The gems in the rings and the stickpin are all false, however. He gives off an air of wealth but is also slightly seedy. He can be quite charming, is fast with a jest, especially an off-color one, and drinks like a fish without ever showing any real effects of the liquor. Does any or all of *that* sound familiar?"

The lengthy description surprised Hannah, but she thought about everything Mr. Smith had said. After a moment, she exclaimed, "Why, shoot, yeah. He was here. I remember a fella who looked like that, and he wore rings and had a fancy stickpin, like you said."

"But he didn't tell you his name?"

She smiled. "He said his name was Jones."

"Ah." Mr. Smith nodded. "Of course."

"He was a nice enough fella. Didn't treat me bad or anything."

Mr. Smith sounded genuinely concerned as he asked, "Do some men treat you badly?"

Hannah sighed. "Well, a little. Now and then. But you just have to expect some of that, Madame Dumont says."

"A shame," Mr. Smith muttered. "A terrible shame. When was this fellow Jones here?"

Right back to business, he was. And not the kind of business Hannah had expected they'd be doing when she brought him up here. But if all he wanted was to talk about that other fella, she wasn't going to argue with him.

"It was five nights ago. Maybe six. I'm not sure. After a while, the fellas . . . well, they all sort of start to run together."

"I can only imagine. You haven't seen him since that time?"

Hannah shook her head. "No, that was the one and only time I ever saw him."

Mr. Smith drew in a deep breath, as if whatever he was about to ask was very important. "Did he happen to mention where he was going from Denver?"

"He never said a word to me about it."

Mr. Smith looked disappointed at that. He opened his mouth, and Hannah figured he was about to ask her if she was certain.

That's why she went on quickly, "But I did hear him asking Ulysses . . . that's the bartender downstairs . . . a question before he left. He asked Ulysses the best way to get to Big Rock."

Mr. Smith's hands were still resting on his knees, but he leaned forward a little and looked excited. "Big Rock," he repeated. "Is that a . . . geographical landmark?"

"It's a town," Hannah said. "Not too awful far from here. The train goes there. It's less than a day's ride. That's what Ulysses told him."

"So he was going to Big Rock," Mr. Smith mused, as much to himself as to Hannah.

"Now, I don't know that for a fact," she said. "I just heard him asking about it, that's all. But it doesn't seem like he would have asked about it if he wasn't intending to go there. Does it seem like it to you?"

"No, indeed," he said. "I believe there's a very good chance this Big Rock was Delroy's destination."

"Why are you looking for him?" she asked. She

got a canny look on her face as she added, "He did something bad, didn't he? Done you wrong?"

Mr. Smith shook his head. "I'm afraid I never actually met the man. But I do have an interest in locating him, and I think there's a good chance you've been very helpful to my cause, Flossie."

"Hannah," she said.

"I beg your pardon?"

She looked down again and said, "Hannah. That's my real name. Girls in places like this . . . well, we don't tell the men our right names. Hardly ever."

"I can imagine that's the case," he said again.

"But you seem like a nice fella, *Mr. Smith*."

She put a little extra emphasis on the words, thinking that maybe he'd tell her his real name in return, but if he noticed, he didn't give any sign of it. Instead, he stood up, stepped over to the dresser, and picked up his hat.

"Wait a minute," she said. "You're not leaving?"

"I'm afraid so," he said.

"But we didn't . . ." She gestured vaguely toward the bed.

"I know, but I got what I needed. And that's what I paid for, after all."

She sighed. "Maybe so. But it's not often I meet a fella as nice as you, Mr. Smith. Seems a shame to waste it."

"Don't believe I'm as nice as you seem to think

I am," he told her. He put his hat on. "But I *am* obliged to you for the help you've given me." He paused as he opened the door. "Perhaps I can repay the favor some way."

Then he was gone.

Hannah stared at the empty doorway for a moment and then sighed. It took all kinds, she told herself. And working in Madame Dumont's Academy for Young Ladies, she was liable to run into all of them before it was over.

She was already dressed, such as it was, so she went back downstairs to the parlor. Several of the other girls were there, still looking a little sleepy. Even though the hour was well past noon, it was still early in the day for them.

Hannah hadn't been sitting next to the piano for more than two minutes when another man came in and picked her out. He wasn't dressed near as nice as Mr. Smith and looked a lot rougher, but as she had told him, a girl in her line of work had to expect some of that. She smiled and flirted and linked arms with this man, then told him her name was Flossie and asked his.

"Miller," he said.

"Well, it sure is a pleasure to make your acquaintance, Mr. Miller."

Also, unlike Mr. Smith, he didn't want to talk once they got into the room. But he wasn't as rough as he looked, and all in all it wasn't bad. Hannah couldn't help but wonder what it would have been like with Mr. Smith, though, as she lay back, sighed, and looked up at the ceiling that had a few water spots on it.

She stayed there while Mr. Miller got dressed, left some coins beside the basin, and came back to the bed. He leaned over, and she thought he was going to kiss her. She was ready to turn her head away, because she didn't allow the men to do that. A gal had to draw the line somewhere.

But then he smiled, which made his squinty eye squint even more. "Mr. Smith said to tell you he's sorry, Hannah, and the only way he can pay you back is to save you from this life."

She had time to stare at him and start to say, "What?" before his hand moved and she felt something against her skin. She gasped in shock.

Then her eyes widened even more as a couple of quick steps took him out of the room and she was left there gazing down at a stack of gold double eagles resting on her bosom.

Ten of them. Two hundred dollars. Enough to take her a hell of a long way from Madame Dumont's Academy for Young Ladies and let her make a new start in life.

CHAPTER 10

Big Rock

Louis Jensen sat in his office. He placed his hands flat on the desk in front of him and waited. A minute, then two, passed. He smiled and said, "Well, they're not knocking down the door."

No one else was in the office to hear him. The air was still and hot. He had the windows on both sides of the room open a few inches, but not much wind stirred. A fly came in one window, buzzed across the office, and went out the other window.

"I suppose he didn't need legal representation, after all," Louis said.

If his sister had been here, Denny would have told him to stop talking to himself before he went loco. That was probably good advice, thought Louis. Anyway, he hadn't expected a deluge of clients as soon as he hung out his shingle. There were other lawyers, more established lawyers, in Big Rock. He was brand-new. It would take time for people to find him and realize that he could help them with their legal problems.

A week had passed since Louis, Melanie, and Brad arrived in Big Rock on the train. During that time, they had moved into the old Livingston house, a well-kept, two-story structure on one of the nicer residential streets. So far, it was sparsely furnished. They had beds, a dining room table, some chairs, and a wardrobe in each bedroom, all left over from the previous owner. Most of their possessions were still in boxes.

But it took time to turn a house into a home. Melanie seemed to understand that and was already working busily to fix the place up the way she wanted it. Louis's mother and Inez Sandoval had come into town to help with that task, and the women had put Brad to work, as well.

In the meantime, Louis had set up his new office on one of the side streets, but just around the corner from the main thoroughfare, so it wasn't difficult to find. He had a single room, but that was enough since he had no secretary. As his practice grew, he could look for a bigger place. This was enough for his desk, a comfortable swivel chair behind it, two leather chairs for clients in front of it, and a pair of filing cabinets on one wall. On the opposite wall hung a map of Colorado and a portrait of President Theodore Roosevelt. A large painting of an impressive mountain landscape graced the wall behind the desk, flanked by bookcases filled with law books. It was a nice office. All it needed was clients.

The door was open a few inches, like the windows, to let air move through the room. Louis heard people talking as they went by outside, the conversations punctuated by the thud of hoofbeats and the creaking of wagon wheels from passing riders and vehicles. Big Rock was a busy town. It might be an actual city someday.

The rataplan of hoofbeats grew louder, rising to quite a racket and then coming to an abrupt stop. Louis frowned and sat up straighter. From the sound of it, a fairly large group of riders had just come to a halt in front of his office. Was it possible that they were coming to see him?

He considered getting up and going to the door to find out, but instead he opened a law book that was sitting on a corner of the desk and pulled a stack of documents over in front of him. They were papers he had promised his father he would review, even though he hadn't gotten to them yet.

He wanted clients other than his own father— not that he didn't appreciate the business Smoke was throwing his way. And it was nice to know that his father deemed him trustworthy. But if he was going to have a successful practice, he needed to do more than just work for the Sugarloaf.

Horses moved around outside. Footsteps came toward the door. Louis tried to look busy. Whoever was out there didn't come inside, though. Instead, a man's voice called, "Boss, look who's comin'."

More hoofbeats welled up. A different man said, "What in blazes are *they* doing here? I don't like the looks of this."

"Neither do I, boss," the first man said. "They're headed this way."

The second group of riders stopped. A tense silence replaced the hoofbeats, broken after a moment by the second man demanding harshly, "What do you want, Gardner? Did you follow us?"

A third man, evidently one of the newcomers, said, "What business is that of yours, Mullen? And I've got better things to do than follow around the likes of you."

"What do you mean by that? I won't stand here and be insulted—"

"Look out, boss, he's reachin' for a gun!"

The smack of a fist against flesh and bone followed that exclamation. Instantly, men bellowed angry curses, and more blows followed. It sounded like both groups were trying to whale the tar out of each other.

Louis jumped up from his chair and hurried around the desk. He jerked the door open and looked out into the street, gaping at the scene that met his eyes.

At least a dozen men were fighting in front of his office. All of them looked like cowboys, except for one man in a black suit who was in the middle of the tangle, trading punches with a stocky, gray-haired hombre. Fists flew back and forth. Blood spurted from battered noses and welled from split lips. Eyes were already starting

121

to swell shut and get dark rings around them. A cloud of dust rose from booted feet shuffling and lurching back and forth. Two groups of horses, made skittish by the violence, danced away nervously.

Louis shouted, "Stop it! Stop it, you men!"

They ignored him and kept hammering punches at their opponents.

Other people on the street had stopped what they were doing and stood watching the battling men. Louis hoped that someone had gone to fetch Sheriff Monte Carson instead of just gawking. But *he* was just standing there, too, he realized. With a fight of this size, it probably was going to take a few shots fired into the air to make the men stop throwing punches. But maybe there was *something* he could do.

He stepped down off the shallow porch in front of his office and moved toward the nearest pair of fighters.

One of them swung a fist to the jaw of his opponent and landed the blow solidly. The man's head rocked back on his neck. He stumbled backward, bringing him even closer to Louis, who reached out to grab him by the arm.

"You need to stop fighting—" Louis began.

The man he had hold of shook his head as if to clear it, then twisted around violently and hooked a fist into Louis's belly. Louis gasped in shock and pain and bent forward as he let go of the man's arm. That put him in perfect position to take a looping punch to the jaw. He flew backward and sprawled in the dirt at the edge of the porch.

Stunned, Louis lay there for a moment, breathing hard and blinking rapidly. Brain and body both refused to work. As his brain began to clear and his muscles started functioning again, he pushed himself into a sitting position and looked at the swirling knot of men who continued fighting in front of him.

However, he was more concerned at the moment with his own health. Doctors in this country, in England, and elsewhere on the Continent, had made it clear that he shouldn't exert himself. He pressed a hand to his chest and felt his heart beating. His pulse seemed steady and strong enough. Getting knocked on his butt didn't seem to have done any real damage.

Not to his body, anyway, he amended. His pride was hurting. He was a Jensen, and while Jensens sometimes got knocked down—nobody was immune to that, no matter who they were—they *always* got up.

Louis got up.

"Want some more, do you?" The angry shout came from the man who had punched him. The young cowboy stood nearby, fists still clenched, and as Louis came to his feet, the man lunged at him again and threw another punch.

Louis ducked under the blow, which passed harmlessly over his head. That miss caused the cowboy to lose his balance and stumble closer. Louis closed his own right hand into a fist and brought it up with all the strength he could muster behind it. The uppercut caught the cowboy under the chin and lifted him off his feet. He crashed down on his back and lay there moaning.

Louis looked from the cowboy to his fist in amazement, as if he couldn't quite comprehend what he had just done, then he cried out in pain as the startlement wore off and he realized how badly his hand hurt. He waved it back and forth and yelled again as that just made it throb even more.

Cradling the aching hand to his body, he staggered back to the porch. As he stepped up onto it, he saw Monte Carson hurrying toward the brawling figures. The sheriff held a shotgun that he pointed into the air, aiming it so that none of the buckshot would come down where it would hurt anything. He triggered one barrel.

The thunderous boom made the fighters stop what they were doing, just as Louis thought it would. Monte lowered the shotgun and shouted into the stunned silence, "Next varmint throws a punch, I'll blast him to Kingdom Come!"

The men probably knew, logically, that the sheriff wasn't going to unload a charge of buckshot into them at close range, but the mere threat of it, plus staring down the ominous twin barrels of the shotgun, was enough to bring the battle to a grudging end. The men dropped their fists and settled for glaring at each other.

Monte went on, "Roy Gardner, Tony Mullen, I see you both. Call off your men and get away from each other. What in blazes is all this about, anyway? I thought the two of you got along, like neighbors should."

"It's a mighty poor neighbor who fences off thirsty cows from water that's rightfully theirs!" responded the stocky, gray-haired man who had been in the center of the fight.

"That waterhole belongs to me!" argued the man in the black suit who had been trading punches with him. "And my cows need it!"

Louis looked at the two men, and now that he had heard Monte Carson call their names, he remembered them. They owned adjoining ranches on the other side of the valley from the Sugarloaf. Both had been to the Jensen spread in the past, to discuss Cattleman's Association business with Smoke and on social occasions, as well. Louis was pretty sure that both men had been there the day he got married. There hadn't been any trouble between them then.

"I don't know why you two are at each other's throats, but you're not going to bring your trouble into the streets of Big Rock," Monte declared. "If you have business here, you can go about it without fighting. If you can't, I'll cram the whole lot of you into my jail, and you won't like it. It'll be mighty crowded!"

"I've got business here, all right," Roy Gardner said. He flung out a hand and pointed. "I came to see *him!*"

Louis blinked in surprise as he realized that Gardner was pointing at him. "Me?" he said.

"That's right." Gardner motioned for the men who rode for him to move back, away from Tony Mullen's men. As they did so, Gardner started toward Louis. "I got to talk to you about a legal matter."

"Wait just a blasted minute," Mullen said. He jerked a thumb to indicate that his riders should withdraw, as well, then he stomped toward Louis. "I came to town to hire young Jensen."

"You can't hire him," Gardner snapped. "I already did."

"You haven't even talked to him yet!"

"Well, I'm about to," Gardner said as he stopped and squared off against Mullen. Both men clenched their fists again.

"Hold it, hold it, hold it!" Monte Carson yelled. "If you try to start this ruckus up again, I swear I'll bend this shotgun's barrels over your heads." He glanced at Louis. "What do you know about this?"

"Not a thing," he answered honestly. "I was just sitting in my office when these men rode in and went to war out here." He rubbed his still-aching hand over his equally tender belly. "I tried to break it up and got punched in the gut for my trouble."

Gardner cleared his throat and said, "Don't know who walloped you, Louis, but if it was one of my boys, I'm sorry."

"And if it was one of my crew, I apologize," Mullen put in quickly, adding a glare at Gardner.

The sheriff looked around at all of them, then said, "All right, here's what we're gonna do. You boys from the Box RG, you head on up to the Brown Dirt Cowboy Saloon, get yourselves some drinks, and settle the hell down. Ace of Diamonds riders, you go to Blaise's Place. Stay where I'm sending you, and especially stay away from each other, until your bosses come to get you." Monte jerked the shotgun in a commanding gesture. "Now git!"

A tall, lean, silver-haired cowboy said to Mullen, "Boss?"

Mullen sighed and said, "Do what the sheriff told you, Orrie. We're going to try to do this legal and proper-like. Things aren't the way they used to be."

"If they were," Gardner said with a sneer, "me and my boys would've loaded up and cleaned out that rat's nest of a ranch you got, Mullen."

"That's enough," Monte snapped.

The two groups of cowboys drifted off,

muttering curses and eyeing each other warily. They turned in opposite directions along Front Street, though, signaling that the conflict was over . . . for now.

"What about us, Sheriff?" Mullen asked.

Monte frowned at them for a second, then said, "You both came to talk to Louis. So talk to him."

"What?" Louis said.

"Together?" Mullen said.

"That's loco!" Gardner said.

"No, it's not," Monte insisted. "Get on in there. You can both explain what you want him to do, and then Louis can make up his own mind. He can sort all this out." He smiled. "He's a lawyer, after all. Sorting things out is his job."

Louis wasn't happy about this, but he supposed finding out what the two ranchers wanted—and why they evidently hated each other now—was the next logical step. He sighed and said, "All right, gentlemen, come on in, I suppose. Whatever the problem is, we can talk it over like civilized men."

"Hmmph," Gardner snorted. Mullen looked equally disgusted.

Something seemed to occur to Monte. "Louis, you said you got punched. Are you all right? Do you need to go see Doc Steward?"

"I'm fine," Louis replied. He flexed the fingers of his right hand and winced a little. "I think I hurt myself more punching one of those cowboys."

"That was Johnny Dolan you knocked down," Gardner said. "You better keep an eye out for him. He's a young hothead. He's liable to hold a grudge, even though I'll tell him to leave you alone."

"Thanks," Louis said dryly. He gestured toward the door. "Go on in and make yourselves comfortable."

Gardner and Mullen went into the office, still eyeing each other hostilely just as their crews had done. Monte stepped closer to Louis and said quietly, "Good luck with those two."

"Do you know what this is about, Sheriff?"

Monte shook his head. "I don't have any earthly idea. But I've got a hunch that you may have your work cut out for you, Louis."

CHAPTER 11

Most of the saloons in Big Rock opened around mid-morning, even though they wouldn't do much business until lunchtime. Then there would be another lull until the late afternoon and evening rush began.

So this time of day, shortly after opening, was pretty peaceful in Blaise's Place. The only customers were a couple of drivers for one of the freight companies. They stood at the bar nursing beers while they waited for other men to finish loading the wagons they would head out with later this morning.

Blaise Warfield sat at a table in the back of the room, sipping from a cup of coffee as she read the latest issue of the local newspaper. It was shadowy enough in the saloon that the light for reading wasn't very good, but on the other hand, the air hadn't heated up much yet, either.

The fourth person in the room was the day bartender, Charlie Tolliver, who stood stolidly wiping the hardwood with a rag, the usual way of passing the time for most bartenders. A craggy-faced man who had been big once, before the years shrunk him some, Charlie was still tough and could swing a bungstarter well enough that only the most belligerent and foolhardy drunks dared to mess with him.

The batwings creaked as somebody pushed them open. Footsteps started across the room. Charlie called, "Mornin', Marshal."

"Hello, Charlie," a familiar voice replied. Blaise looked up from her paper and smiled at Deputy U.S. Marshal Brice Rogers as he walked toward her.

She was aware that she wore a plain, much less provocative dress than she would be sporting later in the day, when the crowds were bigger. The men who drank at Blaise's Place liked to see the beautiful proprietor in low-cut, spangled gowns that showed off her lovely figure. She knew that and didn't mind taking advantage of it. The girls who worked for her, all of whom were still asleep upstairs, also dressed to please the customers' eyes . . . except when they were *un*dressing to please the customers.

Brice didn't seem to mind that she looked more like a shop clerk than a saloon girl right now. In the time she had known him, he had never been the type to leer, and he always treated her with the respect she deserved. *More* than the respect she deserved, she amended to herself, thinking about some of the things she had done in the past.

But nothing that she hadn't had to do in order to survive, she thought.

She folded the newspaper, tossed it on the table,

and gave him a welcoming smile. "Good morning, Brice," she greeted him. "How are you feeling?"

"Right as rain again," he said. He flexed his left arm, which he no longer carried in a sling. "A little stiff now and then, but no problem."

"I'm glad."

"I had a good nurse."

"Oh, pshaw," she said. "I just dropped in to visit you a few times. I didn't do anything to help your arm heal up."

He put a hand on the back of the chair across from her and cocked his head inquiringly. She gestured for him to sit down. He pulled the chair back and sat.

"Charlie, bring the marshal a cup of coffee," Blaise called to the bartender, who nodded.

Brice took off his hat and set it on the table. "Any doctor will tell you that a patient's frame of mind has an awful lot to do with how well he recovers. Seeing you always put me in a mighty good frame of mind."

"Well, it's good to know that I have some . . . medicinal value," she told him with a smile.

Charlie brought over a cup and saucer and placed it in front of Brice. A few wisps of steam curled up from the black surface of the coffee in the cup.

"Here you go, Marshal," he said.

"Thanks, Charlie. Everything quiet so far this morning?"

"Quiet as can be. It's too early for anybody to even think about causin'—"

Before the bartender could finish his thought, angry voices rose outside, prompting everybody in the room to look toward the entrance. A second later, men appeared and slapped the batwings aside to come stomping into the saloon.

Brice sat up straighter in his chair and muttered, "What the devil?"

The newcomers numbered half a dozen. Several of them looked familiar to Blaise, although she couldn't recall their names. She knew only that she had seen them in here before. They all wore range clothes, and five of them were young. Those went straight to the bar. One of them slapped the hardwood impatiently and said in a loud voice, "We need some drinks here!"

Charlie growled quietly. He didn't like anybody taking that tone, Blaise knew. She said, "It's all right, Charlie. Maybe they'll have their drinks and then leave."

"Yeah, maybe," the bartender said, sounding as if he weren't convinced of that. With a scowl, he moved back to his post.

The sixth man, who had paused for a moment when he came in so that he could look around the room, as if checking it for potential enemies, ambled to the bar and joined his companions. He was older than the others, with silvery hair under a hat with a tightly curled brim and a mustache also streaked with silver. But he stood ramrod straight and carried himself with the air of a younger man.

"I know that fella," Brice said under his breath to Blaise. "Monte and I have talked about him. His name's Striker. There are no reward dodgers on him in Colorado, but Monte thinks he's wanted down in Texas and maybe some other places."

Blaise nodded and said, "I remember seeing him before. All of them ride for one of the ranches around here, don't they?"

"The Ace of Diamonds," Brice replied. "Tony Mullen's spread."

Mullen's name was familiar to Blaise, too, although she didn't think she had ever met the man.

"That's most of Mullen's crew," Brice went on. "I wonder what they're all doing in town at this time of day."

"They seem upset about something," Blaise observed.

Charlie had set up glasses in front of the cowboys. He uncorked a bottle and poured whiskey in those glasses. The punchers snatched them up and threw back the liquor. Almost as if it were a synchronized routine, the empties thumped back onto the hardwood together.

"Fill 'em up again," snapped the young cowboy who had demanded service when they came in.

He was a medium-sized man with tight, sandy curls under his pushed-back hat.

Charlie still had his hand wrapped around the bottle, but he didn't pick it up. "You boys intend on drinkin' the place dry this early in the day?"

The young cowboy put his hands on the bar and leaned forward to say, "What we intend ain't none of your business, old man."

Charlie bristled. Blaise thought he might be about to break that bottle across the obnoxious youngster's nose. Brice must have shared that concern, because he started to his feet.

The silver-haired man spoke first, saying, "Back off, Quince."

The young cowboy jerked his head toward the older man. "But Orrie, this apron mouthed off—"

"I said back off," Orrie Striker responded. His voice was soft but had a steely edge to it. "Go sit down at one of the tables. All of you do that. And take your glasses with you."

Quince looked like he wanted to argue, but one of the other men put a hand on his arm and told him quietly, "We'd better do what he says, Quince. Orrie's the boss when Mr. Mullen ain't around."

After a couple of seconds, Quince jerked his head in a nod. He allowed his friend to steer him away from the bar and toward one of the tables that was big enough for all six of them to sit around it. The other men followed, except for Striker, who still stood at the bar.

"Give me a full bottle, barkeep," he said to Charlie, who glanced at Blaise for confirmation. She nodded. Charlie retrieved an unopened bottle from the backbar, along with another glass, and handed them to Striker, who turned toward the table where the other Ace of Diamonds hands sat.

Brice, who was still standing beside Blaise's table, moved forward to intercept him. "Hold on a minute, Striker. I want to talk to you."

Striker stopped and regarded him coolly. "Hello, Marshal," he said. "Didn't see you back there in the corner. Light ain't that good in here."

Blaise would have been willing to bet that Striker had been completely aware of Brice's presence, and hers, too. He had the look of a man who didn't miss much.

"What can I do for you?" Striker went on.

"Satisfy my curiosity," Brice said. "Why are you and the rest of Mullen's crew in town today?"

Striker's voice held a mocking tone as he drawled, "I'm not sure that falls under federal jurisdiction."

"Like I said, I'm curious."

"First of all, this isn't the whole crew. We left a few men on the ranch. And Mr. Mullen brought us with him just in case there was any trouble."

"What kind of trouble?"

"Never know when you'll run into a bunch of snakes," said Striker. "Like the crew from the Box RG."

"Roy Gardner's spread?"

"Yeah. Good thing the boss brought us along, too."

Once the cowboys were seated at the table instead of standing at the bar, Blaise had noticed that all of them were sporting signs of battle: bruises, scrapes, bloody noses, black eyes. She recalled that a while earlier, she had heard a shotgun go off somewhere in town.

Brice was just as observant and could put the clues together as well as she could. He said, "You got in a brawl with the Box RG, and Sheriff Carson broke it up."

"You've got it all figured out, Marshal." Striker hefted the bottle. "Now, the boys are waitin', if you don't have any more questions . . ."

"Go ahead," Brice told him. "Just don't start anything in here."

"Not likely. Carson sent Gardner's bunch to the Brown Dirt Cowboy and told them to stay there until Gardner and our boss get done with their business."

"What sort of business are you talking about?"

"Unless I miss my guess," Striker said, "it's shaping up to be a range war."

Roy Gardner pounded a fist on Louis's desk and said, "If he wants a war, I'll give him a war, by grab!"

Tony Mullen had leaped to his feet, too, when

Gardner did. "I just want what's legally mine, but if I have to fight for it, I will!"

Since they were standing up, Louis figured he might as well, too. He held out his hands and patted the air as he said, "Gentlemen, gentlemen, there's no need to shout. This office is small enough that we don't have any trouble hearing each other. Now, please, sit down and let's discuss this rationally."

"Nothin' to discuss," Gardner snapped. "He fenced off the waterhole on my northern range."

"That's *my* southern range," Mullen insisted.

"Both spreads were surveyed years ago! You know the boundaries as well as I do!"

"That survey was wrong. It missed my southern boundary by a mile. And I have proof of that."

In response to that claim, Gardner frowned and stared at Mullen, evidently taken by surprise. "What the hell are you talkin' about?"

"The boundary line was drawn incorrectly. That chunk of range . . . and the waterhole . . . belong to me."

At least they were talking at a semi-normal level now and not shouting at each other, thought Louis. He would take any improvement he could get.

"Please, gentlemen, sit down. We'll get this all sorted out to everyone's mutual satisfaction."

He had his doubts, but he had to act as if he believed that, anyway.

Gardner and Mullen glared at each other for a moment longer, then slowly sank into the red leather chairs in front of the desk. When they'd first come into the office and Louis asked them to sit down, they had pulled the chairs farther apart before settling into them, as if each feared that being too close to the other would contaminate him somehow.

When they were seated again, Louis took his own chair and leaned forward to clasp his hands together on the desk in a solemn, studious manner.

"Now," he said, "tell me about this survey that established the boundary between your ranches."

"It was wrong," Mullen said.

"You didn't think so the past eight years," Gardner shot back.

Louis said, "That's how long it's been since the survey was done? Eight years?"

Gardner nodded. "Yeah. You were just a kid, livin' over there in Europe somewhere."

"Yes, I know," Louis said.

Mullen said, "I remember Smoke telling me that's where the best doctors were, and he and Sally didn't want you to have anything less than the best."

Louis didn't particularly want to discuss his medical history with these men, but at least they weren't shouting at each other right now. So to keep them distracted and let their blood cool a little more, he nodded and said, "That's right."

Gardner asked with what seemed to be genuine interest, "How are you feelin' these days, son? Everybody in the valley's always been rootin' for you, what with you bein' Smoke and Sally's boy."

Louis smiled and said, "I'm all right, Mr. Gardner, thank you."

"Being married to a pretty woman will cure a lot of a man's ailments," Mullen said. "I never saw a more beautiful bride than Miss Melanie the day you two got married."

"Neither did I," Gardner said, apparently forgetting for the moment that he was agreeing with Mullen.

"I'm a very lucky man," Louis agreed. "Now, if we could get back to the matter of that survey . . ."

"We had it done eight years ago, like I said," Gardner replied.

"We split the cost," added Mullen, "and both of our crews put up the fence between the spreads."

"The fence that *your* crew moved to close off my waterhole." Gardner's voice began to rise in anger again.

"Because that old survey was wrong."

Before the discussion could turn into an argument again, Louis said, "Mr. Mullen, you mentioned that before and said that you have proof the survey was incorrect."

Mullen nodded. "I do. Concrete proof."

"What is it?"

"A new survey. And it found that the old one missed the boundary by a mile. And that's not just a saying. It's an actual mile I'm talking about."

"Hogwash!" said Gardner. "No surveyor worth his salt would make a mistake like that."

"Who carried out that first survey?" Louis asked. "If it was someone here in Big Rock, we can probably settle this by talking to him."

"Oh, he was in Big Rock," Mullen said, "but he's not anymore."

"Did he move his business somewhere else?"

"Moved it six feet under," said Gardner. "He's dead. Old Clyde Meeker. Dropped dead four, five years ago."

The name was vaguely familiar to Louis from visits to Big Rock when he and Denny were growing up. He'd probably seen a sign for his surveying business while riding along the street. But he didn't know anything else about Meeker.

"Did someone take over his business? Is the office still here in town?"

Mullen shook his head. "He didn't have any family except a grown son who lives out in California. Everything in the office, all the records, got boxed up and shipped off to him."

"But the deeds, the surveys he did, all that should be on file in the county clerk's office in Red Cliff."

"Should be," Gardner agreed, "but when I went over there to check, they told me they had a fire there two years ago and lost some of the records. The survey that showed the boundary between my spread and the Ace of Diamonds was in one of the cabinets that burned up."

Louis sighed. Record-keeping had always been a challenge in frontier courthouses. Many documents had been lost through flood, fire, insect damage, and just pure mismanagement and disorganization. However, that wasn't true just on the frontier, he supposed. Anyway, in this day and age, the West wasn't really a frontier anymore.

"It didn't really matter until now," Mullen said. "Roy and I always got along and didn't have any reason to question the line between us."

"That's what I thought!" Gardner exclaimed.

"But then I decided I ought to have a new survey done. I hired a company out of Denver to come here and take care of it. When I got the report and the new maps from them . . ." Mullen drew in a breath. "That's when I found out he'd been stealing my water all these years!"

"That's a damned lie!" Gardner was back on his feet again, fists clenched and ready to swing. "I never stole anything in my life!"

"Except my range and my waterhole!" Mullen replied as he surged up out of his chair again.

Louis stood and held out his hands, wondering

if he ought to hurry around the desk and try to get between them.

He'd probably just wind up getting punched again himself, he thought as he said, "Gentlemen, gentlemen, please!" But this was his office and he had to do something . . .

"Sounds like I'm interrupting quite a legal discussion here," Smoke Jensen said with a dryly humorous note in his voice as he stepped into the office.

CHAPTER 12

"Smoke!" Gardner and Mullen exclaimed together.

"Hello, boys," Smoke said. He smiled at Louis and went on, "Since you already have a meeting going on, son, I'll go down to Longmont's for a cup of coffee and come back later."

Louis didn't want his father to leave, since it seemed unlikely that Gardner and Mullen would come to blows with Smoke here. But it was his responsibility to handle this problem, not Smoke's. So he nodded and said, "All right, give us a little while—"

"No, I want Smoke to stay," Gardner broke in. "He was here when all this mess started. He knows how it came about. Smoke, you remember when Mullen and me put up that fence between our spreads, don't you?"

Smoke glanced at Louis as if to ask if Louis wanted him involving himself in this affair. Louis didn't hesitate. He nodded and waved a hand slightly to indicate that Smoke should answer the question. It was entirely possible that his father could shed some light on the problem, so Louis figured the right thing to do was find out.

"I do remember that," Smoke said, nodding. "By that time, the concept of open range was ending all across the West. It took some getting used to, especially for those of us who'd been ranching for a while, but I reckon in the long run, bringing in fences and definite boundaries was a good thing."

"Except when those boundaries were drawn incorrectly, like the one between the Box RG and the Ace of Diamonds," said Mullen.

Gardner opened his mouth to protest, but before he could, Smoke said, "This is the first I've heard about that, Tony."

Gardner said, "The first *I* heard about it was when his cowboys fenced off my waterhole."

"It's *my* waterhole," Mullen responded coldly.

Louis had to make an effort to hold on to his temper as he said, "Yes, you've both made your respective claims over and over again. But we're no closer to arriving at the truth."

Mullen said, "My horse is tied up outside. Give me a minute, and I'll show you the proof of what I've been saying. I brought the new survey map with me."

Louis wanted to ask him why he hadn't said that before now, but the question wouldn't serve any purpose. Instead, he nodded and said, "That would be very helpful, Mr. Mullen."

"I'll be right back," Mullen said. He left the office.

Gardner turned to Smoke and said, "He's loco. You knew Clyde Meeker, Smoke. Maybe he didn't get every survey perfect right down

145

to the last inch, but he wouldn't have missed a boundary line by a mile!"

"That doesn't seem likely," Smoke agreed, "but I haven't seen that new survey map of Tony's yet. When it comes to legal matters, it's usually best to keep an open mind. Isn't that right, Louis?"

"We have to go by the evidence, whatever that turns out to be," Louis said.

Gardner shook his head and said, "Well, I'll have to see it with my own eyes to believe it. And I ain't makin' any promises about that!"

Mullen returned a minute later carrying a tube of the sort in which maps were stored. He took the cap off it and reached in to pull out a large, rolled-up piece of paper.

Louis moved documents aside and said, "Spread it out here on the desk, please, Mr. Mullen."

The rancher did so. Louis got some law books to hold down the corners and positioned them. Then he leaned over from behind the desk to study the map. Mullen was in front of the desk. Smoke and Gardner took the two ends.

"Here, you can see for yourself," said Mullen as he rested a fingertip on the map. "This dotted line, that's the old boundary. The new one comes down farther south and then across to the eastern line."

He traced his finger across the map to indicate what he was talking about.

Gardner jerked his hand in a curt wave and said, "Anybody can draw lines on a map. This don't prove anything."

"But you can also see the notation of the latitude and longitude," Mullen went on. "The surveyor took those readings and then compared them to the boundaries established on the original claim."

"I thought you said those were destroyed by the fire at the courthouse in Red Cliff," Louis said.

"They were, but there was a copy of my claim at the land office in Denver."

Gardner frowned at him. "What are you talkin' about? Why would there be a copy of your claim but not mine?"

"Well, mine was actually the original claim filed by Travis Holtby twenty years ago."

Smoke said, "I remember Holtby. He was the first owner of that spread. Only it was called the Rocking H back in those days."

Mullen nodded. "Indeed, it was." He smiled. "I renamed it after I caught that ace I needed to fill out a royal flush and won enough to buy the place from him when he wanted to sell. You remember, Smoke, I'd had my eye out for a good spread where I could settle down and be a cattleman instead of a gambler."

"I remember," Smoke agreed. "And it makes sense, I reckon, that Holtby's original claim could still be on file, even if the paperwork transferring it to you later on is lost. And those numbers that establish the bounds of the spread wouldn't change."

Louis said, "Mr. Mullen, do you have that original document in your possession, as well?"

"I do," Mullen said. "It's locked up in the safe in my office at the ranch."

"How did you happen to be aware of its existence?"

"That surveyor I told you about, Edgar Padgett, the one who made this new map, he found it." When Mullen said the name, he pointed to neat, precise printing in the lower right-hand corner of the map, reminiscent of an artist's signature on a painting, only a lot clearer. "Mr. Padgett said he couldn't do it unless he had a starting place, so when we found out about the fire in Red Cliff, he did some digging in Denver."

"Yes, but why did you request a new survey in the first place?" Louis asked.

Mullen grimaced. "All my waterholes are starting to dry up. None of them have gone dry yet, but they're getting there. My cows are getting thirsty."

"You think mine aren't?" Gardner said.

Mullen acted like he hadn't heard the question. He went on, "My foreman told me the waterhole just over the line on the Box RG was still in pretty good shape. I thought about trying to make a deal with Gardner to let some of my stock water there."

"I wouldn't have been able to do it," Gardner said. "I need that water for my own cows."

"I knew that's what you'd say. So I got to wondering if maybe there had been a mistake, all those years ago, and I actually had a right to that water." Mullen shrugged. "Call it wishful thinking if you want, but I figured it wouldn't hurt anything to look into it. And sure enough, it didn't. In fact, it solved my problem. So once I had this map"—he tapped it where it lay on the desk—"I had my crew get to work moving the fence."

Gardner stared at him and blustered, "So you figured it was all right to do that without ever sayin' a damned word to me about it?"

"I know how stubborn and hotheaded you are." Mullen folded his arms across his chest. "I thought it was better to go ahead and get it done before you knew anything about it. It's a, uh, *fait accompli*, isn't that what they call it?"

"It's damned theft, that's what it is!"

"That waterhole is behind my fence. And possession is nine-tenths of the law, isn't that right, Louis?"

"That's an old saying, not an actual legal doctrine," Louis replied. He shrugged. "Although it is applied in court sometimes. Generally, though, only in cases where there isn't any physical evidence by which the case can be adjudicated. You have your survey map, as well as that original claim from the previous owner, *and* the property in question is in your physical possession—"

"Are you sayin' he's in the right?" Gardner demanded.

"I'm saying that in a court case, Mr. Mullen would appear to have the advantage. That's no guarantee that a judge or a jury would find in his favor. It's simply an indication of likelihood."

"What if I sue him? Can I hire you?"

"You can't hire him," Mullen shot back at his neighbor. "I'm hiring Louis to defend my claim. I was here first."

"We came in the door at the same time!"

"But my men and I rode up first."

Gardner looked at Louis. "You don't think I can beat him? I'll pay you for your legal opinion."

Louis held up a hand. "No charge, Mr. Gardner. Under the circumstances, I believe there's approximately a one-in-five chance that you would prevail in a lawsuit."

"That ain't good odds."

"No, not really."

Gardner stared at him for a long moment and then said in a bleak voice, "So I'm beat."

"Perhaps we can work out a compromise—"

"It ain't a compromise when one fella gets what he wants and the other's left out in the cold," Gardner said. He turned to Mullen and went on, "All right, you've got the waterhole. But let's see if you can *keep it*."

He turned on his heel and stalked toward the door. Mullen called after him, "Wait just a damned minute!" But Gardner ignored him and stomped out.

Mullen turned to Louis and Smoke and said, "You heard him. He threatened me!"

"Well, not in so many words," Louis said. "It was more of . . . an observation."

"You know good and well he means to take that waterhole back by force."

Smoke said, "Roy's a good man. A law-abiding man. He'll cool off, Tony. You'll see."

"And if he doesn't? If he tries anything, I'll fight back, Smoke. You know that. I won't let anybody steal what's mine, even a man I used to regard as a friend."

"Be careful, Mr. Mullen," Louis said. "If *you* start making threats, it'll hurt your case if the matter ever does go to court. And I'll charge you the same for that bit of legal advice as I did Mr. Gardner—nothing."

Mullen shook his head slowly. "I'm afraid it's gone beyond court now, Louis. Gardner's a stubborn old bull. He's not going to back down. And neither am I." He rolled up the map and slipped it back into its carrying tube. "But I'm obliged to you for your advice. Be seeing you, Smoke."

With a nod to both of them, Mullen left the office.

In the silence that followed the rancher's departure, Smoke said, "I just figured I'd ride into town and talk over some Sugarloaf business with you, son. I didn't expect to wind up in the middle of a range war."

"It's not a war yet. Maybe I can think of a way to settle this."

"No offense, but I know those two a lot better than you do. You might be able to talk sense into Tony Mullen . . . maybe. But Roy Gardner has been around a long time. He remembers the old days, when the only real law out here was what a man carried in his holster. If he feels like he's being pushed into a fight, he won't back off."

"So you're saying I should . . . ?"

"Hope for the best," Smoke said, "but get ready for the smell of burning gunpowder."

CHAPTER 13

Brice didn't like the sound of what he'd heard from Orrie Striker, but he didn't press the man for more details. Striker sat down at the table with the other Ace of Diamonds hands, uncorked the bottle of whiskey, and started it on its rounds.

Brice went back to Blaise's table and sat down with her. She asked, "What was that about a range war?"

"I don't know," he replied with a shake of his head. "But if it comes about, we'll all hear about it, more than likely sooner rather than later."

"If there's trouble, will it reach into town?"

"That's hard to say. It could, if the two sides happen to be here in Big Rock at the same time, like they were earlier."

Blaise sighed. "I hope that whatever it is, they can settle the problem without a lot of violence. Everything is going well for me, for a change, and selfish or not, I'd like for it to stay that way."

A distant train whistle punctuated her words with its mournful sound. Brice wasn't sure what she meant by that comment about things going well for a change, but he sensed that she wouldn't respond well if he pressed her for an explanation.

The Ace of Diamonds riders were still drinking. They hadn't killed the bottle yet, but they had made a good start on it. Brice overheard several loud, angry comments about the Box RG. The men sounded like they were ready to fight again and were just waiting for an excuse.

Brice was acquainted with Roy Gardner, who owned the other spread. Gardner was middle-aged and proddy. Brice figured that if he were pushed, he wouldn't hesitate to push back. Brice had no idea what the argument was over, but the conflict might reach a point where the cause didn't matter. Then there would be fighting for fighting's sake.

"You look worried," Blaise said. "You feel like you should do something about whatever this is."

"It's more of a problem for Monte and the county sheriff over at Red Cliff," Brice said. "But when you carry a badge and you see trouble building up right in front of you, you can't help but feel like you ought to try to head it off." He shrugged. "I'll go talk to Monte later, try to find out more about what's going on." He managed to get a smile back onto his face. "Right now, I'd rather just visit with you for a while longer and try not to think about what might happen."

"That sounds good to me," agreed Blaise as she lifted her coffee cup and made a little toasting motion toward him.

They continued chatting. The whiskey was having an effect on the cowboys sitting across the room. Several of them had calmed down and started to look sleepy. The others were still agitated, but less so. It wouldn't take much to get them all riled up again, Brice knew, but with any luck, maybe that wouldn't happen.

Several more customers had drifted in as the middle of the day approached. All of them were townsmen, Brice noted, clerks and shopkeepers and livery stable hostlers and freight company loaders.

Except for one, a well-dressed middle-aged man in a tweed suit and black hat. Brice didn't recall ever seeing him before. The stranger went to the bar, nodded to Charlie, and said, "I'll have a brandy, if you please, my friend."

"Not much call for brandy around here," Charlie responded. He reached under the bar. "But I've got a bottle of cog-nack here, if that'll do."

"Cognac," the man said with a smile, correcting Charlie's pronunciation. "And yes, thank you, that will do just fine."

Charlie blew dust off the bottle, pulled the cork, and poured the amber liquor into a glass.

"I'll have a beer with it, too," the stranger said.

"Now, that I can fix you up with, no problem." Charlie picked up a mug and pulled the handle on the tap, filling it with the foamy brew.

Brice had watched and listened to the conversation out of idle curiosity. The same emotion prompted him to glance over at Blaise.

Then he sat up straighter as he saw she was staring at the newcomer with the same sort of expression that might have been on her face if she spotted a rattlesnake slithering across the table toward her.

"Blaise, what's wrong?" he asked.

With an obvious effort, she pulled her gaze away from the stranger at the bar and put an obviously fake smile on her face.

"Nothing," she said. "Nothing's wrong. Why do you ask?"

"Well, you looked like you'd just seen a ghost, or worse."

Blaise shook her head. "Oh, no, nothing like that. A little spot of indigestion, maybe. I'm fine now."

Brice didn't believe that for a second. But he sensed that Blaise might not take it well if he pressed her for an explanation. Probably it would be better to drop the matter . . . for now.

But if he got the chance, Brice promised himself, he would find out who that hombre was and why he had such an effect on Blaise.

The next moment, he had to put that question aside. Tony Mullen, owner of the Ace of Diamonds, pushed through the batwings, spotted his men sitting at the large table, and walked toward them.

They saw him coming and stood up. Orrie Striker asked, "How did it go, boss?"

The sandy-haired young cowboy called Quince added, "Are we gonna have it out with those Box RG varmints?"

"Not today, boys," Mullen said. "We talked it over with Louis Jensen, and he thinks the Ace of Diamonds will win if it ever comes down to a court case."

"Court," Striker scoffed. "Was a time we didn't bother trying to settle things in court."

Mullen nodded. "I know. But those days are gone, Orrie, and we have to at least try to do things legally and properly. If they push us too much, though . . . well, then, we have a legal right to defend ourselves, don't we?"

"Now you're talkin', boss!" Quince exclaimed.

Striker glanced toward Brice and lowered his voice, but not enough that Brice couldn't hear him as he said, "Maybe we'd better be careful what we say. There's a lawman in here."

"What do you—" Mullen began as he glanced around and saw Brice sitting at the table with Blaise. "Oh."

The Ace of Diamonds owner motioned for his men to stay where they were and walked over to the other table. He nodded politely and pinched the brim of his hat to Blaise.

"Good morning, Miss Warfield. You look as lovely as ever."

She smiled and said, "I know that's not true, Mr. Mullen, but I appreciate the sentiment. Join us?"

"No, thank you." Mullen turned to Brice and went on, "I suppose you heard that discussion, Marshal."

"Most of it," Brice admitted. "Enough to know that there's trouble between you and Roy Gardner at the Box RG."

"The law is on my side. Louis Jensen said so."

"Well . . . without casting any aspersions on Louis's legal education, I don't work for him. I work for Chief Marshal Long, and above him, the U.S. Department of Justice."

"Which doesn't have any jurisdiction over a local boundary dispute."

"No, it doesn't," Brice admitted. "So, if you're worried about me sticking my nose into your business, don't be. As long as you keep the peace, I won't have any reason to get involved." His voice hardened. "But if people start getting hurt, I'm still a lawman and I'll be duty-bound to try to put a stop to it."

"If there's any trouble, it won't be Ace of Diamonds that fires the first shot. You can count on that. But like I was just telling my men, they have a legal right to defend themselves."

"That they do," Brice agreed. "See that it doesn't go beyond that."

"That'll be up to Roy Gardner." Mullen nodded again to Blaise, then went back to his men. He jerked his head for them to follow him and started toward the door. Quince picked up the bottle, which had only a single swallow left in it, and downed the whiskey, then wiped the back of his hand across his mouth and followed the others.

Brice watched them leave, then turned to Blaise. "I don't care what he says, there's going to be trouble. I can feel it in my bones."

"I don't feel well, and it's not just my bones," she said. "I hope you'll excuse me. I'm going back upstairs for a while before things get busier later in the day."

"Sure, that's fine," he told her as he quickly got to his feet to hold her chair for her. "If there's anything I can do to help—"

"No, I'll be fine. Thank you, anyway." She managed another insincere smile and headed for the stairs. Brice watched her go to the second floor, where her living quarters were located, and then turned his attention to the bar, wondering if the well-dressed stranger was the reason Blaise had gotten the wind up. That seemed likely.

But the stranger was gone. Brice hadn't noticed him leaving, so he must have slipped out during the strained conversation with Tony Mullen.

Brice was still curious about the whole thing, but if that man really had upset Blaise, he hoped the son of a gun stayed gone.

Blaise's living quarters were located at the far end of the second-floor hallway, past the balcony overlooking the saloon's main room, so by the time she reached her door, she knew Brice couldn't see her anymore. She had felt him watching her all the way up the stairs and as she proceeded along the balcony.

Now she stopped where no one could see her, leaned her right shoulder against the wall, covered her face with both hands, and tried to suppress the trembling that was going all through her.

She was shaken, no doubt about that, but she wasn't going to allow herself to cry. She had known this day might come, even though she had done her best to see that it never did. She had traveled a long way to leave her past behind.

But she shouldn't have used her real name, she supposed. Not only that, but she had plastered it right there on the name of the business. Maybe that was the way he had tracked her down, maybe it wasn't, but it was still a foolish thing to have done, regardless.

Blaise got control over her raging emotions. She lowered her hands from her face and took a deep breath, then another. Her heart was still racing, but not quite as fast as it had been a moment earlier.

It was a shame Brice had to be here to see that, she mused. He was observant. He had noticed her reaction. And he was smart enough to figure out what had actually caused it, despite her flimsy excuse of indigestion. She was relieved that he hadn't pressured her for answers to his obvious questions. But just because he had let it go for now, that didn't mean he would continue to do so.

She would have to take that as it came, Blaise told herself. A small part of her hoped that Martin would just move on, that it was pure luck—bad luck—that had brought him here and he wasn't actually looking for her. Maybe he would just leave Big Rock, as he had left the saloon a few minutes earlier . . .

She knew that was too much to expect, though, so she wasn't really surprised at all when she opened the door to her sitting room and found Martin Delroy lounging on the loveseat. His hat was off, his legs were crossed, and he had a drink in his hand. He looked completely at home.

"Hello, my dear," he said. "Don't just stand there. Come inside and close the door."

For a second, Blaise thought about turning and running away—but there was nowhere to run. Even though she hadn't been in Big Rock all that long, she had made a life for herself here, and she was reluctant to abandon it.

Anyway, Martin had found her once, hadn't he? He could find her again if that was what he wanted to do.

Maybe it would be better to settle this now, rather than running the rest of her life.

She stepped into the room and eased the door

shut behind her. "How did you get in here?" she asked coolly.

"I knew you'd have your quarters up here," he replied. "You always talked about owning and living in a saloon. So I came up the rear stairs and looked around until I found a locked door."

"As you said, the door was locked."

Martin sipped his drink and smiled. "You don't really believe that any lock in a cow country town like this would keep me out for long, do you?"

"No, you always were good at breaking and entering."

"I never had to put much effort into it with you, did I?" He sounded very satisfied with himself.

Blaise suppressed the anger and fear she felt welling up inside her. "What do you want, Martin?"

"Why, I wanted to see you again, my dear. I missed you. My life just wasn't the same without you."

"I'll bet it wasn't," she snapped. "You probably had to work harder than you like to afford fancy clothes and liquor and those high-stakes poker games you love so much."

His deep-set eyes glittered for a second, but whether the reaction was prompted by rage or amusement, she couldn't tell. He threw back the rest of the whiskey and set the empty glass on the little table at the end of the love seat. Then he rose to his feet and took a step toward her.

Blaise took a step away from him and felt her back press against the door. "Don't you come near me," she said. "I'm warning you, Martin."

"Settle down, Blaise," he told her. "There's no need for you to get upset. I understand why you left me. Hell, if the situation had been reversed, I might have done the same thing. If you're worried that I might be holding a grudge, you can ease your mind. Although . . . that *was* a considerable amount of money you took with you when you disappeared, and not all of it was rightfully yours."

"I felt like I earned it." She heard her voice tremble a little as she spoke and hated herself for it.

Martin waved his right hand. The midday light coming in through the gauzy curtains reflected from the gem in the ring he wore.

"That's all water under the bridge, as they say. You've made a fresh start here, and I admire you for that. But from now on, you and I are going to make a fresh start, too."

Blaise shook her head. "No. Absolutely not. We're finished, Martin. If . . . if you need money so you can move on somewhere else, I'm sure we can come to an agreement—"

"Now you wound me," he said as he moved closer and pressed his left hand to the front of the fancy vest he wore. That hand had a sparkling ring on one of the fingers, too. "After all this time, do you honestly believe that I care more about money than I do about you?"

"You always seemed to before," she practically spat at him.

"As always, you misinterpret my intentions. Whatever has been damaged between us in the past, I want to repair it now, so that we can be together—"

"You just want to share what I'm building here. What I've already built!"

His smooth façade slipped for a second as his mouth tried to twist into a snarl under the neatly trimmed mustache. "Considering that you built it with my money, that seems only fair," he declared.

"I told you, I *earned* that money. Now get out!"

He eased closer. "You could at least see your way clear to letting me enjoy a brief reunion—"

He stopped short as her hand dipped into a pocket on her dress and came out with a derringer. The little pistol was nickel-plated, had pearl grips, and carried two .41 caliber cartridges in its over-and-under barrels. Blaise pointed it at Martin and said, "That's far enough."

His eyes widened in surprise, but he didn't seem particularly frightened. "Do you honestly mean to say that you'd *shoot* me?"

"If you try to attack me, I will."

He shook his head pityingly. "Blaise, Blaise, Blaise. Have I ever forced you into anything?

164

As I recall, it was *you* who volunteered to do anything I wanted if I would rescue you from those terrible straits in which you found yourself. Anything at all, I believe you said."

"That was a long time ago," she said, her voice quivering again.

"Not that long, really. And, if you're being truthful, you'll have to admit that I was never less than gentle and considerate with you, was I?"

"You . . . I . . . the things you made me do . . ."

She wanted to pull the trigger. At this range, the slug would put a nice-sized hole right in the middle of his face.

Martin frowned. "Most of the things we did, *you* came up with the idea for them. You know that as well as I do. I'm starting to lose my patience here, Blaise. I've come to you and made no demands . . . and you know that I could have . . . I have every legal right—"

The talking distracted her. He probably knew it would. She hadn't noticed that somehow he had gotten within arm's reach. Then, without warning, his left hand flashed up and the back of it struck her right wrist, knocking that arm aside. The derringer flew out of her fingers, struck the wall, and fell to the floor. Luckily, it didn't go off when it landed.

At the same time, Martin stepped forward, cupped his right hand at the back of her neck, and jerked her toward him. As she collided with him, she was reminded of how hard and muscular his body was, even though when he was dressed, he didn't appear to be all that well-built. His left arm went around her waist, trapping her against him.

"I'm sorry, my dear," he murmured, not meaning a word of it. "But as I said, I have every right to this."

His mouth came down hard on hers. She tried to twist her head away, but his hand on the back of her neck was too strong. She couldn't escape. She thought about trying to hit him, but she knew he would just shrug off the blows. His mustache scraped her upper lip as he continued kissing her for what seemed like an eternity.

Finally, he lifted his head and smiled at her as she panted in rage. "You'll soon come around to my way of thinking," he said with maddening smugness. "And if you don't . . . well, it doesn't really matter, does it? I'm your husband. I'll take what I want."

CHAPTER 14

San Francisco, one year earlier

Harrison Wheeler cupped Blaise's chin, leaned closer to her so he could peer into her brown eyes, and said, "Deborah, my dear, you're the most ravishing creature I've ever seen."

She laughed softly and told him, "Harrison, you're drunk."

"Drunk on your beauty, that's what I am. You're the most intoxicating woman I've met in my life."

In truth, he had had quite a bit to drink. During dinner at this expensive, luxurious restaurant, Blaise had subtly encouraged Wheeler to have the waiter keep the champagne flowing. She had plenty of practice at not actually drinking as much as she appeared to, but Wheeler guzzled the stuff down like it was water.

That was fine with Blaise. If he was drunk enough by the time they got back to his mansion on Nob Hill, he might just go to sleep as soon as he stretched out on the silk sheets of the huge four-poster in the master bedroom.

If he didn't . . . well, it wasn't as if she would have to put up with any more than she had endured many times in the past. And in truth,

Harrison Wheeler wasn't as unpleasant to be with as many of the men she had known.

Certainly, he was large and brawny and a little rough at times when he got carried away, as could be expected from a man who had started out as a deck hand on a China Clipper and risen to become a shipping tycoon whose companies reached around the globe like the fingers of grasping hands. He was utterly ruthless in business and didn't mind crushing a competitor—of whom he didn't have many these days—or an enemy. He still had plenty of those.

But he treated her decently, wining and dining her in the best restaurants in the city by the bay. He lavished presents on her, including the gown she wore this evening and the jeweled rings on her slender fingers.

True, he expected certain things from her, things that his wife—ill in a sanitarium from which she would never emerge—could no longer provide, if she ever had. But that was just . . . business. Wheeler might delude himself that it was more than that, but Blaise never did.

"Are you ready to go, my dear?" he asked now as he leaned back in his chair and regarded the remains of the delicious dinner they had just enjoyed, the fine china and silver and crystal spread across the snowy expanse of white linen.

Blaise eyed the neck of the champagne bottle sticking up from the ice bucket and said, "Surely you don't want the rest of that exquisite bubbly going to waste, Harrison, darling."

"You're right." Wheeler reached out, snagged the bottle's neck, and pulled it, dripping, from the half-melted ice. He started to pour some of the champagne in her glass.

Quickly, she said, "Oh, no more for me. My head is positively spinning already. Any more and I'm sure I shall be sound asleep by the time we get home." She smiled. "We don't want that."

"Indeed, we don't."

"But you're so much more formidable than me. I'm sure you can finish it."

"No doubt about it!"

Wheeler lifted the bottle to his mouth and drank directly from it, the muscles in his throat working as he swallowed. The champagne bubbled as the level in the bottle steadily lowered until it was gone.

Then Wheeler placed the empty bottle on the table and said, "Ah!" He lurched to his feet, swayed for a second before steadying himself, and went on, "Come along, my dear."

He was drunk, Blaise was sure of that, but he had the will and determination not to show it much as he led her from the restaurant and helped her into the waiting carriage. Even though the season was summer, this was San Francisco, and there was always a chill in the air at night, making Blaise glad for the fur wrap she wore.

The carriage barely had gotten started when Wheeler put his arms around her and started kissing her, being very free with his hands as he did so. Blaise put up with it for a moment, then fended him off with a laugh.

"Goodness! Can't you wait until we get home?"

"You drive me mad, Deborah, you know that." Wheeler sighed. "But I'll do as you wish, of course. I don't want to upset you."

And he truly didn't, she knew. He actually did care about her, as much as he was capable of caring about anyone other than himself. For that reason, she felt a little bad about the money she and Martin planned to steal from him . . . but only a little.

As the carriage rolled toward Nob Hill, Wheeler took out a cigar and lit it with a match he struck on an iron-hard thumbnail, just as he would have when he was a sailor. After puffing a moment and exhaling a cloud of fragrant smoke, he said, "Where's that blasted brother of yours these days? Haven't seen him at the club for almost a week." He gestured with the fat cigar. "He won a considerable amount of money from me the last time we played cards. He needs to give me a chance to win it back."

The money Martin Delroy had won from Wheeler amounted to little more than pocket change to the shipping magnate, but he didn't like losing anything to anyone, no matter how much it was. Once Blaise had realized that, she had started to worry that perhaps it wasn't wise to target him after all, but Martin had waved off her concern.

"We'll take enough from him that he'll never be able to find us," Martin had assured her. "Besides, a man with Wheeler's pride isn't going to want to admit that he got taken. He'll just forget about it."

Blaise hoped Martin was right about that.

Tonight, Blaise said in response to Wheeler's comment, "Oh, he's been busy with some sort of business deal. You know Charles. He always has so many different irons in the fire."

Wheeler grunted. "Yeah. I like that about the man. He reminds me of . . . me, I suppose. *And* he has the most beautiful sister in the world. Hard not to like him for that, too."

Martin was the one who had actually made contact with Wheeler first, wangling an invitation into a poker game that included Wheeler among its regular players. Martin had introduced himself as Charles Carrington and pretended to be a successful businessman from back East who was in San Francisco looking for a new enterprise with which to involve himself.

The two men had struck up a friendship over cards. Martin could charm and persuade anyone into anything. If he had been at the Little Bighorn, he would have had Custer and the Indians sitting down to have a picnic together.

From there, it was a simple step for Martin to introduce Wheeler to Blaise, telling him that she was his sister Deborah, visiting from the family's ancestral home in New England. Once Wheeler laid eyes on her, he had been doomed. Doomed to lose a considerable amount of money, anyway.

Their affair had proceeded rapidly, with Blaise putting up only token resistance. The sooner this was over, the better, as far as she was concerned. Not that she found Harrison Wheeler repulsive. It was just that sleeping with him made her feel like a prostitute, and she had believed that life was behind her when she married Martin Delroy.

Since then, they had swindled half a dozen men out of various sums of money, but Blaise hadn't had to go to bed with any of them, only tease and promise and never go through with it. Wheeler was different, Martin said. They had to set the hook properly to reel him in. This would be the only time, he vowed. After this, they were through . . .

The carriage turned in at the stone gate in the high fence around Wheeler's mansion. Wheeler was already snoring a little as he swayed back and forth to the carriage's rhythm. He might rouse long enough to make it inside and up to bed without any help, but then a sound, champagne-induced sleep would claim him.

And she and Martin would be one night closer to the fortune they needed to escape from this life, Blaise told herself.

• • •

Since he was supposed to be her brother, there was nothing unusual about Martin visiting her at Wheeler's mansion. One of the servants ushered him into the sitting room where Blaise was waiting.

She stood up and went to him, lowering her voice as she said, "I think it's time."

He put his hands on her shoulders, smiled, and asked, "Is that any way to greet your loving brother?" before leaning in and brushing his lips across her cheek.

"I'm serious, Charles," she said, using the false name in case any of the servants were eavesdropping. "Harrison is becoming . . . demanding."

He frowned. "I'm sorry, my dear, but we agreed that certain sacrifices were necessary—"

"He's insisting that I should marry him," Blaise broke in. "He doesn't want to damage my reputation." She laughed, a sound that had a thin edge of hysteria in it. "As if it weren't already damaged by me openly being his mistress."

"With the money that Harrison Wheeler has, no one is going to say too much about him . . . or those close to him," Martin insisted. "Has he actually proposed?"

"Yes. I've asked him to allow me some time before I give him my answer."

"Was there a ring involved?"

"There was."

"And how much would you say it's worth?" Martin asked. "I know you have a good eye for things like that."

She had to tighten her jaw to keep from responding angrily. If she gave in to her emotions, she might slip and call him by his real name.

"That doesn't matter," she said. She lowered her voice even more. "I'm not going to marry him. You know I can't."

"If you mean because you and I . . ." He angled a hand to indicate the truth of the relationship between them. "Under the circumstances . . ."

"No." Blaise shook her head. "No."

Martin looked at her intently for a moment, then sighed and nodded. He squeezed her shoulders again and said, "You're right, of course. It's out of the question. We'll go ahead, just as you say."

"Thank you," she whispered.

"No, thank *you,* my dear. You're the one who makes it all possible."

He was right about that, she thought. Without her, he had nothing.

Perhaps it was time to ponder a bit more on that fact.

"Fifty thousand dollars is a great deal of money," Harrison Wheeler said. He pursed his lips and frowned, then said again, "A great deal."

"I'm well aware of that, old boy," Martin

said. "That's why I didn't want to even bring the matter up. But Deborah insisted that you wouldn't be upset. In fact, she assured me that you would be insulted if I *didn't* at least suggest the idea to you."

"And she was right, of course," Wheeler said with a glance toward Blaise, who stood on the other side of the room chatting with some of Wheeler's other dinner guests. "Your sister is very special to me, and you've been a good friend, Charles." Wheeler's fingertips stroked his chin. "Besides, this could turn into a very lucrative investment when that spur line goes through. You're sure about it?"

"I trust your opinion when it comes to shipping, old boy. You can trust me when it comes to railroads." Martin laughed. "I have no doubts about the potential of this deal. None at all."

Wheeler studied him intently for a moment more and then jerked his head in a curt nod.

"All right. You'll have the money. I'll get my lawyers started drawing up the papers—"

"I'm sorry, Harrison," Martin interrupted him, "but I'm afraid there's no time to waste. My contacts require the money immediately, and in cash, I'm sorry to say." He smiled and shrugged. "It's an unfortunate fact of life that not everyone is as trustworthy as you and I are, and as a consequence, they don't extend trust to others. I have to meet with them later tonight, and they'll be expecting their money if the deal is to go through without a hitch."

"Good Lord, man!" exclaimed Wheeler. "You have to have the fifty thousand in cash *tonight?*"

"Those aren't my terms, you understand. I'm being pushed into it. However, I understand your reluctance to part with a sum like that to someone who isn't even family yet. Why don't you wait to give me the money until those lawyers have done their work? I'd get them started on it first thing in the morning, though, if I were you. The longer the delay, the greater the chance that our prospective partners will become impatient and secure their financing elsewhere."

"Wait a minute, wait a minute." Harrison frowned. "You said that you're not a member of the family *yet?*"

Martin let a rueful smile creep over his expression. He chuckled and said, "I've spoken out of turn."

"Not at all. You know something about . . . about a decision your sister is going to make?"

Martin held up a hand. "Really, Harrison, I can't say any more. It just wouldn't be right. Not my place at all. Now, if our business is concluded until tomorrow . . ."

"Wait, wait. You really think that we might get cut out of this deal if we drag our feet?"

Martin spread his hands. "Probably not, but it's impossible to say for sure."

"All right." Wheeler nodded again. "I don't want to run that risk. I'll get the cash together. You'll have it when you leave here tonight."

Martin couldn't keep the surprise out of his voice as he said, "You have that much money here in the house?"

"No, but I can make a telephone call to my banker and have it brought here. That won't be a problem." Wheeler smiled. "By the time you leave tonight, you'll have that money and we'll both be on our way to an even bigger fortune. And maybe there'll be an important change in my personal life, as well."

"I wouldn't doubt it a bit," Martin said.

Blaise had gotten the high sign from Martin and had to make an effort to contain the excitement she felt. Wheeler had agreed to turn over the money. This long ordeal was almost finished.

Wheeler had a maddening smirk on his rugged face all during dinner. Blaise supposed that Martin had dropped hints she was ready to accept his proposal. He probably needed to do that in order to seal the deal, she mused. That was all right; she could play along for a little while longer.

After dinner, the gentlemen retired to Wheeler's spacious study for cigars and brandy, while the ladies sipped port and gossiped in the dining room. Before they parted, however, Wheeler pressed Blaise's arm and leaned in to whisper, "I believe we're going to have a very important conversation later."

"I believe so, too," she murmured.

Then he was gone with the others, including Martin, and she was left to navigate the dangerous waters of San Francisco society.

She managed well. She knew some of these women looked down on her, but Harrison Wheeler was too rich, too influential, and had too many fingers in their husbands' business dealings for them to say anything too cutting. She wouldn't be the first woman to go seamlessly from being a rich man's mistress to being his wife, and they had to guard their tongues against that day.

Besides, as far as they knew, she was from a very wealthy family back in New England, and that gave her more latitude, as well.

Finally, the interminable evening was over, and the guests began to leave. Wheeler and Blaise said their good nights together, as if they were already married. Wheeler slipped an arm possessively around her shoulders, which were left mostly bare by the gown she wore.

When Martin was the last one there, Blaise said, "Harrison, dear, Charles has asked me to go back to his hotel with him this evening."

Wheeler frowned. "What?"

"I'm sorry, but he's taken it into his head that he needs to play the protective older brother.

You see . . . he knows what I plan to say to you tomorrow, and he believes that, for propriety's sake, once our . . . arrangement . . . is official, it would be better for us to live apart until the time that we'll never be parted again."

Wheeler looked like he was having trouble taking all that in. "Confound it!" he burst out. "I thought we were going to settle this tonight."

"One more day, dear. That's all I need."

"When I asked you to marry me, I didn't think you'd be moving out," Wheeler said with a disappointed glare.

"I know, but it's just for a short period of time, until we can get everything arranged suitably. A matter of weeks, that's all."

"Weeks," repeated Wheeler. "Weeks without you. I don't know if I can stand it."

She laughed lightly. "You won't be without me. I'll still see you every day. But I'd really like to get everything off to a good start, Harrison. On the right foot, so to speak. You understand, don't you?"

He sighed and nodded and said with obvious reluctance, "I suppose so." Forcing a smile onto his face, he went on, "Whatever you want, my dear, is what I want, too. But tomorrow—"

"Tomorrow, we'll have brunch together in the garden, and speak of serious things together."

"All right."

One of the servants brought her wrap. She

kissed Wheeler good night and joined Martin in the great, marble-floored foyer. Martin shook hands with Harrison and gave him a wink.

"Here's to a bright future for all of us," Martin said.

"Very bright indeed," Blaise added.

Then they were out of there, in Wheeler's carriage, headed toward the hotel where Martin had been staying—the hotel that had eaten up almost all of their remaining money.

But now, things had changed. In the rear seat, Blaise leaned forward and said in a low voice, "You have it?"

"In this valise," Martin replied, reaching down to pat the carpetbag at his feet.

"The whole thing?"

"The whole thing," he assured her.

He proved that, when they reached the hotel and went up to his room, by opening the bag and dumping the contents on the bed. Blaise looked at the piles of money and wanted to scoop them up and let them run through her fingers.

"We did it," she said. "We really did it."

"And we had better get out of town tonight," Martin told her. "With this much money, we can travel far enough that Wheeler will never find us, but I've heard stories about the man and what he's like when he's crossed. I really think it would be a good idea if we got as much of a head start on him as we can."

"I agree," Blaise said. She slipped her hand into the bag she carried and closed her fingers around the handle of the blackjack inside it. It was loaded with lead shot, and she'd had it for several years. She had been very good at using it, too, at one time, although she hadn't had any need for it in a while.

Until tonight.

Martin was standing beside the bed, hands on hips, gazing down raptly at the cash. He couldn't take his eyes off the money, which was good because Blaise needed time to set herself and get ready. She knew she would have only one chance.

"I think we should be proud of ourselves," he said. "It's not everyone who can bilk a man like Harrison Wheeler. We did really good work here."

She was the one who had done the work, Blaise told herself. She had earned this money, not Martin Delroy.

That thought was uppermost in her mind as she struck, slamming the blackjack against his head behind the right ear with such precision that his knees buckled and he went down hard, out cold. He landed beside the bed in a crumpled heap and didn't move as she scooped up the money, put it back in the valise, and got the hell out of there.

It was possible to kill a man with one blow from a blackjack, she knew, and as she left the hotel, Blaise wondered idly if Martin actually was dead instead of unconscious.

Considering everything she had done at his insistence, she couldn't bring herself to care one way or the other about the answer to that question.

CHAPTER 15

Big Rock

Denny opened the door and stepped into Louis's office. She had ridden into town on horseback today—although not on Rocket—and wore range clothes: jeans that clung to her legs and were tucked into high-topped, dark brown boots; a white shirt with the sleeves rolled up a couple of turns on her tanned forearms; a brown vest and a matching brown hat on her blond curls. Her Colt Lightning rode in the holster attached to the gun belt strapped around her trim hips.

It was a scandalous outfit for a young woman to be wearing, as her mother had informed her more than once, but most folks around here had gotten used to seeing Denny dressed like that. Denny knew, too, that Sally had worn similar garb many times during the early days, when she and Smoke were just getting the Sugarloaf started. Smoke had declared proudly many times that in those days, Sally had been able to ride and handle a lasso better than most men.

She had been good with a gun when she needed to be, too, although neither she nor Smoke talked about those occasions very much.

Denny's brother looked up from his desk,

which was covered with papers and open law books, and asked, "Is the entire Jensen family in Big Rock today? I suppose Mother will come waltzing in here next."

"Well, I'm glad to see you, too," Denny said dryly.

Louis shook his head and stood up. "I'm sorry, Denny. It's been a busy morning, for a change. What can I do for you?"

"I thought maybe you'd like to have lunch with me. But now that you've mentioned it, I want to hear all about this busy morning you've had."

Louis leaned back in his chair and waved a hand toward the red leather chairs in front of the desk. "Father came by earlier to talk about ranch business," he said, "but when he got here, I already had two potential clients in the office."

Denny raised an eyebrow in surprise as she sat down. She took off her hat and tossed it on the desk, letting her hair spill around her shoulders.

"That's a good thing, isn't it? Having clients in the office, I mean."

"Potential clients, I said. And normally, yes. However, in this case, neither of them hired me. In fact, I wound up giving legal advice to both of them . . . free of charge."

"Well, I'm no lawyer," Denny commented with a shake of her head, "but that's not the way it's supposed to work, is it?"

"Not really. Did you happen to meet Father

on the way into town? Have you already heard all about this and are you just stringing me along?"

"I haven't seen him since breakfast this morning," Denny replied honestly. "I don't have any idea what you're talking about."

"It's not good." Louis sighed and then launched into a recital of the conflict between the Box RG and the Ace of Diamonds over the boundary line and ownership of the waterhole. Denny listened with more interest than she would have thought she could muster over a discussion of surveys, longitude, and latitude.

"So you think Mr. Mullen is in the right?" she asked when Louis was finished.

"Oh, I wouldn't go so far as to say that. On the face of the evidence, he has a stronger case, that's all I can say definitively at this point. If I was going to be involved in litigating the case on either side, I'd want to conduct a thorough investigation. That probably would require taking a deposition from the surveyor who carried out this new survey for Mr. Mullen as well as perhaps getting a corroborating survey."

"Like all those second and third opinions you got from different doctors."

"Exactly."

"So, are you going to do that?" asked Denny.

Louis frowned across the desk at her in confusion and asked, "Do what?"

"Conduct a thorough investigation," she said, repeating his words back to him.

"Why in the world would I do that when I don't even have a client?"

"So you'll be ready when one of those ranchers hires you. You don't actually think they'll just let the matter drop, do you?"

Louis hesitated, then said, "I believe that's a very unlikely possibility."

"Yeah, so do I. Mullen might be willing to, especially since it looks like he's getting what he wants, for now, anyway. But Roy Gardner's been in this valley almost as long as our folks. He's not the sort of man to just sit back and take it when he believes he's been done wrong."

Denny paused, unsure whether to proceed with what was in her mind, but then she forged ahead. She had always been honest with her brother, and she wasn't going to change now.

"You know why they both wanted to hire you, don't you?" she asked.

Louis laughed. The sound had a slight edge of bitterness to it. "You mean, why would two successful ranchers want to hire a brand-new lawyer who's never even had a client before? Of course, I know, Denny. They wanted to hire me because my father is Smoke Jensen."

She shrugged and said, "That's what occurred to me. Pa's one of the best-known and most influential men in this part of the country. If you were sitting on a jury and listening to legal arguments, you might give more weight to the ones coming from Smoke Jensen's son."

"That's not the way the law works."

"That's not the way the law is *supposed* to work. But the legal system is made up of human beings, and they all have their flaws and prejudices. There's no way to litigate those out of existence."

"You're right," he admitted. "And I know Mr. Mullen and Mr. Gardner didn't show up here and start fighting over my services because they were impressed with how well I did at Harvard." Louis shook his head. "It doesn't really matter. Neither of them hired me, and there's certainly no guarantee that they will in the future. I hate to say it, but it's more likely that an old-fashioned range war will break out between them. And that's liable to lead to a lot of bloodshed."

An idea that had been playing around the edges of Denny's mind already suddenly seized it. She leaned forward and said, "Maybe you could head that off."

"Head what off? The range war?"

"That's right."

"How do you expect me to do that?"

"With that thorough investigation you talked about." Denny leaned forward as the idea came together. "You could find out the truth, and if the law is really on Mr. Mullen's side, and you can convince Mr. Gardner of that, I think he would back off. He may be a proddy old-timer, but he's a law-abiding man."

"He always has been, at least as far as I know," Louis allowed.

"That would show folks around here how smart you are when it comes to this law business, and they'd be lining up out the door trying to hire you."

"I suppose helping to prevent a range war *would* be good publicity," he mused.

Denny played her hole card. "And I could help you."

Louis started to nod, then stopped and said, "What? What do you mean, you could help me?"

"With the investigation."

Louis frowned and shook his head. "You're not a lawyer."

"No, but I know how to poke into things and find out what I want to know."

"You always have been pretty good about sticking your nose in other people's business, I'll give you that."

"Now you're just being obnoxious." Denny stood up, unable to stay seated as excitement gripped her. She paced back and forth in front of the desk. "You said the man who did the new survey is in Denver."

"That's right. Padgett, I believe his name was."

"I could go there and see him, confirm that he's certain the original survey was wrong."

"I could do that myself," Louis pointed out.

Denny shook her head. "You have to stay here and run your office. You might get some other clients." Denny couldn't resist adding a little gibe. "Paying ones, this time."

Louis glared at her for a second, then chuckled. "You're right that now wouldn't be a good time to leave Big Rock, just as I'm trying to get my practice established. It would be different if I'd actually been hired to represent one of those ranchers. But since I wasn't, anything that you did to assist me would have to be simply as a volunteer. You wouldn't be getting paid, either."

"But I'd have an excuse to go to Denver, wouldn't I?"

"Was that what you were looking for all along? You don't need an excuse, Denny. No one would stop you from going there. In fact, I'm sure Mother would be glad to go with you and do some shopping."

Denny made a face. "That doesn't sound as interesting as conducting an investigation. Like Sherlock Holmes or Sexton Blake."

Louis sat back and shook his head, saying, "All right, if you're determined to play detective, have at it. And if you do find out anything that turns out to be useful, I'll appreciate it. I'll even make sure that the client, if there is one, knows about your contribution to the case."

"You've got a deal. Now, why don't we go

on down to Longmont's and get that lunch I mentioned?"

Louis stood up and reached for his hat. "That's actually the best suggestion I've heard all day."

"And we can talk about how we're going to proceed on this investigation."

Louis didn't argue. Denny figured that by now, he knew it would be a waste of time.

CHAPTER 16

The Ace of Diamonds

Tony Mullen didn't trust Roy Gardner any farther than he could throw him, so even though the Ace of Diamonds seemed to have prevailed in the legal showdown in Louis Jensen's office, Mullen wasn't convinced the Box RG crew wouldn't try something. They might come in the dead of night—or hell, even in broad daylight if they were daring enough—and try to cut that fence. Once the barbed wire was down, they could run some of Gardner's cows through the gap and let them drink their fill at the disputed waterhole.

Mullen wasn't going to allow that to happen, so he posted guards there. At least three riders patrolled in the vicinity of the waterhole, twenty-four hours a day.

Of course, that left him a little short-handed for other ranch chores that needed to be done, but it couldn't be helped. It was more important to make sure the Box RG didn't get away with anything.

After three days and nights in which nothing troublesome happened, though, Mullen began to wonder if maybe Roy Gardner had decided not to be his usual mule-headed self. He dropped the number of men guarding the waterhole to two at a time.

Quince Jessup was one of the pair assigned to watch the waterhole today. The young cowboy was teamed with a slightly older puncher named Kimbrough, who, as far as Quince was concerned, was as dumb as one of those posts on which the barbed wire strands were tacked.

They were sitting in the trees, about a quarter of a mile from the waterhole but with a good view of it. Mullen had told them to stay out of sight. He didn't put it beyond those Box RG polecats to try their hands at some bushwhacking, so there was no point in giving them easy targets.

"Anyway, that fella busted a chair over my head," big, flaxen-haired Kimbrough was saying. His nose had been broken more than once and hadn't healed back correctly any of those times. "But that wasn't enough to knock me out, so he whaled on my skull with his gun for a spell. That was a dumb thing to do. Knocked the barrel plumb out of line, he did."

"Uh-huh," Quince said, not really paying attention to whatever yarn Kimbrough was spinning.

"After a while, that got annoyin', so I picked him up and heaved him through the front window of that saloon. The fella who ran the place got mighty peeved with me for breakin' the glass that way, so he took a bungstarter to my head and walloped me a few times. That made me sleepy, so I took a nap."

The sheer ridiculousness of the story finally caught Quince's interest. "Wait a minute," he said. "You're telling me that you got a chair broken over your head, then a fella pistol-whipped you, and finally another hombre walloped you with a bungstarter."

"That's what happened, all right," Kimbrough replied solemnly. "He hit me with that bungstarter, oh, half a dozen times, I reckon."

"And it just made you sleepy?"

"Yep."

"Hell, that should've busted your head all to pieces!"

"Oh, no," Kimbrough said, shaking his head. "My mama always told me my skull was as thick and hard as the Rocky Mountains. She dropped me on it ain't no tellin' how many times when I was a baby."

Quince snorted. He could believe that more than he could put any stock in most of the other things Kimbrough said.

"I don't think anybody could take all the punishment you claim you have without dyin'," he said. "It just ain't natural-like."

"Why, Quince, I wouldn't lie about nothin' like that. And that little scrap in the saloon weren't near as bad as some of the other things, like the time the beer wagon run over me and then run over me again when the driver turned around to see what he'd hit. He said he figured there must'a been a log a-layin' across the road, but it was just me. That was another time I got sleepy and had to lay down and take a nap."

"Getting run over by a beer wagon . . . twice! . . . didn't break every bone in your body?"

"Nope. I was a mite sore for a few days, though."

"Where'd this happen? I'm gonna go there and ask folks if they remember you."

"Why, it was in . . . uh . . ." Kimbrough took off his hat and scratched with blunt fingertips in the tangled thatch of hair atop his blocky head. "Um, down in Texas, maybe, or it could'a been up Montana way. I have a hard time recollectin' things like that."

The two cowboys were sitting with the backs propped against tree trunks. About fifty feet behind them, on the other side of the little grove where they couldn't be seen from the waterhole, their horses were tied, cropping at the sparse grass. From time to time, Quince could hear the animals moving around back there.

Then a different sound came to his ears, so quiet that at first he didn't realize he had even heard it. It nagged at him, though, making him sit up straighter and reach for the Winchester lying on the ground beside him.

Somebody was moving in the trees. Sneaking up on them.

Kimbrough was still yammering, saying, "I hope you ain't doubtin' what I been tellin' you, Quince. It'd sure hurt my feelin's if you was to think I was a liar—"

"Hush up," Quince said in a low, sharp tone. "Listen. You hear anything?"

"Just them horses stompin' around."

"No, I think somebody's out here with us—"

The gunshot that interrupted him was deafeningly loud under the canopy of branches. The muzzle flash cut through the shadowy gloom. Quince twisted and came up on his knees, bringing the rifle with him. From the corner of his eye, he saw Kimbrough slumping over. Blood welled from the hole in the side of the big puncher's head.

Kimbrough's skull really would have had to be as thick and hard as the Rocky Mountains to withstand the shattering impact of a bullet like that. Unfortunately for him, it wasn't.

Quince opened fire, aiming where he thought he'd seen the muzzle flash. He cranked off three rounds as fast as he could work the Winchester's lever. Then he surged to his feet and leaped toward another tree. He knew he couldn't stay where he was and let the bushwhacker draw a bead on him. He had to keep moving, maybe get to his horse and light a shuck out of there.

Another gun blasted to his left. He felt the wind-rip of the bullet as it sizzled past his ear. *Damn it!* There were two of them—at least. Quince yanked out his Colt and thumbed off a wild shot in the general direction of whoever had fired that last one.

In his haste, he tripped over something, stumbled, and fell. That probably saved his life, because two more shots roared just then. The slugs went over him and thudded into tree trunks, spraying splinters. Panicking, Quince rolled over a couple of times and flung shots in all directions. He jerked the Colt's trigger until the hammer fell on an empty chamber.

He didn't know where the killers were or if his shots had hit either of them. He leaped up, his eyes so wide they bulged from their sockets and his heart pounding so wildly in his chest it seemed about to burst free from his body. He ran blindly through the trees and was lucky he didn't dash his brains out on a trunk or a low-hanging branch.

Then he broke out into the sunlight and spotted his horse and Kimbrough's mount. Both animals were tied to a bush, but the gunfire had spooked them and they were dancing around nervously. Quince knew that if they kept that up much longer, they might break free and bolt. If they ran away, he wouldn't be able to catch them. Then he would be at the bushwhackers' mercy.

He couldn't hold in a frightened yell as he

lunged toward his horse. The cow pony jerked back and pulled its reins loose from the bush. Quince made a desperate grab and caught them.

"Hold still, blast your hide!" he shouted as he hauled down on the reins and tried to bring the horse under control. He stabbed his left foot at the stirrup and missed a couple of times before he got a toe in there.

He expected to feel the hammer-blow of a bullet striking him at any second.

But all he could do was keep trying to get away. He grabbed the saddle horn and jerked himself up, flinging his right leg across the saddle. He landed hard enough to make him groan, but he ignored the pain and leaned forward as he jabbed his heels into the horse's flanks. The horse bounded forward into a gallop.

Quince realized he had dropped his empty gun somewhere. He didn't even remember it slipping from his hand. His rifle was gone, too. So he couldn't have stayed and put up a fight even if he wanted to, he told himself. As he urged the horse on to greater speed, he tried to bring his fear under control. He was still alive, he thought. Still alive . . .

And with that realization came a mixture of fury and shame that made his face blaze with heat. He was running away from a fight, something he had sworn he would never do. But he had heard bullets singing past his head, closer than he had ever experienced such a thing before, and he had seen the surprised look on the face of big, dumb Kimbrough and the dark red blood that had run down the battered features and the limp way the seemingly indestructible lummox had toppled over. Quince didn't believe he was a coward, but things like that were enough to give any man the fantods.

He turned his head to look over his shoulder. Nobody was coming after him. No riders were in sight anywhere as the waterhole and the fence fell behind him. He was abandoning his post, he realized, disobeying the orders that Mullen and Orrie Striker had given him. But he had come so close to dying—and Kimbrough actually was dead—that he hoped they would understand.

And then, once he had told them what had happened here, the whole crew would mount up and head for the Box RG. The blood of an Ace of Diamonds rider was on their hands. No other response was possible.

Blood would answer blood . . .

Chet Holloway didn't have any trouble following the rogue bull as it tried to get away from him. It was making as much racket as an army as it crashed through the brush. After taking one look at him, the bull had turned and plunged into the thicket instead of attacking, as it had been known to do in the past.

Instead of following directly on the troublesome animal's trail, Chet had decided to do the smart thing. He could ride *around* the thicket as fast as the bull could force its way through, and then he'd be waiting to dab a loop on the loco critter.

The bull, a throwback to some of the longhorns that had been brought up here from Texas more than forty years earlier, was more than half wild and had been charging some of the cowboys when they were out on the range. Mr. Gardner wanted it caught, brought down to the ranch headquarters, and corralled where it couldn't do any harm.

In fact, the boss had offered a bonus to the man or men who captured the wild bull. Some members of the crew were working together because they didn't want to tangle with the bull by themselves. Those horns weren't just long, they were wicked sharp.

But Chet, while riding alone on the range today, had spotted the bull and gone after it. He wanted that fifty dollars for his own self.

Now he was on the verge of outsmarting the critter. He rounded the brush thicket and came out with a broad, open pasture stretching off to his left.

On the far side of that pasture rode about twenty men, coming toward him. Chet reined in sharply when he spotted them. The bull, still rampaging around in the brush, was forgotten. The riders were two hundred yards away, but Chet was young and had good eyes. He recognized not only Tony Mullen but also Orrie Striker, and he knew without doubt that that was the whole Ace of Diamonds crew he was looking at. And they were on Box RG range.

There was no good explanation for that. None at all. Chet knew as soon as he laid eyes on them why they were here.

They were on their way to attack the Box RG headquarters, a couple of miles south of here.

The Ace of Diamonds bunch came to an abrupt halt, too. Chet felt them staring at him across the open ground. He didn't know what had happened, what had provoked this raid, but it didn't matter. Those men across there were invaders, and as a Box RG hand, it was his duty to repel them.

Yeah, and if he charged them, he'd wind up dead with a pound of lead in him, the sensible part of his brain said. And there wouldn't be anybody to warn Mr. Gardner and Ben Hendricks and Johnny Dolan and the rest of the boys.

That tense confrontation lasted only a couple of heartbeats. Then Chet whirled his horse around and rammed his boot heels into its flanks. The cow pony leaped ahead and after a couple of bounds settled into a gallop. Chet looked over his shoulder and saw the Ace of Diamonds riders coming after him. A few spurts of powder smoke told him that they were shooting at him, but at this range, with a moving target, it would be pure luck if they hit him.

Bad luck for him, good luck for them. Not much for a fella to bet his life on.

Ahead of him to the right, the longhorn bull burst out of the brush. It barely had time to spot him and bellow furiously before Chet flashed past it. That fifty-dollar bonus didn't mean a blasted thing now.

Maybe the bull would see the men chasing him and go after them. That would slow them down. Chet could hope for such a development, anyway, although he knew it was unlikely.

Then he settled down and leaned forward in the saddle to urge as much speed as he could get out of his horse. This was a race for life and death now.

CHAPTER 17

Brice Rogers hadn't been to Blaise's Place for several days. He had gotten a telegram from Chief Marshal Long instructing him to ride north to a small town near the Colorado/Wyoming border and locate a witness whose testimony was needed in a federal court case. Brice didn't know what the case was about, but such knowledge wasn't necessary for him to do his job.

Marshal Long said it was urgent, so Brice didn't even have time to say goodbye to Blaise, let alone ride out to the Sugarloaf and let Denny know that he was going to be out of town for a few days, as he might have done if matters hadn't been so pressing.

One of these days, he told himself—and not for the first time—he needed to sit down with Denny and have a talk with her. They had to figure out if they were just friends or something more than that.

Of course, in order to do that, he would have to find a time when Conrad Morgan wasn't sniffing around.

Brice put all that out of his mind. Getting caught up in personal drama could be dangerous, especially when a man ought to be concentrating on his job.

In this case, that job turned out to be pretty tedious and not all dangerous. It took him two days to track down the man he was searching for, a drifting cowpuncher who had no idea the law was looking for him. Since he wasn't in trouble, he came back to Big Rock with Brice without putting up a fight. Brice had watched him get on a train bound for Denver. He hoped the fella wouldn't take it in his head to slip off again, but Brice had carried out his assignment. If anything else happened, it wasn't his fault.

He headed for Blaise's Place, ready for a cold beer and some pleasant company.

Instead, he got a shock like a slap across the face when he stepped into the saloon.

Blaise stood at the far end of the bar, her usual spot at this time of day. She wore a dark red dress cut low enough to reveal the creamy swells of her breasts. Her dark brown hair was put up in an elaborate arrangement of curls. A feather the same shade as her dress stuck up from her hair. She looked lovely and gave off a sensuous air that would take any man's breath away and make his heart pound faster.

That wasn't what shocked Brice. He had seen Blaise looking that good many times in the past. What made him stop in his tracks was the sight of the man with her, his left arm curved possessively around her waist. He was laughing about something, and even though Blaise had a smile on her face, Brice sensed that she didn't actually join in the man's amusement.

Brice needed only a second to start recovering from his surprise and realize that the man standing there with Blaise was the same stranger who had come into the saloon a few days earlier and provoked such an apprehensive reaction from her. Having seen the way she looked then, Brice couldn't wrap his head around the idea that she would have befriended the man in such a short amount of time.

Especially when the hombre let his hand stray a mite, so that his thumb brushed the underside of her left breast in the clinging gown. The gesture held such intimacy that Brice immediately felt a surge of jealousy and anger. He had never been that forward with Blaise in all the time he had known her. What gave this fella the right to do such a thing?

The saloon was fairly busy for the middle of the afternoon, with a couple of poker games going on, the roulette wheel spinning, and almost a dozen men lined up at the bar drinking. None of them paid any attention to Blaise and the stranger, which told Brice they were already used to the man being here. He must have staked his claim on Blaise the same day he'd arrived in town, after Brice left the saloon. Brice had never had a chance to stop back by . . . until now.

He put his surprised reaction aside. He wanted

to get to the bottom of this, so he strode along the bar toward the far end, where the two of them stood.

Blaise saw him coming. Alarm leaped into her eyes. Brice waited for her to shake her head in a signal for him not to approach, but that didn't happen. So he walked right up to them, nodded, and said, "Howdy, Blaise. Who's your friend?"

The blunt question didn't seem to bother the stranger. He slid his arm from around Blaise's waist and turned to face Brice more squarely as he thrust out his hand. "Martin Delroy," he introduced himself. Proving he had noticed Brice's badge, he went on, "It's nice to meet you, Marshal . . . ?"

"Rogers. Brice Rogers." Brice clasped the man's hand. Delroy had a firm grip.

"Welcome to Blaise's Place." Delroy's voice had a proprietary tone to it, as if this were *his* saloon.

"Oh, I've been here before. Plenty of times."

Delroy's grin widened. "Then you know what an excellent establishment it is. Please, have a drink on me." He waved to the bartender, who came over and asked Brice what he would have.

"Beer," Brice told him, then turned to Blaise and went on, "Hello, Blaise. You look mighty pretty today."

"Doesn't she, though?" Delroy responded with a laugh before Blaise could say anything.

"I'm just about the luckiest man west of the Mississippi. Or east of it, as well, I'd venture."

"Hello, Brice," Blaise said when Delroy let her get a word in. "I haven't seen you for a few days."

"I've been out of town."

"On a job for the law?" asked Delroy.

"That's right," Brice replied.

"Nothing too dangerous, I hope."

"As it turned out, not dangerous at all. But I'm sorry I had to leave in a hurry, since I never got a chance to say goodbye."

That was addressed to Blaise. She nodded, just a tiny motion of her head.

"Well, you're back now," Delroy said heartily as the bartender placed a foaming mug of beer on the hardwood in front of Brice. "Drink up, my friend."

Brice wanted to tell Delroy that they weren't amigos, but he decided that wouldn't serve any purpose except maybe to make him feel a mite better. He wanted to find out who Delroy was and what was going on here, but he could tell he wouldn't be able to discover those things until he had a chance to talk privately with Blaise. So he nodded, picked up the beer and raised the mug in a gesture of thanks, and took a healthy swallow. The beer was cold and good; that was one thing about Blaise's Place that hadn't changed, thank goodness.

A man in a white shirt, vest, and string tie came

over and said, "Mr. Delroy, a fella wants to make a bigger bet than the house limit on the roulette wheel. Do I let him do it?"

Brice recognized the man as Rollie Hammond, who ran the roulette wheel for Blaise. But now, judging by Rollie's attitude, he worked for Martin Delroy. The uneasy feeling inside Brice got even stronger at this revelation.

"I'll go speak to the gent and size him up, Rollie," Delroy said. "You did well to come and get me." He leaned over and brushed his lips across Blaise's cheek, just above the beauty mark near her mouth. "I'll be back, my dear."

Delroy slid a cheroot from his vest pocket and clamped it between his teeth, unlit, as he followed Rollie Hammond toward the roulette wheel.

Brice looked at Blaise and said, "What in—"

That was as far as he got before Blaise broke in to say, "Let it go, Brice. Martin's my husband. We're married and this place is as much his as it is mine."

Martin Delroy hooked his thumbs in his vest pockets and said, "Now, what can I do for you?"

The man he was addressing smiled at him. "I just expressed an interest in making a larger wager than the house limit, and this gentleman"—a nod toward Rollie Hammond—"said he would have to speak to the owner." The stranger paused for a second, then asked, "Are you Mr. Blaise?"

Delroy chuckled. "Not exactly."

"But I don't understand," the stranger said. "The sign outside says clearly that this is Blaise's Place."

"Indeed, it is. My wife's name is Blaise. That's her over there at the end of the bar."

Delroy nodded toward her. The stranger followed the indication and stared momentarily before dropping his gaze. "The, ah, very lovely woman in the dark red gown?" He sounded a little embarrassed.

"That's right, my friend. I know what you're thinking. I'm a lucky man. A very lucky man, indeed."

"I apologize for staring—"

"Never apologize for appreciating great beauty. Now, how much did you want to bet?"

Rollie spoke up, saying, "He's been on a hot streak, boss, and is letting it ride. He's got close to six hundred dollars there, and five hundred's the usual house limit."

"And you want to let it ride again?" asked Delroy. "On black?"

"That's right."

Delroy considered for a couple of seconds, then nodded. "Go ahead, Rollie."

Hammond said to the other players gathered around the wheel, "All right, fellas, get your bets down."

When all the bets were placed, he spun the wheel. Delroy watched the stranger while, in turn, the man intently watched the revolving wheel and the bouncing ball.

The stranger was around forty, Delroy judged, although the skin of his narrow face was smooth and unlined for the most part. He had a few strands of gray in the brown hair under his derby hat. His Adam's apple bulged prominently in his skinny neck. He wore a pair of rimless spectacles. Short and slightly built, in his suit and derby he looked like a traveling salesman of some sort. Ladies' undergarments, maybe. As the wheel began to slow, he reached up, put a finger against the spectacles' frame, and pushed them higher up on his thin nose.

The ball bounced to a stop. "Thirty-one," Rollie announced, then looked up and added, "Black."

Delroy laughed and clapped a hand on the stranger's shoulder. "Well done, my friend," he congratulated the man. "That's a nice tidy sum you've just won. Are you going to let it ride again?"

Smiling faintly, the man shook his head. "No, I don't believe in pushing my luck," he said. "Besides, I've gotten what I came in here for."

"A good time?" asked Delroy. "The camaraderie of like-minded souls?"

"Of course," the stranger agreed. "What else could a man want?"

Conrad Morgan pushed the batwings aside and stepped into the saloon. The mines had kept him very busy for several days. He had been riding up and down the valley, troubleshooting problems at the various operations, from before dawn until well after dark each day. A couple of those evenings, he had considered coming to Blaise's Place after he got back to Big Rock, but he was just too blasted tired.

Today was the first day in a while there weren't any problems that needed his attention, at least not that he knew of, so he'd strolled around to the saloon, thinking that he would partake of the free lunch, have a beer or two, and visit with Blaise.

There was a chance Brice Rogers would be there, Conrad knew. Blaise's Place seemed to be the deputy marshal's unofficial headquarters these days.

That was all right. Blaise Warfield was a beautiful woman and charming company, but if he was being honest with himself, Conrad knew that most of his attention, when he had time for anything other than work, was focused on Denny Jensen. Denny was the most intriguing woman Conrad had met since his late wife Rebel, and that included the fiery, auburn-haired bounty hunter Lace McCall.

Brice had shared numerous adventures with Denny, and some folks had the idea that *they* were a couple, Conrad knew. But Denny had never said as much to *him,* so he figured Brice didn't have any real claim staked there, to be blunt about it. As soon as he got a chance, he intended to ride out to the Sugarloaf and pay another visit to Denny.

Today, though, he didn't really have time for that, so he stepped into Blaise's Place instead—and stopped short at the sight of the saloon's beautiful proprietor in apparently earnest conversation with Deputy Marshal Brice Rogers.

A small, slightly built man in a suit and derby hat said, "Excuse me, sir." Conrad barely glanced at the gent as he moved aside to let the man leave the saloon. He was still looking at Blaise and Brice.

Then things got even more interesting as a man Conrad had never seen before walked over to Blaise and put his arm around her, acting as if he had every right to do so. Blaise didn't pull away from him, either. She smiled, but Conrad, who'd had considerable experience with women, didn't believe the expression was completely genuine.

Brice didn't look happy, either. Conrad didn't mind that development, but it increased his curiosity about the stranger's identity—and his relationship with Blaise.

Conrad walked toward the little group at the far end of the bar. All three of them saw him coming. Brice looked annoyed, the stranger looked curious, and Blaise . . . well, Conrad couldn't read Blaise's expression. He had a feeling she wasn't happy to see him, but beyond that, he wouldn't venture a guess.

He greeted her first, with a nod and a pinch of his hat brim. "Miss Warfield," he said. "It's good to see you again."

"Hello, Conrad," she said. Her voice was as carefully guarded as her expression.

"Morgan," Brice said with a curt nod.

Conrad returned that nod with a smile. "Marshal."

The stranger extended his hand. "Martin Delroy," he introduced himself. "And I hate to correct someone I'm just meeting for the first time, but you have this lovely lady's name wrong. She's Mrs. Delroy."

As a businessman, Conrad had been in plenty of tense, tricky negotiations where he couldn't afford to show what he was feeling. During the time of his life when he had called himself Kid Morgan and followed the lonely trails of a drifting gunfighter, he had also found himself in many dangerous situations where his life depended on keeping his face impassive. Because of that, he was able to keep from displaying the surprise that went through him at that unexpected revelation.

"Is that so?" he murmured coolly. "I must have missed the wedding."

"It was a while back," Delroy said without offering any further explanation. His hand was still out, so Conrad took it and gave it a quick shake.

He didn't like Martin Delroy at all. When he clasped the man's hand, his instincts reacted as if he had just wrapped his fingers around the scaly, writhing body of a diamondback rattler. He let go and felt relieved.

"So you're helping Blaise run the saloon now?"

"That's right. We're running it together." Delroy tightened his arm around Blaise's shoulders. "Isn't that right, my dear?"

"Of course," she said.

"And what do you do, Mr. Morgan?"

Brice said, "He owns gold mines."

Delroy's dark eyebrows, which were touched with silver, rose considerably. "Is that right?" he said. Avarice glittered in his deep-set eyes.

Conrad shrugged. "I have some mining interests, among other things."

"What's the name of that company you run that sort of has everything gathered up in one place?" asked Brice. "The Browning Holdings? Something like that?"

"That's it," Conrad responded, his jaw tight with irritation. It was fair to say that he and Brice didn't like each other. Brice knew he didn't care for talking about his wealth and would just as soon that it didn't come up in conversation.

"Wait a minute," Delroy said. "You're Conrad *Browning?*"

"I go by Morgan now. That's my father's name, and I prefer to use it these days, although I still have a great deal of respect and affection for my late stepfather."

"His real pa is Frank Morgan, the gunfighter," Brice supplied.

Delroy shook his head. "I don't believe I know the name. But I've heard of the Browning Holdings, of course. Railroads, shipping, mining, banking . . . Is there anything you *don't* have a financial interest in, Mr. Morgan?"

"Plenty of things," Conrad replied. "For example, I don't own any saloons. So you're ahead of me there, Mr. Delroy."

That put a satisfied smirk on the man's face. Clearly, the man was ahead in other ways, too, thought Conrad, if he truly was married to Blaise . . .

His thoughts didn't have a chance to run any further in that direction, because at that moment, rapid hoofbeats sounded from the street outside, mixed with several excited shouts. Conrad couldn't make out the words, but the tone was unmistakable. As he glanced at Brice Rogers, he saw that the lawman had recognized the same thing.

Trouble had just galloped into Big Rock.

CHAPTER 18

The Box RG, a short time earlier

Chet Holloway was still about fifty yards ahead of the pursuing Ace of Diamonds riders when he came in sight of Roy Gardner's ranch house. The raiders continued shooting at him, but most of their bullets fell short. Occasionally, Chet saw a slug kick up dirt to one side or the other of him and knew that if this chase lasted long enough, the men trying to kill him would get the range.

With any luck, that wouldn't happen, since he could see the ranch ahead of him now. And just to make sure that the rest of the crew was alerted to the danger galloping toward them, Chet pulled his Colt from its holster and started firing into the air. Between each shot, he whooped at the top of his lungs.

Probably fewer than half the hands were at the ranch headquarters at this time of day. That gang from the Ace of Diamonds might be intending to kill everybody they found there and burn the house and barn. Chet wouldn't put it past that snake-blooded bunch.

But if Mr. Gardner could get a few boys with rifles scattered around the place, they might be able to hold off the attackers long enough for the rest of the crew to hear the shots and come a-runnin'. That was what Chet hoped, anyway.

He saw a man hurry out of the barn and look toward him, holding up a hand to shade his eyes. Chet could tell by the way the man moved that he was old Ike Armitage, the horse wrangler. Ike was too stove-up to ride the range much anymore, so he was usually around the barn working on some chore. After staring at Chet for a couple of seconds, he took off for the house at an awkward run. Chet figured Ike was yelling his head off.

Two men emerged from the bunkhouse. Chet recognized them, too: Ben Hendricks and Farley Grant. They took a look, realized trouble was fogging toward them, and ran back in the bunkhouse to grab rifles. They had Winchesters in their hands when they reappeared a moment later.

Ike had disappeared into the house. He popped back into sight on the porch, followed by Roy Gardner. They carried rifles, too, and waved Chet on.

Four men, Chet thought as his heart sank. Well, five counting him. Would that be enough to defend the place against the whole Ace of Diamonds crew? Chet knew that wasn't likely. The odds would be four to one.

Then two riders came around the corner of the barn, moving fast. Johnny Dolan and Clint Stillwater. Chet knew them by their horses and the way they rode. They must have been close enough to hear the commotion and had raced back to the ranch. They jerked Winchesters from saddle boots and piled off. Ben Hendricks waved them into the barn.

Chet's cow pony was starting to falter a little. The horse had run a gallant race, but it was about to play out. Chet was close now, though. He holstered his gun, kicked his feet out of the stirrups, and leaped from horseback. He landed running. Momentum kept him upright and moving for several long strides before he tripped and went down in an ungainly roll.

Ben Hendricks was there to grasp his arm and help him to his feet when he came up again. "What the hell!" Ben yelled.

"Ace . . . Ace of Diamonds!" Chet said, a little out of breath from the hard ride and the reckless dismount. "They're comin' to wipe us out!"

"How do you know that?"

"I recognized 'em, and they been shootin' at me for more'n a mile!"

"Yeah, I reckon that'll do it," Ben muttered. A bullet whined overhead, close enough to hear. "Come on, get in the bunkhouse with me and Farley! We'll run those varmints off!"

Chet thought that was a mite too hopeful, but it wouldn't do any good to give up. He raced for the bunkhouse with Ben. Farley Grant stood beside the door, his rifle lifted to his shoulder now. He fired a pair of shots at the charging Ace of Diamonds riders.

Mr. Gardner and Ike Armitage opened up from the front porch of the house. More shots came from the barn. Bullets kicked up dust not far from Chet's and Ben's feet as they ran, but the attackers were starting to slow up now. Some of them even peeled away as the return fire intensified.

"Yee-haw! We got 'em on the run!" Johnny Dolan yelled from the barn. He knelt in the opening into the loft where hay could be put in or taken out. It was a good vantage point from which to aim at the Ace of Diamonds bunch.

But it exposed him to their fire, as well, and Johnny yelped in alarm as a bullet hit the wall beside him. He lost his balance and fell backward, out of sight. Chet saw that as he and Ben hustled into the bunkhouse. He hoped Johnny was all right.

Farley howled. Ben grated a curse and reached back out to grab his arm and pull him into the bunkhouse. "Are you hit?"

Blood trickled down the left side of Farley's neck. "I think the no-good skunks shot my ear off!"

"Lemme take a look." Ben grabbed Farley's chin and moved his head to the side. "No, you've still got your ear. Most of it, anyway."

"Most of it!"

"They might've shot off a piddlin' little piece of it," Ben allowed. "It's just bleedin' like a stuck pig, is all."

Farley blew out a breath. "All right. As long as I don't lose so much blood I pass out, I can still shoot. Let's get to the windows and throw some more lead at that bunch."

There were several rifles in the bunkhouse. Chet picked up one of them and got a box of cartridges from the gear stored under his bunk. He hurried to one of the windows that looked out toward the area where the raiders had drawn back and regrouped. The shooting had stopped, but only for the moment, Chet figured. Tony Mullen's crew was a salty one, and the foreman, Orrie Striker, was the next thing to an outlaw. They wouldn't give up just because the Box RG men had shown a little fight.

"Ben!" The shout came from the house. Chet recognized Mr. Gardner's voice. "Ben, are you boys all right over there?"

"For now, boss!" Ben replied. "Farley got a little nick, but he ain't hurt bad!"

"Ain't hurt bad," muttered Farley. "Feels like half my dang ear's shot off!"

Mr. Gardner went on, "One of you fellas see if you can get to the barn, throw a saddle on a horse, and light a shuck for Big Rock!"

Ben looked startled by the order. He called back, "You mean one of us should run out on you?"

"No, I mean you should go fetch help, you addle-brained pup!" Roy Gardner didn't mince words. "Tell Monte Carson that the Ace o' Diamonds is tryin' to wipe us out! He'll raise a posse and put a stop to it!"

That might well be true, thought Chet. Monte Carson wasn't actually the county sheriff, but through a tacit agreement with that official, he had always enforced the law in the vicinity of Big Rock. In his estimation, that vicinity extended up the broad, rich valley where several successful ranches were located, as well as the gold mines owned by Conrad Morgan. Monte Carson wouldn't stand by and allow the Ace of Diamonds to murder everybody here.

Ben must have agreed with that, because he said, "The boss is right. Chet, crawl out the back window and hustle over to the barn. Saddle the fastest horse there and rattle your hocks for Big Rock."

"Me?" Chet said. "I just got here! I'm the one who warned you fellas, remember? I've already had one hard ride today."

"And you're the best rider on the spread," Ben countered.

"Johnny's littler. He don't weigh as much."

"Yeah, but Johnny sometimes falls off if he tries to ride too fast. We can't afford for him to take a tumble and break his neck. Besides, he's a lot better shot than you are, so he'll do us more good here."

Chet could have argued that point, too, but deep down, he knew Ben and Mr. Gardner were right. If they were going to have any hope of surviving this treacherous attack, those chances would be best served by him going to fetch help.

"All right," he said disgustedly as he tossed the unfired Winchester on a bunk. "I'll go. Just don't kill all of those Ace of Diamonds polecats before I get back!"

Louis was in his office when he got a couple of unexpected but very welcome visitors. Melanie and Brad came in, with Melanie carrying a picnic basket with a cloth spread over the food it contained. Louis smelled fresh bread, among other intriguing aromas.

"We decided to bring your lunch to you today, instead of you coming home to eat," Melanie explained after Louis had greeted her and kissed her on the cheek.

"We even stopped by Mr. Goldstein's store and got some bottles of sarsaparilla," Brad said as he proudly displayed the glass bottles he held.

"That sounds wonderful," Louis told them. "Let me clear off my desk so we'll have room for the food."

He was doing that when the sound of rapid hoofbeats came from outside. Remembering that other morning when the crews from the Ace of Diamonds and the Box RG had converged on his office, Louis looked up and frowned slightly.

He wasn't the only one who heard the commotion. Brad set the bottles on the desk and hurried to the door as someone shouted outside. "I'll see what's goin' on!" Brad threw over his shoulder as he raced out.

"Bradley, come back here," Melanie called after him, but Brad ignored her and disappeared.

Louis said, "I'll get him," and followed his stepson from the office.

A haze of dust still hung in the air from where the shouting rider had swept swiftly past. Louis didn't see Brad and felt a sudden pang of fear. In his excitement, Brad might have run right out in front of whoever was galloping into town.

That fear was allayed a moment later as Louis spotted Brad hurrying back toward the office. The boy waved an arm and called, "Louis! Louis! There's trouble up the valley!"

He sounded almost like an adult, thought Louis. He moved forward to intercept Brad and asked, "What are you talking about?"

"That cowboy who rode into town yellin' his fool head off said the Box RG was under attack and needs help. That's one of the ranches on the other side of the valley, ain't it?" He looked around quickly, as if checking to see if his mother was in earshot. Even though she wasn't, he played it safe by adding, "I mean, isn't it?"

Louis put a hand on Brad's shoulder and asked, "Are you sure he said the Box RG?"

"Yes, sir. I followed him around the corner. Looked like he reined in at the sheriff's office."

Louis didn't know what was going on, but since Roy Gardner had come to him for help, he felt compelled to find out, even though Gardner hadn't hired him.

"You reckon it's Injuns?"

Louis felt a moment of confusion. "What?"

"You reckon it's Injuns attackin' the ranch?" asked Brad.

"No," Louis told the boy with a shake of his head. "There hasn't been any Indian trouble around here for a long time. I'm sure it's something else."

Like the Ace of Diamonds? Had that dispute over the waterhole erupted into open war, as both sides had feared it might?

That seemed the most likely answer to Louis, but he wanted to find out for sure. He said to Brad, "Go back to the office and tell your mother I have to check on something. I'll be back in a few minutes, I hope. But if I'm not . . ."

"You're goin' out there with the sheriff's posse, aren't you?"

Brad was a shrewd youngster, and he knew Louis well. "I may have to," Louis said. "But I'll be careful."

"Can I come with you?"

"No! Certainly not. If there really is trouble, it could be dangerous."

"But you're goin', even if it is dangerous, aren't you?"

"I have a duty to the law," Louis tried to explain. "Mr. Gardner consulted me on a legal matter—"

"Is he your client?"

"Well, no, but—"

"You just want to get in on the fightin'!"

Louis suppressed the impatience growing inside him. "If there's fighting, I want to help put a stop to it. I don't want anyone to get hurt."

"Probably too late for that, the way that cowpuncher was carryin' on."

"Just go on back to the office," Louis said, sharper than he intended. "I'll be there when I can."

Brad frowned but didn't argue anymore. He turned and headed toward the office, scuffing his booted feet angrily in the dirt street as he went.

Louis was sorry he had snapped at the boy, but he was Brad's father now, and Brad needed to know that there were times when he had to do what his father said.

Moving quickly, Louis rounded the corner into Front Street and saw the crowd gathered in front of Sheriff Monte Carson's office. He joined them and listened to the conversation flowing around him. The Box RG was under attack, just as Brad had reported, and according to the rumors flowing among the crowd, Tony Mullen's Ace of Diamonds was responsible for the raid. Louis hated to hear that the dispute between neighbors had turned violent, but he wasn't the least bit surprised.

He spotted Brice Rogers and Conrad Morgan on the sheriff's office porch with Monte Carson and a rawboned cowboy who looked vaguely familiar. Louis figured that was probably the man who had brought word of the attack to town.

He knew Brice and Conrad didn't get along that well and suspected that their feelings for his sister had something to do with that. But right now, they were standing together with Monte, who raised his arms for quiet. It took a moment for the hubbub to settle down. When it did, the sheriff said, "I want half a dozen men to come with me and Marshal Rogers. We'll find out what's going on at the Gardner ranch."

"I told you what's goin' on, Sheriff," the lanky cowboy said. "Mullen and his men are tryin' to massa-cree Mr. Gardner and the rest of the crew!"

"And if that's true, we'll put a stop to it," Monte promised. "Whoever wants to come along, we're riding out in five minutes!"

The crowd began to disperse quickly as men hurried to get horses and guns. Monte had asked for six good men to come with him, but more than likely he would get three or four times that number. The townsmen were eager to grasp any opportunity for excitement, even if it might bring danger with it.

Louis stepped up to the porch, caught Monte's

eye, and said, "I'm coming with you, Sheriff."

The lawman frowned. "Now, Louis, I appreciate that, but I don't know if it's a good idea—"

"I know what the trouble is about," Louis broke in. "At some point, you're going to have to try to talk sense into the heads of those men. Maybe I can help you with that."

Brice said, "Your sister won't like it if you get yourself shot, Louis."

"Neither will your folks," Conrad added.

"You let me worry about Denny and my parents," Louis said. "I'm going to get my saddle horse."

He kept a mount at the livery stable in case he needed to ride out and see a client. So far, that hadn't been necessary, but it looked like that might change today.

Conrad hopped nimbly from the porch to the street. "I'll come with you," he said. "I need to get my horse, too."

Brice joined them. "So do I."

They made an odd trio, Louis mused as they headed along the street: a federal lawman, a millionaire adventurer, and a fledgling attorney . . . all of them with a connection to Denny.

It was a good thing she wasn't here, he told himself, or she would have wanted to get right into the big middle of the action, too!

CHAPTER 19

Denver

Denny had spent enough time in Colorado's capital city to know her way around. When she got off the train in Denver's Union Station that morning, she crossed the high-ceilinged lobby to the station manager's office. In the outer office, she asked the young, bespectacled man sitting at a desk behind a wooden railing if anyone there had a city directory.

He had been pecking around on a typewriter, but he glanced up at her question and then quickly looked again, coming to his feet and heading around the desk.

"What was that, miss?" he asked. "How can I help you?"

"I asked if you or anyone else here had a city directory," Denny repeated, smiling. She took note of the keen interest in the young man's eyes and didn't see any harm in using that to help her in what she had come here to do.

She wasn't wearing her usual range garb today. Instead, she wore a simple, light gray traveling dress and a darker gray hat with a little feather on it. Her hair was pulled behind her head and fashioned there with a clasp. The outfit was restrained and conservative, but the dress was form-fitting enough that the supple curves of her body were apparent. Together with her pretty, tanned face, blue eyes, and thick blond hair, that was enough to make the young man in the station manager's office eager to help her.

"As a matter of fact, there's a city directory in my desk," he told her. "I'll get it for you."

"Thank you." She knew the smile she gave him put a dimple in her cheek. The young man was so distracted by the sight that he bumped into a corner of the desk as he tried to go around it.

He said, "I'm sorry," to her, as if he felt that he ought to apologize for running into his own desk. Hurriedly, he opened one of the drawers, reached inside, and brought out a thick, leather-bound volume. He set it on the desk, went back to the railing, and opened the gate in it.

"Here, come inside," he invited. "You can sit at my desk and look up whatever you need to."

"Are you sure that's all right?"

"I'm positive."

Denny went to the desk, sat down, and opened the book. The pages were thin, and there were a lot of them. She knew the name she was looking for and turned first to the Ps. If Edgar Padgett was a public surveyor, he probably had his own business and it would be listed under his name.

However, Edgar Padgett wasn't listed. No Padgett at all, in fact.

The young man must have seen the disappointment on her face. "Can't find what you're looking for?" he asked.

"Not yet," Denny said. "Is there a way to look up different kinds of businesses?"

"Yes, there in the back. Let me show you."

He stood next to the chair, bent over, and flipped through the thick book to the proper section. When he came to it, he asked, "What sort of business are you looking for?"

"Surveyors," she said. "Or any sort of company that does things like that."

"Well, let's see . . ."

For the next few minutes, they pored over the directory. At first Denny thought the young man might be trying to draw this out just to keep her around, but then she decided he actually was trying to help her and locate the information she needed. They came to the conclusion that there were only three surveying firms in the city. Denny wrote down the names and addresses of all three, using a pencil and a pad of paper the young man provided.

"I can't tell you how much I appreciate your help," she said as she got to her feet.

"That's what I'm here for, to help people," he assured her.

She smiled again. "I'm pretty sure your job has something to do with making sure the depot operates the way it's supposed to, not humoring crazy women who wander in off the platform."

"You're not crazy at all. I don't know why

you're looking for this particular surveyor—"

"It has to do with a legal case," Denny told him. "My brother is a lawyer. I'm helping him."

"Well, I hope you find him." He gestured toward the piece of paper in her hand. "You're not going to walk around to all of those places, are you?"

"That's what I plan to do, especially if you can give me directions."

"I can do better than that," he said. He reached for a hat hanging on a hook. "My lunch hour is about to start. We can get a carriage right outside on Wynkoop Street. I'll make sure that you find all of them, and you won't have to travel all around Denver by yourself that way." He paused. "By the way, my name is Sam Webster. I'm one of the assistant stationmasters."

"I'm perfectly capable of taking care of myself and finding my way around Denver, Mr. Webster," she said. "But that is a good idea about hiring a carriage."

"I understand," he replied with a disappointed shrug. "You never laid eyes on me until half an hour ago. You don't want to ride around town with a perfect stranger. You'd have every right to be nervous."

"I'm not nervous," Denny said. That was the truth. She had a small pocket pistol in the bag she carried and was confident that she could get it out and into action faster than Mr. Sam Webster could try anything funny, if he was of a mind to.

However, she didn't really believe that was his intention. He seemed nice and sincere and willing to help. So, she went on, "I appreciate the offer, Mr. Webster, and I accept. And *my* name is Denise Jensen."

"I'm very pleased to meet you, Miss Jensen. It *is* Miss?"

"It is," she confirmed.

"And afterwards, if there's time, perhaps I could take you to lunch . . . ?"

"We'll see," Denny said. "First I have to locate Mr. Edgar Padgett and get the answers to some questions from him."

"I don't understand it," Denny said an hour later as she and Sam Webster stood outside the building housing the last of the surveying companies on her list. "Not only does Edgar Padgett not work at any of these places, nobody at any of them has ever heard of him!"

Webster nodded and said, "Surveyors are a fairly close-knit bunch, from what I've heard about them. You'd think that if this fellow Padgett was working in Denver or the surrounding area, somebody would have known him." He hesitated. "You're sure you have the name correct, Miss Jensen?"

"Well, I didn't see it myself," Denny admitted, "but my brother got a good look at a survey map

Padgett did, and he said the name was printed clearly on it. Even though I wouldn't want him to hear me say it, Louis is exceptionally smart and very good with details. I don't think he'd make a mistake about something like that."

"How recent was that map?"

"I believe it was made in the past month or so, according to what my brother told me."

"Then I don't know what to tell you," Webster said, shaking his head. "Maybe Padgett just got started in the surveying business, and that's why nobody has heard of him. Or maybe he's working somewhere besides Denver." The young man frowned in thought. "I have an idea. Surveyors probably have to be licensed by the state. You could go to the Capitol and ask there if there's a list of licensed surveyors. That particular office might be in some other building, but they ought to be able to point you in the right direction, at least."

Denny considered the idea and then nodded. "I should give that a try."

"Unfortunately, I don't think I'll be able to assist you with it." Webster took a watch from his vest pocket, flipped it open, and checked the time. "I need to get back to Union Station."

"Oh, and you never got to have lunch! You were too busy helping me."

"Don't worry about that," he told her as he put the watch away. "You didn't eat, either."

"Yes, but I still can, while you have to go back

to your job."

He smiled. "Believe me, Miss Jensen, spending the past hour with you has been well worth a few hunger pangs—"

"You two hush your jabberin' and put your hands up!"

The harsh voice took Denny by surprise. She looked around quickly and saw an unshaven, shabbily dressed man standing a few feet away. He held his ragged coat open enough to show that his right hand was wrapped around the butt of a gun shoved in his waistband.

"Good Lord!" Sam Webster exclaimed. He grabbed Denny's shoulders and pulled her behind him, putting himself between her and the man glaring at them.

"Put your hands up, I said," the man ordered again. "I ain't gonna tell you a third time. I'll just shoot you both and take what I want!"

"Calm down," Webster said. His voice revealed some strain, but Denny could tell he was trying to stay cool under pressure and keep the man from doing anything violent. "What is it you want?"

"That watch you was just lookin' at, for one thing," the would-be robber said as his lips twisted in a snarl. "And any money you got in your pockets. I'll take whatever the gal's got in her handbag, too."

Denny looked around. This was an area filled with office buildings and warehouses, not the sort of businesses that attracted a lot of people. A few pedestrians were on the street, but none of them were paying any attention to this confrontation. They weren't close by, either.

"I could scream for help," she said.

The man's unshaven face darkened with anger. "You do, and it'll be the last sound that ever comes outta your mouth, missy, I promise you that."

Webster still had the pocket watch in his left hand. He extended the right hand toward the thief, palm out. "Please, don't shoot. I'll give you the watch and all my money. There won't be any trouble. Just leave the lady alone."

A half-grin, half-leer stretched across the man's face. "Sweet on her, are you? Well, I don't care! Hand over the watch!"

Carefully, Webster pulled the watch chain and the fob at the end of it from the other pocket on his vest. He held it out. The robber let go of his coat with his left hand and used that one to snatch the watch from Webster's grip. He kept his right hand under the coat on the gun.

After stuffing the watch in his pocket, he held out his left hand again. "Now your pocketbook, mister. Quick! I can't stand around here all day."

Webster's back stiffened. "I'm not giving it to you until you promise to leave the lady alone. You'll just have to shoot me, and I don't think you want that."

"That's a damn foolish bet to make, since you'll

be riskin' your life."

"I don't care," insisted Webster.

Denny knew she had to take a hand in this, or else the young man who had tried to be so helpful to her was going to get himself hurt. She said, "Please, Mr. Webster . . . Sam . . . let's just give this man what he wants."

Webster glanced back at her. "Are you sure?"

"I'm certain. Give him your money, and then he can have what's in my handbag."

Webster still looked like he wanted to protest, but he sighed and reached under his coat to take out his wallet. He handed it over to the robber, who grabbed it and stuffed it into the same pocket as the watch.

"Now step aside," the thief ordered. "Gimme your money, lady."

Webster didn't budge until Denny said, "It's all right." Then he sighed and eased out of her way.

The robber leered at her again. "What do you got for me, missy?"

"This," Denny said as she lifted the pistol from her bag and shot him in the right shoulder.

At the sharp crack of the shot, the man lurched backward and yelled in pain. Denny's bullet had shattered bone. His right hand fell away from the gun in his waistband as that arm dropped uselessly to his side.

He managed to stay on his feet, though, and as he continued yelling, he reached under his coat with his left hand and fumbled at the gun butt.

"Don't try it," Denny warned him.

He didn't stop. As he grasped the gun and pulled it free, Denny shot him again, this time in the left shoulder. The pistol slipped from his fingers and thudded to the cobblestone street. A second later, his knees buckled and he dropped onto them, staying upright but swaying a little.

Denny stepped forward, past Sam Webster, lifted her right foot, and drove the heel of the sturdy shoe she wore against the luckless criminal's chest. He went over backward, and his head thudded hard against the street. He lay there moaning softly and bleeding from both shoulders. Farther up the street, people yelled in alarm at the gunfire and hurried toward them to see what had happened.

"You . . . you shot him!" Webster said, staring at her in shock.

"Just being polite," Denny said as she kept her pistol trained on the wounded robber, even though he was stunned and helpless. "He wanted what was in my handbag, and I gave it to him."

CHAPTER 20

The Box RG

Louis heard the gunfire well before he and the other members of the posse from Big Rock came in sight of Roy Gardner's ranch headquarters. Sheriff Carson held up his hand in a signal for the group of riders to stop.

Monte said, "Louis, you aren't armed, and you're not a fighter. No offense, just stating the facts. I want you to stay back until we calm things down a mite."

The sheriff's firm tone didn't allow any room for argument, so even though Louis felt like protesting, he nodded.

"All right," he said. "I hope you don't have to kill anyone."

"Yeah, I hope so, too." Monte looked around at the other members of the posse, including Conrad Morgan and Brice Rogers. "Nobody starts shooting unless I do, understand?"

"I'm not used to people shooting at me and not shooting back, Sheriff," said Conrad.

"If it comes to that, we'll defend ourselves, don't you worry. But I'd like to put a stop to this without any killing . . . or any more than there has been already," Monte added grimly. "Come on!"

237

The riders galloped ahead. Louis hung back for just a second and then followed them, blinking a little at the dust their horses raised stung his eyes.

They rode through a saddle between some hills, and the ranch came into view below at the bottom of an easy slope. Even from this distance, Louis could see the haze of powder smoke that hung over the place. Muzzle flame spurted from windows in the main house and the bunkhouse, as well as from the loft opening in the barn. The raiders had taken cover behind corrals, water troughs, and a parked wagon. They poured lead at the buildings from those vantage points.

Louis didn't spot any bodies lying in the open, so he supposed that was a good sign.

Monte had brought along a shotgun. He pulled it from the saddle sheath in which it rode and angled the twin barrels skyward as he triggered both of them. The boom of the double discharge rolled over the landscape like a peal of thunder.

Quickly, Monte broke the shotgun open and thumbed a couple of fresh shells into the chambers. The shooting around the ranch had tapered off in response to the first report. The second double blast made everyone hold their fire and look in his direction.

Monte rode forward slowly, reloading the shotgun again as he did so. The rest of the posse followed closely behind him, with Louis bringing up the rear. Into the surprised silence, Monte bellowed, "Hold your fire down there! Hold your fire! I'll arrest the next man who pulls a trigger!"

Louis felt the tension in the air as they closed in on the ranch headquarters. The shooting had stopped—for now—but it wouldn't take much of a spark to blow up that momentary truce and start a swarm of lead flying through the air again.

Monte waved for the men following him to stop, then rode boldly into the ranch yard, putting himself between the two hostile forces. He reined in and called, "Roy Gardner! Tony Mullen! You two get out here where I can see you!"

From inside the house, Gardner replied, "You want me to step out into the open where those Ace of Diamonds skunks can take potshots at me? No thanks! I don't reckon I feel like dyin' today, Sheriff!"

"Neither did my man Kimbrough!" Mullen's voice came from behind the wagon. "But that didn't stop your Box RG bushwhackers from murdering him!"

"What the hell are you talking about?" demanded Gardner. "Nobody from this ranch killed one of your men!"

A different member of the Ace of Diamonds crew shouted, "That's a damned lie! I was with Kimbrough when your men shot him in the head! He never had a chance, the big dumb ox! At least we came to clean out this rat's nest straight on, not like yellow-bellied bushwhackers!"

Monte gestured sharply with the reloaded shotgun and said, "That's enough, blast it! Throwing accusations back and forth isn't going to settle anything. I'll say it again. Mullen, Gardner, come out here where I can talk to you without yelling."

A moment with no response from either side stretched out. Then the screen door on the ranch house opened with a squeal of hinges. Rifle in hand, ready to fire, Roy Gardner stepped onto the porch.

"All right, Sheriff," he said. "But if those varmints gun me down, I expect you to bring them to justice."

"My men will hold their fire," Mullen said. "See that yours do the same, Gardner!"

The Ace of Diamonds owner rose from his crouch behind the wagon and started forward. Even with dust coating his suit and his face and hands grimed by burning powder, Mullen managed to look dapper. He held a Colt, but he holstered it as he started forward.

"Get out here, Roy," Monte said to Gardner, who came down the steps from the porch with obvious reluctance. He scowled and pointed the rifle at the ground.

The sheriff dismounted and waited for the two ranchers to join him. Louis edged his horse forward so that he could hear the conversation better. He ought to be part of the discussion, he thought, but so far Monte hadn't invited him to join in.

The same thought must have occurred to the lawman, because he looked around and then beckoned as he said, "Come on up here, Louis. You know more about this mess than I do."

"Young Jensen's not my lawyer, Sheriff," Mullen said.

"Nor mine," added Gardner.

"Maybe not, but both of you have consulted him, according to what I've been told, and he knows the law. So he's going to help us get to the bottom of this."

Gardner grunted. "Nothin' to get to the bottom of. It's as plain as the nose on my face. That gang of crooks from the Ace of Diamonds invaded my ranch and attacked us."

"Only to settle the score for my man who was murdered," Mullen snapped back at him.

"Not by any of us, damn it!"

"There you both go again," Monte said. "Roy, hush for now. Tony, tell me about this man of yours who got shot."

"But we didn't—" Gardner began.

"Quiet, I said. You'll get your turn." Monte nodded to Mullen. "Go ahead."

Mullen said, "I've been having men stand guard over my south waterhole—"

"You mean my north waterhole," Gardner broke in. "The one you're tryin' to steal from me." The sheriff gave him a warning glare, and he added, "Sorry, Monte, but it's true."

"As I was explaining," Mullen said coldly, "I had guards on that waterhole. Quince Jessup was there, along with another of my hands named Kimbrough."

"I know Jessup," Monte said. "I've had him in my jail a few times for getting drunk and starting fights."

From behind the wagon, the young man in question called, "Hey, that's not fair—"

"Shut up, Quince," snapped Mullen as he turned his head toward the wagon. "This isn't about your previous escapades." He looked at Monte and went on, "Jessup and Kimbrough were there, doing their jobs, when somebody started shooting at them. A bullet struck Kimbrough in the head and killed him instantly. Jessup managed to get away and brought word of the ambush to ranch headquarters." Mullen shook his head. "I'm sorry, Sheriff, but I can't let the cold-blooded murder of one of my men pass."

"You could have come to Big Rock and reported it."

"I could have," Mullen allowed. "But that's not the way things used to be handled around here, and I'm starting to think maybe the old ways are best."

And the rest of his men, no doubt outraged by the death of one of their own, probably wouldn't have paid any attention to a law-and-order speech, anyway, Louis mused.

He stepped up and said, "Mr. Mullen, do you know for a fact that what you just told the sheriff is actually what happened?"

Mullen frowned at him. "What do you mean?"

"You're certain that someone shot your man from ambush?"

"I damned well know he's dead! We stopped by the waterhole on our way here. I saw Kimbrough's body with my own eyes, Louis. We put him on a horse and I sent one of the men back to the ranch with him. Told him to put the body in a wagon and take it to Big Rock to the undertaking parlor. Is that good enough for you?"

"I don't doubt that the man is dead, sir, but what I'm asking is, do you know for a fact that he was shot from ambush?"

"But if he wasn't, then who else could have—"

That was as far as he got before one of the Ace of Diamonds hands burst out from behind the wagon and yelled, "He's sayin' *I* shot poor Kimbrough! Get outta the way, boss! And you, fancy lawyer man, go for your gun!"

Even as he shouted and charged forward, Quince Jessup was clawing at the holstered revolver on his hip. Louis barely had time to widen his eyes in surprise before Conrad Morgan and Brice Rogers appeared in front of him, both men moving almost too fast for the eye to follow.

Their guns flashed out and leveled at Jessup before the cowboy was able to clear leather.

"Let go of that gun, mister," Brice warned. "Louis isn't packing iron."

Jessup's face was flushed dark red with fury, but he wasn't so completely caught up in his anger that he failed to realize he was staring down the barrels of two guns. His hand opened, and his Colt slid back down into the holster.

He raised that hand and aimed a pointing finger between Brice and Conrad at Louis. "You just called me a liar *and* a murderer, you damned dude! I ain't gonna forget that!"

"I didn't do either of those things," Louis responded. "I just pointed out that the only witness to Mr. Kimbrough's death appears to be you."

"And the no-good skunk who shot him!"

Gardner said, "It wasn't any of my men, I can tell you that much."

"How do you know that?" asked Monte.

"Well . . . I've given 'em strict orders to stay away from that waterhole, until I've figured out what I'm gonna do next." Gardner glared at Mullen. "I didn't want to give this tinhorn any excuse to start more trouble . . . but it looks like he's gone and done it anyway."

"We didn't start anything—" Mullen began before Monte held up a hand to stop him.

Louis said, "Mr. Gardner, are all of your men here at the ranch?"

Gardner frowned and shook his head. "No, some of 'em are out on the range doin' their jobs. Which *don't* include shootin' at those Ace of Diamonds polecats."

"But if they're not here, you don't know for certain what they might have done, do you?"

"I know they're good hands," insisted Gardner. "They ain't bushwhackin' killers."

"Tell that to Kimbrough," Jessup growled. He glared at Brice and Conrad, who had pouched their irons and backed off a step but stood ready to take action again if they needed to.

"We're not getting anywhere," Monte said. "Have you two managed to get anybody else killed in this ruckus you've been having?"

"I got a couple of wounded men," Gardner said, "but nobody dead."

"Same here," said Mullen. "Kimbrough's the only man I've lost."

Monte shook his head. "You're both mighty damned lucky, then. As much powder as you were burning, I'm surprised there's not bodies littering the ground everywhere around here. And then I'd be locking up somebody, probably both of you. Mullen, take your men and get out of here."

"What about Kimbrough?"

"I'm sorry he's dead. Bring your man—Jessup, was it?—Bring Jessup to town tomorrow, once he's cooled down, and I'll take his statement. I'll

245

send it on over to the county seat in Red Cliff. Kimbrough's death will be investigated, I can promise you that. But you're *done* taking the law into your own hands." Monte raised his voice and turned his head so that everyone within earshot could hear him. "Everybody on both sides is done taking the law into your own hands! Anybody who tries won't just wind up behind bars. He's liable to wind up *under* the jail!"

Mullen and Gardner both looked like they wanted to argue, but after a couple of seconds they nodded grudgingly. Mullen looked at a tall, spare, middle-aged man and said, "Round up the boys and head for home, Orrie."

"Sure thing, boss," the man drawled. Louis knew he was Orrie Striker, the Ace of Diamonds' foreman.

Gardner edged away toward his house, as if he didn't want to turn his back on Mullen. Monte let him go without saying anything else.

Instead, the sheriff turned to the townsmen who had accompanied him out here and said, "Looks like it's all over, boys. Thanks for coming with me." He added dryly, "Sorry we didn't get any real fireworks for you."

"That's all right, Sheriff," Conrad said. "At least no one else was hurt."

Louis, acting on impulse, said, "Mr. Mullen, wait a moment, if you don't mind."

Mullen, who had turned to follow Striker,

Jessup, and the rest of the Ace of Diamonds hands, paused and looked back at him. "What is it, Louis?"

"I'd like to take a look at this notorious waterhole, and the place where your man was shot, as well. Would you mind showing me?"

"Well . . . I suppose not. Do you mind if I ask why?"

"I've been involved in this case, even if it was on an unofficial basis, since you and Mr. Gardner both tried to hire me. I'd like to help out if I can."

"For a fee?" Mullen asked with a smile.

"No. Pro bono. That means—"

"I know what it means," Mullen cut in. "Sure, come along if you want. I'll show you the place."

Monte had been listening to the conversation. He said, "Louis, you don't need to be messing around a place where a murder happened."

"I won't bother any evidence we might find, Sheriff," Louis promised. "As an attorney, I'm an officer of the court and bound by the same laws and regulations you are."

Monte considered for a moment and then nodded. "All right, I reckon you're smart enough not to tamper with anything. And you might see something I wouldn't."

"Hold on a minute," said Conrad. "I'm coming with you, Louis."

"So am I," Brice added.

Louis looked at both of them in surprise. "Why

would the two of you do that?" Then, before either of them could answer, understanding dawned on him. "Oh, I get it. You think you need to nursemaid me, since I'm not exactly a two-fisted gunfighter like my father."

"Now, that's not what I was thinking—" Conrad began.

"And you believe that by looking after me, you'll be more likely to get on my sister's good side, don't you?"

Conrad and Brice glanced at each other, the glances quickly becoming scowls.

"I'm a lawman," Brice said. "It's my duty to look out for citizens."

"And I'd like to think that I'm your friend, Louis," said Conrad.

"I've known you longer than he has," Brice said.

Mullen said, "You two can wrangle about it for however long you want. I'm going back to the Ace of Diamonds like the sheriff told me to, and you're welcome to come along, Louis, but we're going now." Mullen made a face. "There's a bad smell in the air around here."

"I heard that!" Gardner yelled from the porch, then went inside and slammed the door behind him.

CHAPTER 21

Mullen sent most of the Ace of Diamonds hands back to the spread's headquarters, but he kept Orrie Striker and Quince Jessup with him as he led Louis, Conrad, and Brice toward the disputed waterhole.

They had to take an indirect route, since the waterhole lay on the other side of the fence Mullen's crew had put up. There was a gate a mile to the west.

"How far does this fence extend?" Louis asked.

"A couple of miles on either side of the waterhole," replied Mullen. "There are natural obstacles beyond those points that would make it difficult for Gardner to drive his cattle around and reach it that way. Not impossible, mind you, but I'll just build more fence if he pushes me to it."

The gate was only wide enough for one rider. A herd of cattle could be pushed through it, but that would be a long, difficult task, and the gate would be easy to defend from the other side. There were trees close enough to provide cover, so a couple of men with rifles could hold off intruders without much trouble.

"It's a shame you can't work out an arrangement with Mr. Gardner so that he could water his stock," Louis suggested. "Deals like that are fairly common."

Mullen snorted. "Sure . . . and his cows would drink it dry in a month." He shook his head. "With the weather as dry as it is right now, I just can't afford to take that risk. Besides, I'm not going to give an inch to that muleheaded son of a gun."

They approached the waterhole a few minutes later. Jessup pointed to a nearby grove of trees and said, "That's where me and Kimbrough were, right there. I can find the exact spot. It won't be hard. You ought to still be able to see poor Kimbrough's blood on the ground."

"Were you waiting in the trees so that you'd be out of sight?" Louis asked.

"Yeah, that's right. We could see any Box RG riders comin' toward us from the south. The ground's pretty open in that direction."

Jessup waved an arm to indicate where he was talking about.

Louis nodded and said, "If you were in the trees, how did the bushwhackers see you to shoot at you?"

"Well, they were in there with us, of course," Jessup said, his tone impatient as if he were trying to explain something to a child. "They snuck up on us."

"But not from the Box RG." Louis nodded toward the area on the other side of the fence. "As you said, you would have seen them coming."

"They must've circled around. We just did that ourselves. It ain't that hard. They didn't have to come through the gate, neither. A man on horseback can make it around the far ends of the fence, even though it'd be hard to drive a herd of cattle that way."

"So the killers circled around and slipped up on you."

"That's right," said Jessup. "I heard 'em movin' through the brush, just before they opened up on us. It wasn't in time to save Kimbrough, though. They got him with the first shot. And it wasn't for lack of tryin' that they didn't get me, let me tell you. Bullets came mighty close to partin' my hair more than once."

Brice spoke up, asking, "Could you tell how many of them there were?"

"At least two," Jessup said. "I think that was all, but I'm not sure."

"Show us where it happened," Brice said. He sounded like a lawman conducting an investigation now, thought Louis. Which he was, although it was an unofficial one since murder didn't fall under federal jurisdiction.

But as Brice had said, he had an obligation to stand up for law and order, just as Louis did.

Jessup took them to the spot. As he had predicted, the dark, spattered stain of Kimbrough's blood was still visible on leaves and pine needles where he had toppled over, although it had soaked into the ground by now.

"Could you tell where the men shooting at you were?" Louis asked.

Jessup glared and shook his head. "Not for sure. A fella tends not to think too straight when there's bullets whizzin' past his ears. Somewhere north and east of us, if I had to guess."

"Let's have a look," Brice said. He glanced at Conrad. "Why don't we split up, Morgan?"

"Good idea," Conrad agreed. "We can cover more ground that way. Why don't you stay here, Louis?"

Louis felt like they were leaving him behind because they didn't think he would be able to spot any telltale signs of the bushwhackers as well as they could. Unfortunately, that assumption probably was correct, so he nodded and said, "All right."

While Brice and Conrad were prowling through the woods, Quince Jessup said disgustedly, "This is all just a waste of time. We know who killed Kimbrough. It had to be somebody from the Box RG. Nobody else would have any reason to start shootin' at us."

"You're sure about that?" asked Louis. "You don't have any other enemies who might want to settle a score with you? Sheriff Carson said that you'd been in trouble in town for fighting—"

"Everybody has to blow off some steam now

and then," Jessup said. "That's all it was. None of those fracases actually meant anything."

"Maybe they didn't to you. You can't be sure they didn't mean something to someone else. Something bad enough for them to come after you."

Jessup shook his head stubbornly. "It was the Box RG. I don't care if you believe that or not, lawyer man. I know what happened."

Louis didn't want to waste any more time arguing with the young cowboy. Jessup wasn't going to change his mind. Even if Brice or Conrad came back with proof that Roy Gardner's men weren't responsible for the ambush, Jessup probably still wouldn't believe it.

Brice and Conrad didn't return with proof of anything. Brice rattled some brass empties in his palm and said, "We found these shells, but they're just regular .44-40 rounds. There are bound to be several hundred Winchesters in Eagle County that could have fired them."

"I saw some boot prints, too," added Conrad, "but there was nothing special about them. I'd say, judging by their depth, that the man who made them was a normal weight, not too heavy or light. There were no scratches or other marks to make them distinctive."

Jessup was excited by the discoveries, though. "See, I told you we were ambushed. Those tracks and the empty shells are proof of that, ain't they?"

Louis shrugged. "The evidence, such as it is, seems to support your story, Mr. Jessup. At the very least, it doesn't contradict what you said."

"That's because I told the truth."

Mullen asked, "Are you satisfied now, Louis? I'd like to get back to the ranch and see how my wounded men are doing."

Louis looked around and nodded. "I think we've seen all we're going to here. I still have a few questions I'd like to ask you, though."

"Come on to the ranch with me, then," Mullen suggested.

Louis thought about Melanie and Brad waiting for him back in Big Rock. That picnic lunch Melanie had planned was already ruined by now, and he was sure she'd be angry with him.

So he might as well go on to the Ace of Diamonds headquarters, he told himself. A man whose wife was already mad at him didn't have much left to lose.

"All right," he told Mullen. "Thank you." To Brice and Conrad, he added, "I suppose the two of you—"

"Are coming along, too," Conrad said.

"That's right," Brice said. He didn't come right out and say that they weren't going to take their eyes off him, thought Louis, but they might as well have.

The six men mounted and rode north.

The Ace of Diamonds was a good-sized spread.

It took the little group of riders an hour to reach the ranch headquarters from the southern boundary of Mullen's range.

They hadn't talked much during the ride. Louis hadn't asked the questions to which he wanted answers. Instead, Mullen had chatted about life in the valley and his friendship with Smoke, as if to remind Louis that he was on good terms with his father.

Louis knew that, but he wasn't going to allow the fact to change the way he approached this problem. Smoke and Roy Gardner were friends, too. It didn't mean either of the two feuding cattlemen was in the right.

As they rode up, one of Mullen's cowboys came out of the bunkhouse and hailed them. "What is it, Baxter?" Mullen asked.

"Figured you'd want to know that we got the wounded men patched up, boss," Baxter replied. "A couple of 'em are in bad-enough shape that I figure they ought to see Doc Steward in Big Rock, but the wagon ain't here because Curly already used it to take Kimbrough's body in."

Mullen nodded and said, "Get my cousin's buggy out of the barn and use it."

"I thought about that but didn't know if I ought to ask Mr. Bristol until you got back."

"I'm sure it would have been fine."

Baxter rubbed his beard-stubbled jaw. "Yeah, but we don't know him as well as you do, boss."

"I'll check with him. But in the meantime, go ahead and start hitching a team to the buggy."

Baxter nodded and hurried off to carry out the order. Orrie Striker said, "Jessup and I will go along to the bunkhouse if you don't need us, Mr. Mullen."

"No, that's all right," Mullen said with a little wave of his hand. "Check on those wounded men for me, will you?"

"Sure," Striker said. He and Jessup turned their horses toward the barn.

"Come on," Mullen said to Louis, Brice, and Conrad. "We can leave our horses at the house. Someone will come and tend to them."

As they rode slowly toward the house, a two-story, whitewashed frame structure, Louis said, "Who's this fellow Bristol your man mentioned, Mr. Mullen? The name's not familiar to me."

"That's because he's my cousin and just visiting me from St. Louis," Mullen replied. "You'll meet him momentarily, I'm sure."

As if the man had overheard Mullen's comment, a stranger stepped out onto the porch and watched the four riders coming closer. He was tall and thin, with a shock of rusty red hair and a drooping mustache of the same shade. He wore gray tweed trousers, a white shirt, and a vest. A string tie was cinched around his skinny neck, and a pair of spectacles rested on his prominent nose. He had a studious air about him and reminded Louis of some of the professors he'd had at Harvard.

The man said, "I hadn't expected you to return from your errand with company, Anthony."

Quietly, Mullen said to the trio with him, "I didn't tell Richard we were going to settle the score with Gardner and his men. He knew something had happened, but I didn't want to upset him with too many details."

"Did you get everything settled?" the stranger went on as the four men reined up and dismounted.

"For now," Mullen said. "Gentlemen, this is my cousin, Richard Bristol. Richard, this is Louis Jensen, Conrad Morgan, and Brice Rogers. Mr. Jensen is an attorney, Mr. Rogers is a deputy U.S. marshal, and Mr. Morgan is a prominent businessman here in the valley."

Bristol's bushy eyebrows rose. "My goodness, you've arrived in distinguished company, Anthony." The surprised look turned into a frown. "I hope the presence of a peace officer and an attorney doesn't mean that there's trouble."

"Well . . . there has been some, I'm afraid."

Bristol sighed and shook his head. "I knew from the uproar earlier that *something* had happened. I hoped that it was nothing too bad. But now I insist that you tell me what's going on. It might be something I can help with."

"I don't think so, but I suppose I owe you some

honest answers, after the help you've given me since you've been here." Mullen inclined his head toward the house and added to the three visitors, "Come on in. There'll be coffee on the stove. My cook always keeps a pot warm."

A few minutes later, the five of them were sitting in the ranch house's kitchen with cups of coffee. Louis's stomach was very aware that he had missed lunch, but Mullen hadn't offered them anything to eat.

Bristol, seated at one end of the kitchen table, said, "Tell me what the trouble is, Anthony. I want to help if I can."

"I don't think there's anything you can do, Richard. You know, of course, about the new survey I had Mr. Padgett make."

"Certainly," said Bristol, nodding.

"And you know that it showed a mistake in the original survey by Clyde Meeker."

"Indeed. Your ranch now encompasses more land than it used to, by a considerable amount."

"And that new range has a waterhole on it," Mullen said. "A waterhole that the fella who *thought* he owned it doesn't want to give up."

Bristol sipped his coffee and said, "I've overheard enough conversations between you and your men that I'm aware there's been trouble with the other ranch, Anthony. I know you'd like to shield me from such things, but really, it's not necessary. I may be an Easterner, but I know that things are different here in the West. Sometimes things are settled with gunplay, isn't that right?"

Louis spoke up, saying, "That's the way it used to be, Mr. Bristol. This is a new century, though. The West is civilized. We're all modern men and capable of settling things according to the law."

"You're right," Mullen said grudgingly. "I let my men go off half-cocked today, and I suppose I did the same thing." He looked across the table at Bristol. "Richard, one of my ranch hands was killed this morning, down near that waterhole. The rest of the crew and I went to settle the score with the Box RG."

"Good heavens!" Bristol exclaimed. "A man was killed, you say?"

"Yes, but luckily, no one else was, even though there was a lot of gunplay before the sheriff arrived from Big Rock to break it up. Roy Gardner, the man who owns the Box RG, claims that none of his men were responsible for the killing of my puncher."

"But you don't believe him, do you?"

Mullen thumped a fist on the table. "How can I believe him? Nobody else would've had any reason to shoot Kimbrough!"

"Take it easy," Brice advised. "You don't want to get worked up again, Mr. Mullen."

Bristol said, "You're a lawman, Marshal Rogers. Are you going to find the killer and arrest him?"

"I'm a federal lawman," Brice pointed out. "I don't really have any jurisdiction in cases like this. I'm just helping out the local sheriff."

"But if the matter isn't settled, the dispute will continue to simmer, and hard feelings will just get worse until violence breaks out again."

Mullen sighed and said, "That's probably what's going to happen, all right, unless Roy Gardner comes to his senses. And I don't expect that to happen. He's a stubborn old coot!"

Louis had been sipping his coffee and listening to the discussion. Now he said, "There's something I'm curious about, Mr. Mullen."

"That's right," Mullen responded. "You said there were some questions you wanted to ask me."

"This whole thing came about because of the new survey."

"That's right."

"What prompted you to have that done in the first place?"

"I lost confidence in Meeker's survey," Mullen said. "I found out later that he made mistakes on other surveys he did, before he ever came to Big Rock."

"You went along with it at the time," Louis pointed out.

Mullen shrugged. "I hadn't been in these parts all that long. I wanted to get along with my neighbors, and Gardner seemed like a good sort.

I had plenty of range and water, so I didn't figure that it really mattered."

"But then we had a dry spring and summer, and water became more important," Louis said. "Is that it?"

"That's a lot of it. But blast it, that land and that waterhole are mine by rights. The original claim and the Padgett survey prove that." Mullen flung his hands out in exasperation. "I don't know why anybody's even arguing about it. The law's on my side."

"A jury hasn't found that to be the case yet." Louis leaned forward. "If you want to do this the right way, I think you're going to have to go to court and get a judgment in your favor."

"No court document will stop a bushwhacker's bullet."

Bristol said, "I think you should listen to the young man, Anthony. Acting like a ruffian isn't going to solve anything in the long run. Only the law will do that."

Louis looked at the newcomer to the valley and said, "You sound like an attorney yourself, Mr. Bristol."

Bristol chuckled and shook his head. "No, not at all. I'm a geologist."

"You are?" said Conrad, sounding interested. "I'm involved with mining, myself."

"I thought I recognized your name, Mr. Morgan.

261

You used to be known as Conrad Browning, didn't you?"

"That's right."

"I've followed your activities here in Colorado. You're doing quite well with hydraulic mining."

"It's very productive, when it's done properly," Conrad said. "I agree with President Roosevelt, though. We have to conserve the land, even as we're making use of it."

"Indeed. I couldn't agree more."

"Well, I'm making use of it to raise cattle, and I think that's important, too," Mullen said. "I need that water, though, and I don't want a range war." He sighed and nodded. "You're right, Louis. I suppose this will have to be settled in court. Will you take the case?"

Louis didn't really want to take the side of one of his father's friends against another of the valley's pioneers, but he didn't see any other way to proceed. He nodded and said, "Yes, Mr. Mullen, I will."

CHAPTER 22

Louis went straight to his house when he got back to Big Rock late that afternoon.

Melanie was in the parlor when he walked in. She was mending something and didn't look up from the task as she said, "You might find something fit to eat in the kitchen, if you haven't had lunch already."

"I'm sorry," Louis said. "That trouble between the Box RG and the Ace of Diamonds exploded again. I had to ride out there with Sheriff Carson and a posse he put together."

That made Melanie lift her gaze to him as a worried frown creased her forehead. "Was there shooting?"

Louis nodded. "A man was killed," he said, then added quickly, "earlier in the day, I mean. When the sheriff and I and the other men got there, the fighting stopped."

"Nobody shot at you?"

"No. Like I said, Sheriff Carson put a stop to it as soon as we got there."

"Well, I'm relieved to hear *that,* anyway." She set the mending aside. "What happened?"

"One of Mr. Mullen's cowboys was shot from ambush and killed. The crew from the Ace of Diamonds attacked the Box RG in retaliation.

Thankfully, no one else was killed, although a few men on each side were wounded."

Melanie shook her head. "That's terrible. The fighting, I mean. I'm glad you weren't in the middle of it." She sighed. "I suppose trying to stop a range war is more important than a picnic with your wife and son. So I'll just be a little put out with you, instead of actually being angry."

Louis smiled, bent toward her, and kissed her forehead. "I appreciate that."

"What's going to happen between those two ranchers? Did they settle things?"

"Not yet. Mr. Mullen has decided to bring suit against Mr. Gardner to establish the new boundary line legally. I agreed to represent him."

"So you have a client?"

"I do," Louis said. "I didn't want to take sides, but this seems like the most effective way of ending the dispute and bringing about a lasting peace between the two ranches."

Melanie got to her feet. "With all that going on, I suppose you never got to eat?'

"Well, no, I didn't."

She smiled. "Come on in the kitchen. We'll find something for you."

When Conrad and Brice got back to the livery stable, the deputy marshal asked, "What are you going to do now?"

Conrad cocked an eyebrow in surprise. "I'm

not sure that's any of your business. But I thought I might head back to Blaise's Place, since things didn't go exactly the way I expected when I stopped by there earlier."

"You mean because of that cowboy from the Box RG riding into town with news of the fight out there."

"Among other things," Conrad said.

Brice looked shrewdly at him and said, "Now you're talking about that so-called husband of hers."

"What do you mean *so-called?* We don't have any reason to doubt what he told us, do we?"

"No, I suppose not," Brice admitted with obvious reluctance. "And Blaise didn't contradict what he said. But I still don't like the fella. Something about him just rubs me the wrong way."

Conrad laughed. "For once, Brice, we're in complete agreement. I didn't care for Mr. Martin Delroy, either."

"Well, if you're going over there, so am I."

"Fine. It's a free country, or it was, the last time I checked, anyway."

They made an unlikely pair, Conrad reflected as they walked together toward Blaise's Place. They weren't friends, by any means. And even though Conrad was actually more interested in Denny Jensen than he was in Blaise Warfield, he supposed that he and Brice would have to be considered rivals—for both of those young women. Instead of a romantic triangle, this was more of a rectangle.

Late in the afternoon like this, the saloon was starting to get busier. When Conrad and Brice went in, the places along the bar were mostly full, several men gathered around the roulette wheel, and a couple of poker games were going on. Men sat and drank at some of the other tables.

Martin Delroy was playing in one of the poker games. Blaise wasn't in the room, as far as Conrad could see. He and Brice went to the bar and ordered beers.

"Where's Blaise?" Conrad put the blunt question to the bartender.

The man shook his head and said, "You're asking the wrong fella, mister. I don't keep up with where the boss is or what she's doing."

Brice nodded toward the table where one of the poker games was going on and said, "I thought Mr. Delroy was the boss around here now."

The bartender shrugged. "I just work here, mister. I don't get mixed up in anybody's personal business."

Seeing that they weren't going to get anywhere with the bartender, Conrad just nodded, sipped his beer, and fell silent. Brice stood beside him, sipping from the mug of foamy amber liquid. Several minutes passed before the tension between them grew strong enough to be awkward.

Brice drained the last of his beer and said, "I'd best be going. Need to check at the telegraph office and make sure there haven't been any messages from my boss."

Conrad just nodded and didn't say anything. There weren't going to be any lengthy goodbyes between the two of them.

Brice returned the nod and left the saloon. Conrad stayed where he was, taking his time about finishing his beer. When he finally did, the bartender nodded to the empty mug and asked, "Get you another?"

"No, thanks. I believe I've had enough."

Conrad turned away from the bar, but instead of heading for the batwings, he acted on impulse. He went to the stairs that led to the second floor and started up them.

The bartender called, "Hey, mister," but Conrad ignored him. Most of the time, when men went upstairs here, they were accompanied by one of the girls who worked in the saloon. A man alone represented the potential for trouble. Conrad didn't let that stop him. He wanted to talk to Blaise and make sure she was all right. If she wasn't down here, there was only one place she was likely to be, and that was in her living quarters at the end of the second-floor hallway.

It was too early for much to be going on in the other rooms, but he heard a few telltale noises coming from behind the doors of some of them.

Conrad ignored those, too, and strode along the hall to the last door. He raised his hand and rapped on the panel.

"Come in," Blaise called from the other side of the door.

She was sitting on the love seat with a glass of wine in her hand. Her finely curved eyebrows rose in surprise when Conrad stepped into the room.

"I thought you were going to be Martin," she said, then made a face. "Although why I would think that, I don't know. My husband never would have knocked. He would have just barged in like he owned the place . . . which, I suppose, he does."

Conrad eased the door shut behind him. "It's Delroy I want to talk to you about," he said.

Blaise's chin jutted out defiantly as she said, "I don't see how my marriage is any of your business, Conrad."

"Is it real?" he asked. "Are you really married to that man?"

"Of course, I am. I wouldn't say so if it wasn't true, would I?" That prompted a laugh from her. "Again, what am I thinking? I've said so many things in my life that aren't true, I wouldn't even know where to start counting them."

With that, her expression crumpled a little. She lifted both hands and covered her face. She didn't sob, but Conrad could tell she was holding in tears.

He moved closer to her, reached out and lightly rested the fingertips of his left hand on her right shoulder, which was bared by the low neck of the gown she wore.

"I'm sorry. I didn't mean to upset you. I just had the feeling that you might need help . . ."

Blaise shook her head. "There's nothing you can do to help me. I . . . I should have known that I'd never get away from Martin, no matter how far I ran . . ."

Conrad put his right hand on her left shoulder. She stood up and came into his arms. He folded them around her and held her, trying to comfort her. This time a few choked sobs escaped from her, and he felt the dampness of tears against his shirt.

Or was she just acting? She already admitted that she had a long history of lying.

Conrad's instincts told him that Blaise was genuinely upset, but he remained a little wary anyway as he asked, "Do you want me to see if I can do anything about him?"

Blaise shook her head where it was pressed against his chest. "There's nothing you can do. Nothing anybody can do."

"Maybe Brice could find some reason to arrest him," Conrad suggested. "If nothing else, the threat of it might scare him into leaving town."

She laughed, but there was nothing humorous in the sound. "You don't know Martin Delroy.

269

He's the most . . . the most brazen man I've ever known. Fearless, in his way. He's always been willing to run any risk, make any sacrifice . . . or force someone else to sacrifice . . . to get what he wants."

Conrad knew from her remarks that there was a lot more to the story that he didn't know yet, and Blaise made it sound like she was the victim. Again, he wasn't one hundred percent convinced, but she seemed sincere enough that he still wanted to help her.

He didn't get a chance to figure out how, because at that moment, the door into Blaise's living quarters was thrown open and Martin Delroy stepped into the sitting room, his face twisted with rage.

He ripped out a curse and then said, "I should have known. When I saw this man heading up here, I should have known you just couldn't help yourself, could you, Blaise? You had to be the same sort of slut you've always been!"

Conrad let go of Blaise, moved back a step from her, and turned to face Delroy.

"Watch what you're saying, mister," he warned. "I know you're upset, but that doesn't give you the right to talk to the lady that way."

"No right?" Delroy laughed coldly. "I'm married to the little round-heeled harlot, so I can talk to her any way I please." He looked past Conrad and went on, "I'll give you credit, my dear. You went after the proper target. Mr. Browning here—I mean, Mr. Morgan—is a very rich man. He has a lot more money than that callow deputy marshal I thought you were sweet on."

"I'm not sweet on either of them," snapped Blaise. "They're friends, that's all—"

"And I know quite well how you tend to wind up in bed with your friends," Delroy interrupted her as he moved closer. "Shall I tell Mr. Morgan about some of the things you've done in the past? Do you think he'd be entertained by your little escapades?"

"I never did anything you didn't make me do!" Blaise said as she stepped forward. Her hands clenched instinctively into fists.

"Oh, is that so?" Delroy asked with a sneer. "As I recall, when I met you for the first time, you were already quite experienced—"

"That's enough," Conrad said as he took another step to get between the two of them again. "I think you should leave."

Delroy shook his head. "You can't tell me what to do. Despite what it says on the sign outside, this is *my* place. Bought and paid for with *my* money. Money that she stole from me!"

He pointed an accusing finger at Blaise. His hand trembled from the depth of his anger.

"Enough," Conrad said again. He put a hand on Delroy's shoulder and started to turn the man so he could steer him back out through the door.

But Delroy pulled away and twisted around with an agility that Conrad didn't expect from a man who was probably twenty years older than he was. Delroy's fist flashed up, too fast for Conrad to block the punch. The blow crashed into his jaw and sent him flying backward to collide with Blaise, who let out a startled scream as they went down.

CHAPTER 23

Delroy rushed forward and drew back his leg for a kick while Conrad was tangled up with Blaise. Conrad managed to get loose just in time to fling his hands up and catch the foot that was coming toward his head. He heaved. Delroy stumbled backward, waving his arms as he tried to catch his balance.

Conrad started to get up. Blaise caught hold of his arm and gasped, "No! He'll kill you!"

"He can try," Conrad said as he pulled free and surged to his feet.

Delroy had managed to stay upright. He lunged at Conrad again. The younger man had himself set this time, however, so he was able to block the punch Delroy aimed at his head. The gambler was wide-open for a second. Conrad could have launched a counterpunch of his own and smashed his fist into Delroy's face, but he hesitated. He was all too aware of Delroy's age. The man was almost old enough to be Conrad's father.

But he had started the fight, and Conrad wasn't going to just stand there and let Delroy hit him. Instead, he planted the palm of his right hand against Delroy's chest and gave him a hard shove. Delroy reeled back again.

"Stop it, you damned fool," Conrad said. "I don't want to hurt you."

Delroy was breathing hard, but that didn't stop him from raging, "You have no right to be here! I saw you with . . . with your hands on my wife!"

Blaise had struggled to her feet. She tried to adjust her disarranged gown as she said, "You never worried that much about men putting their hands on me before, Martin. But that was because it was your idea, wasn't it?"

"Shut up!" he shouted at her. "Shut your lying mouth, you slut!"

He charged at Conrad again.

Conrad was glad that Delroy hadn't drawn a gun on him. That could have turned very ugly in a hurry. He pivoted to get out of Delroy's way, and as the gambler threw a punch at him again, Conrad kept turning and grabbed his arm. He used Delroy's own momentum to send him flying into the love seat. Delroy's head struck the wall. He slumped down on the piece of furniture, momentarily knocked senseless.

Conrad turned to Blaise and gripped her arm. "You should get out of here," he told her. "I'll go with you to Sheriff Carson. We can get your husband locked up—"

"No," Blaise broke in. "I don't want that, Conrad. This . . . this is my problem. I have to figure out how to handle it. I don't want you getting into any trouble. Martin could press charges against *you*."

"Me?" Conrad exclaimed. "I didn't do anything except defend myself when he attacked me."

"You were alone with a married woman in her room," Blaise pointed out. "A lot of people would say that you were in the wrong just by being here."

Conrad frowned. He knew she had a point. Most folks were going to side with a woman's husband over another man, no matter what the circumstances.

"Please, Conrad," she went on. "I know that I . . . I'm just a saloon girl, but I'd rather not have people talking about me any more than necessary."

"Well, all right. If you're sure that you're not in any danger from him . . ." He glanced toward the love seat, where Martin Delroy still half-sat, half-lay, groggily shaking his head. His neatly combed hair was askew now, and some of it hung in his face.

"Don't worry, I can handle Martin," she assured him.

Conrad nodded and turned toward the door, pausing after he opened it to say, "If you need help, come and find me. Or even Brice. I know he'd help you any time—"

"Martin!" cried Blaise as, with no warning, Delroy surged up from the love seat and came at him again, brushing Blaise aside.

Conrad didn't have time to get out of the way.

Delroy rammed into him. The collision knocked him out of the room, into the hallway. A couple of doors away, a cowboy and one of the saloon girls had just emerged from another room. They stopped to gawk at Conrad and Delroy as the gambler swung wild punches and Conrad tried to fend them off as he backed away.

A moment later, Conrad ducked, got inside the range of Delroy's blows, and grappled with the man, wrapping his arms around Delroy's torso and forcing him backward, lifting him off his feet. The cowboy and the soiled dove scrambled to get out of the way. Conrad and Delroy landed on the carpet runner in the center of the hallway, with Conrad on top. His weight forced the breath out of Delroy's lungs and left the older man stunned and gasping again.

Conrad pushed himself up, cocked his right fist, and drove it down into Delroy's face. The powerful punch landed cleanly on Delroy's jaw and rocked his head to the side. His eyes rolled up in their sockets, and then he sighed as his eyelids closed. He was out cold.

Conrad put his hand on the floor and braced himself to stand up. As he did so, he saw that his lunging tackle had carried him and Delroy onto the balcony, so that the end of the fight had been visible to the people in the saloon—most of whom were staring up at them in surprise from their places at the bar or at tables in the big room.

It didn't really matter, Conrad told himself. The cowboy and the saloon girl had witnessed the ruckus. Conrad was sure that gossip about the fight would have spread all over Big Rock anyway. But now it was sure to, considering the number of witnesses gaping up at him.

He stepped back up the hall to where his hat had fallen off and bent to pick it up. As he straightened, he saw Blaise standing in the open doorway of the sitting room. He opened his mouth to say something to her, but she shook her head sadly, stepped back, and closed the door.

Conrad stared at it for a second, then shrugged, clapped his hat on his head, and started toward the stairs. As he passed Martin Delroy, the gambler was stirring and moaning as he began to regain consciousness.

By the time Conrad reached the bottom of the stairs, Delroy had fought his way up into a sitting position. He reached over, grabbed the balcony railing, and clung to it as he thrust his face up to the balusters.

"Morgan!" he bellowed through the railing. Curses spewed from his mouth. Conrad didn't look around, even when Delroy shouted, "If you ever set foot in here again, I'll kill you! Do you hear me? *I'll kill you!*"

Conrad slapped the batwings aside and stepped out of the saloon.

Dusk was settling down over Big Rock, but

even in the gloom, Conrad's keen eyes spotted a man standing nearby. Something about him was familiar, and as he looked again, he recognized the short, slightly built man who had won the big bet at the roulette wheel earlier in the day.

"My goodness gracious," the man said. "What's all the uproar in there?"

Conrad wasn't in the mood for conversation, but he was naturally polite enough not to brush off the man's question.

"There was a disagreement," he said. "I was trying to comfort a lady, and her husband objected to it."

"I see." The man's voice held a slightly prim note of disapproval.

"No, you don't," said Conrad. "The lady's just a friend of mine, that's all, and I actually was trying to make her feel better because she was upset. And her husband's the man she was upset about, so don't waste any sympathy on him."

"Was that him yelling and cursing and threatening to kill you?"

"As a matter of fact, it was."

"Well, then," the small man said, "I won't waste any sympathy on him, just as you suggest." He held out his hand. "Hubert Osborne is my name. I'm a newcomer to Big Rock."

"Conrad Morgan," Conrad introduced himself. He clasped the man's hand. "I haven't been around these parts all that long myself."

Hubert Osborne had a surprisingly strong grip for a little fellow. He nodded and said, "I'm glad to meet you, Mr. Morgan. I was about to go inside and try my luck at some of the other games of chance, but I think perhaps under the circumstances, it might not make for a pleasant evening."

Conrad looked back over the batwings. He was worried about leaving Blaise here with Delroy and thought about returning to the saloon himself. He could go upstairs and insist that she return to the hotel with him, where she could get a room and be safe.

But before he could go inside, he saw Blaise descending the stairs. She had straightened up her clothes and the feather in her hair, and she looked like she had washed her face and gathered her composure, too. She smiled brightly at the men staring at her and called, "Don't just stand there with your mouths hanging open, boys. Put them to work. The next round's on the house!"

That brought cheers and laughter from the crowd. Men thronged to the bar. The fight they had witnessed a few minutes earlier was forgotten.

Conrad looked up at the balcony. Martin Delroy had disappeared. Conrad supposed that he was nursing his hatred in Blaise's living quarters.

Blaise was in the middle of the crowd now, laughing and joking with the saloon's customers.

She would be safe as long as she stayed there, he told himself. And Delroy would cool off after a while. Evidently, Blaise had plenty of experience at coping with him, so Conrad figured he would leave her to it. He had sensed upstairs, during the last look they had traded, that she wouldn't appreciate it if he inserted himself in her problems again.

Instead, he turned to Osborne and said, "I think you can go back in and be confident of a good evening. All the trouble's over now. At least, that's what it looks like to me."

"Well, if you think that's the case . . . I suppose I'll risk it. Can I buy you a drink, Mr. Morgan?"

"Maybe some other time. It's been a long day."

"I'll bid you good evening, then."

Osborne pushed the batwings aside and entered the saloon. Conrad walked on to Front Street and turned the corner there.

When he did, he nearly ran into Monte Carson. The lawman stopped and said, "Howdy, Mr. Morgan. You wouldn't happen to be coming from Blaise's Place, would you?"

Conrad mustered up a smile. "As a matter of fact, Sheriff, I am."

"A fella stopped by my office and said there was trouble down here. Something about a big fight." Monte squinted at him in the fading light. "Looks to me like you might've been in a little tussle yourself."

"I was," Conrad admitted. "I'm not proud of myself for doing it, but I got tangled up with Martin Delroy just now."

Monte looked surprised. "That gambler who showed up and claims to be Miss Warfield's husband?"

"I think it must be true. She's not denying it."

"I didn't know you were even acquainted with the hombre, let alone enemies enough to get in a fight."

"Well, the whole thing developed rather quickly," Conrad said ruefully. "And as I said, I'm not proud of it, since Delroy is considerably older than I am, but he left me no choice except to defend myself."

Monte stiffened. "You didn't kill him, did you?"

"No, he was fine when I left him. A little the worse for wear, maybe, but as you noted, so am I."

"The trouble was over Miss Warfield, I reckon?"

"Don't jump to conclusions, Sheriff," Conrad said with a slight edge in his voice. "That's what Delroy did. I consider Blaise a friend, but that's all."

"She's a mighty good-looking gal."

"She is, for a fact. But I still don't have any romantic interest in her. For a while, I thought I might, but I believe it's better this way."

"None of my business," said Monte. "As long as the trouble's over, that's all I was going to check on."

"When I left, Blaise had just bought a round for the house, and everybody was happy."

"I suppose I'll go back to the office, then." Monte looked around. "It would be all right with me if it was a peaceful night in Big Rock." He shook his head. "Even in this new, modern century of ours, that doesn't happen as often as I'd like."

CHAPTER 24

Despite the rather pessimistic note on which Monte Carson had departed from Conrad Morgan, the rest of the night in Big Rock *was* quiet and peaceful.

Denny Jensen had no way of knowing that, however, when she rode into town the next morning to see her brother.

She knew Louis was more likely to be at his office than home, so she went straight there. But she would stop by the house later to say hello to Melanie and Brad, she told herself.

"Well, there you are, looking like Young Wild West, as usual," Louis greeted her as she came in wearing her range garb.

"I'd rather look like a dime novel character than a stuffed shirt," she gibed right back at him. She thumbed her hat back on her blond hair and went on, "But I'm here on law business, so we'd better get down to it."

"You found something in Denver?" he asked, leaning forward in the chair behind the desk.

"Yeah, I found something," Denny replied as she sat down in one of the client's chairs. "Trouble. Some crook tried to rob me and a fellow who was helping me."

"Good Lord," Louis muttered. "Are you all right?"

"Yeah, I'm fine."

"Well, what happened?"

"What do you *think* happened?" Denny wanted to know.

"If I had to venture a guess . . . I'd say you probably shot the man."

Denny laughed. "You bet I did. He looked surprised as all get-out, too, when I pulled out the pistol I had in my bag. He tried to throw down on me anyway—"

"You killed him, didn't you? Did the authorities charge you with manslaughter?"

"No," Denny said, sounding slightly offended. "I didn't kill him. I didn't have to. But he won't be using either arm any time soon, so he'll be pretty uncomfortable in jail."

Louis sighed. "I'm relieved you didn't get in trouble with the law." He sat up straighter. "You didn't, did you?"

"Not at all. The policeman who came to see about the trouble said that I acted in self-defense."

"That's good. But what about the reason you went there? Did you find Edgar Padgett?"

"Now, that's a little odd," said Denny. "I didn't find him, because apparently he doesn't exist."

Louis frowned and shook his head. "What do you mean, he doesn't exist? I saw the survey map he did. It had his name printed on it and everything."

"And it said he's located in Denver?"

"That's right."

"There's no Edgar Padgett . . . nobody named Padgett, period . . . who works for any of the surveying firms in Denver. And he doesn't have his own firm, under that or any other name. Not only that, but the state licenses surveyors, and they don't have any record of an Edgar Padgett working as a surveyor anywhere in Colorado."

Louis looked utterly confused. "I just don't understand. I saw the map with my own eyes."

"Where is it now? At Mr. Mullen's ranch?"

"That's right." Louis shoved his chair back. "I'm going to have to ride up there and find out about this. I want another look at that map."

Denny held out a hand to stop him as he started to get up. "Maybe you'd better think about that idea a little more," she suggested.

He settled back down in the chair but asked, "What's there to think about? I have to make sure that new survey map is authentic. Good grief, I should have done that before I ever agreed to take on this case!" Agitated, Louis ran his fingers through his brown hair. "What a foolish mistake. That's the sort of thing a law *student* would know better than to do, let alone someone who's actually passed the bar."

"Don't be too hard on yourself," Denny told him. "A man had been killed earlier, and you weren't far from being in the middle of a shooting war."

"I've been around violence before, you know. That's no excuse."

"Maybe not, but you've had a lot to handle. Getting married and getting not only a wife but a son, going back East to school, coming home, buying a house, setting up this office . . ." Denny spread her hands. "That's a lot to keep up with. So don't worry about what's happened so far. Figure out what you need to do next."

"I just told you. I have to look at that survey map and satisfy myself that it's the real thing."

"And if it's not, what will that mean?"

"That someone is trying to pull a fast one . . ." Louis blinked a couple of times. "Oh. I see what you mean."

"That's right. I don't want to believe that Tony Mullen is a crook any more than you do. He's been at the Sugarloaf as a friend. He was even at your wedding. But if that map is a fake, I don't see any other explanation for it, and you don't want him knowing you've figured that out when you're right there in the middle of his ranch, surrounded by his men."

Louis shook his head. "He'd never dare hurt me. He's bound to know what would happen to him if he did."

"You're talking about what Pa would do. I agree with you, that wouldn't end well for Mr. Mullen. But sometimes, desperate men don't think straight. You don't want to bet your life on what might happen if you call his bluff."

"All right," Louis said with a sigh. "Then what do *you* think I should do?"

"Send word to the Ace of Diamonds that you need him to come in and talk to you about the court case, and that he should bring the map with him. If it's a fake, he'll probably come up with some excuse why he can't do that."

"He'll suspect that I'm on to him."

"Maybe, maybe not. Anyway, we don't have any proof that the map's not real," Denny went on. "It's kind of suspicious that I couldn't find hide nor hair of Edgar Padgett, but that doesn't guarantee that Mr. Mullen is trying to steal Mr. Gardner's range or that waterhole. Maybe there's some other explanation."

"Maybe," Louis allowed.

"I have an idea. Why don't you let me take the message out there to the Ace of Diamonds?"

Louis narrowed his eyes warily. "Why? So you can shoot somebody else?"

"I'm not going to shoot anybody," Denny scoffed. "But I can tell Mr. Mullen that I'm delivering the message as a favor to you. I mean, even if there's something sinister going on, they're not likely to hurt a poor, defenseless girl, are they?"

"A poor, defenseless girl?" Louis repeated. "I thought you were talking about riding out there yourself."

"That's not funny. Listen, it's a good idea. You know I'm an excellent actress, Louis. I'll just pretend I don't really know anything about it. He won't suspect me of being up to anything."

"Well . . . you're probably right about that."

"I know I am. When do you want him to come into town?"

"How about tomorrow morning? I don't want to rush him too much."

Denny nodded. "That sounds like it'll work." She smiled. "Maybe I should go to law school, if I'm going to help you with your practice."

"I'm not sure you'd like it, Denny. You have to wade through a lot of dry, dusty, boring law books and try to remember just about everything that's in them."

"No, that's not the kind of chore I like," she agreed. "I'll stick to looking for surveyors and delivering messages."

And while she was out on the range anyway, she thought, maybe she could take a look at the waterhole that was the source of so much conflict . . .

Although Denny had met Tony Mullen several times at the Sugarloaf and in Big Rock, she had never been to the Ace of Diamonds ranch. She knew where it was located, though, and had no trouble finding the trail that led to it from the main road through the valley.

According to what Louis had told her, the disputed waterhole was a couple of miles east. When she left the ranch headquarters, she would ride out of sight and then veer off in that direction. She didn't want Mullen to know that she intended to poke around on his range. It never hurt to be careful, although sometimes she had to convince the more reckless side of her personality of that fact.

She figured she had to be nearing the Ace of Diamonds ranch house when she spotted a rider angling toward her across a wide pasture to her right. She reined in to wait, since he appeared to be aiming to intercept her. She had a Winchester carbine in a saddle sheath, and the Colt Lightning rode on her hip, as usual, so she wasn't too worried about her safety.

The man reached the trail and brought his horse to a stop about twenty feet in front of her. He was lean and hatchet-faced, middle-aged with streaks of silver in his hair and mustache. Denny knew she had seen him before but didn't recall his name. She knew he rode for Tony Mullen.

The reins were in her left hand. Her right rested on her jeans-clad thigh. The cold look in the man's eyes made her slide that hand a little closer to the Lightning. She had seen looks like that before, and sometimes they led to gunplay.

"Something I can do for you, Miss Jensen?" he asked. "You *are* Miss Denise Jensen, aren't you?"

"That's right. I'm on my way to the Ace of Diamonds ranch."

"You're already on Ace of Diamonds range. You have business out here?" The man paused, then asked, "Did your pa send you?"

Everybody in these parts knew Smoke. His actions commanded interest and respect. Nobody would cross him . . . unless the stakes were high enough.

Denny didn't know what the stakes were here, but she didn't want to complicate matters with a lie. She said, "No, I'm here to deliver a message for my brother. He's an attorney representing Mr. Mullen."

The man nodded slowly. "I know who your brother is, miss. I'm Mr. Mullen's foreman. Orrie Striker."

Denny remembered the man's name now that he had mentioned it. She nodded, smiled, and said, "Of course. I know who you are, Mr. Striker."

His eyes were still pretty chilly as they rested on her, but maybe not quite as wary now. He turned his horse and said, "Come on. I'll take you to the ranch house."

"Thank you, but I'm sure I can find it. I don't want to take you from your work."

He chuckled humorlessly. "Like I said, I'm the foreman. I decide what my work is. And right now, it's making sure you get where you're going."

And keeping her from wandering around, maybe? That thought nagged at Denny's brain as she urged her mount ahead and fell in alongside Striker.

He didn't seem like he wanted to make small talk as they rode, but she said, "I've heard about the trouble you've been having out here. It's a shame Mr. Mullen and Mr. Gardner can't get along. They were friends and neighbors for quite a while."

"That's the way it happens sometimes. Things change."

"Not without a good reason."

"Doesn't take much to set one man against another."

"No, I suppose not. I know my brother wishes they could work things out."

Striker shook his head. "Things have gone too far for that, more than likely. Blood's been spilled. No way to take that back."

That was his last word on the subject. Everything else she said, he responded with curt monosyllables, if he responded at all. After a few minutes, Denny gave up and they rode in silence.

They came to the ranch headquarters a short time later. Striker nodded to the cluster of buildings and corrals and said, "There you go, miss. I'll be riding on now."

"Thank you, Mr. Striker."

He nodded, turned his horse, and loped off. Denny rode on toward the ranch house.

Someone inside had seen her coming. A tall, thin, rusty-haired man stepped out onto the porch. Denny had never seen him before. She knew he wasn't Tony Mullen.

"Hello," she told him as she reined in.

"Good afternoon," he replied with a smile. "What can I do for you?"

"I'm looking for Mr. Mullen."

"I'm sure he'll be quite devastated to have missed a visit from such a beautiful young woman, but he's out somewhere on the range right at this moment." The stranger laughed. "He's not really that much of a cattleman, you know, but he enjoys acting as if he is, from time to time. By the way, I'm his cousin from back East, Richard Bristol."

"Denny Jensen," Denny introduced herself.

Bristol's shaggy eyebrows rose. "Jensen," he repeated. "The same name as the attorney in Big Rock? Surely you're not his wife?"

That brought a laugh from Denny. "Not hardly! He's my brother. But I'm here on his behalf. I have a message for Mr. Mullen from him."

"Indeed?" Bristol shook his head. "Good heavens, where are my manners? Please, Miss Jensen, come inside. I can offer you a cup of coffee or perhaps some cool water?"

"No, thank you, Mr. Bristol, that's all right. When do you expect Mr. Mullen back?"

Bristol spread his hands and said, "I have no

292

idea. When he left, Anthony didn't say anything about when he expected to return. Sometime before nightfall, I assume."

Denny caught her lower lip between her teeth for a second as she thought about the situation. She didn't want to spend the rest of the day waiting for Tony Mullen to get back to the ranch headquarters.

"Would you mind giving him the message for me?" she asked instead.

"Absolutely not," Bristol answered. "I'd be more than happy to pass along whatever you need to tell him."

"My brother wants him to come to town tomorrow morning, to his office, to discuss the court case he's representing Mr. Mullen in. And Mr. Mullen needs to bring the survey map that shows the new boundary between the Ace of Diamonds and the Box RG with him."

"Is there some problem about the map?" asked Bristol.

"I don't know. I'm just repeating what Louis told me to say to Mr. Mullen. You're sure you don't mind telling him?"

"Of course not. I'll deliver the message just as soon as he returns."

"I appreciate that." Denny started to turn her horse away.

Bristol stopped her by saying, "I'm curious, though, why your brother sent you with the message instead of delivering it himself."

"Oh, I volunteered," Denny said. "I figured I'd save Louis the time and trouble, and besides, it was a good excuse to ride out here on a nice day."

"It *is* a nice day, isn't it? Rather hot, though."

"Well, it's that time of year." Denny raised a finger to the brim of her hat and went on, "Nice to meet you, Mr. Bristol."

"Oh, the pleasure is all mine, Miss Jensen," the man assured her. "Thank you, and good day."

Denny rode away from the ranch. Her forehead creased in a frown as she felt a slight pricking of the skin at the back of her neck. She wanted to glance back over her shoulder at Richard Bristol, but she resisted the impulse. She didn't want to look as if he had spooked her, and anyway, there was no reason for her to react that way. He had seemed to be about as mild-mannered and friendly a fellow as anybody could want to encounter.

She pushed that out of her mind, and when nothing had happened by the time she was well out of sight of the ranch headquarters, she veered off the trail and rode in the direction she believed would bring her to the waterhole.

She wasn't sure what she hoped to find there, but she wanted to lay eyes on the place for herself.

CHAPTER 25

The boss had given orders for the Box RG riders to stay away from the new fence and the waterhole beyond it, but it wasn't Chet Holloway's fault that some of Mr. Gardner's cows had wandered up here.

That was what Chet told himself, anyway, as he rode in sight of the barbed wire fence and looked around for the strays. He had followed their tracks this far, but now he didn't see any sign of them. He'd expected to find them grazing in the pasture just south of the fence.

A mile to the east lay some brushy breaks. Maybe the cows had drifted on over there. If they had, they might have gotten tangled up in the thickets and couldn't get out. Cows were pretty stupid that way, thought Chet.

Of course, since he'd signed on to nursemaid them, maybe that made *him* pretty stupid, too. But cowboying was the only way of life he'd ever known. The only way of life he wanted to know, in fact. He was never quite as happy and satisfied as when he was out riding the range.

He followed the fence toward the breaks. To his left, he could see the disputed waterhole. The sight of it reminded him of everything that had happened. He felt anger welling up inside him at the memories. Several of his friends were still nursing injuries from the Ace of Diamonds raid on the Box RG. It just wasn't right that those varmints were going to get away with that.

Chet tried to push the anger and resentment out of his mind and concentrate on the job that had brought him here. He wanted to find those cows. He wasn't sure how far the fence ran in this direction, but it was possible that if the cattle had gotten up into the breaks, they might eventually work their way around the end of it and wind up on Mullen's range. If that happened, probably it would lead to more trouble, so Chet wanted to make sure that it didn't.

The breaks came in sight, a wide stretch of brush-choked gullies and ravines, slashed by sharp-crested ridges. The fence dipped down and ran through a couple of shallow gullies, then stopped at the edge of the first ravine. The drop-off there was too steep for it to continue. That was exactly what Chet expected to find.

He studied the ground and spotted not only cattle tracks but also several piles of what looked to be fairly fresh droppings. Those blasted cows had wandered over here, all right, also as he'd suspected. More than likely, once they were down in that first gully, they had turned and followed it, rather than going to the trouble of climbing out of it. With the fence still in place, they would be forced to head back south, onto Box RG range.

Even though that theory made sense to Chet, he knew he would have to confirm it. You could never assume what cows would do, because they would surprise you from time to time with their bizarre behavior. They were notional critters, as the old-timers said.

Chet heeled his horse forward and rode down the slope into the first gully. He was wearing chaps, so he wasn't too worried about the brush clawing his legs. He would have to be careful where he rode for his horse's sake, though. He would find the easiest route he could.

He had just reached the bottom of the gully and turned to the south when he heard crackling in the brush behind him, on the other side of the fence.

Chet reined in and looked over his shoulder. That was strange, he thought. Sounded like a good-sized animal moving around over there. Probably one of the Ace of Diamonds cows and none of his business, he told himself. He looked at the fence. It was intact. None of Mr. Gardner's stock had gotten through there, so whatever was making that racket, it wasn't his responsibility.

However, as the noises in the brush continued, Chet's curiosity got the better of him. One of the Ace of Diamonds hands might have gotten tangled up and couldn't get loose. Even though the two spreads were in a state of war, as far as Chet was concerned, and peace was maintained only by an uneasy truce, he couldn't turn his back on another cowboy in trouble, no matter what brand the hombre rode for. That just wasn't the way he was brought up.

Chet turned around and rode to the fence. Resting his hands on the saddle horn, he leaned forward and called, "Hey, is anybody in there? You need a hand? Are you hung up in all that brush?"

Nobody answered, but the noises stopped. Chet couldn't figure it out. Ultimately, though, anything that happened on that side of the line wasn't his responsibility. He lifted his reins and got ready to search for those wandering cows again.

He heard a sharp crack, felt a tremendous blow against his head, and tumbled from the saddle as his horse suddenly shied at the sound of the shot. He didn't know anything after that, never even felt himself hit the ground.

When consciousness seeped back into Chet's brain, it brought with it pounding explosions of pain worse than any he had experienced. Rhythmic agony filled his head to the point that with each throb, each beat of his heart, he felt as if his skull was going to shatter and fly apart.

On top of that, he realized that he was sick to his stomach. His guts twisted and heaved, but nothing came out. If it had, that might have been a relief. Chet was denied even that small bit of comfort, however.

Gradually, he realized that hurting so bad and being sick were good things. They meant that he was still alive. If that bushwhacker had blown his brains out, he wouldn't be aware of anything now, unless it was clouds and harp music, if the sky pilots were right about what was waiting on the other side of the divide. Chet had never quite been able to make up his mind if he was looking forward to that or not.

But since he was alive right now, he damned sure wanted to stay that way, so he began trying to take stock of himself and his surroundings, even though it hurt to think. Everything hurt no matter what he did, so it didn't really matter, he told himself. He might as well try to figure things out.

He was in darkness, but subtle shifts in that darkness made him realize that he had his eyes closed. He would leave them that way for now, he decided, until he had more information.

His head and arms hung down, and so did his legs. He swayed some, back and forth. He knew that feeling. He was on a horse. The way he was hanging on both sides and something hard was pressing against his middle told him that whoever had shot him had thrown him over his saddle and now was leading his horse somewhere.

He tensed his arm muscles but couldn't move

them. The rough fibers of a rope scraped his wrists. His arms were tied to his legs under the horse's belly. Whoever had positioned him up here didn't want him to fall off.

That meant he couldn't do anything to free himself, even if he'd had the strength, which he didn't. He could tell his muscles probably wouldn't work if he tried to use them. That meant he had to wait until the bushwhacker got wherever he was going. Once they were there, wherever *there* was, maybe the varmint would cut him loose and he could get some feeling and strength back in his limbs.

In the meantime, Chet figured it would be safer to keep quiet and let the would-be killer believe he was unconscious, even though he wanted to groan every time the horse took a step and a fresh bomb burst of pain went off inside his head.

That ride seemed to take forever. Chet tried to distract himself from the pain by thinking of other things, but his thoughts kept coming back to the no-good skunks who rode for the Ace of Diamonds. The shot had come from their side of the fence. Chet was convinced that one of Mullen's crew had tried to kill him.

An idea crept slowly into his head. Maybe the bushwhacker believed that he *had* killed him. A head wound like the one he had suffered was bound to bleed a lot. He was sure it looked pretty bad. It was possible the bushwhacker had thought he was slinging a corpse over the horse's back.

But if that was true, then where was the varmint taking him . . . and why? If all the man wanted to do was kill him, why hadn't he just left Chet where he'd fallen?

Chet didn't have answers to any of those questions. He didn't know if there was any truth to the speculation that the bushwhacker thought he was dead. Again, all he could do was wait and hope he would get a chance to strike back somehow at the man who had tried to kill him.

Finally, after what seemed like a week but was probably just an hour or so, the horse stopped. By now, Chet had heard other hoofbeats and figured out that a rider was leading the horse he was on. Both mounts came to a halt as the hoofbeats fell silent. Saddle leather creaked as the other man swung down. Footsteps approached.

Something tugged at his wrists. Chet felt cold steel against his skin. The bushwhacker was cutting the rope that bound his wrists to his legs. As it came free, the man grabbed hold of Chet's belt at the small of his back and heaved. Chet slid off the saddle and fell hard to the ground.

He might have tried to break his fall with his hands, but he realized at the last second that if he wanted his captor to continue believing that he was either unconscious or dead, he couldn't do that. He had to go limp and stay that way.

Even so, his hands struck the ground first

because that's the way he came off the horse, and that blunted the impact slightly. His head and shoulders still struck the ground pretty hard, though. The pain in his head had subsided a little, but this fresh assault on his skull made more agony blossom like a flower opening up. He gritted his teeth to keep from crying out.

That resolve was tested even more a second later as the bushwhacker kicked him. Chet managed not to grunt as the boot toe dug into his ribs, but it wasn't easy.

The man walked off. Chet heard his footsteps. He didn't seem to go very far, but at least he wasn't looming over the wounded cowboy anymore. Chet lay there trying to gather what strength he could, breathing as shallowly as possible just in case the varmint did believe he was dead.

A loud *twang* suddenly split the air.

What in blazes?

A moment later, there was another *twang,* followed by another and another. By the time Chet heard the last one, he had realized what was causing the sound. That was tight-strung strands of barbed wire fence coming apart as they were cut. The bushwhacker had brought him back to some spot along the fence, and now he was cutting it for some reason that Chet couldn't fathom.

The footsteps returned. A man said, "You made

it easy for me, you dumb puncher. I figured I'd have to hunt down one of you Box RG hands, but you just rode right up to the fence and sat there waiting for me to shoot you, like you had a big target painted on you. This ought to set off some fireworks, me gunning you down right after I caught you cutting the Ace of Diamonds fence."

The voice was familiar, even though Chet couldn't place it right away. The words made it pretty obvious, though, that the man rode for the Ace of Diamonds and was trying to start more trouble between the two spreads.

"Reckon I'd better make it look a little more like self-defense, though," the man continued, acting like he was talking to Chet even though he was actually just musing to himself. "It's a good thing I picked up your gun after it fell out of your holster. I'll fire a few shots from it and drop it beside you, so it'll look like you were shooting at me when I dropped you." The man laughed. "Hell, since I've got to roll you over on your back, I'll put the last one right in your heart, just to make sure . . ."

Chet felt that boot toe nudge under his shoulder and knew this would be his last chance to maybe save his life. As the bushwhacker grunted with effort and started to roll him over, Chet surged up on his knees, wrapped his arms around the man's leg, and heaved.

● ● ●

Denny was looking for the waterhole when she
heard the sharp crack of a rifle shot somewhere
off to the east. She had found the fence, all
right, and was following it because she knew the
waterhole ought to be somewhere ahead of her.
She didn't think she could miss it.

She reined in when she heard the shot. There
was only one report. It didn't have to mean
anything, she told herself as she frowned.
Punchers carried rifles for a good reason when
they were out riding the range. It was common
to come across a varmint that needed killing,
whether it was a snake or a mountain lion or
even, on very rare occasions, a bear.

Denny couldn't tell which side of the fence
the shot had come from, Ace of Diamonds or
Box RG. Either way, she didn't particularly
want anybody catching her snooping around, so
when she heeled her horse into motion again, she
headed for some nearby trees. She would get out
of sight and wait for a while to see if anything
else happened, she decided.

By the time she reached the trees, she had
spotted the waterhole up ahead, just as she'd
expected. It looked like a hundred other waterholes, with nothing about it to indicate that it was
the source of so much trouble.

She moved into the shade under the branches
and waited, listening for another shot that didn't

come. The fact that she'd heard only one shot was a further indication that its origin was innocent enough. Just some cowboy shooting a rattler, more than likely.

Then a rider came in sight on the other side of the fence, following it toward the waterhole at a leisurely pace. The man led another horse behind his mount. Draped over the saddle and tied in place was a shape that Denny recognized.

The second horse was hauling a corpse.

Denny knew now that the shot she'd heard hadn't been aimed at a snake or some other kind of varmint. It had been aimed at the man who now hung limply over his saddle. But she had no idea who he was or why he had been shot.

She recognized the man leading the second horse with its grim burden, though. She had seen and talked with him earlier today, in fact.

He was Orrie Striker, the Ace of Diamonds foreman. But what was he doing on the Box RG side of the fence with a dead man?

Denny told herself that if she kept watching, she might find out.

Sure enough, Striker came to a halt a little farther on, when he was due south of the waterhole. He dismounted and dropped his reins, leaving the horse ground-hitched. The horse carrying the corpse had stopped, too, and stood there stolidly as Striker opened a clasp knife and used it to cut the bonds holding the dead man's arms and legs together underneath the horse's belly. The corpse slid off and thudded to the ground. Denny couldn't hear the impact, but watching the dead man land made her wince, anyway.

Denny's jaw tightened as she saw Striker draw back his foot and kick the corpse in the side. That was a pretty low-down thing to do, but after her earlier encounter with Striker, she wasn't really surprised. That coldness she had seen in his eyes had been positively reptilian.

Striker's strange and sinister behavior continued. He put away the knife and got something from one of his saddlebags. He went to the fence. Sunlight reflected off the metal object in his hand. The top strand of wire parted with a noise loud enough for Denny to hear it, even at a distance. Striker stepped back quickly to avoid the wire as it sprang and twisted.

He was cutting the fence. Why?

Striker worked with the wire-cutters until all four strands of barbed wire had leaped and coiled away to create an opening. He put the tool back in his saddlebag and then went to the corpse again. Was he going to drag the man onto Ace of Diamonds range? If the dead man was a Box RG puncher, Striker could claim that he'd caught him cutting the fence and shot him for that crime. Clearly, though, that wasn't what had happened. Denny's keen mind thought it much more likely Striker had ambushed the man. By setting it up to look otherwise, Striker was bound to cause more trouble between the two ranches . . .

Which was probably exactly what he was trying to do, Denny realized. She caught her breath as she wondered if *Striker* was the one who had bushwhacked the two Ace of Diamonds hands and killed one of them, sparking the battle a few days earlier.

That theory had just started to form in her mind as she watched Striker standing over the sprawled corpse. Then the Ace of Diamonds foreman started to roll the dead man onto his back . . .

And the "dead man" exploded into action, grabbing Striker's leg and throwing the man backward off his feet. The Box RG puncher, if that was what he was, tried to get up and go after Striker, who was already clawing at the gun on his hip. But the man Denny had taken for a corpse didn't have the strength to keep up the fight. He reeled and fell again and rolled, and Striker's gun swung toward him.

He would be a dead man for real in a matter of heartbeats. The only one who could prevent that was Denny. Without even realizing what she was doing, she had pulled her carbine from its sheath already. She brought the weapon to her shoulder and cranked off three rounds as fast as she would work the Winchester's lever, aiming over Striker's head . . . but not *too* far over.

Then she kicked her horse into a run, exploded from the trees, and galloped toward the fence.

CHAPTER 26

Chet Holloway figured he was looking the Grim Reaper right straight in the face for the second time today as he saw the gun in Orrie Striker's hand tracking toward him. He recognized Striker now and knew the man wouldn't miss again. Striker had a reputation as a killer. Every part of Chet's mind wanted to get up and make a fight of it, but his body just wouldn't cooperate. He had managed a brief moment of resistance, but that was all.

Then, before Striker could pull the trigger, shots blasted from somewhere nearby. Bullets whined through the air above Striker's head, close enough for Chet to hear them, too.

Striker's instincts must have kicked in when he realized he was under attack from a different direction. He twisted around on his knees to meet the new threat.

Chet stared, dumbfounded with amazement, at the rider galloping toward them from the north. Her hat had come off and hung behind her neck from its chin strap. Thick blond curls streamed out in the wind from her swift passage. She looked like an angel, thought Chet . . . an avenging angel on horseback, with a Winchester carbine in her slim hands.

He knew that only one gal in these parts looked like that: Denny Jensen, Smoke Jensen's daughter.

Striker must have recognized her, too, and hesitated because no man in his right mind, even a cold-blooded killer like Striker, wanted to take a shot at Denny Jensen and maybe have Smoke come after him to avenge his daughter's death. He didn't return Denny's fire, and that gave Chet just long enough to force his muscles to function again. He pushed himself up and lunged at Striker from behind, ramming his shoulder into the man's back in a diving tackle.

Chet was a good-sized young man. The impact drove Striker forward and smashed him facedown to the ground. The gun flew out of his hand. Chet's head was swimming, but he managed to plant a knee in the middle of Striker's back and pin him to the ground for a few seconds. Chet heaved his body up, clubbed his hands together, and brought them down on the back of Striker's neck. He hoped to knock Striker out with the blow. Hell, he wouldn't mind if he *killed* the son of a buck.

Chet just didn't have the strength for that at the moment. Striker groaned but heaved himself upward, arching his back and throwing Chet off to the side. Striker rolled the other way to put some distance between them. He came up on hands and knees and crawled toward the gun he had lost.

The swift rataplan of hoofbeats filled the air as Denny swept up to them. Striker's hand was only inches from the gun's butt when Denny's carbine cracked again. The bullet struck the Colt's walnut grips and shattered them, kicking the weapon farther away from Striker.

Denny had reined in just on the other side of the opening Striker had cut in the fence. She called in a clear voice, "Stay away from that gun, Striker! I'll be aiming at *you* next time!"

Striker's thin-lipped mouth twisted in a snarl as he looked up at her on horseback. "What the hell are you doing here, you witch?" he demanded. "You're still on Ace of Diamonds range!"

"And you're on Box RG range," she replied coolly, "about to murder a Box RG puncher, from the looks of it."

Striker pushed himself unsteadily to his feet. He had lost his hat, and his thinning, silvery hair was askew. His hatchet face was flushed with rage.

"I had every right to shoot him! He cut the boss's fence!"

"That's a damn lie!" exclaimed Chet. "Pardon my language, Miss Jensen, but that don't make what I said any less true. I never cut no fence."

The carbine in Denny's hands was rock-steady as she kept it pointed toward Striker. Without taking her eyes off him, she asked, "What's your name, mister?"

"Chet Holloway, ma'am."

"You're one of Mr. Gardner's hands?"

"I sure am."

"How bad are you hurt? No offense, but you look like somebody dumped a bucket of blood over your head."

Chet was a little surprised to feel himself grinning. He lifted a trembling hand to his head and found a long, sticky gash above his left ear.

"Head wounds always bleed like a son of a gun," he said. "Reckon that varmint creased me pretty good when he bushwhacked me, but I don't think my skull's busted. Hurts like the dickens, though."

"I imagine it does," Denny said. "Can you stand up?"

"I can try." Chet pursed his lips and whistled. His horse, spooked by the gunplay and the smell of blood, hesitated at first but then came over to him. He reached up, grabbed hold of the stirrup, and used it to brace himself as he hauled himself to his feet.

"What happened to you?" asked Denny.

Chet explained about how he had been looking for some straying stock when a gunshot had come from the brush on the north side of the fence and knocked him out of the saddle.

"Striker must've figured I was dead, what with all that blood," Chet went on, "so he threw me on my horse and brought me back here. He was so proud of himself for the plan he came up with that he was braggin' on himself to me, even though he thought I was dead. Said he was tryin' to make it look like I cut that blasted fence, then tried to shoot him. That was gonna be his story, that he gunned me down in self-defense. But he's the one who cut the fence."

"I know," Denny said. "I watched him do it. I'm not sure why, though."

"To stir up more trouble between the two spreads," Chet told her. "Like I said, he bragged about it. That got me to wonderin' if maybe *he's* the one who shot and killed that Ace of Diamonds puncher. That came mighty close to startin' a war, and that seems to be what he wants."

Denny said, "The same thought occurred to me."

Striker had stood there stony-faced and silent during the conversation between Chet and Denny, but now he spoke up, saying, "You can't prove any of this."

"I saw you cut that fence," Denny said again. "I can prove that much."

"And I know you shot me," Chet added.

"No, you don't, you dumb ox. You never laid eyes on me before you got shot, did you?"

"Well . . . no, I reckon not. But who else could've done it, and how do you know I didn't see you if you weren't the one who did it?"

That was some pretty complicated thinking, Chet told himself, especially for him.

Striker just sneered. He turned back to Denny and said, "Cutting a fence is against the law, but around here it's just a fine if you get caught. So you go ahead and tell whatever story you want, girl. I'll just deny it, and the worst you can do is get me fired."

Denny stared coldly at him for a moment, then said, "Maybe. But I'm betting if Mr. Mullen fires you and the law starts looking into what you've done, they'll find out what you've been up to. *And* they'll find out who you're really working for."

Panic flared up in Striker's eyes. Chet had moved forward enough that he could see the man's face while he talked to Denny. Striker suddenly had the look of a cornered animal. He really was involved in something crooked, and there was too much of a chance it would come out if the sheriff started looking into his activities.

In addition to that, Chet wondered if Striker was afraid of his real boss. The hombre would have to be pretty bad to affect an icy-nerved gunman such as Orrie Striker like that.

"You're not as smart as you think you are, witch," said Striker. "Maybe I'll just tell a different story, about how I came across this cowboy right after he attacked you and killed you, and I had to shoot him—"

"Hey, watch out!" Chet yelled as Striker's hand flashed to the small of his back with blinding speed. Chet saw the butt of the gun under the man's shirt and realized it had been hidden there all along. And he was fast, fast on the draw and fast on his feet as he lunged toward Chet, trying to use the cowboy as a human shield.

Striker never made it. Denny's carbine cracked. Striker twisted halfway around as the bullet ripped through him. He had yanked his hide-out gun from its concealed holster and managed to jerk the trigger, but the slug went harmlessly into the ground. The gun slipped from Striker's nerveless fingers before he could fire again. His knees buckled and he pitched forward. His fingers dug at the dirt for a second and then went still.

The echoes of the two shots were still rolling away across the valley when a rumble of hoof-beats welled up. Half a dozen riders emerged from the trees and pounded toward Chet and Denny. Chet hung on to his horse's saddle horn as the newcomers swept up, their hands bristling with guns. Denny sat calmly on her horse with the carbine's butt resting on her thigh and the barrel angled toward the sky. A tendril of powder smoke still curled from the muzzle.

Tony Mullen, at the head of the group, reined in, stared at Orrie Striker's body lying facedown on the ground, and exclaimed, "What the hell just happened here?" He swung his startled gaze to Denny and went on, "Miss Jensen, I think you've got some explaining to do."

• • •

As she looked around at the newcomers, Denny knew that despite being female—and Smoke Jensen's daughter—she might be in trouble here. Those Ace of Diamonds cowboys worked with Orrie Striker, and clearly, they knew she had just shot him. She saw some of the men ease their hands closer to their guns as they glared at her.

She didn't think Tony Mullen would allow things to get out of hand, though. At least, she hoped not. She said to him, "I'll be happy to explain, but I'd like it better if your men backed off some. They look a little proddy right now."

"She shot Orrie!" a young puncher exclaimed as he jabbed an accusatory finger at her. "Don't listen to her, boss. She's bound to lie about it."

"Be quiet, Jessup," Mullen snapped. "I asked the young lady a question, and I want to hear her answer."

Chet Holloway spoke up, saying, "She saved my life. Striker shot me and was gonna kill me."

Mullen regarded him coldly. "Seeing as how you ride for the Box RG, mister, I'm not sure you're helping Miss Jensen's case."

"You want the truth," Denny said, "and I'll give it to you. But I warn you, you probably won't like it."

"Go ahead," Mullen told her. "Start with why you're on my range."

"That's easy. My brother sent me out here to talk to you. I went to your house first, looking for you. You can ask your cousin about that. I talked to him."

"You spoke to Richard?" Mullen asked with a frown.

"That's right. I gave him the message I intended to deliver to you. Obviously, you haven't been back there since I left, so I'll go ahead and tell you, too. Louis wants to see you in town tomorrow morning, and you need to bring that new survey map with you."

"That map's locked up in my safe, and it's going to stay there where nothing can happen to it. I wouldn't put it past Gardner to try to destroy it." Mullen gave a little shake of his head. "But that doesn't explain what you're doing *here,* and why my foreman's lying there dead."

"I wanted to have a look at that infamous waterhole for myself." Denny shrugged. "I was curious. That's all. But then I heard a shot and decided to investigate."

She went on, describing how she had watched Striker ride up to the fence on the Box RG side, leading Chet's horse with the wounded and senseless cowboy draped over the saddle.

"I thought Holloway was dead," she said. "He was bloody enough that it was a reasonable assumption. But then, after Striker cut that gap in the fence, Holloway fought back. Striker was about to shoot him, so I fired some warning shots over his head. He turned to fire at me, but

Holloway tackled him from behind and kept him busy enough for me to ride up and get the drop on him."

"He cut the fence so he could frame me for doin' it and shoot me," Chet put in. "He bragged about how he was gonna do it and said that'd stir up more trouble between the two spreads for sure."

Mullen looked sharply at Denny. "Did you hear Striker say that?"

She shook her head. "No, I wasn't close enough at that point. But it makes sense. He'd already bushwhacked Holloway. He slipped up and pretty much admitted that when he said that Holloway couldn't have seen him fire the shot. And I saw him cut the fence with my own eyes. Put all that together, Mr. Mullen, and it's the only reasonable explanation."

The young Ace of Diamonds hand called Jessup burst out, "That's just loco, Mr. Mullen! They're just makin' stuff up to try to get out of killin' Orrie."

"How *did* Striker wind up dead?" Mullen asked as he looked intently at Denny.

"He had a hide-out gun and made a play for it when I said we were going to find out who he was really working for, *after* boasting that he was going to kill me and Holloway and frame Holloway for my murder. Does that sound like a man you want to defend?"

"You both heard him say that?"

Chet said, "My hand on the Bible, Mr. Mullen,

I sure did. Miss Jensen didn't have no choice but to ventilate him, because he sure as blazes meant to kill both of us."

"Boss—" Jessup began.

"Shut up, Quince," Mullen said. "I appreciate your loyalty, but Orrie Striker had a reputation as a man fully capable of doing such things. Just because he appeared to be staying on the right side of the law since he came to work for me doesn't mean he actually was."

"So you believe these two?" Jessup asked incredulously.

"I know Denny Jensen, and I know her father even better. Jensens aren't the type to lie."

Sensing that Mullen was coming around to believing her, Denny said, "Here's something else to consider. If Striker's been trying to stir up trouble between you and Roy Gardner, it's possible he's the one who bushwhacked your men a few days ago and killed one of them."

Mullen's forehead creased deeply as he thought about that. He turned to look at Jessup. "You said you never saw who fired the shot that killed Kimbrough, Quince."

"Well, no, I didn't, but . . . but . . . that don't mean—"

"The rest of you think back," Mullen said to the other cowboys. "Do any of you know for a fact where Striker was when Kimbrough was killed?"

Some muttering and murmuring went on. A

couple of the men shook their heads. No one spoke up to offer Striker an alibi.

Mullen looked at Denny again and said, "None of this will stand up in a court of law."

"No, it won't," she admitted. "But it all fits together, and I think you know that, Mr. Mullen. What you have to ask yourself now is who would benefit from a range war between you and the Box RG." Something else occurred to her, breaking in her brain with a flash like a ray from the rising sun. "Did somebody else suggest to you that the boundary might be wrong and that you ought to get a new survey done? Maybe even offer to help you with it by finding a good surveyor for you?"

Denny hadn't even told him yet that Edgar Padgett, who had made that new map, evidently didn't exist. That would be the next card to play, if necessary.

She didn't need to, because a stricken look came over Tony Mullen's face as he thought about what she had just asked him. In a hollow voice, he said, "Yes, as a matter of fact, someone *did* recommend that I look into the boundary. And he said that he knew a good surveyor because of his background as a geologist."

"Who would that be, Mr. Mullen?" Denny asked, even though she had a hunch she already knew the answer.

"My cousin. Richard Bristol."

CHAPTER 27

Louis had walked home for lunch with Melanie and Brad, and now he was back at work in his office. Half a dozen open law books were spread out on his desk as he used a pencil to make notes on a pad of paper. He jotted down a long list of citations from his research on cases involving property lines and surveys. He was going to be prepared when he went into court.

He heard hoofbeats and the sound of a buggy pulling up outside. The door was closed to keep out dust, so he didn't know what was going on until it opened and a tall man in a tweed suit and bowler hat stepped into the office.

Louis remembered him immediately. His visitor was Richard Bristol, Tony Mullen's cousin from somewhere back East who was visiting the Ace of Diamonds. Louis said, "Hello, Mr. Bristol. I wasn't expecting to see you again, but welcome to my office. Please, come in and have a seat."

"Thank you," Bristol said as he took off his hat and placed it on a corner of the desk not covered by law books. He sat down in one of the leather chairs.

Louis resumed his seat behind the desk and said, "I sent word to your cousin's ranch that I wanted to see him, but there was no need for you to ride into town, Mr. Bristol. And I didn't expect to see Mr. Mullen until tomorrow."

Bristol crossed his legs and rested his hands on his knees. "Yes, your lovely sister delivered the message to me when she didn't find Anthony at home. I'm afraid I wasn't fully forthcoming with her."

"Oh?" Louis said with some interest.

"Yes, I knew I was going to need to discuss this matter with you, so I didn't see any point in burdening her with it."

Louis shook his head and said, "I don't think I follow, Mr. Bristol."

"No, of course not. There's no reason you would. I've been talking matters over with Anthony, and we've reached an agreement whereby I'm going to purchase a half interest in the Ace of Diamonds from him. We'd like for you to draw up a partnership agreement."

Louis was surprised, but he tried not to show it. His clients had a right to do whatever they wanted, as long as it was within the law, and it was his job to facilitate those wishes. But he knew that Tony Mullen seemed to enjoy his life as a cattleman after spending most of his life as a gambler, and he wouldn't have expected Mullen to take on a partner. Of course, Bristol and Mullen were cousins, so maybe that had something to do with it.

"I can certainly do that for you," said Louis. "When do you need it?"

"This afternoon would be good."

Louis couldn't keep from frowning this time. "That's pretty fast, isn't it? And I'll have to have Mr. Mullen come into town, too, in order to execute the document. Or I could ride back out to the Ace of Diamonds with you."

"Neither of those things will be necessary." Bristol reached inside his coat and withdrew an envelope. "I have here a power of attorney signed by Anthony, giving me the right to negotiate and sign documents on his behalf."

Louis sat back in his seat. "That's rather irregular—"

"But allowable, under the law, I believe."

"Well, yes." Louis held out his hand. "Do you mind if I take a look at that document?"

"Of course." Bristol smiled and passed the envelope across the desk.

Louis opened it and took out the folded sheet of paper inside. He scanned the words printed on it in a neat, very readable script. It was a standard power of attorney. At the bottom were two signatures, those of Anthony Mullen and Richard Bristol.

"Everything is in order, I trust?" asked Bristol.

"It appears to be. It would be better if your cousin had been here with you and both of you had signed it in front of me, but that's not absolutely necessary. Colorado state law doesn't require either witnesses or notarization for a power of attorney, only the signatures of the two people involved."

"Which you have there," Bristol said.

"That's right." Louis started to fold the legal document again so he could slip it back in the envelope, but then he paused. "Let me just look at one thing here . . ."

Bristol leaned forward in his chair. "A problem?"

Louis's heart slugged hard in his chest as he studied the neatly printed words. He had noticed something about them, and a closer look made a realization burst in his mind that caused his pulse to jump.

But he forced a smile onto his face and refolded the power of attorney. "Just making sure it's dated properly," he said as he placed it back in the envelope.

"Isn't it?"

"Yes, it certainly is. Everything is in order." He handed the envelope back to Bristol.

"So you don't need anything else before you draw up that partnership agreement?"

"I just need to know the heirs for both of you, so that if anything happens to one of you, their share will go to the right person."

"Well, that's quite simple," Bristol said with a smile. "Anthony and I have no other living relatives, as far as either of us are aware, so the ranch would go to the surviving partner, of course."

"Of course," Louis said, nodding. "That *does* simplify matters. All right, I'll get started on this. But it's going to take a while, and you don't want to sit in this hot office while I'm working on it. Why don't you go somewhere more pleasant— I'd suggest Longmont's Saloon and Restaurant— and come back in, say, two hours?"

"Do you really think it will take that long?"

"To do it correctly, it will, and also, of course, I'll have to make more than one copy. You and Mr. Mullen will each want one, and there'll be a copy filed in the county clerk's office."

Bristol uncrossed his legs and stood up. "Very well," he said as he reached for his hat. "Longmont's, you said?"

Louis told him how to find the place. Bristol told him thanks, clapped his hat on his head, and left the office.

Louis sat back, placed his hands flat on the desk, and thought hard for a long moment.

Then he stood up and reached for his own hat where it hung on a hook behind the desk.

Tony Mullen told his men to load Striker's body on his horse and take him back to the ranch headquarters. Then he turned to Denny and said, "I want to talk to your brother."

"I'm sure he'll want to talk to you, too," Denny told him. "You and Louis can sit down and figure this out . . . without anybody else getting killed."

Mullen sighed. "I hope so. It's hard for me to believe that my own cousin would scheme against me like this, but with everything I've seen and heard today, I can't come up with any other explanation, either."

"I'm sorry, Mr. Mullen. But it's better to get to the bottom of it."

"Yes." Mullen looked over at Chet Holloway. "Can you get back to the Box RG all right? You need to get that head looked at."

"I reckon I can make it," Chet replied. "I'll just get my horse—" He swayed and had to grab hold of his mount's harness to hold himself up. "Maybe I *am* a mite light-headed."

"I'll send one of my men with you," said Mullen. "Your friends won't start shooting at him because he rides for the Ace of Diamonds, will they?"

"Not if he's with me, they won't. I'm obliged to you, Mr. Mullen."

Mullen rubbed his chin, grimaced, and said, "Well, if Gardner and I were set against each other under false pretenses, things need to be made right. And we can start by getting you home so you can be patched up, Holloway."

Mullen picked out one of his riders to go with Chet, then said, "Quince, you and Jordan and Larkin will come with me to town. I want to keep my eye on you."

"What do you mean by that, boss? Don't you

trust me? I'd never double-cross you like Striker did . . . if that whole crazy story really is true."

"I trust you, son, but I know you're a little on the hotheaded side. Until we figure out what's really been going on, you ride with me."

"Sure, if that's what you want."

Denny said, "I'll come with you to see Louis, too. There's actually something else about that survey you don't know yet."

Mullen groaned. "Something else to show how Richard played me for a fool?"

"Nobody's going to blame you for trusting a relative," Denny said. She turned her horse and fell in alongside Mullen as they followed the fence toward the trail leading to Big Rock. Quince Jessup and the other two Ace of Diamonds hands followed. "I'm just sorting it all out in my own mind, but I know that your cousin was playing a mighty deep game. I'm not sure why, though. How did he hope to benefit from starting a range war?"

"I don't know, but I'm going to get your brother and Sheriff Carson, and after we've talked it over, I intend to come back out here and get some answers."

That sounded like a good plan to Denny.

They could have crossed over onto Box RG range through the gap Orrie Striker had cut in the fence, but they waited instead to use the gate. Once on the other side, the trail was close by. Jessup rode ahead, opened the gate, and then pulled his horse aside so Mullen could go through first.

Mullen was about to do that when Denny spotted afternoon sunlight reflecting from something on top of a bluff about fifty yards away. Acting on pure instinct at the sight of that flash, she dug her boot heels into her horse's flanks and caused the animal to leap ahead and collide with Mullen's horse, which reacted with a lunge to the side.

Denny felt as much as heard the wind-rip of a bullet as it passed between her head and Mullen's, accompanied by the bark of a rifle shot. She knew that if not for her swift action, there was a good chance the slug would have drilled Mullen.

"Ambush!" yelled Jessup as he yanked his pistol from its holster. "It's the Box RG!"

Denny doubted that, but now wasn't the time to argue. Whoever was up there, he was trying to kill Tony Mullen, or perhaps even all of them. She pulled her carbine from the saddle boot and called, "Spread out! He's on the bluff!"

She lifted the Winchester to her shoulder and sent three rapid shots toward the spot where she had seen the sun glint off metal. More than likely, the reflection had come from the barrel of the rifle that fired the shot at Mullen. She figured the odds were pretty slim that she would hit the bushwhacker, but maybe she could distract him, make him duck for cover.

⚔ None of the four men with her would admit to taking orders from a young woman, but common sense was on Denny's side. They spread out as she had told them to, yanked out their guns, and blazed away at the bluff, too. The range was pretty far for a revolver, but not out of reach. Denny figured the ambusher had to have his head down by now, so she kneed her mount into a run and dashed through the open gate. Leaning forward in the saddle, she headed toward the bluff.

A muzzle flash and a puff of smoke from the top of the slope told her that the bushwhacker hadn't given up. The bullet kicked up dirt and dust to her right, too close for comfort. She veered the horse in that direction, thinking that the rifleman would try to adjust his aim the other way, and sure enough, more dirt flew to her left from a third shot.

She pulled the sure-footed cow pony farther to the right, trying to stay ahead of the bush-whacker's thinking. A slug whined past her. Given enough time, he would get the range.

Denny was closing the gap to the bottom of the slope pretty quickly, though. A few more seconds, and the bushwhacker wouldn't have a good angle on her anymore. Rifles cracked behind her. She knew that Mullen and the others had used the distraction she'd given them to pouch their irons and haul out their Winchesters.

She leaned back and slowed the horse as she reached the bottom of the bluff. She was out of the saddle before the animal stopped moving completely. Momentum carried her in a run to the bluff's base, where she pressed her back to the sandstone slope and craned her neck to look up.

The bluff's face wasn't sheer and was deeply scored by cracks. Denny knew she could climb it. She leaned her rifle against the sandstone, turned, and began the ascent, hoping that Mullen and the others would keep the bushwhacker pinned down until she could reach the top. If he appeared right above her, there would be no place for her to hide.

Lithe and athletic, Denny had little trouble with the climb, although she slipped a couple of times and had to hold on tightly with both hands while she found another foothold. The shooting continued, including sharp reports from the hidden rifleman above her and to her right.

Because of her tight-drawn nerves, reaching the top seemed to take longer than it actually did. When she got there, she ventured a look and saw a clump of trees and boulders about twenty yards to her right. A haze of powder smoke floating over the rocks confirmed that was where the ambusher was still forted up. His rifle blasted again.

Then, just as she pulled herself up and over and

rolled away from the brink, he burst out of hiding and dashed toward a bulky shape farther back in the trees that had to be his horse. He was giving up, lighting a shuck out of here.

Denny didn't intend to let him get away that easily.

Her roll carried her up onto one knee. She filled her hand with the Lightning and triggered the double-action weapon twice.

The fleeing man stopped short as the bullets smacked into the ground around his feet. He pivoted toward Denny and lifted the rifle he still held.

"Don't do it!" she shouted.

He ignored the warning and fired. The bullet flew wide past Denny. She didn't give him another chance. The Lightning blasted again. The bushwhacker rocked back with blood welling from his bullet-shattered right shoulder. He dropped the rifle, stumbled, and fell.

Denny leaped up and raced toward him. The way he was bleeding, he might die in a matter of minutes. Denny didn't intend to let that happen.

The man wore a handgun, but he seemed to be in too much pain to reach for it. He pawed at his wounded shoulder and whimpered. Keeping the Lightning trained on him, Denny reached down, wrapped her other hand around the hot barrel of the Winchester the man had dropped, and tossed the rifle farther way, well out of reach. She bent again, snagged the revolver from its holster on the man's hip, and flung it after the rifle.

"Miss Jensen! Denny!" The shout from Tony Mullen came from the bottom of the bluff. "Are you all right?"

"I'm fine," she called back, "but I could use a hand up here."

The bushwhacker continued to whimper and mewl as Denny stood a few feet away, keeping him covered. She wanted to stop the bleeding from his wound, but even though he appeared to be too badly hurt to put up a fight, she didn't trust him.

The young cowboy called Jessup appeared at the edge of the bluff, having scrambled up the slope first. He stopped short and exclaimed, "Baxter!" as he stared at the wounded man.

"One of the Ace of Diamonds hands, I suppose?" Denny asked dryly.

"Yeah, but . . . but . . ."

"But he just did his best to kill your boss, and the rest of us, too." Denny thought back to the events of a few days earlier. "Didn't you say there were two bushwhackers when you and that other puncher were attacked while guarding the waterhole?"

"Yeah, I reckon there were." Jessup shook his head. "I never dreamed one of 'em would turn out to be Baxter!"

"That's why a double-cross works. Nobody sees it coming."

Jessup had drawn his gun when he reached the top of the bluff and still held it, so Denny slipped her Lightning back in its holster and went on, "Keep him covered while I try to stop the bleeding from his shoulder. I don't want him dying before he can tell us the truth about who he and Striker were working for!"

CHAPTER 28

When Louis Jensen left his office, he headed toward Front Street. He wanted to talk to Sheriff Monte Carson. He wished he could ask his father about the theory that had formed in his mind, but Smoke was out at the Sugarloaf, and he didn't want to take the time to ride out there before approaching Monte.

If he was right, a man's life could be in danger, so he had to act as quickly as possible.

He turned the corner and started toward the sheriff's office but had gone less than a block when someone called his name softly from a narrow alley he was passing.

Louis stopped and looked into the shadows, then stiffened in shock at what he saw. Richard Bristol stood about ten feet away with his arm looped around Brad's throat, choking off any outcry. Bristol's other hand held a pistol jammed cruelly against Brad's head.

"Not a word, Jensen," Bristol said quietly. "Not a damned word. I've nothing to lose now, so I'll pull the trigger and kill the boy if you don't cooperate."

"Please—" Louis began.

"Shut up and listen to me. I know you've figured out what's going on with that survey.

That's why you sent word for Anthony to bring it into town tomorrow. Step into the alley where you won't be so noticeable."

Louis's heart was racing wildly again. He knew that wasn't good for him. He was supposed to stay calm and not exert himself too much.

But how could he remain calm when a man had a gun pressed to his stepson's head?

"I told you to step into the alley," snapped Bristol.

Louis found his voice. He had always been able to speak persuasively. That was one reason he had become a lawyer. He prayed that talent wouldn't desert him now.

"Take it easy," he said as he moved into the alley. He kept his hands in plain sight, not wanting to spook Bristol. "I'll do what you say. Just don't hurt my son."

"I've no intention of hurting anyone, but I have to prevent you from paying a visit to the sheriff. That *is* where you were headed, isn't it? Instead of working on that partnership agreement like you were supposed to?"

Instead of answering the question directly, Louis said, "You mean to use that agreement to steal the Ace of Diamonds from your cousin, don't you? Or is Tony Mullen even your cousin, really?"

"Of course, he is!" Bristol sounded annoyed that Louis would doubt the relationship. "We've known each other since we were boys."

"And yet you'd steal his ranch from him. Even kill him if that's what it takes to get what you want."

Bristol drew in a deep breath. "Sometimes a man is placed in a position where he's forced to make unpleasant choices. Such as making use of this lad to ensure your cooperation. I ran into him outside your office. He was on his way to see you, I believe. But I convinced him to show me around Big Rock instead. By doing that, I was able to keep an eye on *you* . . . and when I saw you leave your office and come this direction, I knew I had to act."

"You're a madman, Bristol." Louis couldn't hold in the outrage he felt at the sight of the gun being held to Brad's head.

Bristol didn't seem to take offense at the accusation. In fact, he smiled. "Not mad at all," he said. "Just desperate. There's a difference."

"What is it you want from me?" Louis asked.

"Come with me. Cooperate, and nothing will happen to you or this youngster. I give you my word on that."

Louis didn't believe Bristol was sincere, but his hands were tied. As long as Brad was in danger, he had to play along with the man . . . for now.

"Where are we going?"

"Follow me."

Bristol backed away, forcing Brad to come with him. Louis followed. He looked at the boy, locking his gaze with Brad's and trying to make him see that he would never allow anything bad to happen to him. Even if it cost him his own life, Louis would get Brad out of this.

They came to an open area behind the row of buildings. To one side was a large storage shed with a number of crates stacked in it. Louis gave it a moment's thought and figured out that the shed was behind a hardware store facing another street.

Bristol jerked his head toward it and said, "In there."

The shed had side walls and a roof but no front. Tall wooden fences with gates in them closed off the alleys on either side of the store. Even though they were in the middle of Big Rock, this was a small, isolated area where no one would be likely to see them.

Bristol pulled Brad into the shadows under the shed roof. The stacks of crates made it even gloomier in there. Louis followed them and asked, "What are we doing here?"

"We're going to wait right here, out of sight, and don't get any ideas about raising a commotion, Jensen."

Louis shook his head. "I won't. But I'd like to know why you're doing this. You don't strike me as a man who's trying to take over a ranch because he wants to raise cattle."

"Hardly!"

"Wait a minute," Louis said. The longer he could keep Bristol talking, the better. Also, his inquisitive mind really wanted to figure this out. "You said you're a geologist."

"That is correct."

"Everybody already knows there's gold in the valley. Conrad Morgan is mining for it, and my father had a gold mine on the Sugarloaf for a long time, even though it's not producing anymore. So it can't be gold you're after. If there was any on the Ace of Diamonds, it would have been found before now."

Bristol chuckled, which infuriated Louis even more, although he managed not to show it. How could the man laugh while he was holding a gun on a defenseless, innocent boy?

"Not regular gold, anyway," said Bristol.

That comment made no sense to Louis. There was only one kind of gold, unless Bristol was talking about fool's gold . . .

Then, suddenly, Louis realized he was wrong. There *was* another kind of gold that people had begun to seek out in recent years.

Black Gold.

"This is about oil," he said in a half-whisper.

"It is, indeed," Bristol admitted.

"You came here looking for it?"

"Not at all. I came to visit my cousin because I'm deeply in debt and I thought perhaps I could convince him to square that obligation with the very unpleasant people who are pressing me for payment. However, I hadn't been here for long before I realized that all the signs point to a substantial pool of oil underneath both Anthony's ranch and the property to the south."

"The Box RG." Louis felt a moment of annoyance with himself. "Now it's all starting to make sense! You tried to start a range war because you want to get your hands on both spreads."

"I was able to put off the men who threatened me by promising them a share of something much more lucrative," Bristol said. "If I'm correct in my assessment, we can all become rich men when that oil field is developed."

"But only if you take over those ranches." Louis shook his head. "You're going to have your cousin killed, aren't you? That's why you wanted me to rush on that partnership agreement. You planned to sign it for both of you, using your power of attorney, and then Mr. Mullen would die, leaving you to take over." Now that all the pieces of the puzzle were lining up in Louis's head, the words continued coming from him. "You'd blame his death on the Box RG, and this time the Ace of Diamonds crew would be so incensed that they'd wipe out Mr. Gardner and his men. Probably quite a few of them would be killed, too . . . which I assume would be all right with you, since you wouldn't need cowboys to pump oil."

"You're a very shrewd young man. I see now that I underestimated you. I wasn't worried about some inexperienced frontier lawyer—"

"And that's what caused you to overplay your hand with that power of attorney."

Bristol's mouth tightened under the mustache. "What was it about that that gave me away? I could tell by the look on your face while we were talking that I'd made a mistake. Really, Jensen, you need to control your expression better than that if you're going to be a good litigator."

"It was the writing. The same writing that was on the survey map where Edgar Padgett's name was. Because, I suppose, *you're* the non-existent Mr. Padgett."

Bristol's eyebrows drew down. "You know that there's no such person?"

"I do," Louis told him. "And so does my sister. So, before somebody else gets hurt or killed, my advice to you would be to let go of my son, put that gun away, and get out of Big Rock as fast as you can. I won't try to stop you." Louis drew in a breath. "Let go of Brad, and I'll even give you a head start before I talk to Sheriff Carson."

Brad's eyes widened. He couldn't say anything with Bristol's arm clamped across his throat, but he managed to shake his head just a tiny bit, telling Louis not to cooperate with his captor.

Bristol glared at Louis and said, "You act as if all my plans are defeated."

"As far as I can see, they are. You'll never get your hands on the Ace of Diamonds now, even if whoever's working with you succeeds in killing Mr. Mullen. There's no partnership agreement."

"But I *am* his only surviving relative, and he has no last will and testament. That should be enough for the estate to come to me." Bristol sighed. "As you said, I overplayed my hand with that power of attorney. I was just trying to make sure there were no slip-ups. No chance for anything to go wrong." He shook his head. "Ah, well. I'll simply have to do the best I can. Once Anthony is dead and the war between the Ace of Diamonds and the Box RG has wiped out everyone else—and it will, my associates will see to that—I should still be able to salvage the operation."

"I don't see how," said Louis. "With what I know . . ."

His voice trailed off as he realized that it didn't matter what he knew, at least as far as Richard Bristol was concerned. Because Bristol intended to kill him and always had, and he would kill Brad, too, since he couldn't leave a witness behind.

"Let's not forget your sister," Bristol said. "If she proves to be troublesome, I'm sure she can be dealt with, too. Now—"

"You can't shoot us," Louis said, hating the way his voice shook a little. "People will hear. You won't be able to get away."

"Turn around and back up closer to me. Do it now, Jensen."

Louis knew what the man intended to do. If he came close enough, Bristol could knock him out with the pistol, do the same to Brad, and then cut their throats, quietly and quickly. Louis had no doubt Bristol had a knife hidden somewhere on him.

So this was the end. No more cooperating in the hope that Bristol would spare Brad's life. Neither of them really had anything to lose anymore, because Bristol had planned all along to kill them. He had just enjoyed gloating for a few minutes first.

Bristol's patience ran out. He pulled the gun away from Brad's head and leveled it at Louis. "I'll risk a shot if need be," he rasped. "Get over here, Jensen. Now!"

He took his attention off Brad to threaten Louis, and his grip on the boy eased. Not much, but Brad was slippery and agile and didn't need much of an opportunity. He seized the one he was given and twisted loose just enough to reach Bristol's left wrist and bite down on it as hard as he could.

Bristol yelled in pain, tried to pull away, and then slashed at Brad's head with the pistol in his other hand. The blow never landed, because by that time Louis had launched himself across the space between them. He grabbed Bristol's gun arm, and a split-second later, his shoulder rammed into the older man's chest.

Brad was able to free himself completely as Bristol staggered backward from the impact. Without looking around at the boy, Louis clung to Bristol's arm and shouted, "Run, Brad, run! Get help!"

"Louis—" Brad began.

"Go!"

Louis heard Brad's rapid footsteps pelting away from the shed as he and Bristol lurched back and forth in the gloom. He let go of Bristol's arm with his right hand and hooked a punch into the man's stomach. Louis wasn't much of a fighter, but he had been in a few scuffles in his time. Not many, because of his poor health. But he was fighting for his life here, and that made a difference.

Bristol went, *"Oooff!"* as Louis's fist sunk in his belly. But Louis couldn't hang on with one hand, and Bristol tore his gun arm loose. He swiped at Louis's head with the weapon. The blow he landed was a glancing one, but it was enough to make Louis's head spin, and for a second, he was stunned.

Bristol tried to bring the gun to bear, but Louis slipped and fell and that took him out of the line of fire again. He wrapped his arms around Bristol's knees. Bristol's balance deserted him. He yelled in alarm as he went down.

Louis was vaguely aware of pain in his chest,

but he ignored it. His chest had hurt plenty of times in the past. It hadn't killed him yet. And if it did today . . . well, Brad was safe, and Louis would go out fighting, wouldn't he?

Like a Jensen.

He levered himself up and threw himself at Bristol. Both hands clamped around the wrist of Bristol's gun hand. Louis slammed it against the ground. The pistol slipped away from the older man. Louis drove his right elbow into Bristol's jaw and jerked the man's head to the side. With an awkward but effective lunge, Louis planted both knees on Bristol's chest and started hitting him. His fists rose and fell, smashing into Bristol's face each time they came down.

Louis had no idea how many times he had hit Bristol, only that the man's face was swollen and covered with blood, and so were Louis's hands, by the time somebody grabbed him under the arms from behind and hauled him off the geologist. Louis started to struggle and try to pull away from whoever had hold of him, but then a familiar voice said, "Stop that! It's all over, Louis. You got him."

Panting, Louis said, "D-Denny?"

"Yeah," his sister said. "If I let go of you, you won't go loco again, will you?"

"He . . . he held a gun to Brad's head. He said he was going to kill him."

"I'm not surprised. But he won't do anything like that now." There was a note of pride in Denny's voice as she added, "You saw to that, didn't you, brother?"

CHAPTER 29

Melanie tightened her arm around Brad's shoulders as she held him snuggled against her on the sofa in the parlor of their house.

"I still don't see how that terrible man ever thought he could get away with his plan," she said.

"Like a lot of men who turn to crime, he believed he could outsmart everybody," Sheriff Monte Carson said. He was sitting in a comfortable chair with a cup of coffee in his hand.

The room was a little crowded. Louis was on the sofa with Melanie and Brad. Denny was there, as well, in a chair by the fireplace, and so were Tony Mullen and Roy Gardner. Gardner had been summoned from the Box RG so Louis could explain to him everything that had happened and put the feud between him and Mullen to rest. Louis hadn't wanted to try to cram everyone into his office, so he had called the meeting for here at his home, instead.

"And he stood at least a chance of getting away with it," Louis said. "Enough of a chance that he felt like he had to risk it."

Frowning, Roy Gardner shook his head and said, "I'm still not sure I understand the whole thing. I get bits and pieces of it, but I'm having trouble puttin' it all together in my head."

With what Louis had learned from Denny, as well as Tony Mullen, along with the confessions from Richard Bristol and the wounded hardcase called Baxter, he had a pretty clear picture of the scheme in his head. He leaned forward, clasped his hands together between his knees, and said, "It started with Richard Bristol getting in financial difficulties back in St. Louis. He had a habit of gambling too much, among other things—"

Melanie cleared her throat and shot a warning glance toward Louis, cautioning him not to go into detail about Bristol's more sordid activities.

"And he wound up owing a lot of money to some pretty rough fellows," Louis went on. "They were pressuring him to pay it back and threatening him if he didn't. So he came out here to his cousin's ranch, hoping that he could hide out there or persuade Mr. Mullen to loan him the money he needed."

"I probably would have done it, too, if he'd asked," said Mullen. "I know what it's like to be in trouble like that. I might not have been able to raise enough cash to square his debt completely, but I could have gotten those men off his back for a while, anyway."

Denny asked, "How long had it been since you'd seen him?"

"Quite a few years," Mullen answered with a shrug. "But I knew him right away, and I was glad to see him. I don't have any other relatives."

"And that was what gave Bristol the idea of taking over the Ace of Diamonds," said Louis. "That was an especially attractive option once he looked at the terrain with a geologist's eye and saw that there might be oil under the ranch, as well as under your ranch, Mr. Gardner."

"I wouldn't know about that, one way or the other," the old cattleman said, "but what *good* is the blasted stuff?"

"They make fuel out of it and use it for a lot of other things," Louis explained. "They've been pumping it out of the ground back East in Pennsylvania and other places for quite some time now, and just in the past year or so there's been a big boom in it down in Texas and out in California. It's the coming thing, or so they say."

Gardner snorted. "Just a bunch of sticky, smelly, useless stuff to me."

"Richard Bristol really wanted to get his hands on it, though. So he came up with the idea of provoking a range war between the two of you. He hired Orrie Striker and Baxter to help him. He overheard some of the hands talking about Striker's reputation as a gunman and decided to approach him, and Striker brought Baxter in on the deal.

"That was the first step. The next was to convince you, Mr. Mullen, that the original survey was wrong and the boundary line between the two ranches should be a mile farther south. Once he'd stirred up suspicion in your mind, he volunteered to find a new surveyor for you . . . but he produced the survey map himself and made it look real."

"So there was never any Edgar Padgett," Mullen said.

Denny said, "That's right. I found out that much when I tried to track him down, and then Louis figured out Padgett was really Bristol when he saw the writing on that power of attorney."

"That was his overconfidence coming back to haunt him," said Louis. "It didn't occur to him that I'd recognize his writing after only seeing the survey map once." He smiled. "I'm pretty good about remembering details like that, though."

"All your life, all you had to do was look at something to remember it," Denny said. "That's how you got through school as easy as you did."

"I wouldn't say it was easy . . . but my memory certainly helped." Louis paused for a second, then continued, "The power of attorney was his undoing, all right, and the ironic thing is that it was unnecessary, as was that partnership agreement he wanted me to draw up. It was the third prong of a three-pronged plan. Striker was out trying to stir up another battle between the Ace of Diamonds and the Box RG by killing one of Mr. Gardner's hands and framing him for cutting the fence, and Baxter's assignment was to ambush and kill you, Mr. Mullen. If those two parts of the plan had succeeded . . ."

Mullen said, "The crews from the two spreads would have wiped each other out. Striker would have made it his mission to see that Roy died, for sure, leaving both ranches without owners."

Louis nodded and said, "That's how it was supposed to play out. That would have been enough for Bristol to take over the Ace of Diamonds and his partners to move in on the Box RG. But then he had the bright idea of forging the power of attorney . . . he really does have a deft touch with such things . . . and getting me to draw up a partnership agreement leaving everything to him if anything happened to his cousin. He didn't want to take a chance on anybody challenging his ownership in court." Louis shook his head ruefully. "But then he realized I was on to his scheme, and he felt like he was trapped in a corner. When he ran into Brad outside the office . . ."

"I'm sorry I went with him," Brad said. "He told me he was one of your clients, Louis, and said he was new in town, so when he asked me to show him around . . ." The youngster shrugged. "I didn't think there would be anything wrong with it."

"Of course, you didn't," Melanie told him. "But you have to be careful about trusting people."

Denny said, "You don't want to get to where you think everybody's out to double-cross you . . . but there's nothing wrong in being in the habit of figuring out what you'll do if there's trouble."

Brad nodded and said, "Yeah, I reckon so. Things always happen in Big Rock, don't they?"

Monte chuckled. "More than I like to admit, Brad. There's a lot more law and order than there used to be, say, twenty years ago, but the place isn't exactly tame yet."

Melanie said, "How in the world did that awful man believe he could get away with . . . with killing the two of you?"

"Aw, he never had a chance of that," Brad said. "I always knew Louis would stop him from hurtin' us."

"I appreciate that, Brad," Louis said, without mentioning that if the youngster was telling the truth, he'd been a lot more confident at the time than Louis himself had been. He continued in answer to Melanie's question, "If he had managed to . . . dispose of us . . . without any witnesses, it might have worked. No one else really knew that he'd paid a visit to my office or anything about what he asked me to do. He probably would have taken everything valuable so it would look like we were killed by a thief. It's unlikely anyone would have connected our deaths to Mr. Mullen being ambushed and killed on the same day."

"Except that Striker was dead, Baxter was

wounded, and we already knew what was going on," Denny pointed out.

With a smile, Louis said, "Ah, but Bristol wasn't aware of any of those things. He just knew he'd made a mistake, and he was trying to rectify it the only way he saw how."

"What will happen to him?" asked Melanie.

Monte Carson said, "He'll go to prison, him and Baxter both, not much doubt about that. Nobody was killed except that Ace of Diamonds hand, Kimbrough, and Baxter is telling anybody who'll listen that Striker actually pulled the trigger on that shot. Whether that's true or not . . ." The lawman shrugged. "I don't reckon it'll ever be proven, one way or the other. But Bristol and Baxter are accessories to Kimbrough's killing, plus there'll be charges of attempted murder against both of them. They'll wind up behind bars for a long time."

"And Bristol still has to worry about those fellas who have a grudge against him," Denny added. "They won't be happy when they hear about what's happened."

"Yeah, there's that, too," Monte allowed with a nod. "Bristol doesn't have much to look forward to except trouble . . . and that's the way it ought to be for a crook like him."

Tony Mullen sighed and said, "I don't disagree with anything you just said, Sheriff, but I remember what it was like when we were both boys, back in Missouri. It's a shame that things had to turn out this way."

"I reckon it is, sure enough," Roy Gardner said. "But it wound up with the two of us bein' friends again, I hope."

Mullen smiled and nodded. "Indeed, it did. I hope you can forgive me for starting all this trouble, Roy."

"For believin' what kinfolks told you, you mean? Shoot, I can't hold that against you. You've always been a fine neighbor, and I reckon you will be again."

"I'm certainly going to try. For starters, I'll have my men move that boundary fence back to where it really belongs, right away."

Gardner shook his head. "You might want to hold off on that for a little while. The waterhole's still in pretty good shape, and with the fence cut, my stock can get to it, too. No reason we can't share it for a spell."

"But if it doesn't rain—"

"We'll deal with that when the time comes."

Gardner stuck out his hand. Mullen didn't hesitate in reaching over to clasp it firmly. Both men nodded, and nothing else needed to be said.

"I'm glad that's settled," Louis told them. "Even though it looks like I don't have a client anymore."

"Oh, I wouldn't say that," Mullen responded. "Any legal work I need done from now on, you'll be handling it, Louis."

"Same here," Gardner added. "And I plan on tellin' all my friends that they ought to bring any legal needin's they have to you, too."

"Thank you," Louis said. "Word of mouth like that is the best endorsement any attorney can have."

"Just please," said Melanie, "no more trouble."

Denny laughed. "With the last name of Jensen, there's no guarantee of *that!*"

Conrad hadn't been in Blaise's Place since the run-in with Martin Delroy. He wasn't afraid of the gambler, certainly, but he also didn't see any reason to provoke trouble when it wasn't necessary. Longmont's was a much better drinking establishment, anyway, and Louis Longmont also had some beautiful young women working for him.

None as beautiful as Blaise, though.

Besides, Conrad was stubborn enough that he didn't want Delroy believing he had run him off. So this evening, even though it was against his better judgment, Conrad found himself pushing aside the batwings and strolling into Blaise's Place.

Two days had passed since Denny and Louis Jensen had uncovered the plot to take over two ranches in the valley and capitalize on the oil possibly to be found in the ground underneath them. Conrad had heard all about it and was very intrigued by certain aspects of the story.

The Browning Holdings had some small interests in oil production in Pennsylvania, and Conrad had given some thought to expanding into Texas. But if he could explore for oil right here in the valley where he was making his home at present, that might be even better. He needed to talk to Louis, who, he'd heard, represented Tony Mullen and Roy Gardner, about getting leases from the two ranchers and drilling a few test wells.

He had been thinking about that very thing as he walked over here, but such speculation vanished from his mind when he walked in and saw Blaise standing at the far end of the bar.

She was in dark green today and as lovely as ever. She spotted Conrad as soon as he came in and frowned slightly. He looked around the room and didn't see Martin Delroy. Not that he cared, Conrad told himself. He didn't want any more trouble with Delroy, but only because it might upset Blaise, not because he was afraid of the man.

Conrad walked along the bar until he came up to Blaise and nodded a greeting to her. "Good evening," he said. "It's nice to see you again."

"You shouldn't be here, Conrad," she said bluntly. "Martin told you to stay out, and, well, he does own the saloon."

Conrad shook his head. "I'll never be able to think of this place as his. You put your heart and soul into it, Blaise. It's yours by right."

"His money paid for it," she pointed out.

"You're married to him. It ought to be your money, too."

She blew out a breath and shook her head. "It doesn't work that way, and you know it. Besides . . . the circumstances are a little different when you knock someone out, take all the money, and disappear."

Conrad tried not to stare at her. "That's what you did?" he said.

Her chin lifted. "I'm not ashamed of it. I wanted to get away from him, and that seemed like the best way. But since it didn't work out . . . well, some things in life, you just have to put up with. He's my husband. Nothing's going to change that."

"You could divorce him."

"That seldom ends well for a woman. Besides, I'm not going to stand up in court and talk about everything that went on before. I'm just not."

He nodded and said, "That's your right. And if you really want me to leave . . ."

"No, stay a while," she said. "Martin probably won't be down until later. You can get a drink, maybe play some cards. But I'm going to mingle, so that I won't be talking to you when he *does* come down."

"Fair enough," Conrad told her.

She walked off, and Conrad signaled for the bartender to bring him a beer. He had just taken his first drink of the cool, foamy liquid when someone stepped up beside him and said, "Hello, Mr. Morgan. Good to see you again."

Conrad turned his head to see who had spoken to him but had to lower his eyes as he realized the newcomer was a head shorter than him. He recognized the mild-looking, bespectacled little man but couldn't recall his name. "Oh, hello," he said, hesitating before he went on.

"Hubert Osborne," the man supplied. He chuckled. "Don't worry. Almost everybody forgets my name. I'm not the most memorable sort of fellow."

"I wouldn't say that—" Conrad began.

"Then you'd be trying to be considerate of my feelings. It's all right, really. I'm accustomed to it, and it doesn't bother me. In fact, sometimes it comes in handy."

Conrad wasn't sure what Osborne meant by that, but he didn't press the man for an explanation. "Why don't I buy you a drink?" he offered instead.

Osborne smiled. "I won't turn that down. I know from experience that they don't have sherry here, but I can make do perfectly fine with whiskey."

Conrad laughed and said, "Whiskey it is, then."

Even though they were an unlikely pair, Conrad felt an instinctive liking for Hubert Osborne. They drank and chatted for a while, then Conrad asked, "Just what is it that brings you to Big

Rock, anyway, Hubert? What line of work are you in?"

"At the moment, I'm . . . at liberty, shall we say. Looking around for a likely situation."

"Do you know anything about mining?" Conrad thought he might offer the man a job in his office, since Osborne evidently didn't have one.

"Mining? Heavens, no. I don't know a thing, I'm afraid. But I think I know what you had in mind by asking that, and don't worry, I'm fine. I have an independent income."

Conrad nodded and said, "I know about that. I inherited some money. But I like working."

"I do, too, when the circumstances are right, which I believe they will be, very soon now."

Conrad didn't know what he meant by that, and before he could ask Osborne to elaborate, a harsh voice called his name and prompted him to look around.

Martin Delroy was coming down the stairs, a cigar clenched between his teeth at a jaunty angle and an unfriendly scowl on his flushed face.

CHAPTER 30

Conrad glanced around the room and spotted Blaise standing next to the roulette wheel with a worried look on her face. She stayed where she was and didn't try to head off Delroy as he reached the bottom of the stairs and started toward Conrad.

"Oh, dear," Hubert Osborne said softly.

"It's all right, Hubert," Conrad told him. "There's not going to be any trouble."

"I certainly hope you're right. I would prefer not to have to duck any flying bullets."

Despite the tension that gripped him, Conrad had to laugh at that comment. Then he suggested, "Why don't you sidle on down the bar, Hubert, just in case?"

Osborne threw back the half-inch of whiskey that remained in his glass and said, "I believe I'll do that."

Conrad faced Delroy squarely as the gambler came up to him. Delroy hooked his thumbs in his vest pockets. He didn't take the cigar out of his mouth but rather said around it, "I thought I told you that you're not welcome in this saloon anymore, Morgan."

"It's a free country, the last I heard," Conrad replied. "A man has a right to drink where he wants."

"A man also has a right to tell a troublemaker that he's not wanted and to stay out of his business."

"I don't plan on making any trouble. I was just having a drink with a friend."

"My wife—"

"Your wife is on the other side of the room, next to the roulette wheel. I spoke to her briefly when I came in, to be polite, but other than that I've left her alone. You can ask anybody in here about that."

"I'll take your word for it," Delroy said. "Blaise knows better than to tempt fate by giving in to her baser instincts. It's difficult for her, lacking in morals as she is."

Conrad had to hold down the anger that welled up inside him at that crude statement. Instead, he said, "If you want me to leave, I'll do so . . . for Blaise's sake."

Delroy seemed to think about the offer for a moment. Then he shook his head.

"That's not necessary. Go ahead and enjoy your drink. Hell, play poker or try your luck at roulette, if you want. Just stay away from my wife."

"I'll do that."

Delroy nodded curtly and turned away. He went to one of the tables where a poker game was going on, spoke to the men playing, and after a minute or so, when the hand was over, he took one of the empty chairs and sat down, obviously intending to join the game.

Hubert Osborne edged back up to Conrad and said, "Well, that appeared to go more smoothly than I thought it might."

"Delroy and I don't like each other, and we never will," said Conrad. "But I reckon we can get along if we try hard enough." He shrugged. "I suppose I'd better get used to him. From the looks of it, he's going to be around Big Rock for a while."

Conrad got another beer, then turned his back to the bar and rested his elbows on it as he watched the table where Delroy was dealing now. After a few minutes, a perverse impulse began stirring inside him. He drank the beer and told himself not to be crazy. But when he finished the mug, he turned and placed the empty on the bar.

"I feel like playing some cards," he said.

Osborne's eyes widened behind the spectacles. "You mean . . . ?"

"Why not? I want to try my luck, and Delroy, from what I've seen of him, is a pretty good poker player." Conrad grinned. "I like a challenge."

Osborne just shook his head dolefully.

For a few more minutes, Conrad watched the game from where he was. When one of the players stood up at the end of a hand, said, "You've cleaned me out, boys," and walked away from the table, Conrad straightened from his casual pose and moved to take his place.

He rested a hand on the back of the empty chair and said, "I believe I'll sit in for a spell."

Martin Delroy was seated on the other side of the table. He glared up at Conrad. The other players waited nervously to see what was going to happen.

After a moment, Delroy shrugged. "I suppose your money is as good as anyone's, Morgan," he said. "Sit down."

Conrad settled in the chair and asked, "What are we playing?"

"Stud poker," Delroy replied.

Conrad placed a stack of double eagles on the table in front of him and asked, "Is that enough for me to buy in?"

Delroy chuckled. "More than enough. And I'll be happy to take every last cent away from you."

"We'll see," Conrad said.

As usually happened, he got caught up in the flow of the game and momentarily forgot about the grudge he felt toward Delroy. Judging by the intent look on the gambler's face, Delroy felt the same way, more interested in the cards than he was in the resentment he felt toward Conrad. Delroy won the first hand Conrad played, but Conrad took the pot in the second hand. It continued that way, back and forth between them, with an occasional hand being won by another player. It was clear to anyone who knew anything about poker, though, that Conrad and Delroy were the best players at the table.

Delroy had finally lit and smoked the cigar he'd been chewing on earlier when he came downstairs. He slid another cheroot from his vest pocket, snapped a match to life on his thumbnail, and held the flame to the cigar's tip. When he had it going to his satisfaction, he inhaled, blew out a large cloud of smoke, and said, "Why don't we raise the stakes, Morgan?"

"That's fine with me," Conrad said. He was pretty sure he had more resources at his command than Delroy did, although he might not have as much cash in his pocket.

One of the other men spoke up, saying, "Well, it's not all right with me. I've lost enough to you already tonight, Delroy, and if you're raising the stakes, I'm out."

"So am I," another man said. Then he added, "But if you and Morgan are going to turn this into a real high stakes battle, I wouldn't mind staying and watching."

"That's what I'm thinking, too," the remaining player said. He raked up the little pile of cash in front of him, put the money in his pocket, and leaned back in his chair.

Delroy smiled and asked, "Still willing to play if it's just the two of us, Morgan?"

"Of course," Conrad replied without hesitation.

"Then we'll make the ante . . . a hundred dollars?"

"Why not make it two?" suggested Conrad.

That brought a curt nod and a "Fine" from Delroy.

Conrad had enough cash and coins in front of him that he was able to push a stack of ten double eagles into the center of the table. Delroy had won the last hand, so he dealt.

Conrad wasn't, by nature, a conservative player, but he took more chances, bluffed more, counted on luck more in this game than he normally did. He knew Delroy would feel compelled to match him, and that was exactly what happened.

The two of them still appeared to be evenly matched, splitting the hands, but the pots when Conrad won tended to be slightly bigger. As more of the saloon's customers gathered around the table to watch the game, the pile in front of Conrad slowly grew larger. The tension in the air thickened. Delroy puffed harder on the cigar now tightly clamped between his teeth. When he announced his bets, he spoke around it.

Conrad stole a glance at his current hole card, even though he knew perfectly well what it was. They had been betting a hundred or two at a time, but now he picked up some of the greenbacks in front of him and said, "I'll raise five hundred."

That brought impressed murmurs from the spectators.

The tip of Delroy's cigar jumped a little as his teeth clenched harder on it. "You must be mighty sure of your cards," he said.

"Sure enough," Conrad replied.

"I'll see the five hundred . . . and raise a hundred." Delroy shoved coins and bills into the pot.

Conrad eyed the money and said, "I'm not sure there's that much there."

"There's not," snapped Delroy. "It's two hundred short. But I'll give you my marker for that amount."

"All right. Go ahead and do it."

Delroy scowled and called to the bartender to bring him a pencil and paper. When the crowd parted, though, it was Blaise who came to the table.

She dropped the pad of paper and a pencil in front of Delroy and said, "Why don't you put a stop to this while you still can, Martin? You're not proving anything."

"I'm not trying to prove anything. Morgan and I are just enjoying a friendly game of cards." Hate glittered in his eyes as he looked across the table at Conrad. "Isn't that right, Morgan?"

"Just a friendly game of cards," Conrad repeated. His tone was every bit as cold as Delroy's.

Delroy tore off a piece of paper, scribbled on it, and then tossed that onto the pile in the center of the table. Conrad nodded slowly and said, "So that's six hundred to me. I'll see it . . . and raise a thousand."

Delroy bit through the cigar. It fell on the table in front of him. He snatched it up and crushed it in his hand, not even flinching as he extinguished the glowing coal at the end of it. The shreds of tobacco dribbled down. He turned his head and spat out the butt.

"Think you're so damned smart . . ." he rasped.

"No." Conrad saw how pale and drawn Blaise's face was, and he didn't think he was smart at all. He had allowed his pride to push him to this . . . and now that pride wouldn't allow him to back away. "If you can't cover the bet—"

"I never said I couldn't cover the bet. My marker is good."

Delroy printed another IOU and added it to the pot. Conrad glanced regretfully one more time at Blaise, then leaned forward to count the money that was in front of him.

"That adds up to eight hundred," he said. "I'll write a bank draft for seventeen hundred more and make it two thousand five hundred."

Breath hissed in and out through Delroy's clenched teeth. "I don't have that kind of money."

"You have this saloon," Conrad suggested coolly.

"Conrad, no!" exclaimed Blaise. She turned to her husband. "Martin, don't—"

A wave of Conrad's hand stopped her. No matter how much animosity he felt toward Delroy, he realized he couldn't do that to Blaise.

He asked Delroy, "What *can* you handle without wagering the business?"

For a couple of seconds, Delroy didn't answer. Then he said, "Another thousand, on top of what's out there."

"All right. We'll let it go at that. My bank draft will be for two hundred."

"Write it!" barked Delroy.

Conrad chuckled. "I happen to have one in my pocket. If I can borrow your pencil . . . ?"

He took out the folded piece of paper and wrote on it. As he tossed it into the pot, he glanced up and saw Hubert Osborne in the crowd, watching him. Osborne grinned, clearly enjoying himself.

Conrad slid the pencil back across to Delroy, who wrote one final IOU and added it to the pot. "I call," he said.

"You have four diamonds showing," Conrad said to Delroy. "I'm guessing that fifth card will be another one."

Delroy turned it over. The card was a lowly two . . . but it was a diamond.

"And I have two pair, sevens and fours." Conrad was enjoying himself now, and Delroy could tell it. The gambler looked sick, even before Conrad turned over the third four to make a full house.

"Sevens and fours," muttered Delroy. "Sevens and fours!"

"They got the job done, didn't they?"

For a second, Conrad thought Delroy was going to come up out of the chair and lunge across the table at him. His muscles tensed, readying to meet that potential attack.

But then Delroy slumped back in his chair and shook his head. "A damned four," he said hollowly. He drew in a deep breath, let it out in a sigh. "All right. I'm a professional enough to admit it when I'm beaten. You've taken the hand, Morgan. This time." He tossed the deck on the table. "It's your deal. Give me a chance to win it back."

"No, Martin," Blaise said. "Let this be the end of it. Please."

Conrad stretched his arms out and gathered in the pot, including Delroy's IOUs. "You don't have anything left to wager except the saloon," he said, "and I'm not going to take that away from Blaise. So the game is over. As soon as we settle up, that is."

Tiny beads of sweat had popped out on Delroy's tanned face. A vein jumped in his throat. It was obvious that being humiliated like this infuriated him. But there was nothing he could do about it, short of accusing Conrad of cheating. Conrad believed he saw it in Delroy's eyes when that thought crossed the man's mind. The accusation wouldn't stand, though, not with so many witnesses crowded around the table who had watched both players' every move. To level a charge like that would just belittle Delroy even more in everyone's eyes.

"Well played," he said. "If you'll come upstairs with me, Morgan, I'll get the rest of your money."

The crowd was starting to disperse already, now that the game was over. Conrad scraped his chair back and stood up. "All right."

Delroy rose to his feet. "Just one thing first," he said. "Once I've paid you off, I don't want to see you in here again. If you set foot in this saloon, I'll kill you."

That bold but flat-voiced statement made the customers around the table stare at Delroy in surprise. Blaise paled even more, making the small beauty mark near her mouth stand out sharply.

Conrad regarded Delroy coolly. "This isn't the first time someone has threatened to kill me. It isn't even the first time *you've* threatened to kill me. But I'm still kicking. Just pay me and save the empty words."

Delroy jerked his head toward the stairs and then started in that direction, not looking back to see if Conrad was following him.

Blaise put a hand on Conrad's arm and said quietly, "Please, no more trouble."

He smiled at her and shook his head. "I'm just going to get the money he owes me. That's all."

"He's a proud man. Too proud sometimes."

"Not too proud to treat you badly," he pointed out.

"Everyone has flaws. I'm not trying to excuse what he's done, not at all, but I don't want *either* of you getting hurt."

"Don't worry," he assured her. Then he followed Delroy up the stairs.

The gambler had already disappeared into the living quarters at the end of the hallway. The door stood open. Conrad went in and found Delroy standing beside a small writing table.

"Close the door," said Delroy.

"So there won't be any witnesses when you shoot me?" Conrad asked with a mocking smile.

"Just close the damned door," Delroy snapped. "Nobody's going to shoot anybody. I just don't like to reveal all my secrets to anybody who could be looking in."

Conrad glanced over his shoulder. "There's nobody out there in the hall."

"You never know when someone will step out of one of those rooms."

Conrad shrugged and took hold of the door. He pushed it up until the latch clicked. He did that without turning his back on Delroy, since he didn't trust the man as far as he could throw him.

Delroy reached in his vest pocket and brought out a small key. He unlocked the drawer in the writing desk and opened it. He started taking cash out of it, counting the bills as he made a small bundle out of them.

"That's what I owe you," he said. He placed the

bundle on the writing table next to a small but sharp-looking letter opener, closed the drawer, and relocked it. "I have enough left to continue operating . . . barely."

"Contrary to what you may think, Delroy, I didn't set out to break you."

"Maybe not, but you came damned close."

Conrad's voice hardened. "You can thank your wife that I *didn't* wipe you out."

Delroy glared at him with murder in his eyes for a long moment, then rasped, "There's your money. Take it and get the hell out."

He turned and stalked to the door on the other side of the sitting room. He jerked it open, vanished into the bedroom beyond, and slammed the door behind him.

Conrad picked up the stack of bills from the table, folded them, and wedged them into a pocket. Then he left the room, closing the door firmly enough behind him that Delroy would know he was gone.

Most of the eyes in the saloon's main room swung toward him as he came down the stairs. Blaise had moved back over to the end of the bar. Conrad joined her, well aware that the rest of the customers were watching him.

"Have a drink with me," he suggested.

"I don't think so," she said. "Did you get your money?"

"I did."

"Martin told you to leave. Your business here is done."

"I'm not so sure about that," Conrad said. "You really deserve better than him, Blaise."

"Like you, you mean?" she snapped.

Conrad thought about Denny Jensen. He shook his head and said, "No, despite what your husband believes, I really do consider you just a friend, Blaise. A good friend. And as such, I hate to see you trapped in such a bad situation."

She laughed and then repeated bitterly, "I deserve better, you say."

"That's right, you do."

"Well, Conrad . . . you don't know what I deserve. You don't know what I've done in my life."

"I don't care—"

She stopped him by shaking her head. "Have one more drink if you want—on the house—and then please leave and don't come back."

He drew in a sharp breath. "So that's the way it is."

"That's the way it has to be."

"All right." He looked at the bartender. "Whiskey."

The man poured the drink and set it in front of him. Conrad picked it up and turned to Blaise, intending to drink to her one final time, only to see that she was gone. She was walking up the stairs, no doubt heading for the suite she shared with Martin Delroy. Conrad watched until she disappeared along the balcony and into the corridor.

Then he muttered, "So be it," and threw back the drink. As he set the empty glass on the bar, the batwings swung open. Conrad glanced in that direction and saw Brice Rogers come into the saloon.

The deputy marshal was the one who was going to have to give up his ambitions regarding Blaise, thought Conrad. Brice was the one who had actually had hopes of having a future with her. Maybe he ought to warn the young lawman that he was wasting his time, mused Conrad . . .

At that moment, a horrified scream came from upstairs and ripped through the hubbub in the saloon, leaving a stunned silence in its wake.

CHAPTER 31

With no assignments taking him out of Big Rock, Brice Rogers had been around town for several days, but he'd been avoiding Blaise's Place during that time. With Blaise's husband showing up out of the blue like that—and being such an unpleasant hombre, to boot—Brice figured it would be better to avoid her, even though that was a discouraging decision. He had believed they were on the verge of growing close, only to have that potential relationship snatched away.

Tonight, he had given in to a disturbing impulse. He had decided to pay a visit to the saloon and try to catch a moment alone with Blaise. If he was going to give up on the idea of there ever being anything between them, he needed to hear it from her lips that there was no hope.

He heard something from Blaise's lips as soon as he pushed the batwings aside and stepped into the saloon, all right, but it wasn't what he expected.

Instead, her throaty, unmistakable voice came from somewhere upstairs in a scream that made Brice's heart lurch in fear that something had happened to her.

He charged toward the stairs, shouldering past several of the stunned customers on the way. As he passed the end of the bar, from the corner of his eye he saw Conrad Morgan standing there, but he didn't slow down to wonder what Conrad was doing in Blaise's Place. Brice knew that Martin Delroy had warned Conrad to stay out of there after their recent clash.

Brice took the stairs three at a time, bounding up them. Blaise hadn't screamed again, but at this point, Brice didn't know what that meant. He heard footsteps pounding behind him on the stairs and, when he reached the top, glanced over his shoulder to see that Conrad was hot on his heels.

"Stay back!" Brice ordered. "You're not the law!"

"But you might need my help," Conrad countered. He ignored Brice's command and didn't slow down. In fact, his greater height and longer legs allowed him to catch up, so the two young men were side by side as they reached the open door at the end of the hallway.

They couldn't go through at the same time, so they came to an abrupt halt there in the doorway with Brice's left shoulder jammed against Conrad's right shoulder. They stared into the suite's sitting room. The faces of both young men displayed the shock that they felt.

Blaise stood on the other side of the sitting room, next to the chair that sat beside the writing table. Martin Delroy was sprawled in that chair with his legs stretched out in front of him, his arms hanging limp at his sides, and his head tipped back against the wall at a slightly odd angle. That angle was a result of the fact that a gaping wound stretched across his throat. The whole front of Delroy's shirt and vest was sodden with blood, like a red curtain that hung down from his ruined throat.

The letter opener that had caused the hideous wound was still stuck in Delroy's neck on the right side.

Blaise turned toward Brice and Conrad. Brice had never seen her as pale as she was at this moment. Her eyes were open so wide they seemed about to leap from their sockets.

Conrad found his voice and exclaimed, "Good Lord, Blaise! What have you done?"

She stared at him. It took her a moment before she was able to speak.

"I didn't do this," she declared in a quavering voice. "I . . . I never . . . He was like this when I came in here! I found him this way! You know I didn't have time to do this, Conrad. You were with me downstairs. You know that! I never could have overpowered him, anyway."

Conrad nodded, then moved back a step and gestured for Brice to go into the room ahead of him.

Instead, Brice rested his right hand on the butt of the Colt at his hip and said, "No, you go first, Morgan."

The implication was clear, and Conrad flushed angrily at it. "You don't think *I* did this?" he said.

"I don't have any idea who did it," said Brice, "but I'd rather keep you where I can see you, anyway."

Conrad's jaw tightened, but he didn't say anything else. He stepped into the room. Brice followed him.

"Blaise, maybe you'd better step back away from your husband," Brice suggested. "I don't reckon there's any chance he's still alive, so there's nothing you can do for him now."

"Nobody who's lost that much blood is still alive," said Conrad. He added, "I'm sorry, Blaise," when she flinched at his words.

Blaise moved over to the loveseat, sank onto it, and covered her face with her hands. She didn't sob, but clearly she was shocked, even if she wasn't necessarily grieving over Martin Delroy.

Footsteps in the hall made Brice glance around. The bartender and several of the saloon's customers had gathered their courage and come upstairs to see what had happened. They were gawking through the open doorway at the bloody spectacle of Delroy's corpse.

Brice backed to the door, keeping an eye on Conrad as he did so, and told the gaping onlookers, "Somebody fetch Sheriff Carson. You'd better send for the undertaker, too. He'll be needed."

Then he pushed the door shut, closing off the grisly scene.

"Look, Brice, you know me well enough to know that I wouldn't cut a man's throat like this," Conrad said.

Brice shrugged. "It does seem more likely you'd shoot a man, if it came to a showdown, and give him an even break, at that. But there's a saloon full of people right downstairs. A shot would draw a lot of attention. Killing a man with a knife is usually a heap quieter."

"That's not a knife," Conrad pointed out. "It's a letter opener." He grunted, then went on, "Not that it really makes much difference, does it? It's still a blade, and Delroy's throat is still cut."

"Yeah. Have you been downstairs all evening?"

"No." Conrad's voice was a little hollow. "I was up here with Delroy a little while ago."

"What were you doing in here with him?"

"Collecting money he owed me from a poker game." Conrad pulled a folded wad of greenbacks from his pocket and showed it to Brice. "He got the money out of the drawer in that writing table. Now that I think about it, that's where the letter opener was, too, lying on the table."

"So you admit you knew the letter opener was there?"

"Damn it, Brice!" exclaimed Conrad, apparently exasperated. "You know I'm not a murderer."

Blaise finally lowered her hands from her face and looked up at the two men. "But who else could have done it?" she asked. "I'm sorry, Conrad, I really am, but you were up here with him for several minutes, and then you came downstairs and I came up here and . . . and found him. I just don't see how anybody else could have killed him."

"From what I've heard, neither do I," Brice agreed.

Conrad opened his mouth, probably to protest again, but before he could say anything, the door opened and Monte Carson came in. He closed the door quickly behind him, looked at the scene, and shook his head.

"The fella who came and got me said it was pretty gruesome in here, and he wasn't lying," the sheriff said. "That's Martin Delroy, isn't it? Your husband, is that right, Miss Warfield?"

"Yes," Blaise said, her voice hushed. She looked down at the floor. "It's Martin."

"Did you kill him?"

"No!" Blaise's head jerked up. She looked aghast at the question.

"We were just talking about that, Sheriff," Brice said. "From the sound of it, the only one who had the opportunity to kill Delroy was Morgan here."

"Conrad?" Monte looked and sounded surprised.

"I didn't do it, Sheriff," Conrad told him.

"Delroy was alive and well when I left out of here a little while ago. At least, I assume he was. He had gone in the other room and closed the door after telling me to get out."

"What were you doing in here to start with? I thought you and Delroy didn't get along."

"We didn't," Conrad said. He sketched in the details of the poker game and the big final pot he had won from Delroy. "He brought me up here so he could get the rest of the cash to pay me," Conrad concluded. "Blaise saw all of this. She can confirm what I'm telling you. There are probably at least a dozen men downstairs who can, too."

Monte rubbed his chin and frowned in thought. "I don't doubt what you're telling me, son," he said, "but all you've really done is admit that you were alone here with a man who hated you . . . and who had threatened to kill you just a few minutes earlier. It's kind of a logical thing to think that maybe you decided not to give him a chance to but figured you'd get rid of him first."

Conrad shook his head. "That's not the way it happened."

"Maybe not, but we're going to have to look into this killing and get to the bottom of it. While we're doing that . . . I don't see that I have any choice but to arrest you, Conrad."

Conrad stiffened. His hand wasn't far from the butt of the gun at his hip.

"I know you used to be known as Kid Morgan,"

Monte went on, his voice soft. "I know you're mighty fast. But I was a pretty good hand with a gun myself, and Brice is slick on the draw, too. It would be mighty long odds for you to get both of us before one of us got you. Besides, Miss Warfield is right here. You don't want to put her in danger by throwing lead around the room. And if you really are innocent . . . the best thing you can do is let us investigate and prove it."

Conrad's mouth twisted in a grimace. "Yes, lawmen always say that, don't they? But you're right." He lifted his hands and held them well away from his gun. "I'm not going to endanger Blaise. And I *am* innocent."

Monte nodded and drew his Colt. "I'm glad to see you're gonna be reasonable. Turn around."

When Conrad had done so, Brice moved forward, being careful not to get in the sheriff's line of fire, and snagged the broomhandle Mauser from the holster on Conrad's hip. He backed away, holding the German pistol.

"My jail's not nearly as comfortable as what you're used to, I imagine, but I'll do my best to see that you're not too miserable," Monte went on. "And the town has an arrangement with Lambert's to provide meals for prisoners, so you know the food's good."

"Yes, I'm thankful for that," Conrad said dryly over his shoulder. "Can I put my hands down and turn back around now?"

"Sure, go ahead."

Conrad did so. He looked at Blaise, who still sat on the loveseat, and said, "I give you my word, I didn't kill Delroy. But from what I know about the man, I can't say that he didn't have it coming."

"That's enough," Monte said. "Come on now. Brice, you mind clearing out the crowd?"

"Not at all, Sheriff." Brice drew his gun and went first out of the suite, raising his voice and telling the curiosity-seekers who had gathered in the second-floor hallway, "All right, move on downstairs, folks! Back off and clear out!"

Conrad came out with Monte following him, gun in hand. Lots of startled conversation rose from the crowd as Brice prodded them downstairs and then out of the way. He cleared a path to the batwings and went through them, then covered Conrad as he emerged from the saloon.

"There's something you can do for me, Sheriff," Conrad said as the three men turned toward the jail and some of the crowd followed them out of the saloon.

"What's that?" asked Monte.

"I'm going to need a lawyer." Conrad looked around at the sheriff. "I'd appreciate it if you'd send someone for Louis Jensen."

Louis was sitting at the kitchen table with Brad. A chessboard was set up between them, with the black and white pieces scattered across it. Louis had taught the boy to play while they were back East, and Brad had gotten fairly good at it. He had an attitude that was unusual in a youngster, in that he didn't mind losing all that much. As he had told Louis, he learned something from every defeat.

Louis was confident that in a few years, Brad would be able to do more than give him a good game. Louis would be doing well to keep up with him.

Brad moved a knight now and said, "Check."

Louis angled a bishop in from the other side of the board and took the knight. "And that's check," he said.

Brad frowned at the pieces, lifted a hand and used a finger to trace movements in the air, and then looked up at Louis. "You'll have me in checkmate in two more moves, and there's nothing I can do about it, is there?"

Louis smiled and shook his head. "I'm afraid not."

"You trapped me!" Brad was grinning as he said it, though, to show that he wasn't upset.

"Maybe," Louis admitted.

"I'm going to remember that move," Brad said as he put a fingertip on his king and tipped the piece over. Louis's chest swelled with pride at the boy's aplomb.

That was much better than the pain that had

filled his chest a few days earlier, when he'd been tussling with the murderous Richard Bristol. Thankfully, those twinges had receded and hadn't troubled him since.

Someone knocked on the front door, the rapping clearly audible in the kitchen.

A puzzled frown replaced Louis's smile. It was pretty late for someone to be calling. He scraped his chair back and came to his feet.

Melanie was in the parlor doing some needlework. He heard her footsteps as she went to the door to answer the knock. Louis suddenly felt a surge of alarm. He wasn't expecting any trouble, but sometimes it came calling with no warning. As the son of Smoke Jensen, he knew that.

"Melanie, wait," he called as he started toward the front of the house. "Let me get it."

He was too late, he saw as he looked up the hall to the foyer. Melanie stood at the door, swinging it open.

Relief washed through Louis as he recognized the tall, angular man standing there, hat in hand. He stepped up beside Melanie and asked, "What can we do for you, Deputy Chadwick?"

The deputy, who worked for Monte Carson, said, "The sheriff just brung in a prisoner and locked him up, and the fella's askin' for a lawyer. You in particular, Mr. Jensen. So Monte sent me to fetch you."

"At this hour?" said Melanie, frowning in disapproval.

"I'm afraid that's part of being an attorney," Louis told her. "It's like being a doctor. You have to be available twenty-four hours a day, whenever someone needs your help." He looked at the deputy again. "What's this prisoner done? Gotten in a fight? Public drunkenness?"

"No, sir. He's bein' charged with murder."

"Murder!" Melanie said.

"Who in the world . . . ?" Louis said.

"It's Mr. Morgan, sir. You know, that fella who owns all the mines and railroads and such-like," said Deputy Chadwick. "Conrad Morgan."

CHAPTER 32

Big Rock still had the same sheriff's office and jail that had been built when the town was founded, back in the wild days when the settlement was established as an alternative to the outlaw town of Fontana. The building had been expanded a couple of times as the town grew. The cell block was larger now. But it was empty tonight except for one occupant.

Conrad Morgan sat on the bunk in his cell and listened as footsteps echoed hollowly, coming toward him.

Monte Carson appeared, carrying a ring of keys. Behind him was Louis Jensen, wearing a suit but no hat, indicating that he had come to the sheriff's office in a hurry.

"I'll let Louis in there to talk to you," Monte said. "You're not gonna try anything funny, are you, Conrad?"

"You know better than that," Conrad said. "I came along peacefully, Sheriff. I'm placing my faith in the legal system." He sighed. "I hope it doesn't let me down."

"It won't," Louis said. He stepped into the cell as Monte opened the door. The sheriff closed it behind him.

"Sing out when you're ready to go," Monte told him.

Louis nodded. "Thanks, Sheriff."

When Monte was gone, Conrad stood up and said, "Take the bunk, Louis. It's more comfortable than that stool, even if only more marginally so."

"No, I'm all right," Louis said as he sat on the three-legged stool on the other side of the cell. He waved Conrad back onto the bunk and went on, "Tell me what happened."

"I didn't kill Martin Delroy, that's what happened."

"I'm sure you didn't, but I need all the facts of the case."

Conrad nodded and launched into a recital of the evening's events. From time to time, Louis interrupted him to ask for more details. The young lawyer listened with intensity shining in his eyes.

When Conrad was finished, Louis asked, "When you came back downstairs after getting the money from Delroy, you stood at the bar talking to Miss Warfield for several minutes?"

"A few minutes," said Conrad. "I don't know that I'd call it several. Two or three would be more like it."

Louis nodded. "During that time, did you see anyone else go up to the saloon's second floor?"

"I've been thinking about that very thing. That

would mean another suspect." Conrad shook his head. "But that's not what happened. I'm sure no one went upstairs between the time I came down and Blaise went up."

"And you're convinced she couldn't have killed him when she went upstairs?"

Again, Conrad shook his head. "It wouldn't have taken long for Delroy to bleed to death, but I just don't think she had the time to do it. On top of that, there's the matter of her not being able to overpower him."

"She could have taken him by surprise and stuck the letter opener in his throat."

"But he would have fought back," Conrad insisted. "He wouldn't have just sat down in that chair, let her cut his throat the rest of the way across, and then peacefully bled to death."

"Peacefully," repeated Louis. "That brings me to my next question. Could you tell from the room if there had been a struggle?"

Conrad frowned, thought about it, and said, "Didn't look like it to me. Nothing was really out of place, as far as I remember."

"When you and Brice came into the room, did Miss Warfield have any blood on her hands or clothes?"

"No. I'm certain of that." Conrad leaned forward on the bunk. "That's another point in her favor, isn't it? If she'd fought with Delroy, she would have gotten some blood on her."

"We're looking for points in *your* favor," Louis pointed out with a faint smile. "And since the sheriff brought you here straight from the room where the murder took place, and I assume you haven't washed up or changed clothes, the lack of blood on *you* is a very good thing."

"Maybe . . . but I have a longer reach than Blaise. I might have been able to avoid the blood when it came out. Or, if I'd gotten behind Delroy, I could have cut his throat from that angle while I was holding on to him. I would have gotten some blood on my hands, but that's all. And I could have washed it off before I left the suite. I'll bet there's a basin in the bedroom." Conrad smiled and shrugged. "Just playing Devil's advocate, you know."

"Leave that to the district attorney," Louis advised. "But it could be an important point. I need to check and see if there is indeed a basin in that bedroom, and if it had been used to wash off any blood."

"The killer might have gone back and cleaned all that up by now."

Louis nodded. "Unfortunately, you're right. When I leave here, the first thing I need to do is take a look at the scene."

"Don't you have a wife and son at home? You don't want to be out half the night investigating a murder."

"Making sure my client has the best possible

defense is my job," Louis said. "I assume that you *are* going to hire me?"

"You're damned right I am, counselor. You can name your fee."

"We'll talk about that later. Is there anything else you can think of that you haven't told me?"

Conrad thought that over for a long moment and then shook his head. "I believe you know as much as I do, Louis."

"Let's hope that'll be enough." Louis stood up from the stool. "One more thing. What happened to Delroy's body?"

"Sheriff Carson told the bystanders that someone should fetch the undertaker. I assume the man has come and picked it up by now."

"Then I need to hurry," Louis said. He turned to the iron-barred door and called, "Sheriff!"

Louis had to knock several times on the front door of Big Rock's undertaking parlor before he heard it being unlocked on the other side. He had seen a light burning in the back, so he was certain someone was here.

A balding, middle-aged man opened the door. Like most men in his profession, Simon Rone had an affable, unflappable air about him, even in the middle of the night. Enough light spilled through the door for him to recognize the man who had knocked.

"Louis Jensen!" he said. "What in the world?"

Alarm suddenly appeared on his face. "Nothing's happened to any of your family—"

Louis held up a hand to forestall the question. "They're all fine, as far as I know," he said. "I don't need your services, Mr. Rone. I'm here about the body you picked up a short time ago from one of the saloons."

"From Blaise's Place?" Rone nodded. "That's right. I believe the man's name is Delroy. He was married to the woman who owns the saloon." Rone cocked his head to the side, clearly puzzled. "Are you representing her?"

"No, but I'm involved in the case," replied Louis. He didn't go into detail. He didn't think that Monte Carson would forbid him to examine Delroy's body, but he hadn't asked the sheriff's permission, either. He had come straight here instead. "You haven't started the embalming process, have you?"

Rone grunted. "No, I'm still cleaning up the, ah, deceased."

"I'd like to take a look at him, if that's all right."

"Well . . . it's kind of a funny thing, if you ask me, but I don't see any reason why you shouldn't. It's not like the sheriff told me not to let anybody in."

Rone stepped back and opened the door wider. He ushered Louis through the darkened front room and down a hall into a large room at the back where the smell of chemicals and a lingering hint of decaying flesh made Louis wrinkle his nose.

He could see now that Rone wore a thick canvas apron. Louis nodded toward it and asked, "Do I need one of those?"

"Not unless you intend to be my apprentice and help with the work."

Louis shook his head. "No, I don't think so." He had to swallow hard as he looked at a sheet-draped form lying on a table. "I suppose that's Mr. Delroy."

"The only customer I have at the moment." Rone moved to the side of the table, grasped the sheet, and pulled it back enough to reveal Martin Delroy's head, shoulders, and part of his chest.

Louis wanted to take a deep breath, but he realized that probably wouldn't be a good idea, even though Delroy's corpse hadn't had time to start decomposing yet. The undertaker had cleaned it up to a certain extent. The gaping wound in the throat was still quite visible, though, and some dried blood still remained around it.

"What happened to the weapon that killed him?" asked Louis.

"It's right over there," Rone said, pointing to a table sitting against a wall. Louis moved closer and looked down at the letter opener. The blade was about four inches long and had quite a bit of blood dried on it. The letter opener had a plain wooden handle.

"This is basically a knife," Louis commented.

Rone shrugged. "A dagger, more like. And it's not sharp enough to cut a lot of things. An envelope, sure. A man's throat, for somebody who's strong enough. But I wouldn't want to try to saw through a rope with it."

"There's no doubt this is what was used to kill Delroy?"

"Not in my opinion. It was still stuck in his neck. And if you look at the edges of the wound, they're a little ragged, indicating that it took some force to cut through there, like I said."

"You don't think a woman could have done it?"

Rone shook his head. "Very doubtful. It would take a man of normal strength, at least."

That was one more factor ruling out Blaise Warfield as the killer, mused Louis. And one more finger pointing at Conrad Morgan, who was a muscular, powerful young man.

"Are there any other wounds on his body?"

"No." Rone pulled the sheet the rest of the way off. "You can see for yourself."

Louis flinched and was annoyed at himself for doing so. Delroy's pale, flaccid nudity was an all too obvious reminder of mortality. Louis's medical history meant that he always walked a little more in the shadow of death than most people, but most of the time he managed not to think too much about that. To be standing where he was gave him a glimpse of his own certain fate, and he didn't like it.

But he was here to do a job. He had a responsibility to his client. So he stepped closer and looked over Martin Delroy's corpse. There were some fading bruises from the fight with Conrad several days earlier, but as the undertaker had said, there were no other actual wounds—but the one in Delroy's throat was more than enough.

"How long would it have taken him to die?" Louis asked.

"He would have been unconscious in, oh, a couple of minutes, I'd say, and dead a couple of minutes after that."

Louis nodded, deep in thought . . . so deep that he didn't hear Rone's next question, and the undertaker had to repeat himself.

"I asked, do you want to see his back, too?"

"Might as well, I suppose," Louis said, although he actually didn't want to. Being thorough was part of being a good attorney, he reminded himself. More than one of his professors had stressed thoroughness and diligence in preparing a case.

Rone gripped Delroy's right shoulder and thigh and rolled the corpse onto its left side, then stepped back so Louis could get a better look. Louis turned his head as he studied the body from head to toe. He pointed to a tiny red spot on the back of Delroy's neck and asked, "What's that?"

"Flea bite," Rone responded. "Either that or a bedbug. There are several bites like that on him." He pointed to similar marks on Delroy's back and hips.

"All right. I've seen all I need to see. I appreciate your patience, Mr. Rone."

"I'm glad to help, Louis," the undertaker said as he lowered the corpse onto its back again. "Are you defending Conrad Morgan? When I picked up the body, I heard talk about how Monte had arrested him for the killing."

"That's right."

"Well, I wish you luck. From what I heard, most people already seem to believe that he's guilty. *And* that Delroy probably had it coming." Rone pulled the sheet up. "Me, I don't judge anybody. As far as I'm concerned, folks are all the same by the time they get to me."

The next morning

"What the hell were you thinking?"

Monte Carson looked up from his desk, glared, and said stiffly, "I beg your pardon, young lady?"

Denny paused just inside the door she had thrown open. She closed her eyes for a second, drew a deep breath as she tried to control her emotions, and went on, "I'm sorry, Sheriff. I was rude and out of line just now. I'm just surprised that you'd believe Conrad Morgan is a murderer."

Monte pushed back his chair. Morning sunlight flooded into the sheriff's office, and it threw Denny into silhouette as she stood in the doorway. Her hat was hanging behind her head by its chin strap. The light made a golden halo of her blond curls.

"I never said I believed he's a murderer," Monte told her. "That's for a judge and jury to decide. But as far as I can see, he's the most likely to have killed Martin Delroy, so I had to take him into custody. I've already received word this morning from the district attorney in Red Cliff that Conrad will be charged and tried, said trial to commence Monday morning."

"Monday—" Denny choked out. "This is Friday!"

"The law calls for a speedy trial whenever possible, out of fairness to the defendant so he doesn't have to stay behind bars for any longer than necessary."

Denny stepped farther into the office and pushed the door closed behind her.

"And it couldn't be that the district attorney wants to move as fast as possible because Conrad is a rich, important man, and he knows putting someone like that on trial will get him a lot of publicity, now could it?"

Monte shrugged. "It's true there'll be an election this fall, and the district attorney is standing for re-election. A lot of stories in the papers about the conviction of a man as well-known as Conrad wouldn't hurt a fella's chances, I reckon."

Denny blew out a disgusted breath. "Trials are supposed to be about the law, not politics. I've seen enough back East and in Europe to know that it doesn't always work that way, though. I just thought that out here in the West, it would be better. More honest."

"People are people, no matter where you are."

"And politicians are politicians." Denny sighed. "At least Conrad has a good attorney in his corner."

"I know. Your brother. Are you going to help him out with this case, the way you did with that trouble between the Box RG and the Ace of Diamonds?"

The question surprised Denny a little. She answered honestly, "I don't know. I haven't talked to Louis this morning. I just overheard some of the Sugarloaf hands who were in town last night talking about how Conrad was arrested for murder. I jumped on a horse and rode right in." She nodded toward the door into the cell block. "Can I see him?"

"I don't see why not." Monte stood up and took a ring of keys from a peg on the wall. "I can't let you into his cell like I did with Louis, though. Have to do that when a fella's lawyer is visiting him, but not with a . . . uh . . ."

"Just say friend, Sheriff," Denny said, to save Monte from his embarrassment over not knowing what, exactly, she was to Conrad Morgan.

That was understandable, she thought, because she didn't know—exactly—herself.

CHAPTER 33

Conrad had heard Denny's voice through the small, barred window in the cell block door, so he wasn't surprised when Monte Carson brought her back to see him.

"Hello, Conrad," she said as she came to a stop in front of the cell door. He was waiting for her on the other side, with his hands gripping the iron bars.

"It's good to see you," he told her.

"Uh, Denny," Monte ventured, "I'd feel a mite better if you'd give me your gun. I hate to ask, what with you being Smoke's daughter and all, but, well, rules are rules . . ."

"It's all right, Sheriff," she said as she slipped the Colt Lightning from its holster and extended it to him butt-first. "I understand. And so would Smoke."

Monte took the gun and nodded. "Let me know when you're ready to go." He walked out of the cell block and closed the door behind him.

Conrad put a hand through the bars and held it out to her. Denny took it and moved closer. Their eyes met and they stood there silently for a moment, until Conrad cleared his throat and let go of her hand.

"Did Louis send you to see me? Do you have any word from him?"

"Dang it, why does everybody think I'm here because of that blasted brother of mine? I just heard you were in trouble, that's all, and I wanted to see for myself that you're all right."

Conrad smiled and gestured at his surroundings. "As all right as I can be, given the circumstances, I suppose. The sheriff promised me the food would be good, and he was right. Breakfast this morning was excellent. Lambert's has the best rolls I've ever eaten."

"I think you have more important things to worry about than breakfast. If you're found guilty of murder, there's a good chance you'll hang."

Conrad shook his head. "I'm not going to be found guilty, because I didn't kill Martin Delroy."

"Surely you're not naïve enough to think innocence is a guarantee of being found not guilty."

Conrad shrugged and said, "I have to believe so. Otherwise, it would be too easy to give in to despair . . . and I'm not the sort to do that."

"No," Denny said slowly. "No, I know that you're not." She squared her shoulders. "I'm going to go see Louis and find out what he's planning to do. Is there any message you want me to give him?"

"No, I can't think of anything. I know he'll do his very best for me."

"He'd damned well better," muttered Denny. "He'll know that if he doesn't, I'll kick his scrawny rump from here to Cheyenne!"

Conrad laughed and said, "I believe you would, too." He grew more serious as he extended his hand through the bars again. "Denny."

She took his hand and let him pull her closer. Their faces moved to the bars and were only inches apart, then their mouths came together in a kiss. It was awkward with the bars between them, but they managed. They managed quite well for a long, passionate moment . . .

Then Denny stepped back and said, a little breathlessly, "I'll be around."

"Good," Conrad told her.

"Your trial may start as soon as Monday, you know."

That news rocked Conrad a little. He hadn't heard that until now.

"But Louis and I, we won't let it," Denny went on. "We'll have you out of there by then, one way or another."

She went to the door and called for Monte Carson to let her out of the cell block. She was gone before Conrad got his wits back about him enough to wonder what she'd meant by that comment about getting him out of there "one way or another."

Where Denny Jensen was concerned, he realized, you never really knew what she was capable of . . .

Louis looked up as his office door opened and Brice Rogers walked in. He hadn't been expecting to see the deputy U.S. marshal. He leaned back in his chair and said, "Hello, Brice. What brings you here?"

"I came to see you about Conrad Morgan."

"I believe we're sort of on different sides of that case, Marshal. I'm supposed to keep Conrad from being found guilty, and you're supposed to convict him."

Brice took off his hat and shook his head. "Not exactly," he said. "Murder's not a federal offense, so I'm not actually involved in the case. I just gave Sheriff Carson a hand with the arrest because he's a fellow lawman."

"Professional courtesy," Louis said.

"Yeah, you could call it that."

"And the fact that you and Conrad don't get along very well, because of my sister, had nothing to do with it."

Brice turned his hat over a couple of times in his hands, then said, "You can get that idea out of your head, Louis. I might've had some feelings for Denny in the past, I won't deny that, and I still consider us friends, but I don't reckon we were really cut out to be more than that, no matter how much it seemed like fate kept trying to throw us together."

"Is that so?"

"Yeah, it is, and you can believe it or don't, that's up to you. But I'm not holding any grudges against Conrad Morgan, because of Denny or anything else. All the evidence that I could see told me he killed Martin Delroy. That's all there was to it."

Louis sensed that there was something else Brice wanted to say. "But now you feel differently?" he prodded.

"I don't know." Brice gestured with his hat toward the chairs in front of the desk. "All right if I sit down?"

"Of course," replied Louis. He waved a hand at the chairs. "If you have something on your mind about the case, I want to hear it."

Brice settled into the chair to Louis's left, but before he could say anything else, the door opened again. This time it was Denny who came in, all in a rush, but she stopped short at the sight of Brice sitting there.

"You!" she practically spat out.

Brice started to his feet. "Denny—"

"You arrested him," she interrupted as she came forward, scowling darkly at him. "Did that make you feel good, Brice?"

"It didn't make me feel a bit good, if you want to know," he shot back as he stood up and faced her.

"Did you follow him into the saloon hoping he'd get in trouble and you could do something to hurt him?"

"No. As a matter of fact, I didn't follow him or even know he was in there. I went to see Blaise."

Denny blinked a couple of times and drew in a sharp breath. "Oh."

Louis said, "Why don't both of you have a seat and calm down? I get the feeling that all of us want to help Conrad, so why don't we stop arguing, put our heads together, and see what we can come up with?"

Brice nodded and Denny shrugged. They took their seats, although Denny glanced suspiciously at the young lawman a couple of times.

"I guess somebody must have carried word to the Sugarloaf about what happened," Louis said.

"Some of the hands were in town last night and were talking about it in the barn this morning," Denny explained. "That's how I found out. I don't really know any of the details, though. I stopped at Monte's office and saw Conrad for a few minutes, but we didn't, ah, didn't really discuss the case against him . . ."

Louis was a little surprised to realize that Denny was blushing. Only faintly, but a pink flush was visible in her face. In his experience, Denny had always been pretty much shameless about most things. Maybe whatever feelings she had for Conrad Morgan were genuine.

"You were there, Brice," he said. "Why don't you tell Denny what happened?"

Brice looked somewhat reluctant, but he spent the next few minutes filling her in on what he knew about Martin Delroy's killing. Louis listened as intently as Denny did, hoping that Brice might have thought of something else that could prove helpful. Brice laid out the sequence of events exactly as he had the night before, though. He had a lawman's good eye for detail.

When Brice was finished, Louis said, "I talked to Conrad, and he tells the story the same as you do, except that he insists Delroy was alive when he left the suite."

"Conrad's not a liar," said Denny. "Whatever he told you is the truth, Louis."

"I agree with you." Louis paused. "I also paid a visit to Mr. Rone's undertaking parlor last night."

Brice frowned. "You went to take a look at the corpse? Why? It was as plain as the nose on anybody's face that Delroy died from having his throat cut."

"That's right. He had to still be alive when he suffered that wound, or else he wouldn't have bled so much. The heart stops pumping at the moment of death."

Denny said, "That makes sense, I suppose."

"However . . ."

That caused Denny and Brice to look at Louis with renewed interest.

"There were several marks on Delroy's body that made me curious." Louis touched the back of his neck. "Here, and a couple of places on his back, and a few more of them lower down on his hips."

"Are you talking about wounds of some sort?" asked Brice.

"Mr. Rone said they were insect bites. Fleas or bedbugs."

Denny said, "In a saloon like that, I wouldn't be surprised by any kind of vermin."

"Now, that's just not fair," Brice told her. "Blaise runs a clean place."

Before Denny could argue or say anything else disparaging about Blaise, Louis said, "I haven't quite figured it out yet, and those marks may turn out to be nothing at all, but like I said, they made me curious. I also wonder why there were no signs of a struggle in the room. Delroy was a good-sized man. I don't doubt that Conrad could have overcome any resistance he put up, but there should have been some signs of it. From all appearances, Delroy just allowed someone to cut his throat and then sat there and bled to death."

"It doesn't make sense, that's for sure," Denny said. "If Conrad's the only one who had the opportunity to kill him—"

"But he wasn't," Brice broke in. "That's one thing I came to talk to you about, Louis."

Louis sat forward and clasped his hands together on the desk. "What do you mean? Conrad himself said that no one from the saloon went upstairs between the time he came down and Blaise went up to discover the body." He glanced at Denny, thinking that she might be about to speak up. "And it's not possible for Blaise to have killed her husband, for several different reasons."

"Nobody went up the stairs there in the saloon," said Brice, "but I walked by there this morning on my way here. The sitting room and the bedroom both have windows."

"Yes, but they're on the second floor," Louis pointed out, "and there's no balcony. I noticed that when I went by the saloon last night, after visiting the undertaker. Miss Warfield allowed me to take a look around the suite."

"What were you doing there?" asked Brice.

"Checking to see if there was a basin in the bedroom where the killer could have washed the blood off his hands. There was . . . but no sign that the killer used it for that purpose."

"That doesn't matter," Denny said. "There's a window, and somebody could have gotten a ladder and climbed up there. That's what's important. Conrad said Delroy went into the bedroom as he was leaving. The killer was waiting for him in there!"

Brice nodded. "That's exactly what I'm thinking." He looked at Louis. "Isn't that enough?"

"To create reasonable doubt in the minds of a jury?" Louis spread his hands. "I'll admit, that angle hadn't occurred to me, and it's certainly feasible. But it still leaves the question of who else had a reason for wanting Delroy dead other than Conrad and Blaise, not to mention the somewhat odd manner of his death. If you're going to establish enough reasonable doubt for a juryman to vote to acquit, you have to give him more than vague possibilities, or a shadowy, anonymous *someone* who might have done something. You have to give him an alternative explanation for the apparent facts of the case, or else show that the facts are wrong or incomplete."

"You make it sound like nobody's ever found not guilty," complained Denny.

"Not at all. But we have to have solid answers for as many of the questions as possible."

"And we don't have much time to find them. Monte said the trial may start Monday! That's loco."

Louis nodded and said, "I know. I'm going to file a motion later today to postpone the case for a month. I won't get that, but I might get a week or two."

Brice said, "While you're doing that, I'm going to ask around town and see if I can find anybody who might've seen something suspicious around the outside of the saloon last night. That's a longshot, I know, but I'm not sure what else to do."

"What do you want me to do?" Denny asked. "I helped you with that other case, Louis. I know I can help you with this one, too."

Louis shook his head. "Honestly, I can't think of a thing. I suppose you can try to keep Conrad's spirits up. Let him know that we're working on his behalf."

"But . . . but there's got to be something else I can do!"

"I'm sorry, Denny. Right now, there's just nobody for you to shoot."

CHAPTER 34

When folks in the valley got up on Sunday morning, the sky was overcast, and the air felt heavy and oppressive. In every one of Big Rock's churches, the minister made some comment during the service about how maybe the Good Lord was going to see fit to bless them with some rain at long last. The increasingly parched ground could use it, and so could the thirsty livestock and the crops that people hoped to get in during the fall. As congregations walked out of the churches when the preaching was over and gathered in clumps to visit with their friends and neighbors for a spell before heading home, the men looked at the sky, gauged the chances, and nodded solemnly to each other.

But as the afternoon wore on, the clouds thickened some but withheld any life-giving moisture they might be carrying.

In the cell block of Monte Carson's jail, Conrad sat on the bunk with his back propped against the stone wall. The air in the place was stifling. Every so often, Conrad lifted his arm and sleeved beads of sweat from his face.

Denny had been to see him several times over the weekend, including today right after she and her parents had attended church. She had looked beautiful in her Sunday best, but the time they had spent together had been strained and awkward. Denny was frustrated, Conrad knew. A part of her wanted to bust him out of here. Denny believed in direct action. She had suppressed the impulse so far, though.

He hoped she wouldn't stop back by today. It was too miserable in here. Just because he had to suffer didn't mean that she ought to, as well.

Earlier, she had assured him that Louis was working practically around the clock, trying to figure things out. The judge had denied his motion to postpone the trial, which was scheduled to begin at nine o'clock Monday morning. The district attorney from the county seat in Red Cliff had pushed that through. He intended to prosecute the case himself, Louis had told Conrad. A conviction would be quite a feather in his political cap.

Friday afternoon, after Louis had delivered that news, Conrad had written out some wires for him to send. The Browning Holdings had attorneys in Denver, and a couple of them would be on hand by the time the trial started. Conrad had also sent for Claudius Turnbuckle, but it would take longer for him to get here from San Francisco.

After handing the message to Louis, Conrad had said, "I want you to understand something, Louis. *You're* still my lawyer. You can use these other attorneys to help you, but they don't know the case, and they don't know the people involved." He had smiled. "With the exception of Claudius, who's an old friend, none of them know *me* as well as you do. We're just business associates. So my trust, my faith, is still in you."

Louis had sighed. "I hope it's not misplaced. I have some ideas, but nothing concrete, nothing that will point us to the real killer."

"You'll get there." Conrad had clapped a hand on the smaller man's shoulder. "I know you will."

Now, as he sat in the cell and baked in the damp heat, Conrad hoped his trust wasn't misplaced, too.

Down the street and around a corner, Louis Jensen sat in his office, once again surrounded by open law books, a pad of paper in front of him as he scribbled notes with a pencil.

He wasn't actually looking up case law this time, however. He had been going through the volumes hoping they would spark something in his brain. He kept laying out theories on the paper, only to cross through them when he realized they didn't hold water. Because of the oppressive heat, his coat was off, his collar was open, and his tie hung loose around his throat. He had rolled up his sleeves a couple of turns.

A footstep came from the doorway. A man cleared his throat. Louis looked up to see a small, slender, nattily dressed man standing there.

"Mr. Jensen?" he asked.

"That's right," Louis replied. He dropped the pencil he was holding onto the desk. "Can I help you?"

"I wouldn't have thought you'd be in your office on a Sunday afternoon, but I was passing by and noticed that the door was open . . ."

The visitor seemed to be the sort of man who took his time getting around to saying what he meant. Louis didn't really have the patience for that today, so he said, "I'm rather busy with a case. What can I do for you?"

"It's the case you're working on that I wanted to ask you about. You represent Conrad Morgan, isn't that correct?"

"That's right." Louis managed to put a smile on his face. This man, whoever he was, might have some valuable information. "Do you know something about it?"

"Actually, I have a question for you. My name is Hubert Osborne. Has Mr. Morgan happened to mention me?"

Louis thought about it and then shook his head. "No, I'm afraid not."

"Mr. Morgan and I are . . . friendly acquaintances, I suppose you'd say. We had several pleasant conversations at Blaise's Place, and during one of them, he offered to give me a job."

Louis's expectations fell. This didn't sound as

promising as he'd hoped. "I don't know anything about that," he told Osborne. "As I said, Mr. Morgan hasn't mentioned you to me."

"Oh, that's all right. I wasn't inquiring about the job, not really. As I said, Mr. Morgan and I got along well. Is there anything I can do to help with his, ah, situation?"

Louis supposed it wouldn't hurt to ask the man a few questions. He gestured toward the chairs in front of the desk and said, "Please, have a seat."

Osborne sat down and took his hat off, placing it primly in his lap. He toyed with a pearl stickpin in his cravat that had a long pin extending downward through the silk.

"Were you there at Blaise's Place the night Martin Delroy was killed?"

"For a short time, earlier in the evening. I watched the poker game between Mr. Morgan and Mr. Delroy." Osborne smiled. "An epic clash, and quite suspenseful. I say that as one who's not really an aficionado of poker."

"How about when Delroy's body was found?"

Osborne shook his head. "I had departed by that point."

"As you were leaving, did you notice anyone lurking around outside the saloon?"

"A suspicious character, you mean? Someone who might have committed the murder?" Osborne sighed and shook his head. "I wish I could say that I had, Mr. Jensen, because it might prove

414

helpful to Mr. Morgan's case. But unfortunately, I saw nothing of the sort. Surely by now you've turned up other suspects, though. You must have, because based on my conversations with him, I refuse to believe that Mr. Morgan is a murderer!"

Louis grunted. "I can't really go into that, Mr. Osborne. I'm sure you understand."

"Of course, of course," replied Osborne as he rubbed the stickpin's pearl head again. "I didn't mean to pry."

Louis thought that was precisely why Osborne was here, to satisfy a morbid curiosity and also to find out if there was still any chance of him getting that job Conrad had promised him. Louis was starting to get annoyed with the little man now, so he said, "I should get back to work."

"Certainly." Osborne stood up and clapped his hat on. "Thank you for your time, Mr. Jensen. Oh! You're a lawyer. I should pay you—"

"Not at all," Louis interrupted him, eager to get rid of the little pest. "I didn't give you any legal advice. We were just talking."

"Very well. Thank you. And good luck with the case!"

"Leave the door open behind you," Louis called after him as Osborne stepped out of the office.

Osborne looked back. "Yes, this heat is quite oppressive. I wish it would break."

"So does everybody else in the valley."

Osborne nodded and moved on. Louis sat

back in his chair. He pulled a handkerchief from his pocket and used it to mop sweat from his forehead, then put it away and fiddled with the ends of the tie that hung from the open collar around his neck.

His head lifted suddenly. *Was that a rumble of thunder he had heard in the distance?*

The group of riders reined in at the top of a ridge. They were twenty strong, having picked up some men along the way back here. The man in the lead took a pair of field glasses from his saddlebags, lifted them to his eyes, and peered through the lenses at the roofs of the buildings visible in the distance, along with the steeples of several churches.

"There it is," Jess Fenner said. "Big Rock."

The outlaw called Nick asked, "Are we gonna ride on in and start raising hell, Jess? You've got a big score to settle with those folks."

Before Fenner could answer, thunder sounded in the distance, a low, rolling peal full of foreboding. As he listened to it, an evil smile spread across the gang leader's craggy face.

"Sounds like there might be a storm moving in later," said Fenner. "We'll wait a while, Nick. There's not that much daylight left. We'll wait for night. With all these clouds, it'll be a dark one. Nobody will see us coming, so they won't know we're there among 'em until it's too late. A storm, if there is one, will just give us that much more cover."

"Sounds good," Nick said, nodding. "Nature itself is cooperatin' with us." He laughed, an ugly sound that boded well for no one. "Yes, sir, it's gonna be a dark night in Big Rock."

By early evening, the storm had not yet broken, although thunder grumbled every few minutes now and long, jagged fingers of lightning clawed at the darkening sky to the west. The lightning seemed to become even brighter as the last vestiges of daylight faded and a thick, heavy gloom settled over the town like a blanket. In weather like this, anything could happen . . . and most likely, it would be bad.

A looming storm didn't stop the train from running. A whistle shrilled through the gathering night, counterpointing the thunder, as the eastbound approached. It pulled into the depot with the usual clashing of drivers, squeal of brakes, and hissing of steam as smoke billowed from the locomotive's diamond-shaped stack. Porters placed steps at the platforms of the passenger cars so travelers could disembark.

A tall, powerfully built, middle-aged man in an expensive suit was the first one off the train. Half a dozen other men in suits followed him, and a dozen who looked just like them climbed down from the next car. Most of the men wore mustaches. All of them had hard, heavy-featured faces, and if one looked close enough, the bulges of the guns they carried under their suit coats were visible.

Hubert Osborne slipped out of the shadows and came up to the first man off the train. "Mr. Wheeler," he said. "Welcome to Big Rock."

"Osborne," Harrison Wheeler grunted. "Where are the rest of your men?"

"They're around." Osborne glanced at the men who had accompanied his employer. "I didn't expect you to bring this many with you. It shouldn't take but a few men to successfully persuade Mrs. Delroy to leave with you."

"Don't use that name," snapped Wheeler. "It reminds me of how angry I am at you. I never ordered you to kill Martin Delroy."

Osborne nodded and said, "It's true, sir, I used my own initiative. But the opportunity presented itself, and I seized it. And, if I may be so bold as to remind you, I removed a potential rival for Miss Warfield's affections at the same time. Mr. Morgan is in jail, and as far as I can tell, it's all but inevitable he will be found guilty of Delroy's murder."

"All right, all right," Wheeler said impatiently. "What's done is done, and it doesn't matter because I'm not going to give her any choice. I just want to get Blaise and get out of here."

"And kill anyone who gets in your way?"

There was an eager little tremble of anticipation in Osborne's voice.

"That goes without saying," Wheeler replied. "Now, where is she?"

"I'll take you there," Osborne said. With him and Wheeler at their head, the group of hired toughs moved off into the darkness.

All afternoon, something had been nagging at Louis Jensen's mind, but he hadn't been able to figure out exactly what it was. He just had a sense that it was something important. No matter how much he wracked his brain, though, he couldn't figure out what it was.

He had lit the lamp in the office earlier in the day because it was so gloomy, so he didn't really notice how late the hour had gotten and how dark it was outside. When he finally realized what time it was, he knew that Melanie and Brad were probably waiting for him to get home before they ate supper. Scolding himself for not paying enough attention to the important things in life, he started to close the law books, then stopped and left them open like they were. Nobody was going to bother them. He rolled down his sleeves, shrugged into his coat, and buttoned his collar, then blew out the lamp on the desk and headed for the door. When he had stepped out and closed it behind him, he reached for his tie, intending to tie it properly before he went home.

Then he stopped short, staring straight ahead. Light spilled into Big Rock's street from windows in some of the other buildings, but Louis didn't see it.

Instead, in his mind's eye, he was seeing a small red mark on the back of Martin Delroy's neck, as well as other marks lower down on the dead man's body.

Louis stood there motionless for a long moment, turning over the theory that had just formed in his head and examining it from every angle he could think of. It didn't explain everything, by any means, but if he was right, he had a pretty good idea who had killed Delroy.

With a little shake of his head, he broke out of his reverie. He walked to Front Street and turned to the right. He was hurrying, and after a moment his eagerness got the best of him and his rapid walk turned into a run. Somebody noticed and called out to him, but Louis barely heard and didn't slow down, not until he reached a small, neat house behind a picket fence. A sign hung from a post in the well-kept yard.

Louis went up the walk. More lightning flashed across the sky, and the accompanying thunder made the ground shake slightly. Louis stepped up onto the porch and knocked on the front door.

He had to knock twice more before the door opened and the puzzled countenance of Dr. Enoch Steward peered out at him.

"Louis," the physician said. "Are you all right? Is there something I can do for you?"

"I hope so, Doctor," Louis said. "I really hope so. I just need the answer to one question."

CHAPTER 35

What seemed like an impending storm had kept some of Big Rock's citizens off the streets and out of the saloons tonight, including Blaise's Place. She had closed the saloon Saturday; that was the day Martin Delroy had been buried in the town cemetery. He had been a terrible excuse for a husband, and honestly, she had hated him. But there had been a time when she loved him, or at least convinced herself she did, and on occasion he had done nice things for her. Anyway, they had been married, and she had closed the saloon and dressed in black and gone to the funeral, and that was that. She wouldn't have to worry anymore about her past catching up to her.

What she really regretted most about the whole thing was that a decent young man like Conrad Morgan was sitting in jail, accused of killing someone who, if there was any justice in the world, should have come to an ignoble end long before now.

Blaise wasn't sure if she believed Conrad's protestations of innocence. There were probably plenty of people still in the world who would have liked to see Martin dead, but as far as she knew, none of them were in Big Rock. She couldn't figure out who else could have killed him.

It wasn't her job to figure that out, she told herself. Her job was running a saloon.

Her saloon, once again.

But the place was less than half full on this stormy Sunday evening.

Blaise had taken her usual spot at the end of the bar when the batwings curved in and a man stepped between them. Without even looking around the room, he came directly toward her, as if he knew instinctively where she was. Blaise's heart slugged hard in her chest at the sight of him, but she wasn't surprised. Not really. She had told herself that with Martin's death, she no longer had to worry about the past. She had cursed herself with that thought.

More men followed Harrison Wheeler into the saloon, but Blaise was only vaguely aware of them. She watched Wheeler coming toward her and didn't know whether to turn and run or throw herself at him and try to claw his eyes out or simply stand there and wait for him.

She stood and waited.

He looked her up and down, his gaze bold and arrogant as it always had been. With a smile on his lips that didn't reach his agate eyes, he said, "Hello, Blaise. You're as beautiful as ever, my dear."

Somehow, she made her mouth work enough to say, "What are you doing here?"

"I came to finish what we started a year ago. I

423

had a question to ask you, remember? A question I never got an answer to."

Her pulse pounded so hard in her head that it was hard for her to think, but something occurred to her, anyway. She said, "You called me Blaise . . ."

"That's your name, isn't it? Your real name? Or as close to it as you can come. I've had a great many investigators working for me in the past year, learning everything they could about you and your . . . husband. Eventually, they discovered where you were. When they communicated your location to me, I knew I had to see you again." Wheeler shook his head slowly. "I don't intend to let you get away from me this time, my dear."

In a hoarse whisper, Blaise said, "You're insane."

"On the contrary, I know what I want, and I intend to get it. I know *how* to get it and what I'm prepared to do for it. I'd call that the essence of sanity, having a clear goal and a path to obtain it. For example . . ."

He lifted a hand and, with a surprisingly eloquent gesture for a man of his size and crude bearing, indicated the customers in the saloon, some of whom still glanced at him and his companions curiously, although most of them had gone back to their drinking.

"You agree to leave with me tonight and become my wife, or I'll have my men kill everyone in here. That's as simple and direct a choice as you possibly could have."

"Those are innocent men," Blaise husked.

"Of course, they are. If they were monsters, it wouldn't be much of a threat, would it?"

"There's only one monster here."

Wheeler laughed. "I see you still have a considerable amount of spirit. Good. I was afraid you might have lost it." He rubbed his hands together. "Now, I assume your living quarters are upstairs. We'll go up there, and you can pack enough for the trip back to San Francisco. You can get out of that gaudy saloon outfit. Whatever else you need, we'll buy when we get you home. You'll never want for anything again, my dear."

"Except freedom."

"Well . . . there are always trade-offs in life, aren't there?"

"You'd really kill all these men?"

Wheeler said, "I think you know me well enough to know the answer to that."

That was true. Blaise knew that he meant every word of it. And from the looks of the pack of curs he had brought with him, they were fully capable of doing it. Even though all the props had been knocked out from under her and the world seemed to be spinning the wrong way around her, Blaise was nothing if not adaptable. In earlier years, she'd had to be in order to survive. For now, she had to play along with him.

"All right," she told him. "I'll go up and pack. You can wait down here to make sure your men stay in line."

"My men won't do anything without a direct order from me," said Wheeler. "And you, my dear, will never be out of my sight again. You see, I've learned my lesson . . . and now you'll learn yours."

Brice Rogers stood on the boardwalk and frowned. It was odd enough that Louis Jensen would be out roaming around the streets of Big Rock at this time of evening, let alone on a night when it seemed like one rip-roarer of a thunderstorm was about to break any minute. But it was even more strange that Louis had ignored it when Brice called across the street to him.

Brice had watched while Louis engaged in several minutes of earnest conversation with Dr. Enoch Steward, then left the doctor's residence/office and headed back downtown. Still curious, Brice had followed. He didn't try to get Louis's attention this time. He would just wait and see where the lawyer was going.

Louis headed straight to Blaise's Place. That was enough to confirm the hunch growing inside Brice. Louis had discovered something important about the murder. Brice wanted to know what it was, so he started across the street toward the saloon.

He had taken only a few steps when a crash of thunder sounded and the sky finally opened up.

Denny reined her horse to a stop, swung down from the saddle, and looped the reins around the hitch rail in front of the sheriff's office and jail. It was late to be out and about, especially on a stormy night such as this, but she had told Smoke and Sally where she was going before she left the Sugarloaf. They probably hadn't approved, but they hadn't said anything.

Denny wanted to see Conrad again. She knew it was loco, but her instincts told her she needed to be here with him tonight. The trial would be starting in the morning, and it might change everything.

Monte Carson wasn't in the office. Deputy Nate Chadwick was seated at the desk, reading a copy of the *Police Gazette*. He put it down hurriedly and got to his feet.

"Miss Jensen," he said. "Howdy. Uh, what are you doin' here?"

"I want to see the prisoner. You do still have just the one, don't you?"

"Yeah, folks seem to be behavin' theirselves this weekend. Big Rock's nice and quiet for a change." Thunder boomed outside. "Well, the town's quiet, even if the weather ain't."

"So it's all right if I step back into the cell block and visit with Conrad?"

"Monte didn't say nothin' about him not havin' any visitors, so I reckon it's fine. Got to take your gun, though." The lanky deputy blushed. "You ain't got any other weapons, uh, hidden about your person, do you?"

"I give you my word I don't," Denny replied with a smile as she placed the Colt Lightning on the desk.

"Good enough for me," said Chadwick as he got the ring of keys from its peg.

Conrad stood up and hurried to the barred door when the deputy ushered Denny into the cell block. He grasped the iron bars and Denny closed her hands over his. Chadwick gracefully withdrew to give them some privacy.

"I wasn't expecting you back tonight," Conrad told her.

"I couldn't stay away. I had to see you again. Conrad, they just can't send you to prison or . . . or . . ."

"The gallows?" he finished for her. "That's not going to happen. I give you my word."

"How can you promise a thing like that? Yeah, you've got a lot of money, and you can hire plenty of lawyers besides my brother—"

"I have complete faith in Louis."

"So do I, blast it, but crazy things happen in this world. You never know—"

"I know one thing," said Conrad. He didn't have to elaborate because the look in his eyes told Denny very clearly what that one thing was. She leaned toward the bars to kiss him . . .

Before their lips could meet, thunder boomed so loudly that the whole building shook, and as it died away, they heard the rain, sounding like a huge waterfall suddenly had opened up above Big Rock.

Louis had gone to Blaise's Place because he didn't know where else to start looking for Hubert Osborne. Luck was with him, though, he saw as he stepped into the saloon and spotted the little man standing at the bar with a drink in his hand.

As he walked toward Osborne, Louis was aware that several strangers were in the saloon, along with a few of the usual customers. The hard-faced strangers all wore suits and were scattered around the room, a couple at the bar and the rest at tables. With his mind full of everything he had figured out tonight, Louis realized they were there but didn't really pay any attention to them.

Osborne saw him coming and raised his eyebrows in surprise. "Mr. Jensen," he said as Louis walked up to him. "What are you doing here?"

It was an odd question, in a way, since Louis had the right to stop by a saloon like anyone else.

"Looking for you, actually," Louis replied. "I was thinking about our visit earlier today."

"Some thoughts about Mr. Morgan, perhaps?"

"No, just you. That stickpin you wear, actually." Louis gestured toward the pearl-headed pin.

"This?" Osborne touched the pearl and frowned. "I don't understand."

"I just got to thinking that that pin is long enough, and sharp enough, that if you pushed it into the back of a man's neck, you might be able to penetrate his spine with it."

Osborne swallowed hard but shook his head. "That hardly seems possible."

"Oh, it's possible," insisted Louis. "I spoke to our local doctor about it. He agreed that a pin of that length could reach the spine, *and* it could do sufficient damage to paralyze a man from the neck down. Leave him conscious enough to know what's going on, but unable to do anything about it. So whoever did it could stick him several more times, to make the wounds look like insect bites and confuse the issue, and then drag him into another room, prop him up in a chair, and cut his throat with a letter opener that happened to be handy. It would take a strong man to do those things, but not necessarily a large one. Sometimes people just aren't what they seem at first glance."

Osborne's eyes had widened as Louis continued speaking, until it seemed that they were about to pop out of their sockets. When Louis paused, he sputtered, "You . . . you can't . . . you couldn't possibly know—"

"Couldn't possibly know what? How you killed Martin Delroy, after you climbed through the window into his bedroom? Actually, I do. And as I said, our local doctor and I had a very interesting conversation about it a short time ago. He agreed to notify the sheriff while I looked for you. Understand, I have no idea *why* you killed Delroy, but I'm absolutely confident that you did. You admitted that you were here but left the saloon before Conrad Morgan came back down from the living quarters upstairs. You had the means and the opportunity. I'm confident that with a little investigation, we'll find the motive—"

A heavy footstep sounded on the balcony. Louis glanced up, saw Blaise standing there, dressed in a conservative traveling outfit rather than her saloon garb. A big, middle-aged man stood beside her with his left hand clamped around her right arm.

While Louis was looking away, Osborne moved suddenly, reaching under his coat and bringing out a short-barreled pistol. The sight of the gun made the other well-dressed strangers in the saloon leap to their feet and yank guns from under their coats, as well. The saloon's regular customers gaped at the unexpected and threatening sight.

Osborne pointed his pistol at Louis and cried, "He knows about me killing Delroy, Mr.

Wheeler! We have to kill him! We have to kill them all!"

A huge peal of thunder crashed. As torrents of rain began to pour from the sky, Brice Rogers slapped the batwings aside and yelled, "Louis, get down!"

Louis dived to the sawdust-littered floor. Osborne swung his gun toward the deputy U.S. marshal, as did the other armed strangers. Osborne fired first, sending a bullet whipping past Brice's ear as the lawman crouched slightly. Brice triggered a return shot that punched into Osborne's chest and threw the little man backward. His gun thudded to the floor right in front of Louis.

The next instant, Blaise's Place erupted in gun-thunder to rival anything the storm generated outside.

All the shots were directed at Brice. Louis saw him throw himself backward through the entrance as slugs chewed splinters from the batwings and made them swing crazily. Since all the gunmen were looking in that direction, Louis pushed himself to his feet, leaped onto the bar, and rolled over it. As he did, a bullet gouged a trench in the hardwood of the bar. He looked up and saw the man with Blaise firing at him.

Before Louis could return that fire, Blaise rammed herself into the man's shoulder as hard as she could. He was concentrating on shooting at

Louis and must not have had his feet set, because the collision knocked him off balance and forced him against the balcony railing. It cracked and gave way under the impact. Blaise and the man both toppled through the opening and plummeted down onto a table, which shattered under their weight.

Brice fired from the entrance, using the outside wall to one side for cover, and two of the gun-wielding strangers spun off their feet. Several of the townsmen attacked another man and wrestled him to the floor, took his gun away from him, and began beating him with it. Louis aimed carefully and shot another man through the shoulder, causing him to drop his gun, clutch the wound, and collapse.

The thunder and lightning were near-constant now. The storm was chaos outside. Rain blew in through the doorway and bullet-shattered windows. Most of the customers scurried for the side door, willing to dare the storm rather than remain in the middle of the battle going on.

Louis crouched behind the bar as bottles shattered on the shelves behind him and sprayed liquor around. He hadn't inherited his father's skill with a gun, but in this desperate moment, he found that he had at least some of Smoke's cool nerves. He fired again, saw another of the strangers double over and fall. Most of them were down now, and as Brice charged in with his Colt spitting flame, he cut down the final two men. Wind from the storm whipped through the broken windows and pushed the smell of gunpowder from the saloon.

Louis hurried around the end of the bar and checked the fallen Hubert Osborne. The little man stared sightlessly at the ceiling. He was dead.

Keeping his gun leveled and ready, Brice came toward the bar and raised his voice to ask over the tumult, "Louis, are you all right?"

"Yes, I . . . I think so."

Brice looked past Louis, toward the spot where Blaise lay huddled in the debris of the broken table with the man called Wheeler. When he saw her, he cried, "Blaise!" and ran toward them.

At that moment, more shots blasted outside, enough to be heard even over the rolling thunder. It sounded like a war had just broken out in Big Rock.

CHAPTER 36

The huge blast of thunder made Denny gasp and step back from the bars of the cell door. As the echoes faded slightly, she heard excited voices coming from the sheriff's office. She recognized one of them as belonging to Dr. Enoch Steward. A second later, she heard the doctor say Louis's name.

"I'll be right back," she told Conrad. She hurried to the cell block door and called, "Deputy! Deputy Chadwick! What's going on?"

Chadwick appeared on the other side of the thick wooden door and said excitedly through the small, barred opening, "It sounds like that brother o' yours is about to get hisself in some trouble, Miss Jensen! Doc Steward says he's goin' after a murderer!"

"What! Let me out of here, now!" Denny flung a glance over her shoulder at Conrad. "I have to see about Louis."

He nodded and told her, "Go on. And if there's anything I can do to help—"

Denny was gone then, rushing out of the cell block without hearing the rest of what Conrad had to say.

Dr. Steward's hair and clothes were damp but not soaked, as if he had made it to the sheriff's office just as the downpour was starting. Denny said, "Doctor, what was that about my brother?"

"Louis believes he's figured out who actually killed Martin Delroy, and how," Steward said. "He was going to search for the man he thinks is guilty."

"By himself?" Denny groaned. "What a loco thing to do! But it sounds like Louis."

"He asked me to fetch the sheriff and tell Monte to meet him at Blaise's Place. He was going to start there."

"Monte ain't here," said Deputy Chadwick, stating the obvious. He was taking down a Winchester from a rack on the wall. "But I'll go see if I can find your brother, miss—"

At that moment, a wave of gunfire came from somewhere else in town. The three people in the sheriff's office turned toward the door.

"That sounds like Louis found some trouble, all right!" Denny exclaimed.

"Dang it, I better hurry," Chadwick said. He started toward the door.

Denny scooped up the Colt Lightning from the desk. "I'm coming with you," she declared. Chadwick didn't argue with her. They stepped out onto the porch. The rain was coming down so hard, it was difficult to see the buildings across the street. It muffled the shots, but Denny could still hear them, although the blasts seemed to be tapering off.

Before they could head in the direction of the trouble, riders loomed up out of the rain with no warning. Muzzle flashes cut through the gloom. Denny felt the wind-rip of a slug past her cheek.

The mounted attackers veered toward the sheriff's office. Denny reached out, caught hold of Chadwick's collar, and yanked the deputy with her as she lunged back through the still-open door. Bullets thudded into the panels as she kicked the door shut.

"Now what the hell!" yelled Chadwick. "Who in blazes were *those* hombres?"

Denny didn't know, but as the hoofbeats and the gunshots and the shouts continued outside, she knew that whoever they were, they had Big Rock under attack, right in the middle of the biggest thunderstorm in months.

Chadwick used the Winchester's barrel to poke glass out of one of the windows and knelt at the sill to return the fire from outside. He said over his shoulder, "Looks like they're spreadin' out through town, and some of 'em got their hearts set on blastin' their way in here."

"We'll just have to stop them," Denny said as she drew her Colt.

From the cell block, Conrad shouted, "Hey, what's going on out there!"

"The sheriff's office is under attack," Denny called back to him.

"Well, hell, let me out of here! I'll help you fight them off."

Chadwick squeezed off a shot and then said, "I can't do that. Mr. Morgan's a prisoner—"

Dr. Steward interrupted them. "But Deputy, I just told you that Louis Jensen has figured out who the real killer is. The charges against Conrad will be dropped by tomorrow."

"It ain't tomorrow," muttered Chadwick. He ducked as more glass shattered above his head. "But things is gettin' a mite hot, and I reckon we could use an extra gun. Doc, grab them keys off the wall and let Morgan loose. Then you'd better grab a rifle your own self."

Steward got the keys but said, "I won't shoot anyone."

"Suit yourself, Doc." Chadwick triggered another round.

Denny used her Colt to knock glass out of the window on the other side of the door. She dropped to one knee, made herself as small a target as possible, and waited for a muzzle flash. When one came, she snapped a shot at it an instant later. She thought she heard somebody yell, but between the shooting and the storm, with so much racket going on, she couldn't be sure.

Suddenly, Conrad was beside her with a Winchester in his hands. "You should stay down," he told her.

"The hell with that," Denny said as she fired another shot.

Conrad brought the rifle to his shoulder and joined in the battle, cranking off swift shots as he worked the rifle's lever. For a few minutes, bullets flew back and forth furiously and sounded like a swarm of angry bees as some of them passed through the sheriff's office.

Then Chadwick lowered his rifle with smoke still curling from the muzzle and said, "That's the last of 'em, I think. The last of this bunch, anyway. But there's still fightin' goin' on all over town. I got to go out there and put a stop to it."

"I'll come with you, Deputy," said Conrad.

"And so will I," added Denny.

Conrad looked at her. "Will it do any good to argue with you?"

"Not one damned bit."

He sighed and nodded. "That's what I thought. Let's go!"

Brice knelt beside Blaise, got his arms around her shoulders, and lifted her so that he could prop her up against his leg and chest.

"Blaise!" he said urgently. "Blaise, can you hear me?"

She made a little noise and moved her head. Relief flooded through Brice at the knowledge she was still alive, at least. Her eyelids fluttered and then opened. She peered confusedly up into his face for a second and muttered, "Brice . . . ?"

"I'm here," Brice told her. As far as he could see, she didn't have any broken bones or wounds. He hoped the fall had just stunned her for a few moments.

Then she turned her head quickly to look around and said, "Wheeler! Where—"

"If you're talking about that fella who was up on the balcony with you, you don't have to worry about him anymore." Brice nodded to where the man's body lay next to them, his head canted at an unnatural angle on his twisted neck and his eyes glazed over in death. "Looks like he broke his neck when he landed."

Blaise closed her eyes as a shudder ran through her. "Thank God," she whispered. "He . . . he was a devil. While I was getting ready to go, he . . . he boasted about how many men he had killed while he was searching for me." She clutched Brice's sleeve with one hand as her voice got stronger. "One of his men killed Martin, Brice. Conrad Morgan is innocent."

"We'll get all that squared away," Brice promised her. "Come on, let's get you up on your feet, maybe get a drink in you. I reckon you could use one right about now."

"That's the truth," she murmured.

Brice helped her to her feet and kept an arm around her for support as he led her over to the bar.

Louis stood there over the body of a dapper little man. Blaise looked at the corpse and shuddered again.

"That's him," she said. "The one who killed Martin. He works . . . worked . . . for Harrison Wheeler." She inclined her head toward the dead man lying in the wreckage of the table. "He . . . he was a monster. Tortured people . . . killed them . . . like a mad dog, and Harrison was his master. You . . . you wouldn't think it to look at him, would you?"

"No," said Louis, "but people often aren't what they appear to—"

Before he could go on, more gunfire roared outside. Brice and Louis whirled in that direction as Blaise gasped. Brice had been thumbing fresh cartridges into his Colt's cylinder. He snapped it closed and said, "I have to go see about that." He glanced at Blaise. "Get behind the bar and keep your head down. Louis, look after her."

"I can't," Louis said as he bent and scooped up two guns that had fallen from the dead hands of Harrison Wheeler's hired killers. "I'm coming with you."

Big drops of rain pelted Denny as she and Conrad and Deputy Nate Chadwick trotted toward the battle. They hadn't gone ten feet before they were soaked to the skin.

The rest of the mounted invaders had charged

441

along Front Street, pouring lead into the buildings on both sides. Now they reached the far end of the street, wheeled their horses, and started to ride back toward Denny, Conrad, and Chadwick, firing as they came.

The trio stood their ground, flame lancing from the barrels of Denny's revolver and the Winchesters held by Conrad and Chadwick. The flashes competed with the brilliant lightning ripping down from the heavens. One jagged bolt tore through the blackness and struck a church steeple, sending sparks flying in a scintillating display of destruction.

The invaders' charge broke under the withering fire from Denny, Conrad, and the deputy. Men toppled from saddles. Horses collapsed and rolled over their screaming riders. The man in the forefront of the attack remained mounted, though, and thundered toward the town's three defenders. The glare from a lightning bolt that hammered to the ground nearby illuminated his hate-twisted face.

Recognition stabbed into Denny. The man was Jess Fenner, the outlaw whose escape had been foiled when Brice was taking him to the train to turn him over to other deputy marshals. Somehow, Fenner had gotten away from the law before he made it to the gallows in Utah . . . and tonight he had come to take his vengeance on Big Rock.

Denny knew she had one round left in her gun. She lined the sights on Fenner's chest and pulled the trigger at the same instant as Conrad fired his Winchester beside her. Both slugs slammed into Fenner's chest and lifted him out of the saddle. He seemed to hang in the air for a second as his horse galloped out from under him, then he crashed to the street and lay in a limp, lifeless heap in the mud.

Chadwick grunted as more shots suddenly came from the right. The deputy crumpled, obviously hit. Denny and Conrad swung sharply toward the new threat, but Denny's gun was empty, and she wasn't sure if she would have time to reload. Men in suits and derby hats and bowlers—and Denny had no idea where *they* had come from or what they were doing in Big Rock tonight— had opened up on them from the boardwalk on that side of the street. With Chadwick down and Denny's gun empty, Conrad wouldn't stand a chance against what appeared to be six-to-one odds.

Then more shots sounded. Denny's startled gaze flicked toward two men advancing along the boardwalk toward the suit-wearing bushwhackers and scything lead into their ranks. The muzzle flashes revealed the two to be Brice Rogers and none other than Louis, who had a gun in each hand and was firing with methodical precision, mowing down the would-be killers who had the drop on Denny and Conrad. Taken by surprise, the strangers tried to fight back, but one by one, they fell to the deadly fire from Louis and Brice.

When they were all down, Louis dropped the now-empty revolvers and ran into the street. "Denny!" he called. "Denny, are you all right?"

Denny threw her arms around her brother and hugged him tight. "I'm fine," she told him. "What about you?"

Louis just nodded.

Brice came over to join Conrad in helping Deputy Chadwick back to his feet. "Don't go to fussin' over me," the deputy said. "I ain't hit that bad. I tripped over my own two feet as much as anything, I reckon. Durned big ol' clodhoppers."

"How about you, Conrad?" asked Brice.

"I'm all right. You don't seem surprised to see me out of jail, though."

"I'm not. Louis figured out who really killed Martin Delroy. You would have been released by morning, at the latest." Brice glanced around at the carnage. "That is, if all hell hadn't broken loose in Big Rock tonight." He shook his head. "Who *are* all these lunatics who tried to shoot up the town?"

"Jess Fenner and his men account for some of them," Denny told him. "He escaped somehow and came back to settle his score with the town." She nodded toward the suit-clad strangers. "I don't know who those hombres are, but they seemed to want us dead."

"They worked for a man named Harrison Wheeler, I'm guessing," replied Brice. "He's dead now, too, but ultimately, he was responsible for Delroy's murder, even though he didn't commit the crime himself. It's a long story."

"And one best told when we're inside, out of this rain, and in dry clothes," Conrad suggested, which sounded like a mighty good idea to Denny.

Three forces of nature had descended on this dark night in Big Rock: ruthless outlaws bent on vengeance; a rich man mad with injured pride and lust, along with the hired killers working for him; and the biggest, toad-stranglingest thunderstorm folks in these parts had seen in a long time.

The first two had been defeated. The third had gone on its way, the rain slowed to a drizzle now, the lightning just pretty flashes in the distance, the thunder nothing more than rumbling echoes.

Warm and dry, wearing borrowed clothes, Denny, Conrad, and Brice sat in the parlor of Louis's house, drinking coffee that Melanie had brewed. The shirt and trousers Louis had loaned to Brice actually fit him fairly well. Conrad was bigger, so the borrowed garments strained some on him.

Louis and Melanie sat on the sofa with Brad between them. Denny, Conrad, and Brice were in armchairs facing them. For the past half-hour, they had been hashing out everything that had happened, with Louis explaining his theory about how Martin Delroy was killed. Based on what Blaise had told Brice, they now knew why Delroy was murdered, as well. As far as Denny could tell, it all made sense.

"So, like much of the evil in the world, the whole thing had its roots in the past," Louis concluded. "Mistakes were made, decisions were reached in haste and poor judgment and greed, and all of it combines to haunt the present, no matter how much we wish we could put those regrets behind us."

"That's a rather gloomy way to look at it," said Conrad. "Don't you think people can learn from the past, so they don't repeat the same mistakes again?"

"You'd think so," Louis replied with a shrug, "but how often does that actually happen?"

Melanie asked, "Is Deputy Chadwick going to be all right?"

"Yeah, Doc Steward patched him up and said he'd be fine," Brice told her.

"What about the outlaws who weren't killed?" Brad wanted to know.

"I locked up the ones I could find. Some of them probably got away, but I don't reckon they'll want to come back to Big Rock any time soon. Considering the reception they got here, they probably won't ever set foot in these parts again!"

"What about Blaise?" asked Conrad. "Will she get to keep her saloon?"

"I don't see any reason why not."

Denny said, "But she admitted she and Delroy swindled Harrison Wheeler out of that money, and then she stole it from Delroy."

"At this point, who's going to bring charges against her? Wheeler and Delroy are both dead." Brice shrugged. "Anyway, those crimes, if they happened, took place in California. Blaise hasn't broken any laws here in Colorado, as far as I know, and nothing she's done falls under federal jurisdiction."

Denny said, "You're just saying that because you're sweet on her," but she smiled to take any sting out of the words. Brice just looked down into his coffee cup, but he was smiling, too.

"So," Conrad said, "it appears that, despite the odds, everything has worked out all right."

"Yeah," Denny said as she reached over to rest her hand on his arm for a second, "but I know somebody who's going to be mighty disappointed."

"Oh?" Louis frowned. "Who's that?"

"Smoke. I mean, there was a giant gun battle tonight, and there he was, sitting at home, missing the whole thing!"

Center Point Large Print
600 Brooks Road / PO Box 1
Thorndike, ME 04986-0001 USA

(207) 568-3717

US & Canada:
1 800 929-9108
www.centerpointlargeprint.com